The Great Unlife

M. U. Zaetl

Dedicated to my brother, Gar, who remains the man I look up to most.

Sorry about that three year wait between chapters 2 and 3, bro.

There is a world that exists in a reality far from our own. Her name is Wayfarer, but none call her that now. Even the eternal creatures that wander her lands have forgotten.

Wayfarer is a world caught in a terrible cycle of death and rebirth, a cycle overseen by four Elder beings known as the Horsemen. When her life is in Balance, she grows and prospers. When that Balance is lost, the Horsemen call the Ride, venturing out into her lands to purge her inhabitants, to prepare her for death. In a final cataclysm, called the Purification, the Four summon a cleansing magic that engulfs her in elemental chaos.

Millennia later, she emerges from the flames, reborn and restored to Balance. The survivors of the Ride dig themselves free of their sanctuaries, remembering little of what came before, spreading out across her lands to begin the cycle once more. The Horsemen, drained of their power, fade into the shadows to plot and await the time when they are needed once again.

Wayfarer is a world caught in the grasp of two suns: White and Blue. The White Sun is alive, full of power, growing toward the height of its life. The Blue Sun is dying, radiating decay, nearing its end. White fuels the world, bolstering the four elements that form Wayfarer and the life that inhabits it. Blue saps the world, weakening the elements and Wayfarer's inhabitants.

From White is born aether, an energy that can be molded by beings known as elementalists. These creatures are attuned to a single element, drawing and shaping aether of Fire, Wind, Water, or Earth. They wield a power strong enough to revive a dead forest. They wield a power strong enough to return it to ash.

An elementalist sees aether as a geyser. It is bursting and alive. Drawing from it is to race into the inferno, to leap into the tornado, to ride the tsunami, to stand firm against the landslide. Those that can feel and draw and shape aether are in turn shaped by their element. Sometimes to their detriment. Sometimes to their death.

From Blue is born nether, an energy drawn from the decay and rot of the world and the aether that flows through it, an energy wielded by those known as arcanists. Where elementalists are powerful, arcanists are resourceful. Those that gather and shape nether may never be as strong as their kin who walk with the elements, but the forms they craft are endless in number.

An arcanist sees nether as a mire. It is still and stagnant. Drawing from it is to walk through rotting leaves, to taste mouldy bread. Perhaps it is testament to the nature of life that there are more born with the ability to see and draw and shape nether than there are that can touch aether.

Then there are those rare creatures that stand outside the power of the Suns. Most who walk this world do not know they exist, but those that do call them lunarons. Creatures of the Blood Moon, cursed to walk in the light of the Suns but never to touch it. But though lunarons wield no magic, they do have a dark power of their own.

A lunaron is a black hole in the spaces between reality where aether and nether wait. Energy is drawn to them, and then it is gone. An arcanist standing near a lunaron would find the decaying and rotting mire vanished. An elementalist would find the fire extinguished, the wind silent, the water dry, and the earth naught but dust. The Suns have no hold on a lunaron.

Rarer even than lunarons are the creatures known as solarons. A solaron basks in the light of both Suns, wielding not aether nor nether, but a combination of both. Where arcanists and elementalists are hobbled by their inability to see the energy of their opposite, solarons suffer no such limitation.

A solaron sees the blood of both White and Blue, and it is a blazing storm of light, seething with both life and death. Drawing from it is to gaze out into the universe, to walk the edge of oblivion. Wielding the very power of the stars, a solaron is limited only by what their body can sustain.

The life and death of Wayfarer are intrinsically linked with the light of the Suns. Powerful arcanists, known as archons, have laid waste to her lands, leaving nothing but rot behind. Aethons, the strongest of elementalists, have shattered her continents, leaving only dust and ruin. Yet, those creatures' power pales in comparison to that of a solaron.

No one has come closer to killing her entirely, defying the work and power of the Horsemen, than the ones who reached to the very stars and brought astral rage crashing down around them...

a world born in the ruin of the last
too closely linked to the sins of the past
so Death went out to find a soul
so the next one would be whole

bring me one who holds the stars
bring me one who won't stray far
break their spirit, tempt their greed
all so that the rage is freed

and once the horror has been done
the whole world ash beneath the Suns
go on and give to Death his due
and let the game begin anew

1

'You know, there is a reason these things have an expiry date,' Dr. Jacobs said as he patted my arm, 'and yours is well past that. Have you thought about getting a construct, recently?'

I scowled at the man. Irritatingly, my ire was wasted as he had already returned to his ministrations. His practised hands wove intricate patterns over my stricken heart, and I could feel him shaping the nether into the forms that would bring the ailing organ back to its old self.

Well, for a while, anyway.

'We've discussed this, Doctor. It's not something I'm prepared to do. There's got to be another way.'

He clucked his tongue at me as he put his fingers down on my bare chest and I felt the tingle of the magic passing through my skin. 'I know an excellent necromancer just down the street that makes a great flesh construct. Cheaper than metals or plastics, and you can hardly tell the difference between this,' he poked my leg, 'and her work.'

I turned to look at the wall, frustrated. 'I'm somewhat attached to this body,' I said, a bit louder than I meant to. Hanging mockingly on the wall was a leaflet from the Government proclaiming the benefits of transferring to a construct.

Jacobs paused and looked up at me. His face was kindly, but his voice was very serious. 'Mr. Tundra. Martin. Even the strongest will can only hold these together for so long. I can, of course, continue to correct some of the decay through medicine and spells, but eventually your body will break down beyond even my ability to fix. If this heart attack had happened outside of office hours and you had been unable to get an ambulance wyvern in time, nothing short of a favour from Death would have saved you.'

'This body will one day die, Martin. And you with it. And there is no coming back from that. Most people abandon these long before the expiration date, which is, what, a hundred years for a good model? How long have you been in yours, again?'

I looked at him, at his oddly perfect face, at his vivid green irises, at the barely perceptible seams that ran down the sides of his neck, at his impeccably straight hair. I breathed deeply of the purified air, feeling my heart beating strongly in my chest once more. Somewhere at the back of my mind I heard a dark chuckle.

'Two hundred and fifty years,' I answered after a long minute.

2

It had actually been two hundred and sixty-four, but most people stopped counting a century before that, and I was considered somewhat odd already. Why draw more attention to yourself, after all? Besides, few people asked how old you were these days. It wasn't even that it was considered rude. It was considered unimportant.

My watch pinged quietly. Noon. I wiped at its surface out of habit. A hundred years of neglect had dimmed the display and permanently fogged some of the glass. Still, it was a nice watch.

I wandered out into the sun with my body back to its more-or-less usual self. I was glad that the City had an excellent health care system, or my increasingly frequent visits to Dr. Jacobs would have very quickly exhausted my army pension. Granted, there weren't many people that had lived in their original model anywhere near as long as I had. Oh, sure, there were a handful that I knew offhand who were older than a hundred fifty or so, but they didn't have organ failure on a regular basis.

This was my second heart attack this month.

Last month, it had been kidney failure. The month before, we'd discovered a rare form of cancer that I'd survived only because my magical defences were strong and had delayed its spread. That had been touch and go. Even with the tumour stalled out, it had taken the surgeon several hours to remove it. Part of the problem had been that Dr. Jacobs had been playing golf up on the Cloud, so I'd had to take my chances with the nearest emergency ward.

The doctor that had worked on me had done good work but sent me on my way with a quiet, 'See you again soon.' This kind of thing was always best done with your regular doctor, as having a stranger operate on you could take a heavy toll on any body, especially one that had seen as much use as mine.

I found my car sitting quietly at the far end of the parking lot, her pristine paint gleaming in the sunlight. The lot was almost empty today, though that wasn't entirely surprising. Most of Jacobs' patients didn't have the money to own their own vehicles, and took public dragon transit or the giant mole subway. I put my hand on the door handle, felt the familiar tingle as her guardian spells checked me over, and then slid into the seat as the door swung open.

I sat there for a long time, hands on the wheel, staring off into space. It was quiet inside, the spells designed to isolate the occupants from exterior noise and vibration still strong. She was like new, even after having been on the road for over a decade. I took very careful care of her, though I could probably afford to buy a new one if she died.

Feeling a bit tired, I sighed and pulled a small amount of nether from outside the car, shaping it with a quick flick of my wrist, and then lit the ignition fire. The car roared to life, then purred quietly as I idled her out onto the road toward Upper River District and home. Turning on the music player filled the cabin with some classical orchestrated metal. A flyer rocketed past, his goggles slightly askew, smirking at me in my chariot. I flipped him the finger and cranked the volume.

The singer howled something incoherent, which I tried to emulate. It came out in a hoarse whisper. Alright, so maybe my body wasn't quite back to its usual self after all.

I knew it was only a matter of time before something happened to it that couldn't be fixed and then it'd start to rot. After that, my options were to hang some air fresheners on my ears and wait for the end, or go out and get a new model. Most of the people I knew couldn't understand why I'd kept this body as long as I had. Explaining it to them gained me only blank stares or incredulous looks.

Another laugh from deep in my brain. I scowled and pushed the sound away.

My cellphone pierced the fury of the music with a single blast of electronic anger of its own. I spared it a quick glance, saw that it was a text from a friend, and then turned back to the road. If I'd wanted to, I had more than enough skill in the arcane arts to manipulate the phone without ever taking my hands of the wheel, but I was convinced that wasn't any less stupid than handling it physically.

I pulled into my garage and hopped out of the car. The dull thump of her doors sealing behind me seemed incredibly loud in the sudden quiet. She was high quality. I'd personally assisted the worker in her creation. He had been very skilled and hadn't really required my help, but it's common for a car company to allow an owner to participate in his car's birth. I appreciated the gesture.

Walking in the front door, I dropped my keys on the counter. This had been a long day, and I could use a nap. At least I was probably healthy for another month.

There was a sudden fluctuation in the air next to me, and then a small winged creature appeared from nowhere. It opened its tiny, tooth-filled maw and barked out in a sing-song woman's voice, 'Martin, it's Dr. Jacobs. I have bad news.'

3

I turned to the little beast and sighed. It shook its head in a comically sad fashion and said, 'I'm sorry to do this over Imp Messaging, but our phones are down and I have an emergency surgery on an ogre in five minutes.' The Doctor paused, leaving the imp to stare at me in annoyance, wings fluttering wildly to keep its round bulk in the air.

'Better just get to it, Doctor. You wouldn't be telling me here if it wasn't really, really bad,' I said with more than a bit of trepidation.

The irritated imp snapped back into its Jacobs impersonation, and the doctor again spoke through its mouth. 'The cancer's back. And it's past the point where we can correct it. You don't have much time, Martin. The damn thing is spreading at an unbelievable pace. You need to get out of that body, and you need to do it today.'

I fell more than sat in the chair at the counter. The imp had resumed staring at me balefully now that the doctor had once again fallen silent. It swatted at one of my wisps absently. My cellphone sang again. My watch pinged.

Resignedly, I asked, 'how long, Doctor?'

'A month, maybe month and a half. But you will find it pretty unpleasant in there over the next two weeks. You need to get into a construct before your body becomes too weak to handle the transfer spells,' the imp said. It looked frantic.

A distant and ethereal laugh echoed from the depths.

I put my hands over my face and took a few deep breaths. When I felt slightly calmer, I looked back up at the imp. 'Thanks for letting me know, Doctor. I have some things that I need to do, I should go.'

The imp again looked very sad, and said, 'Alright, Martin. Please keep in touch, you may not require my services again after you have transferred, but I would still like to know how you are.' It reached up, patted me roughly on the head, and then vanished with a flash of light and a small pop.

I sat at the counter for a long time after Jacobs had hung up. A wisp settled on my shoulder and watched me quietly. A taxi dragon roared past outside. My neighbour shouted obscenities at his cat.

My phone chimed again, and this time I clicked it out of standby and had a look at my messages. My friend again, demanding to know why I wasn't answering his texts. I chuckled, briefly breaking out of my funk. Nox was never a particularly sunny and happy fellow.

I decided that I'd call him in a bit, and settled back into thinking about my predicament. I idly pulled a bit of nether from the air and shaped it into lights, letting the spell spin around my fingers in tight patterns. Looking out through the walls of reality, I could see the oceans of arcane energy floating in decaying, quiet menace. Energy enough to reduce the world to dust. I smiled bitterly.

The Government classified me as an archon, a creature with a terrifying amount of magical strength, but right now, that didn't mean a whole lot. My magical talents were almost entirely on the violent side of the spectrum. I could shape forms that annihilated whole Districts, but I couldn't heal so much as a paper cut. I couldn't save this body any more than Jacobs could.

Which meant a construct. I shivered and immediately turned away from the thought. Transfer was just as bad as death, as far as I was concerned. And I'd go to my grave before I'd meet my end in a transferring rite.

The alternative was to ask Death for a reprieve, but that was a long shot at best. The Horseman would need a pretty compelling reason to stay his hand, especially as I'd avoided his grasp for so long already. His brethren could also give me a stay of execution through their powerful magic, but War was keeping a low profile and Famine and Pestilence were absent. No one knew where the two sisters were.

No, the Four Horsemen were not going to be my salvation. There were other elder beings like them that might have the power to help me - the Green Lady, maybe - but they were unpredictable at best and were just as likely to take my life as to save it.

My watch pinged, and shortly after so did my phone. Two texts: one from Nox, this time stating that he'd come to my place and eat me if I didn't respond; and one from the Government, reminding me that my pension would end the day after I met my demise, as per the conditions of my retirement package.

I put my head against the counter and wondered how the day could get worse.

4

I decided that I'd go for a walk to try and clear my head, taking the time to send Nox a quick message letting him know that I wouldn't be particularly tasty and that I'd talk to him later. I didn't get a response, so I threw on a better jacket and headed out.

I left my house, shooing away the horde of wisps that tried to follow me out the door. A gremlin bolted past as I walked down my sidewalk, the beast was clutching a battered fedora and cackling madly. A few seconds later, a particularly angry steam construct went crashing by. I stood aside for it, as I was pretty sure my ailing body wouldn't take kindly to a head on collision with two metres of metal and magic. Across the street, an imp floated along next to a man, the two arguing with each other rather animatedly. I briefly wondered if the imp was working or if it was offline. It reached out, poked the man in the nose, and then floated up out of reach as it continued yelling. The man swatted at it angrily from below.

I soon left the residential areas behind me and entered into the parkland that ringed the District. It was quiet here, and I frequently walked this way when I needed to think. The breeze whistled through the ancient trees. I could hear birdsong from somewhere in there, though it may have been a sprite. I hoped it wasn't. I was direly allergic to their damned powder.

Ignoring my surroundings for the moment, I considered my situation. I could try some of my contacts in the Government. I'd spent the better part of a hundred years fighting in the Department of Enforcement and later the Department of Operations. Maybe Research had something experimental that could help.

I shook my head. And owls could teach me to two-step.

Constructs again circled through my head, and I frowned. I understood the draws that transferring had. There were a lot of good reasons to want to get a new model. Maybe the original was dying, or had a genetic flaw of some kind, or the owner didn't identify with the gender they'd been born in, or even just the desire to be someone or something else.

I stopped and frowned. Then I turned my gaze inward and whispered, 'Are you there?'

For a long moment, there was nothing. I had just started to give up in disgust when I heard the familiar laugh from far below.

I'm always here, Martin.

I shivered, as I always did when talking to him. I usually longed for a hot shower after I did. 'Anything you care to add to save ourself?' I asked. The question echoed hollowly through the darkness. There was more silence, and then suddenly I felt his presence erupt from the depths, crashing up against the surface in a roiling geyser. I staggered and felt nauseous. Through the sickness of him being near, I heard his voice.

You can let me out.

I gathered my wits and with a fair amount of willpower, gathered him up and threw him back into the pit. He laughed the whole way.

I shook my head violently, and gulped for air. My mind was empty once more, though I thought I could hear him cackling from far away. Having recovered enough to move, I snarled something obscene beneath my breath. I should have known better than to speak to him.

He's a monster.

I don't talk to the Other often. I have to keep my guard up or he might break loose. Usually, he's content to haunt the dark recesses of my brain, watching. Sometimes he gets in close and pushes the walls and I have to push back. Sometimes he pushes the walls when I'm not at my best, and then I'm the one in the box. Being in the box while that psychopath is in control is not a fun experience. I always get the wheel back, though. Eventually.

A hand took mine, and a familiar and pleasant scent filled the air. I smiled without looking over at my new companion. Thoughts of constructs and death and the Other vanished, and I felt my day brighten.

'Hello, Ceile,' I said, squeezing her hand.

'Hello, Old Man,' she said, squeezing my hand back.

Ceile is my oldest and greatest friend. I met her on a crazy New Year's Night, the one where the Cloud was finally released and tethered to the Morning District. I don't remember a whole lot about the night, but I woke up in her hotel room and she woke up in mine. We've been steadfast friends ever since.

She called me Old Man, despite the fact that she was over a decade older than me. Of course, you couldn't tell. Ceile had abandoned her body long before I'd met her, having been in her flesh construct for over a hundred and fifty years. The necromancer who had built her new body had done an amazing job. Her light brown skin was so smooth and felt so much like original model flesh that unless you got a really good look at her, you'd never know. The seams were very subtle, the usual tremor of magic running beneath the surface almost unnoticeable.

My friend looked like she was thirty. And she would forever.

She rubbed some dust off of the ornate bracer on her right arm, and said, 'I am sorry I was not able to get here sooner. The dwarves were acting up along the old water tunnels under Lower Eight and we went in to make sure they remembered who lost the war. I got your text while I was five kilometres down.' She squeezed my hand again, looking worried as she gave my body the once-over.

Ceile wasn't a powerful magic user, having virtually no training and little natural strength, but much like Dr. Jacobs her skills with healing and other medical spells made me look like I had no talent at all. My friend made a gesture with her free hand, and I felt the alien tingle of one of her scanning spells. Unlike me, Ceile was an elementalist, shaping her magic from aether of the element of water. Not only was that living energy invisible to me as it flowed around us, but the feel of it was also completely different than that of something shaped from nether.

It made me uneasy, even after all my years. Not because it was different, but because being touched by aether made you feel alive, whereas being touched by nether felt like being dipped in oil.

Unless the spell in question was a fireball, then the two energies felt very similar.

Whatever Ceile saw during her scan made her shake her head in dismay. I gave her a laugh, 'Jacobs is one of the best medical wizards in the City. If he says it's over, then it's over.'

Ceile stopped walking and pulled me around to face her. She was almost half a foot taller than me, and staggeringly beautiful. She had chosen to appear as an elf when she had transferred into her flesh construct, and carried herself very much like a member of that aloof species.

She looked thoughtful and then pulled me into a tight hug. Turning us around, she started walking back up the path while gently pulling me into step next to her. With the barest hint of a smirk on her face, she said, 'Let's go get a drink. I have someone I want you to meet.'

5

We made our way back to my place to grab my car. Ceile could move like a banshee when she wanted, but I was an old man and forty blocks was a long way for me to walk, even with my ticker ticking away properly.

The guardian spells let my friend in first, as usual. I was pretty sure the car had a thing for her. Once we were both settled in the cabin, I fired up the engine. My chariot rolled down the driveway while I closed the garage door with a quick spell and then we were roaring down the road.

Ceile was quiet and kept giving me covert looks as I drove. I looked over and gave her a roguish grin, to which she wrinkled her nose in amusement and turned away.

Truth be told, I was feeling almost giddy. The cloud I'd been under for most of the day had faded away in her presence. She'd told me once that I had the same effect on her, but I'd always wondered if she was only humouring me. Ceile was the strongest person I knew.

We arrived in the Uge District and I pulled into one of the dingy parking lots that peppered the area. Rolling down my window, I swept my phone past the ticket kiosk screen to pay the ridiculous fee, and then left the printed ticket on my dash. The sound as the car locked behind us was almost mournful.

My watch pinged, and I absently wiped at its display as Ceile and I walked out into the Uge. The almost-giddiness had started to dissipate. This District was loud, colourful, and potentially dangerous. Coming here alone would have been a mistake. Sure, I could turn this block into a river of molten lava, but my body would fall apart from the strain.

It'd been a long time since I'd been able to reach anywhere near my potential.

No, I wouldn't be much use in a fight if we got jumped, but I wasn't alone. Ceile was a soldier, and one of the best. She was more dangerous than pretty much anyone in the Uge. You'd have to be pretty stupid to attack her.

'What does he think about all this?' Ceile quietly asked, giving my hand a tight squeeze. I knew who she was talking about without having to ask. Both she and Nox knew about the Other.

'He thinks it's funny, for the most part. Hasn't had much to say about it, though. He's been unusually quiet, other than a half-hearted attempt to break free earlier,' I answered after a moment. My companion fell silent again.

I suddenly felt eyes on me, and rightfully so. The Uge was packed to the gills with every type of construct available. There were virtually no original models here, and even the most unobservant person could tell I was very much original. There were dangerous looks being shot my way, and I knew that many people here took the presence of people like me very, very poorly.

A group of metal constructs, titanium maybe, watched me intently from across the street, and there was not an ounce of friendliness in their looks. Ceile didn't spare them a glance, but she did take my hand again.

I occasionally felt like a child when she was around. I wasn't strong anymore, despite the power that lurked at my fingertips. Over two centuries of medicinal and magical treatments to keep this frail body intact hadn't kept it from slowly tiring. Now, even a short walk could leave me breathing hard. A construct could take me apart pretty easily, but Ceile could hold her own against almost anything. It was mesmerizing to watch her fight.

As we headed for our destination, the group followed along. There were a lot of them. Not for the first time tonight did I think meeting Ceile's contact at a Basilisk & Castle back in the Upper River District would have made more sense. We were only a short way from the entrance to the pub and its neon sign depicting a cat in the process of being electrocuted when the group made its move.

'Hey! Fleshy!' one of them yelled as they all rapidly closed the distance. Knowing what was coming, I slowly turned and readied myself. I felt bad. This wasn't going to work out for them at all.

6

'Look at this one, Cogs,' one of them sneered as the group moved to surround us, 'he's gotta be a millennium old!' The others all cackled evilly, and the sound of metal lips clanging filled the street. I noticed that the area was suddenly devoid of people. Oh good, these guys have a reputation.

'What, you too good for a replacement model, fleshy? You think you're better than us? Huh?' another of them snarled. More laughter. Ceile's hand tightened on mine, and I knew she was just waiting for one of them to get a little too brave. One of the constructs turned away from me and looked her up and down.

'Look at you. Still clinging to who you used to be, and trying to look pretty. I could give you a ride you'd never forget,' it said in a nasty tone, making an obscene gesture and then reaching forward to prod her roughly in the chest.

I cringed a little inside.

Ceile let go of my hand gently, and in one smooth motion bent the Cog's arm in half. The construct squealed in electronic pain and fell away. The others roared and closed in on us, the first of which caught a kick to the abdomen that caved its plating in and sent it flying back into the street.

I tried to stay with her, mainly to make sure I didn't catch a wild swipe from one of the constructs by accident. Ceile moved like a viper, striking and moving so fast that she quickly overrode the ability of myself or the constructs to keep up with her. Still, there were a lot of them, and my friend could only do so much against that big of a group. One of them managed to lay a hand on her and tore away a large chunk of flesh from her shoulder.

Ceile howled and kicked that Cog in the face, almost ripping its head from its shoulders. It dropped like a rock, spewing oil and electric screams.

The constructs hadn't bothered with me yet, obviously not considering me a threat. From somewhere at the back of my mind, I felt something shift. Movement in the depths.

Let me out, Martin, and I'll teach every last one of these dogs to behave.

I shook my head, pushing his presence back toward the shadows. 'I've got this, go back to your box,' I said, under my breath. He laughed.

Ceile got hit again, and this time the blow threw her backward against a car, caving the driver's side door in. The Cogs swarmed toward her, and now I had to do something. I steeled myself, reached out and drew nether into my hands, prepared to shape it into the forms that would tear all of them apart.

Just in time to catch a punch to my face that knocked me flat and took my breath away. The nether flashed away, back into the oceans roiling behind the curtain. Spots danced across my vision, and I could just barely see Ceile being lifted from the cratered car and a couple Cogs drawing out wicked knives and grinning. A foot dropped into view in front of my face and then I was lifted high into the air, coming nose to nose with a smirking construct that was saying something about tearing my head in half.

In the middle of the chaos I felt the Other rush forward, hitting the surface in an explosion that rocked my mind. I tried to stop what was about to happen but I was too dazed and I couldn't push back

and then I pulled aether from the air around me, fingers already shaping the gusts. In a split second, I tore the head off of the construct holding me in the air and threw its body across the street to smash into several of its buddies. I slowly floated to the ground, the forms dancing around my feet, summoning the wind to further do my bidding. I laughed manically.

I was free. I could taste the elements again. I could feel the wind.

I could hear Martin angrily yelling from deep in my mind, but I didn't bother listening long enough to know what he was saying. It was probably boring anyway.

Some of the other Cogs had noticed my performance, and were turning to come punish me. I laughed even louder, filled my arms with aether, and began folding it repeatedly. I gave the nearest construct a dirty look and a grin.

The wind suddenly rose from a breeze to a gale. The sky far above went grey, and then lightning blasted down from the clouds, hitting one of the Cogs and leaving it a smoking mess on the ground. I heard Ceile scream something, saw her staring at me in desperation. I ignored her, too. Besides, the thunder was too delightfully loud to hear her anyway.

I continued shaping the spells, reaching into the vortex to bow it to my will. I hit one of the Cogs with a bolt that sheared off its right arm and threw it into a building down the street. The aether rippled around me, begging me to turn it into destruction. To use it to devastate the block. To destroy the District. I decided that was a great idea.

Drawing ever more aether to me, I reached to the sky to pull down the tornado that would take the Uge down to the bedrock, grind it to dust, but something was wrong. My arm wouldn't rise above shoulder height, and I felt weak. My vision went fuzzy, and I felt dizzy and nauseous. Both Martin and Ceile were screaming at me, but my ears were full of a buzzing noise.

My chest felt suddenly tight, and I dropped to my knees. I snarled against this betrayal by my body, but the effort to do much more than that eluded me. I tried to stand back up, but I was so tired. The wind was gone, the sky once again full of fading sunlight. I looked up and I could see one of the Cogs standing over me, its arms reaching down to my head, a hand on either side.

Martin shook the bars of his cage in fury, and I tried to shoo him away. 'Not now, Martin. I'm busy dying here,' I whispered, hoarsely.

I suddenly felt pressure and pain as the construct began to squeeze, its face full of demented pleasure. I struggled to stay conscious and I felt Martin throw all of his strength against the bars

and then I put my hands weakly up to try and stop the construct from crushing my head, barely aware of the Other's hoarse and angry cries from the depths at the back of my mind. I'd regained control, but all I think I was going to succeed in doing was dying at the wheel. The Cog suddenly looked up over my head and yelled something.

The pressure was suddenly gone, and the construct's feet flew up into the air out of my vision. I heard something snarl loudly beside me as I dropped unceremoniously to the ground.

The Cogs turned as one to the new sound, their faces full of anger and rage. One of them charged at the newcomer, and I had just enough of a view to watch it go flying back in two pieces.

'Do we have a problem here?' rumbled a voice that was deep and mostly growl.

The intact constructs fled.

Ceile was instantly at my side, and while I tried to speak, I could barely breathe. I could see her lips moving and healing magic darted across my body. Some of the tightness eased. She looked really angry.

A massive, furry, clawed hand dropped roughly onto my shoulder, and a huge wolfish face moved into view, glaring down at me. I gasped for air, but I was smiling.

'Hello, Nox,' I whispered hoarsely.

'Martin,' the werewolf growled back.

7

Ceile was an accomplished healer, but she was no doctor. Fortunately, it didn't look like my heart had decided to take the day off after all, and after a few minutes I was able to stand on my own legs. Nox had a strong hold on the back of my jacket anyway. As we walked down the street, I was pretty sure I could have stopped my legs and kept right on moving like a string-less marionette.

The street was chock full of people again, some stepping gingerly around the fallen constructs, others helping them up and into the shadows, others still scavenging pieces from the less fortunate. Most of them would be fine, as their head cases were all intact and could be transferred or rebuilt without much trouble. Well, provided they could get someone to take their head to an engineer to do it.

Ceile had a painful grip on my hand. She was pretty angry, and she spent most of the walk to the local medical outlet muttering angrily about the Other. In return, I could hear him weakly giggling at her. I kept quiet, because she was wrong. If he hadn't broken free, she and I would probably be dead and Nox would be busy ripping every Cog into tiny pieces.

Not that I was happy about the Other running the show. There was a good chance that left to his own devices long enough, he'd either kill everyone around him or himself and by virtue of that, me.

Regardless, if Nox hadn't shown up, my head would be in multiple pieces and places at once and Ceile not much better off. The big 'wolf walked just over my shoulder, scanning the crowd around us for threats. I could tell he was angry, though that wasn't entirely surprising. Nox was almost always angry at something or another.

'You spend the morning in a damn hospital and you come here of all places?' he growled, menacingly. The crowd was already giving us a wide berth, but it thinned out even more at the sight and sound of the grumpy beast.

Ceile answered first. 'This was my idea, Nox. We are meeting someone at the Cat once we are done putting the old man back together,' she said. Nox snorted.

'Then you're both idiotic and I should drag you out of the District. Martin should be in bed, not fighting 'struct gangs. You're lucky that was just strain and not another heart attack,' the 'wolf growled, though quieter this time. 'As it is, once we're done with the medics I'm taking you back to your fancy car and sending you on your way.'

Ceile slammed to a stop and started to let Nox know just how likely it'd be that he could send her anywhere when I put a hand on her shoulder and turned to face the 'wolf.

'I'm dying, Nox,' is all I said.

He looked down at me, and for a brief moment his wolfish face was filled with fuzzy sadness. He shook his head slowly and said, 'I know.' Sighing deeply, he caught hold of my jacket, lifted me off the ground, and continued our march toward the medical facility. I tried to reach the pavement and walk on my own for a few futile strides and then finally gave up.

Ceile caught up with us and took my hand after giving Nox a glare. I shrugged my shoulders as best I could and gave her a grin. For a brief instant that glare settled on me, and then she also shook her head and a slight smile cracked her face.

We walked - well, they walked - in silence for a couple blocks, until Nox startled me by saying, 'you obviously aren't here to get yourself a construct, and I don't imagine that's what you planned for him either, Ceile. So what's the deal?' She shook her head and pointed ahead.

We had arrived at the medical building, all white and sterile cleanliness. It stood out like a sore thumb against the chaos of neon and illusion outside. 'Let us get this sorted out and I will give you the details,' Ceile quietly said as we walked up the stairs and in the glass doors.

We didn't have to wait long. In a neighbourhood of constructs, a medical team doesn't have much to do. The young tech who took care of us laughed unconcernedly about some big fight that had just happened down the street, unaware that we had a little something to do with it. Afterward, he filled the exam room with a healing mist, asked us to stay for about ten minutes, and then went back to watching the television at the front desk.

I looked around at my companions, and barely concealed a weak grin. We were an odd trio.

The exam room was spacious enough for the three of us and a technician, but the chairs were not designed for something like Nox. Almost three metres of blond furred fury, he loomed over me and Ceile, clicking his nightmarish claws on the counter impatiently. His vivid blue eyes were constantly in motion, taking in everything around him at a speed that few others could match, much less exceed. There was a reason the Government required people like him to be licensed and closely monitored. Even lucid permanent therianthropes were very dangerous.

He said nothing, just looked angry even though he was probably only irritated. The 'wolf's face rarely showed anything other than anger or angrier. The shaggy hand that wasn't trying to vandalize the marble counter scratched idly at the fur under his chin.

By contrast, Ceile no longer looked angry, just serene. She always amazed me. My friend could fall into a terrifying rage or bitterly cold fury, but it was when she allowed herself to quiet and calm and settle that she was her strongest. Her attacks would flow like water, fast and smooth and deadly. She had to be pretty upset to have let the Cogs get the jump on her.

Her lightly pointed ears poked out of her mostly short-cropped dark hair, and I think she might have fit in well walking the streets of an elven city. At least until the elves realized she was a flesh construct, and then things might get ugly. Elves and humans might not be in active hostilities with each other like we were with the dwarves, but they weren't happy to have us wandering around their cities either.

She stared at nothing, lost in thought, eyes focused on some distant object. I had questions for her, but I didn't want to interrupt and I knew that she would tell me when she was ready. She wouldn't have risked my life here in the Uge unless it was for a real good reason. If she wanted me to meet someone, it was important that I do.

And what about me, Martin?

I frowned but didn't respond. The Other laughed and floated along, just beneath the surface. Watching. He wouldn't bother trying to break free right now, but it was still disconcerting whenever he hung around.

The tech reappeared, breaking some of the discomfort, and waved us toward the exit with a flamboyant flourish. Nox lifted me to my feet, despite my squawk of complaint. I gave him a sour look, but the big 'wolf just snorted and ducked out the door.

We walked out into the night, Ceile on my left, once again holding my hand but gently now, and Nox on my right, no longer holding me up but walking very closely just over my shoulder, his big furry head scanning everything around us for trouble. The presence of my friends made me feel stronger, and I tried to maintain a steady pace, knowing that they were both drastically slowing their strides to match mine.

The familiar electrocuted neon cat materialized out of the fog of lights, and as we neared the entrance I had a quick scan of my own around the area. The constructs were all gone, and what damage there had been to property or street was already repaired. They didn't mess around in the Uge. Its denizens liked the noise and chaos of the place, but if anything was out of order, they had it fixed very quickly.

Nox took hold of the door handle, which seemed tiny in his hand, and held it open for us. I gave Ceile a wink and walked on through, my companions following me into the brightly lit interior. As the door slowly closed behind us, a sign appeared to our right.

'Welcome to the Electric Cat,' it said as the pub's neon mascot rode the lightning forever.

8

Compared to the din and racket outside, the Cat was pretty quiet. I'd been to the Uge District a handful of times over the years, but had never set foot in this place. Ceile came here a couple of times a week with some of the soldiers we'd fought alongside over the years, and she had a reputation. The Cogs were either new to the area or just stupid, as pretty much everyone here knew my friend could mangle a steam construct with her bare hands if she wanted to.

A bulky plastic construct nervously walked up to us, wringing his hands and looking like he wanted to be anywhere else. The pub's bouncer, and a new one from the looks of it. He came to a stumbling halt in front of us, and his eyes twitched back and forth between the floor and Nox.

'I'm very sorry, sir, but I must see your license,' the poor fellow stammered out, trying hard to seem intimidating and authoritative but failing miserably in the face of the werewolf towering over him.

Nox snorted, which nearly sent the newcomer scrambling for cover, and then reached down to his belt. Flicking a pouch open, he reached in and carefully pulled an identification package out with two of his very large claws. Looking down at the bouncer, he dropped the document into the withering construct's hands, crossed his arms and began tapping the claws on his feet against the tiles impatiently.

The bouncer looked his prize over, nodded with relief, and then haltingly passed the package back. 'Thank you, Agent. No slight intended, just following regulations,' he said as he slowly backed away. He gave a half salute and then turned and fled.

Nox sneered at the construct as he vanished into the back room. The big 'wolf put the document back into its pouch and went back to scanning for threats. He didn't have much patience for bureaucracy, even if he understood the reasons for it.

Along with having to be licensed, permanent therianthropes - as they were labeled by the Government - were usually pressured into working with the Department of Enforcement. Mostly to keep tabs on them but also to take advantage of their strengths. Nox was no exception. He'd been an Agent with Enforcement for almost ninety years, having been taken in by the Government when he was just fourteen.

Unless Ceile had summoned him here to meet us, his presence here meant something big was up in the District. Enforcement policed the whole City, but the people here weren't any happier about extra-humans than they were original models. Sending Nox in meant the Government needed muscle, either to take down a big target or to keep the place quiet. He was adept at either.

I had questions for both friends. This was turning into a really weird day.

If you ask me-

'And I'm not asking you. Shut up,' I said, under my breath. Ceile gave me a funny look, but I waved her off. The Other just chuckled and vanished into the depths.

We sat at one of the split-level tables, with Ceile and me on the upper seat, Nox on the lower. These booths served the dual purpose of being more comfortable for big patrons and also putting everyone at roughly eye level. The 'wolf settled in, not looking pleased but at least looking slightly less irritated. My less-monstrous companion put a hand on my leg and looked around the pub intently.

'Alright, who wants to go first? Ceile, who're we here to see? Nox, what're you doing here? Unless Ceile called you in, something bad must be going on in the District,' I asked. My voice was shaky, but after the day I'd been having, I was okay with that.

Nox gave a low growl and then stopped his scanning to look at me. He shook his head slowly, then said, 'the Department sent me here to bring the District back into order. We'd been getting reports of some of the old gangs reforming, so I was to find some of them and tear them apart.' He lifted a claw and pointed at me with a sneer, 'and it's a good thing I'm here. That group was huge, and they were going to rob or kill you both right in the busiest part of the Uge. That's either a lot of guts or a lot of stupidity. Once we're done here, I'll have to go and make sure they don't get to do it again.'

I looked at the werewolf and I was reminded that as much as I regarded him as my friend, he was very much a monster and a weapon. The Government didn't exactly keep him on the payroll for his stunning intellect, though he wasn't an idiot. No, they kept him because there wasn't much out there that he couldn't kill.

Ceile and I liked to joke that he could take a dragon.

What would be more interesting is to see which of your friends could take the other.

I snarled in my head and lashed out with all my will, sending the Other spinning away into the depths of my mind. He laughed as he vanished into the darkness.

Nox had fallen silent and returned to gazing around the room. The other patrons were avoiding his gaze as much as possible, though one goblin in the corner made brief eye contact and then fled for the washrooms with a squeak of fear.

I turned to Ceile and raised an eyebrow at her. She quietly looked at me, her crystal blue eyes intense and unblinking, and said, 'There is a man that has agreed to meet with us. He is a wizard, and a powerful one, but his true power lies in gathering information. And he has information that I think you very much need.'

Seeing my look of confusion, my friend reached up and touched my check. Her soft, light brown skin was warm against my face.

'The Fountain of Youth, Martin. He knows of an artifact that can restore your body. Do you not see? You are going to live forever with me.'

9

I stared at her, mouth agape, and out of the corner of my eye I could see Nox was doing a fair approximation of that as well. The laughter in the dark corners of my mind had gone dead silent. My watch pinged.

After a long moment me, Nox, and the Other all started talking at once. Though the big 'wolf's voice was quiet, at least for him, he drowned my own out. 'What are you talking about, Angael?' he snarled, 'There's no such thing.'

Ceile ignored him, just continued looking at me. I frowned and said, 'How, Ceile? That kind of magic doesn't exist. Science either. And I won't transfer to a construct.' That last part echoed through my head. As far as I knew, a construct was the only thing that would save me. If I chose not to take one, then I'd be gone. But Ceile would live on forever, provided her body wasn't completely destroyed somehow, swapping from construct to construct.

She'd live on forever. Without me.

Ceile must have seen something in my eyes, as she took both of my hands and held them tight. Moving in very close, she stared at me intently. Out of the corner of my eye, I could see Nox staring at nothing just over her shoulder.

'You are right. No spell, no surgery, no medicine will work. I have researched every option to exhaustion and came up with nothing. A hundred years, I have looked! All for nothing,' she said, her voice briefly tinged with desperation. 'And when I had almost given up hope, prepared to accept that my greatest friend would one day be gone forever, this man came to me with an answer.'

Now I was really shocked. For so long, I'd just let everything slide, thinking I'd figure something out when my health got bad and all along, Ceile had been looking for a solution. I suddenly felt ashamed and looked away.

Ceile put a hand under my chin and pulled my head over to look into her eyes. 'Do you trust me?' she asked.

I nodded without hesitating. I trusted her with my life. If she thought there was a chance this man knew how to save me, then it might work. I squeezed her hands. She smiled, brilliantly.

'His name is Bill. He is,' she paused briefly, 'a bit odd. But he has a reputation, and a very good one, for finding things out. He had heard of my search and he was intrigued.'

Nox was staring at us silently, his face pensive, one bushy eyebrow slightly raised. He looked almost comical, though mentioning that to him would have probably been a mistake. I could feel the Other hovering just below the surface, listening. Ceile smiled at me again, and then turned toward the pub floor and beckoned.

From out of nowhere, a thin man appeared. Garbed in flowing, rainbow robes covered in chaotic patterns, he would have been almost perfectly camouflaged in the cacophony of neon in the streets outside. He had unruly brown hair and a ridiculously twirled mustache. Ornate brilliant blue rings decorated each of his fingers. He strode forward with purpose, stopping at the foot of our table. He bowed deeply.

'Hello, my friends! I am Bill. And I know everything.'

10

Bill sat himself down on the upper seat, having chosen a spot where all three of us could easily see, hear, and speak to him. Ceile smiled at the wizard. Nox did not.

The Other lurked, uncharacteristically quiet.

'I imagine you all have a lot of questions, and I will attempt to provide answers for each but this is not the place for such discussions. Instead, I'll give you my five minute pitch, you decide if I'm making everything up, and then we can go to a slightly more private location,' Bill said, arms gesturing wildly.

I struggled to wrap my head around the constantly shifting cadence of the strange fellow's speech. If he was hiding an accent, he was doing a good job. I couldn't begin to pick a region he might be from.

'Your friend Ceile Angael is correct. I am in constant search of knowledge, traveling the world looking for the answers to things I do not know. Listening for tales that might turn out to be true.' The wizard paused for effect. Nox snorted and clicked his claws on the table.

'And somewhere out there is something that can somehow do what magic and science can't, wizard? This is ridiculous. Ceile, I can't believe you fell for this. Martin, let's get out of this dump,' the big 'wolf growled and started to stand. I looked over at him and was about to say something when Bill abruptly slammed his hand down on the table, palm down. Each of his rings flared red.

The lights in the pub went out, and the other patrons faded into shadow, their noises deadening and then vanishing altogether. A brilliant red light sprung into existence behind the wizard, back-lighting him in crimson. Wind had sprung up from nowhere, and Bill's hair and cloak billowed out. Then he spoke, and his voice echoed through the void we now found ourselves in.

'Stay, friends! I am Bill, who was once known as Peter and will one day be known again as Poe! I have walked through terrible lands and nightmare realms! I have spoken to fell creatures and beings older than this world itself! I've parlayed with Death, the Eldest of the Horsemen; swapped riddles with the Earthmonger, King of the Dwarves; sung a dire dirge with the Harrowtree, Lord of Wolves and Ravens! I have walked among dwarves and elves and kobolds and dragons! I have traveled to the Reyan Desert in the deep south and dipped a toe in the poisoned ocean at its edge, and journeyed to the very end of the Ravenmyre in the far north and looked into oblivion! I've learned magic from archons, the greatest of wizards, and shared stories with an aethon, an elementalist of truly mind-boggling power!

I have ventured to the tallest mountains and to the deepest caves!' the wizard roared.

'And there, my friends, in a vault far below the earth, lies an artifact. A relic from a distant time, built when the human species created horrors simply because they could. This device can regenerate a human body, give it back its youth and vigour,' the wizard said, his voice quieter. 'The particulars I can give you later, should you choose to hire my services. Suffice it to say that this item can save your life, Martin Tundra, and extend it well into the future. If we go get it, that is.'

With that, the wizard lifted his hand from the table and the pub returned to normal. His rings slowly went dark and then back to brilliant blue. I blinked in the sudden light and looked around to find the other patrons completely oblivious to Bill's magic.

Nox was looking at the wizard with disbelief and distrust written plainly on his face. His claws were frozen over the tabletop. Ceile, on the other hand, was looking at me with hope in her eyes. It was obvious that she believed that Bill was not only telling the truth but also that his prize might do what he says it does.

I wanted to believe that, too.

'How long, Bill? How long to go get this thing?' I asked. Nox started to growl something at me, but I put my hand up and he grudgingly went silent. Turning back to the wizard, I continued, 'How long? Will it be dangerous?'

Bill gave me a smile, and said, 'Two weeks. Longer if things go wrong. And yes, we're going to run into trouble.'

Two weeks. Longer if things go wrong. That put this little adventure past the two weeks of relative healthiness that the doctor had given me and closing on the date range of my death. So, that meant the last bit of this journey was going to be unpleasant, if I chose to go.

If I chose to go. I didn't have a lot of choices, really. If I declined Bill's services, then what would I spend my last days doing? Obviously I'd spend them with Ceile and Nox whenever they had the time. Get nostalgic with them, laugh over old stories and a pint, at least until my body deteriorated to the point where I was stuck at home or in a hospital. And then I'd lie there and wait to die. Or I could continue searching for some escape from my doom, pour over the libraries, scour the dark parts of the lower Districts for a less-than-legal solution of some kind.

Or I could buy a construct and undergo the transfer rites.

I shook my head slowly. No, none of those would be my fate. I wouldn't lie in a bed, my body disintegrating around me until the end came. I wouldn't find my salvation in the City. Any areas I hadn't already searched would have been poured over by Ceile.

And as far as I was concerned, transfer was a bit misleading. Cloning, more like, and cloning where the original is destroyed. Oh, that wasn't what the Government and such would like you to believe, of course. They've been supporters for centuries. No, as far as the vast majority were concerned, transferring your consciousness into a construct was the natural progression of things. Ceile's reason for abandoning her birth body was different, but she still believed that once your original model had reached its end, the next step was transfer.

I broke out of my thoughts to find everyone staring at me with very different expressions. Bill was smiling gently, fingers steepled beneath his chin. Ceile looked excited, continuing to squeeze my hand tightly. Nox had returned to his seat and was now glaring at me in disbelief.

'You're thinking about this. You're actually thinking about going on this trip, and you don't know anything about it,' the 'wolf quietly growled.

I looked at him for a moment, and then nodded. 'I've got weeks but not months, Nox. And I'm not interested in going to shake hands with Death quite yet. What else can I do?' I said, then turned back to Bill. 'Alright, Bill, let's hear the details. I'm interested.'

The wizard clapped his hands and a broad grin split his mustachioed face. 'Excellent, but not here. Some things should be spoken of only in private. My home isn't far, we can discuss the adventure there,' he said. Then he lifted free of his chair as though he were a marionette with invisible strings and floated to the pub floor behind him. With a flourish, he waved us all toward the door and then strode away with a spin.

Ceile burst into laughter, squeezed my arm lightly, and then slid off the bench after dropping some coins on the table to cover our drinks. She was still laughing as we walked to the door and its neon cat, with Nox thundering along behind us, his wolfish face dour.

From somewhere at the back of my mind, I felt the Other smile.

And so it begins.

11

Bill walked us to my car, giving us his address and directions to get there. He was friendly, smiling and gesturing animatedly as he talked about his home. When we reached my car, he shook my hand with a firm grip and then kissed Ceile's as he winked at her. He briefly considered Nox and the 'wolf's clawed hand before giving him a salute instead. Nox chuckled, darkly.

The wizard then knelt to the ground, head bowed, and arms wide. With a dramatic flourish, he lifted his head to the sky and launched himself into the air, rocketing away. A few seconds later, he'd vanished.

Nox, Ceile, and I watched him go. The big 'wolf turned to look at us in amusement, then said, 'If he's a fraud, I'm going to eat him. Maybe if he isn't one, too.' He paused and put a hand to his stomach, then continued, 'It's possible I'm hungry.' He gave us a terrifying and toothy grin and then shot off across the parking lot in pursuit of the wizard.

He'd probably get there well before us.

The guardian spells spun around my and Ceile's hands and then the car's doors swung open. We hopped in and soon enough we were on our way. Traffic was light. Night and rain were falling, which both intensified and muted the neon chaos of the Uge. An electric fox leapt from sign to sign as it chased us down the street. I recognized it from a pub several blocks back.

We passed through the massive wall that divided the District from the next and left the beastie behind.

'Tell me about him,' I said to Ceile after we'd driven in comfortable silence through the Green Lakes District for a while. She looked over and smiled at me.

'I first met him a few years ago. I had just finished running into another dead end when my contact in Lower Eight suggested that it could get me in touch with a man who could possibly help. I was running out of avenues to search, so I asked it to do so. A week or so later, Bill appeared from nowhere while I was going through some of the old necromancy texts in the Library.'

She paused for breath and then continued, 'He told me that he was fascinated by my search and your situation, and wanted to offer his services. He said he could find what I was looking for. For a suitable price, of course.' She looked away and fell silent for a long moment.

My watch pinged quietly. 'Price?' I asked her.

'I told him to begin immediately. He gave me a bow, told me he would be in touch, and then I did not hear from him for over two years,' she continued, ignoring my question. 'Last week, he walked out of the wall of the barracks and told me he had found what I had been looking for.'

'And what was it?' I asked, mind racing. Ceile shook her head.

'He explained that it would regenerate your body, drastically increasing your lifespan, but would not go into specifics. Said he would give us the details once our party was all together, asked me to set up a meeting with you,' she said.

I thought about all of that for a bit, then said, 'And here we are. What do you suppose he meant by 'party'? Did he know that Nox was going to be there, somehow?'

My friend shook her head again. 'I do not know. I never mentioned the werewolf, and I did not ask him to meet us today. Maybe there are others Bill will be bringing along if we go,' she said, looking out the window. She suddenly burst into laughter. 'Oh, Martin. I think we are here,' she said, pointing out into the rain.

I glanced out Ceile's window and laughed just as my cellphone played a tone to say we had arrived at our destination. Bill's house fit the man's extravagant personality perfectly. Most of the homes in this section of the Lakes were fairly upscale bungalows or two stories. The wizard's home was a tower that rose four stories above a barren dirt lot, lit by rings of small, brilliant, multi-coloured lights placed regularly from base to top. It was obnoxiously loud.

I brought the car to a stop in front of Bill's yard, and found Nox standing on the sidewalk in the rain, looking the wizard's tower up and down with a bemused look on his face. As Ceile and I got out and joined him, he looked over at us.

'He really wants everyone to know he's a wizard, doesn't he?' the big 'wolf growled, shaking his head.

Ceile smiled and gave his arm a squeeze. 'Let us go see what Bill has to say, shall we?' she asked, and stepped forward into the dirt of the wizard's yard, heading for the door.

As soon as her foot hit the ground she vanished. There was the sound of a door slamming, and then it was just Nox and I standing shocked in the rain.

From deep in my mind, the Other laughed.

12

I drew some nether from below me and shaped it into detection forms, letting my magic poke and prod along the edge of Bill's lawn. I gave up after a few minutes. If the yard was trapped, the wizard had hid it well.

Nox paced angrily behind me, stopping every once in a while to growl toward the tower. The door taunted us from across the dirt. There was no motion from within, no shadows at any of the windows. The brilliant lights continued to gleam in the rain and dark.

'Well, what is it, Tundra? What happened to Ceile? What do we do next?' the big 'wolf snarled at me, punctuating each question with a vicious jab toward the door.

I shook my head. 'I can't tell what took her. There's no trace of magic here, so I can't try and counter it. All I can say is that the trigger was definitely when she stepped on the ground,' I said in frustration.

'In the ground, huh,' Nox said. I recognized his tone of voice, turned toward him and started to tell him to stop. Before I could, the 'wolf had caught hold of my jacket, flung me over his shoulder, and then we were hurtling through the air toward the door.

Then nine hundred pounds of werewolf reduced it to rubble, the two of us crashing through both the door and some of the walls around it. Before we'd even come to a stop, Nox had gently thrown me into the safety of the debris near the door and rolled to his feet. Dust and splinters blasted past him into the hall.

For a long moment, the werewolf stood, arms outstretched, claws at the ready, eyes slowly scanning the area. We appeared to be alone, but dust shrouded the far end of the hall. Nox sniffed the air, teeth bared.

'I can smell her,' he growled.

I looked around. We hadn't made the most strategic entrance. I was going to have to have a chat with the big 'wolf sometime about tactics. He made a hell of a shock trooper, though. 'Well, we've just made a subtle entrance into a building we know nothing about. So, that's something. We'd best move fast, who knows what defences there are. Can you track Ceile?' I asked.

Nox nodded and said, 'Stay close, she isn't far.'

He moved forward quickly, and I got to my feet and followed as best I could. The dust swirled around us as we went, the gloom back lit by the odd multi-coloured lights. The far end of the hall opened up into a large chamber, and the two of us slowed and entered it cautiously. As visibility steadily improved, the 'wolf and I found ourselves standing in front of six cloaked figures, arrayed in a half circle.

Each of them was carrying a shock cannon at the ready.

Kill them all, Martin. Break them, and let's go get your friend.

I ignored him as I took up position just to Nox's side and slightly behind. The big 'wolf was crouched and ready, teeth bared and claws clacking together menacingly.

'Holy crap, he's big,' one of them whispered. His neighbours shushed him.

'Well, that was a spectacular way to invite yourselves in,' one of the figures said, stepping forward a couple metres. 'Could you have just used the front walk? That door is for ornamental purposes!' he continued, shaking his head and gesturing in irritation at the ruin behind us.

I realized that none of the six were taller than a metre and a half, and something about them was familiar.

'You're gnomes. Bill has gnomes for security,' I said, chuckling.

The gnomes all drew themselves up in indignation and started talking at once. The leader tried to maintain some professionalism, attempting to get his minions to be quiet, but soon the six were animatedly arguing amongst themselves.

Nox shook his head in amusement. 'Gnomes,' he growled. We probably could have walked right past them at this point without being noticed. I wondered if Bill actually expected the gnomes to provide security or if they were just one more addition to the theatrics.

The 'wolf looked at me expectantly. I smiled at him and said, 'We can probably get them to take us to Ceile. Get their attention.' My friend bared his teeth in a terrifying grin and then turned back to the arguing gnomes. He took a deep breath.

And then he howled.

There isn't much in this world that can make a sound like that. A few of the other big 'thropes could. 'Lions and 'tigers. 'Bears, of course. Dragons. Some elementals. When Nox cut loose, anyone caught unaware might think the world was coming to an end. As it was, the room violently shook and the gnomes dropped to the floor in shock and terror. Hands reached up to cover their ears, their weapons falling to the floor, forgotten.

The werewolf stamped forward and snatched the leader off of the floor, lifting the poor gnome up until they were nose to nose. The little fellow immediately started shrieking.

'I'm just a gardener! We dress up as security when the boss is elsewhere! Don't eat me!' he yelled. Eyes wide, he gestured wildly over his shoulder and hoarsely whispered, 'they're much tastier. The one second from the back on the right probably tastes like chicken!'

Nox growled and bared his teeth. I stepped forward to stand next to the gnome's knees, which were dangling around level with my face.

'Our friend stepped onto the lawn and vanished. Where did she go?' I asked him. He looked back and forth between me and the 'wolf.

'Oh. Oh! The boss must have left the door step on when he left. Your friend is fine! Please don't eat me!' he said in a rush.

I was about to ask another question, but I realized that it had suddenly gotten very cold in the room. Recognizing the feeling, I spun around and yelled, 'Nox, sorcery!' The big 'wolf instantly dumped the gnome into the midst of his colleagues and turned with a snarl.

Bill floated in the air not three metres away, arms out and palms up. His cloak and robes snapped and fluttered in a conjured wind. He was wearing a hat that was so stereotypically wizard that I almost laughed. The air above his hands glittered, and I could feel the cold emanating from him.

'How rude of you both! Breaking my tower and scaring my staff!' he roared, his voice echoing down the hall and through the chamber. The glitter over his palms became jagged ice that spun wildly around his arms. 'Perhaps I will cancel our deal. Perhaps I will send you home,' the wizard snarled, lifting a hand into the air. Then he pointed at me with the other, his eyes narrowing and mouth twisting into a sneer.

'Perhaps I will teach you some manners.'

13

'Seriously, though. You should have just called me. I forgot to shut the step off when I got back,' the wizard suddenly said, dropping gently to the ground with a wide grin. The ice and wind slowly faded away. He strode right up to us and bowed deep.

'The front path is triggered when someone sets foot on the ground. Ms. Angael was wrapped in a stasis field and deposited at the main entrance below ground. When the step is off, a traditional set of stairs leads to the real door. The decoy door,' the wizard said with a chuckle, 'is just there to look pretty.'

Nox looked like he was still planning to tear Bill's head off, and the claws on his right hand were clacking together sporadically. I didn't know what to think. The explanation was just weird enough to be true, considering we were dealing with the wizard.

Bill didn't seem to notice our unease, and turned away, waving us to follow. 'I have Ceile settled upstairs with some tea. She wanted to come, but I thought it'd be funnier if I came alone.' Looking over at the pile of beleaguered gnomes, he chuckled and said, 'C'mon, you lot. We need to feed our guests.'

With a wave of his hand, a massive staircase descended slowly from the ceiling above him, coming to rest with the bottom step only inches behind the wizard's feet. He snapped his fingers with a deep laugh, and then charged up the stairs. 'Come!' he yelled over his shoulder. There was a clatter as the gnomes gathered themselves and their gear up and jostled their way up the stairs after him.

I stood there, shaking my head, and looked over at Nox. The 'wolf was watching the gnomes as they one by one vanished into the ceiling. When they were gone, he looked down at me and growled, 'Well, this isn't exactly how I figured the evening was going to go. Figure this is a trap?'

'Well, you go first and then you can let me know,' I laughed, clapping him on the elbow. The big 'wolf snorted and then stomped forward. Gingerly setting a foot on the lower step, he tested his weight and then slowly progressed upward. I trailed along behind him, drawing nether to me and shaping forms that flickered through the air in search of malevolent magic. I found nothing. With a shrug, I formed new shapes that blew the dust and debris off of the 'wolf and me.

We climbed for some time, and I started to wonder how we hadn't yet poked out through the roof of the tower. Just as I was prepared to tell Nox to start tearing up the walls, the next set of stairs opened up into a wide chamber that contained a massive fireplace, benches and loungers of all kinds arrayed around it, a fully stocked bar and kitchen, several tables and chairs pulled up in a rough triangle, and bookshelves. Dozens of them. Stacked to the high ceiling with millions of books and scrolls and what appeared to be compact discs. I shook my head. Who uses those relics anymore?

'Welcome!' Bill roared from the kitchen. He appeared to be making pancakes. The gnomes had vanished.

I burst into laughter at the absurdity of everything, taking in the whole room in amusement. I paused my examination when I found a familiar face sitting in one of the loungers in front of the fireplace. Ceile waved, a big grin on her face and a mug of tea in her hand.

Nox and I made our way over to her. I squeezed her shoulder and then dropped into the chair next to hers. Nox crouched down beside us, his wolfish head still standing taller than me and eye-to-eye with Ceile.

'You're alright?' I asked her. She nodded.

'Fine. The stasis ride was a bit surprising, but Bill was waiting in the entry chamber to apologize and explain. He is quite the character. He had just turned the step off when we heard you crash through the wall upstairs. I was alarmed, but after a few seconds of staring off into space, Bill laughed and explained that you and Nox had gotten impatient and wanted to beat us to the hot chocolate,' she said with a laugh. 'He summoned a gnome from nowhere - a gnome! - and said I should follow the little fellow up and get myself some tea while he went to collect you two.'

She paused for a moment, gesturing around the room before continuing, 'Just look at this place. It is wonderful. I could spend days reading in one of these chairs in front of the fire.' She smiled happily. I didn't think I'd ever seen quite that look on her face.

'It reminds me of home,' she said suddenly, and sadness ringed her voice. I was surprised. My friend had never really spoken about where she had come from. I didn't know anything about her home and the only thing I knew about her childhood was that the people in her life hadn't taken it well when she had come out as a trans-woman. Saying this place reminded her of home was more of a clue than I'd gotten in the hundred and fifty years I'd known her.

Today was going to be full of surprises.

'Well, he's lucky I didn't decide to wear his head for a hat,' Nox growled loudly, interrupting my thoughts. There was a chuckle from the kitchen.

'Can I get you gentlemen something to drink?' said a quiet voice from over my shoulder. We all turned to find a gnome woman dressed in a server's uniform standing between me and Nox. She couldn't have been a metre and a half tall.

I decided that with my death lurking somewhere in the not-so-distant future I was just going to go with it. I smiled at her, still enjoying the novelty of seeing gnomes, and said, 'Do you have any dark ale, miss?'

She nodded at me with a small smile and then turned to Nox. Looking not a bit nervous, she said, 'And you, Agent?' The big 'wolf looked at her for a long moment, and then chuckled.

'If you've got a mug I can hold without shattering, I'll have whatever dark ale you're going to poison my friend with,' he said in amusement. The gnome nodded, patted the 'wolf's knee, and then darted away.

Nox looked back and forth between me and Ceile, and shook his head. 'Where did he find gnomes, of all things?' he growled quietly. I started to answer but was interrupted by the sight of the largest, most comfortable-looking lounger I'd ever seen coming to a perfect landing just across from the three of us.

Bill lounged in the pillows, a plate of pancakes resting next to him, lifting a hand in greeting to us as his odd chariot came to a halt. I felt a sizable mug pressed into my hand, and turned to find our server valiantly trying to wrestle a massive pitcher off of a serving cart. 'I'm sorry, Agent, I can't lift it,' she said, puffing with the exertion. Nox grinned a toothy grin and gingerly lifted the huge glass into his lap with one clawed hand.

Nox and I both thanked her and she beamed back happily.

'Don't drink all of that at once,' I said to the 'wolf as I looked back at Bill. Nox growled in mock anger. Ceile chuckled.

Bill clapped his hands, and the light in the room lowered. 'Now that we are all settled, I will tell you what I know, what I have for you, and what will be required of you. You have made no bargains and signed no contracts. You are free to leave at any time, preferably without further damaging my home. I think you will agree, Martin, that time is of the essence and that you have run out of options,' the wizard said, his voice once again echoing through the chamber.

I nodded silently. Ceile reached over and took my hand. Nox patted me roughly on the head. I smiled my thanks at the two when it occurred to me that I hadn't heard or felt the Other in almost an hour. I was immediately suspicious. Bill once again interrupted, clearing his throat and then speaking.

'Let us begin,' the wizard said.

14

'This is what I know, Martin Tundra, Ceile Angael, and Nox of the Wolfmoon. Martin, you have kept your body alive long past its time through the use of powerful medicine and magic. In my centuries of investigation, I have never known of an original model that had survived for more than one hundred and ninety-four years before dying. Your willpower has been second to none in pushing yourself and your body forward despite the odds,' Bill said, gesturing grandiosely with each sentence.

'Your time, however, has arrived. The cancer you fought so hard to beat several months ago is back, and there is nothing left to kill it with. Your doctor has given you a couple of weeks before your health begins to deteriorate beyond its already weakened state. Your doctor has further given you four to six weeks before your body is no longer able to sustain life, at which point you will die.'

I frowned, wondering how the wizard came by that information.

'Your only option, that you knew of, was to have a construct built for you and then have your consciousness transferred into this new body. Alas, this is no option at all, at least for you. You firmly believe that the procedure known as transferring is no transfer at all, but is instead a copy. A copy in which the original self is destroyed,' Bill continued.

I felt Ceile tense up, and her grip went tight. She and I had never really discussed it, though she knew what I believed. And, honestly, I didn't like to talk about it. It was a terrifying topic for me. There were more than a billion constructs in the City, some of whom had transferred more than once. I had lived here for all of my two hundred and sixty-four years, and as they went by, I could only stare out into the City and shudder. Everyone was a copy. No one was who they really were. How many people had disappeared into that flash of light, gone without a trace, with a stranger walking around in their image, the copy believing itself the original.

Ceile had been in her current body for more than two hundred years. From the little that I knew about her early life, it had been a horrifying mess of bigotry and abuse, simply because she'd been born with the wrong genitalia. When she'd finally escaped that hell, and had been able to afford to do so, she'd immediately transferred to a body that reflected who she was, finally free of the flawed one she was born in.

If I was right, that meant that the Ceile I know was not the Ceile that had survived those terrible years. That that Ceile was long gone, erased in the magic that gave my Ceile a body that she loved. That the things that had shaped her life and who she is had never happened to her. That that part of her life was a lie.

I was sure that the reason we'd never talked about it was because neither of us wanted to say that out loud.

'Whether you are correct in your belief or not is irrelevant. That option is off the table and now you have nothing else,' Bill said, and then paused for dramatic effect.

'Wizard, all the dark ale in the world won't keep you alive if you don't keep this monologue moving,' Nox snarled. Bill laughed.

'I'll speed things up a notch, then. The truth, my friends, is that Martin does indeed have an option. My search initially covered the usual suspects. Radical surgeons, the Grafters, reckless healing wizards. The Grafters offered the strongest solution, jamming your head onto a full-fledged android body, however I do not believe that that is much better in your eyes than the transfer.'

'Truth be told, I did not believe I would find a result in those camps, as Ms. Angael had poured over them thoroughly and yourself as well, to a lesser extent. So I turned my eyes outward from the City. I spoke with many of the Elders, with little luck. Death flat out refused to rejuvenate your body, and suggested that he ought to take your life away instead. War thought it might be funny to heal you just to anger his brother but turned me away in the end. The Green Lady offered to give you back the years of your life, on the condition that you stay with her forever in her realm. I did not believe that you were interested in that, and so I declined her generous offer. Coronais refused to even hear me, and I had to fight my way free of her domain.'

'I then crossed the world in search of aethons,' he said with an odd tone, and then stopped.

Aethons. Elementalists whose power could shatter cities. Decimate countries. The strongest among them had been responsible for some of the most terrifying cataclysms in the world's history.

I can turn this world to dust. Free me. My power can keep us alive.

The voice sends shock waves through my mind and I struggled to keep upright. The Other's presence crashed against the surface of my consciousness and suddenly I was fighting to maintain control.

I was vaguely aware that Ceile was out of her chair and clutching both of my hands, that Nox was on the other side, wolfish face pressed close, scanning my face with concern, that Bill was watching me with a sad smile.

I will be free, Martin. You can't keep me locked in here forever.

I snarled and tried to gather the strength to throw him back but his attack was relentless. The bastard was stronger than I'd ever seen him. I huddled in on myself and tried to bring my magic to bare *and then* I sat back up and looked around. Martin howled from his cage at the back of my mind. Ceile and Nox are very close, both of them looking comically concerned.

'Let go of me,' I said, neutrally. Nox growled in anger. Ceile hissed in dismay and backed away. Looking at the big 'wolf, I quietly repeated, 'Let go of me, 'wolf.'

For a long moment, I thought he might tear me in half, but then he shoved me backward lightly and backed away.

'You!' Ceile snarled. I looked at her dismissively and then turned to Bill. The wizard was looking back with a strange expression.

'Keep talking, wizard,' I said.

15

'Ah, excellent. I'd hoped to meet you before we set off. And power! You practically radiate it,' Bill excitedly said, leaning forward from his perch to look me up and down.

'I can arrange for you to get a first-hand demonstration if you're so inclined. But I want to hear what you have to say. So get to it,' I said, quietly.

The wizard smiled and bowed. 'So be it. I trust Martin can still hear what I have to say?' he asked and, when I nodded, continued, 'Having found nothing but dead ends, I turned my experienced eye in a different direction. The destruction of the last world scattered artifacts and relics from the civilizations that died with it across what would become our world.'

'Millions of these are completely useless, damaged, destroyed, or unfathomable. In my travels, however, I've come across dozens that still function, many of which perform tasks that our own technology and magic cannot. Many of which can heal bodies in ways our own technology and magic cannot.'

He paused to take a gulp of whatever was in the mug next to his pancakes. Out of the corner of my eye, I could see Ceile glaring at me. Nox had moved to stand beside her, and while he wasn't looking at me, I knew the big 'wolf was angry.

Martin had finally fallen silent. He knew he'd get control back eventually. My lip curled involuntarily at that. This wasn't an arrangement I was very happy with.

'It wasn't long before I learned of a relic that had the potential to be what I was looking for. Intact. Functional. And, importantly, well tested,' Bill continued, before pausing again.

My patience was wearing, and I reached out for aether in the surrounding air. I started to shape it into forms that would make the wizard a little more likely to talk faster and Bill's face suddenly went serious.

'That would be very impolite of you, my friend. Perhaps we'll talk another day,' he said, frowning.

I snarled and said, 'What are you talking about? Keep talking, wizard, or I'll-' but Bill pointed his fingers at me and snapped them *and then* I rocked backward, nearly falling out of my chair. Ceile caught hold of my arm, and Nox was over our chairs and crouching next to me again in a single leap.

'Martin? Bill, how did you do that?' Ceile asked. I shook my head, trying to clear my mind. The Other was dead silent, floating stunned deep below the surface.

'Just a little bit of magic that I've learnt for similar occasions. Are you alright, Martin?' Bill said, looking at me with concern.

I gulped air for a moment, managing to right myself, and then said, 'Yeah, I'm alright. What was that? He isn't usually able to do that, normally I have to be hurt or really distracted. How did you send him away?'

Bill waved me away, and smiled. 'Another time. The night grows late and my speech has been delayed enough already. Ms. Glaiya, another round for our guests, please,' he said, settling back into his pillows and waving at the gnome woman, who had been sitting in a seat just off to the side that was much too large for her. She nodded with a big grin and bolted off.

'Please, please. Get comfortable, you won't have to worry about your little cellmate for the rest of the night, I imagine,' Bill said, turning back to us with a smile. He cleared his throat.

'Where was I? Ah, yes. The relic. My friends, I spent some time looking into it, and it is a truly special device. This device regenerates biological tissue. Rejuvenates it to a younger and healthier state, right down to its very core. Removes the genes that might lead to cancer, or heart disease, or mental illness.'

Then he stopped and smiled down at me. 'Removes the genes that might cause ageing,' he said.

There was silence in the room. Ms. Glaiya appeared at my elbow and passed me my drink. My mind raced, trying to wrap my head around that information.

'That's right, my friends. A hit from this relic could give someone eternal life. Well, unless they were vaporized or dismembered or something. But otherwise keeping them alive in their original model forever,' Bill continued.

'Assuming this whole story isn't full of crap, why aren't you selling this thing's services to every fat, rich slug in the City and making millions? You want Martin to be your lab rat? And if this thing is so powerful, why aren't any of its builders still around?' Nox growled. My chair creaked as the big 'wolf's grip tightened in anger.

'Excellent questions, my furry friend, and the answer is that this device has strict limitations on just who can use it,' Bill answered, one hand thrusting into the air theatrically. 'In fact, the relic, known as the regeneration chamber, might only work for Martin. My investigation into it turned up technical documents, and from what I was able to decipher, it would only work on the very elderly, and only if they were unmodified.'

He looked thoughtful. 'If a subject had so much as a finger replaced, the chamber would reject him. And you must understand, the civilization that built this device was one where science and engineering had run wild. Cyborgs weren't rare like they are today. Almost everyone had at least one mechanical part,' he said, then paused.

He dropped his hand and looked excitedly down at me. 'You have no enhancements. Your body is decades older than the test cases in the documentation. This thing can help you, Martin! And maybe only you!' the wizard said.

He leaned way forward from his chair, mouth smiling wide. 'This thing can save you, my friend,' he said, quietly.

I looked at him, and I fought to digest everything the wizard had said. If the artifact did what he said it did, then it was the answer to everything. If it didn't, then I'd spend my last days on a dangerous trek into unknown lands which would ultimately be meaningless.

Other than the meaningless part, that actually sounded pretty exciting.

What choice did I have? Die in a hospital bed or die in a far away land? 'Where is it, Bill?' I asked, finally. The wizard grinned and gave me a wink.

'The dwarves have it,' he said.

16

My watch pinged. Midnight.

No one spoke. Nox and I stared at Bill. Bill and Ceile were watching me.

The wizard finally cackled, and all of his rings flared red 'It's true, my friends! The device has fallen into the possession of the dastardly dwarves, who have tucked it away in chamber full of such curiosities, deep within their kingdom. They have more or our ancestor's relics than we do,' he said, grandiosely.

I started to say something and Nox wasn't far behind. Bill threw his hands up and shouted, 'Wait! Wait, my friends! Hear everything I have to say before passing judgement.'

I fell silent. Nox looked over at me and then crouched back down. Bill took a deep breath and then continued his speech, arms raised dramatically.

'That's right, my friends. The dwarves are a species of archaeologists, every one of their number fascinated by things left behind by the march of time. Their kingdoms lie deep, and as they expand they uncover thousands of things that are thousands of years old. They know more about our history than we do. A miner was working on a dig to expand a chamber and broke through into a room from another time. A room that had once been part of an ancient human building, whose purpose is long lost. Within that room were many artifacts from millennia ago, among which was the regeneration chamber.'

I had spent years fighting in the Dwarf Wars. A hundred years ago, when I was still old but not as old as I am now. And even before and after that decade of full-fledged warfare between the City and the three dwarf kingdoms - what they called krekts - beneath it, Ceile and I had spent years fighting to keep the treaty borders intact. I knew it was a dangerous mindset, but I had trouble thinking of dwarves as anything other than ruthless enemies with technology that rivaled the power of any magic.

'Make no mistake, Martin!' Bill yelled out, pointing at me. 'The dwarves know what they have but not what to do with it. They have experimented with it for decades, first on themselves and then on captured humans. None of the dwarf subjects survived, and most of the humans also suffered horrifying deaths a short time after exposure to the chamber. Most! See, the dwarves made a startling discovery during their tests.'

'The older human subjects not only briefly survived their test, but also displayed a level of tissue regeneration. And the older the subject was, the longer they lived afterward and the more their bodies were rejuvenated.'

Nox abruptly stood up, towering over us and bristling with anger. 'And you'd have Martin use this murder machine? Give him his youth back for a few minutes and then die a horrible death? Are you insane, mage?' the big 'wolf roared. All of the gnomes vanished. Bill flinched but held his ground.

'Hear me out, Nox of the Wolfmoon! Hear me out, Martin Tundra!' he added, probably noticing the less than positive look on my face. 'Yes, the artifact can cause terrible damage to unsuitable subjects, but the dwarves did thousands of tests using this device and their captives, and their research notes and papers are second to none. Forty years ago, they ended their testing and concluded that a subject of two hundred and fifty-seven years of age or older could safely use the regeneration chamber to completely regenerate their body without the unwanted side effect of 'complete cellular breakdown',' the wizard said, his face full of excitement. He leapt down from his lounger and came forward to crouch down in between me and Ceile's chairs.

'Think about it, Martin! The dwarves are unparalleled scientists. Their documentation is meticulous. Their tests incredibly thorough. If their conclusion was that a human of two hundred and fifty-seven was the lower end for safe use of this artifact, then that's that truth. Their oldest subjects, who were in the sub-two hundred bracket, were still alive a century after their exposure. A century! And the dwarves calculated that the lifespan increase was exponential based on the subject's age.'

Now he reached over and grabbed my arm. 'If those youngsters survived for at least another century after, you might live for thousands,' he said, voice full of conviction. Then he paused for a moment, took a deep breath, and said, 'You might live to see the end of this world, my friend.'

I didn't hesitate. 'I'm in. What do we do next?' I asked.

Bill clapped his hands excitedly.

Ceile reached over and grabbed my hand tight, her face beaming. I gave her a searching look. 'You knew all of this already. You weren't at all surprised,' I said. She smiled.

'Yes. I would never have had you meet Bill if I thought it was not worth it. He may be a bit silly,' she gestured lazily at the wizard, who acknowledged it with a nod, 'but he knows what he is talking about and I believe he can get us to the only thing that can save you now. And, yes, of course I am coming with you.'

I smiled at her, and nodded. Even if I had misgivings about her coming, it wouldn't matter. When my friend made up her mind, she was unstoppable. I looked back at Nox.

'Well, Nox? Where we're going, I imagine we could use your help,' I asked the big 'wolf. He looked resigned.

'You're going whether I come or not, I imagine. You're right, you're going to need my help. Alright, then. I'm sure the City won't burn down if I'm gone for a few weeks,' he said. Then he turned to Ceile. 'We'll have to let Enforcement know we're leaving or they might be a bit angry when we don't show for our next shifts,' he rumbled. Ceile nodded at him.

'Sent my notice off during Bill's speech,' she answered, patting the multifunction bracer on her left arm. The wizard looked affronted.

Nox chuckled, then said, 'Looks like we're all crazy, then. I'll have a chat with my supervisor via IM once our little chat is done here. I don't think it'll be a problem to get the time off, they usually give me whatever I want.'

I gave the werewolf a clap on the shoulder and started to turn back to Bill when there was a rumble from the depths. I felt the Other slowly float free from the depths and lie sedately beneath the surface.

You believe this thing is real? That it'll do what the wizard says?

'Do we have a choice? If this body dies, we both die. Is that what you want? Are you going to fight me the whole way?' I asked, under my breath. The others looked at me quizzically, but I waved them off.

The Other was silent for a long moment, and I started to prepare myself for his attack.

I don't want to die. I want to be free of this prison.

I felt him move up to drift along the edge of my consciousness. I felt nauseous as his presence rippled across my mind.

I will help you. If you help me. Once we've healed our body, you'll help find a way to free me.

I thought about that for a moment. Everyone watched me with concern.

'You'll behave? You won't impede our journey?' I whispered. Ceile and Nox suddenly had suspicious looks on their face.

I'll watch from a distance. So long as you don't endanger our body. Just remember my strength, Martin. There'll come a time when you have to unleash me. Don't fight it.

I nodded. 'Deal,' I said. Now Nox and Ceile really looked concerned. Bill smirked. The Other radiated dark pleasure and sank away into the murk.

The deal is made. Good hunting, Martin.

I turned back to everyone else and put my hands up to forestall any questions. 'He'll behave during the trip. It's not like we can leave him behind anyway,' I said, then paused. 'And as awful as it is, he could be useful. We might need his power if things get really dire.'

The others looked unconvinced. 'Do you think he'll really behave? The last time we said that, I had to stop him from ripping a dwarven building out of the ground to kill a single dwarf. Who was running away!' Ceile said, darkly.

'He'll behave. Trust me,' I said, though I wasn't convinced that he would, either. I turned to Bill before Nox had a chance to jump in on the reminiscing.

'Looks like we've got a party,' I told him. The wizard smiled.

'Well, I do have a couple members of my own that will be joining us. They have specialized knowledge that we'll need to get to where we're going, and we're going to need all the help we can get,' he said, then looked over his shoulder. 'Come in!' he yelled.

All the gnomes in the room vanished.

Bill got to his feet and raised his arms over his head with a flourish. At the same time, his lounger lifted from the ground and floated away, revealing two figures walking toward us from a rapidly-closing door near the fireplace. It was tough to make them out in the half-light of the room.

One of them was a short woman in mechanic's overalls and a large variety of firearms. The other appeared to be some sort of steam construct.

Suddenly, Nox growled angrily and I heard his claws clack against each other furiously. Ceile leapt out of her lounger, drawing her combat pistol and training it on the newcomers. I was confounded, looking at my friends for an explanation and then looking back. Then I kicked my chair aside and reached for nether from the building.

Bill laughed and roared, 'Nox of the Wolfmoon, Martin Tundra, Ceile Angael, meet my associates Robin Mrek-Two and Petrel Mrek-Eight of Krekt Fourteen!'

The two came to a stop, each at one of the wizard's shoulders. Robin had a vicious grin on her face. Petrel's held no emotion, just metal neutrality.

They were dwarves.

17

It was a tense house for a couple minutes as the two sides stared at each other. Petrel and Bill watched us impassively. Robin smirked dismissively. Ceile held a shooter's stance, her pistol up and ready to take that smirk off of the dwarf's face forever. Nox had stepped forward a metre and was now low to the ground next to me, claws taut, teeth bared, snarling, brilliant blue eyes darkened almost to black.

The Other was laughing, the sound of it echoing through my mind.

Nether writhed around my hands, and I was prepared to shape it into the forms that would do terrible things to the newcomers if need be. I could feel the world decaying, rotting, dying around me. I ignored it. That was the sacrifice arcanists made for their power. To intimately know that their world speeds toward its end.

And I was well aware that I was doing the same.

'Easy, my friends! There's no need for violence here! I have told you that the artifact is held in a chamber deep in a dwarven kingdom, and so it is. Krekt Twelve. I have been down there to see it!' Bill roared, his arms wide and his cloak flapping in a wind that touched nothing else. Then he dropped his arms and hunched over with an exhausted look.

'I was able to get to the relic chamber without being detected, but it was close. The chamber itself, however, has been sealed for decades, and getting in brought the whole of the fortress' defences down on my head. It was a foolish decision, going down without assistance. I barely escaped, even with my prodigious power. And that mistake may have made our task that much more difficult, as the dwarves of Krekt Twelve are likely alert to further attempts on their artifacts,' the wizard said, his voice barely more than a whisper.

He fell silent, looking almost comically sad. After a long moment had passed, he straightened up, and said, 'But the regeneration chamber is not lost to us. There are other paths, other ways we will take to descend to it. And we will have assistance!'

The wizard gestured to the two dwarves standing next to him. 'Robin and Petrel are dwarves of Krekt Fourteen, a small kingdom with no love for nor loyalty to the others. They are deep miners, who work mostly in isolation in dangerous areas for large sums of credits. Their many talents will be of immense use to us,' he said. Robin nodded. Petrel didn't move.

I narrowed my eyes. 'And what incentive do you two have to help get us there safely and uncaptured?' I asked, a bit rougher than I meant. The dwarf woman turned her hazel eyes to me.

'Greed, friend. The lab that your artifact is sitting in is full of other artifacts. More than enough to get my help. Enough to get both of our help,' she said, pointing at the other dwarf. 'In return for our delving expertise, you and your pals are going to provide some muscle for us on the way out.'

She stepped forward a couple metres, and her eyes were full of excitement. I got ready to disintegrate her face if she did anything rash. Instead, her grin went from dismissive to a close approximation of friendly.

'We get you down to the regeneration chamber. You guys do your thing. Petrel and I collect some loot. You get us back up. Seems like a pretty solid deal to me,' the dwarf woman said. Bill nodded in agreement.

I looked at her searchingly, then turned to the wizard. 'And you, Bill? What do you get out of all of this? I imagine you aren't helping us out purely from the bottom of your heart,' I said. The wizard laughed.

'You are correct, my elderly friend. I am not a charity. I usually demand a large sum for my services but I know that you aren't capable of paying a large sum and that your situation is quite unique. So I have been content to, up until this point, operate for free,' he said. Then he leaned forward.

'On my perilous trip to visit the artifact, I had a brief time to investigate the lab before the security systems tripped. As Robin has so graciously explained, there are many other artifacts in there. Among them is a single item that I will take as compensation for my assistance. Once I have collected that item and the dwarves have taken all they can carry, the three of you may take whatever else you can. So long as you are able to protect us on the way out,' the wizard finished with a nod.

I continued to look at him for a few seconds, scanned the dwarves, and then said to Ceile and Nox, 'What do you think?' without turning away.

The werewolf was first. 'I don't like it, but if Bill's telling the truth than we'll need the help,' he growled hesitantly. He stepped back a bit and straightened up, letting his arms fall into a more casual position.

Ceile's soft voice came next. 'I trust Bill. If he thinks we need the dwarves, then we need the dwarves,' she said. She sounded convinced. I heard her holster her pistol.

I knew that most of my disapproval came from my time fighting the dwarves in Krekts One through Three. I didn't know much about the kingdoms outside of the City's borders.

I sighed. I didn't have a choice, really. I had to do this.

I let the nether dissipate and then stepped forward to offer my hand to Robin. She looked surprised, then took it and gave a solid shake before smiling and letting go.

'It's a deal, then. Alright, Bill. What else do we need to know?' I asked, looking over at the wizard. Bill chuckled and bowed theatrically.

'Well, my friend. We have to make a stop in Woodsholme,' he said with a grin.

I'd heard the name before, but couldn't place it. I turned to look at my friends to see if they had a better idea and stopped dead when I saw Ceile.

My friend's face was white, and she looked terrified. I reached out to grab her arm in confused support. I'd never seen her with that look on her face. She turned to me and I could see the ghosts in her eyes.

'Woodsholme, Martin. The greatest of the elven cities.'

18

'Correct, Ms. Angael! Woodsholme is the closest of the seven elven nations, and the nearest to our entrance into Krekt Twelve. I have a contact there, who I've dealt with on a number of excursions,' Bill said, coming forward to stand a metre from Ceile and me.

My friend still looked upset, but the horror in her eyes had faded and her face had returned to its natural light chocolate colour. She held my hand tightly while she listened to Bill. Nox stood worriedly over her other shoulder. He'd never seen her react like that either, and we shared a confused glance before turning back to the wizard.

'My contact will get us into the dwarf kingdom quietly. Petrel and Robin will get us down to the lab unnoticed. After that, it'll get dangerous. I probably don't have to tell any of you how the dwarves will respond to intruders in there with their artifacts,' he said with a slow nod. 'We'll have to be quiet, we'll have to be quick. But I wouldn't be going along if I thought we weren't coming back,' the wizard finished.

With a flourish, Bill spun on his heel and walked toward the fireplace. Petrel stamped mechanically around and followed. Robin gave me a wink, turned quickly in a whirlwind of long red hair, and walked down to stand near the wizard.

Without turning back to us, Bill raised an arm over his head and snapped his fingers. The chairs and benches around him lifted free of the floor and spun lazily around the wizard's head. 'Enough words, my friends! It is well past time for us to be off. Come!' he yelled, spinning and beckoning us to him.

Ceile gave me a weak smile and pulled me forward as she stood and moved to join the wizard. 'We're leaving now?' I asked, bemused. Nox looked equally startled.

'No time like the present, Mr. Tundra. You are on a tight schedule, my friend! And besides,' he said with a sad smile, 'you have nothing you need to do before we go.'

I frowned, but as we came to stand with the wizard and the dwarves beneath the whirlwind of furniture, I realized he was right. I had no family, no friends beyond Ceile and Nox. I had no employer to notify, and the few bills I still received would be paid automatically as usual. My house was locked up, the Government no longer had reason to check up on me, and my wisps didn't need food. They'd get bored and probably clog the ventilation system for amusement, but they were otherwise fine.

I had a sudden thought. 'My car. I can't leave her on your street, I should take her home.'

Ceile and Bill both burst into laughter. 'Oh, Martin, you should see the look on your face!' the wizard said, chuckling. 'I had no intention of leaving your lovely car here in the rain. But I have a better idea than simply driving her home. Come! You will see soon enough'

Suddenly, the maelstrom of furniture quickly formed up into a single flat platform just behind Bill's feet. He stepped backward onto it without looking, just as the final piece slid into place. It was more than large enough for all of us.

The wizard moved to the back of the platform, and beckoned us all forward. The dwarves didn't hesitate, they followed him up close on his heels, settling in one at each shoulder. Ceile was close behind, leaving Nox and me standing amongst a crowd of gnomes that had appeared from out of nowhere. They watched us excitedly.

I looked up at the big 'wolf and found him watching me with a strange expression. 'What do you think?' I asked him, quietly. He was silent for a moment, then nodded toward Ceile.

'Ceile's no idiot. She's up there because she's sure this thing will work for you,' he growled softly. 'So let's go get you patched up.' And then he stepped forward and up onto the platform. Ceile squeezed his arm with a smile. Nox patted her roughly on the head.

Now it was just me. Several of the gnomes near me were holding their breath, their hands over their mouths in anticipation. I sighed.

'Alright, let's do this. But you better be careful with my car,' I said as I joined my friends.

There was a loud cheer and thunderous applause from the gnomes. They started dancing around the platform. Bill rolled his eyes, then lifted his hands toward the ceiling.

'Away we go!' he yelled, snapping his fingers loudly. The platform lurched free of the ground and floated upward. As we neared the ceiling, a hole appeared, just wide enough for our makeshift elevator to pass through. Then we were out on the roof of the tower.

Into the middle of a storm.

Whatever forms Bill was shaping to manipulate the platform also appeared to provide us shelter from the elements. Which was good, as the rain was coming down around us in sheets and the wind was howling.

Wind.

I narrowed my eyes. The Other was an aethon of wind. His power was immense to begin with, but in this storm it would be even stronger. Here, the element was in turmoil, a force of chaos. The aether around us would be feeding off of that, growing in strength.

Anytime he got loose, the Other was dangerous. In this storm, he would be almost unstoppable. Or would be, if our body wasn't on the verge of death.

Relax, Martin. I said I'd play nice.

'We'll see,' I whispered beneath my breath.

The gloom of the storm shrouded most of the roof top, but as the platform drifted forward a massive shape appeared in the murk, eventually looming above us. As we closed with its base, I finally realized what it was.

'You have an airship,' I said, my voice full of wonder.

19

Sure enough, as we moved further underneath the shadow, cutting out the rain and most of the wind, we got a better look at Bill's ship. Airships were rare here in the City. The Government used them, but very few private citizens did. I'd never been on one. I'd always wanted to.

'I certainly do, my friend! This chariot will take us to our destination and back in comfort and style. And make no mistake! She appears bigger than she is, and she's fast! I've augmented her with spells for everything from defence to speed to seat cushioning. I haven't had a chance to test her out fully, but if everything works out we may even arrive at the artifact chamber a few days early,' Bill said, gesturing wildly with the hand that wasn't guiding our platform.

'Her name is the Red Flag,' he finished.

We finally came to a slow stop at the Red Flag's loading bay, and in the stark lights that ringed the airship's tail, I could see that the original shape I'd seen in the shadows was some sort of structure. The ship hung from three massive rails above it.

I could see three bladed propulsion engines, at least two cannons of some kind, plus something that might have been a missile launcher but had arcane sigils scrawled all over it in neat, orderly rows. Judging by the placement of the weapons, I figured there were at least two more at the front of the ship.

The Red Flag was a pretty serious beast.

The platform had settled gently to the ground, and Bill was already strolling past us into the loading bay. Bags and supplies on the floor shifted into neat piles as he walked by, talking animatedly to himself. He soon vanished into the ship.

Petrel was off right behind him, the big steel dwarf thumping along without a word, the pistons on his legs and arms clicking and hissing quietly. He too disappeared without stopping.

The rest of us got down together, and as the last of us stepped off the platform, it split into its component pieces of furniture and sank through the roof top. As we watched, the hole slowly filled itself in and then there was no trace of our strange ride left.

Robin chuckled. 'Bill's always been weird. C'mon, let's get out of the cold, you're gonna love this thing,' she said with a smile, slapping my arm playfully as she passed, headed for the bay.

Nox watched her go with a frown. 'That's going to take some getting used to. I'll bet having that pair around is making you two uncomfortable,' he growled, softly. Shaking his head, he started moving and then continued, 'I hope they built this thing with 'thropes in mind. Using a human-sized washroom isn't pleasant.' He promptly banged his head on the loading bay door. The big 'wolf snarled in irritation as he too moved out of eyesight.

Ceile stifled a laugh, then sobered as she turned to me. 'Are you ready for this, Martin? I do not think this will be an easy task. I trust Bill, but I believe he has downplayed some of what we will face,' she said, reaching out for my hand.

I looked down. Her flesh was so smooth, and mine so wrinkled. I was old. She'd never be.

She put her other hand under my chin and lifted my head gently until I was looking up into her emerald eyes. 'Just imagine, Martin. Your body young once more. Your power restored. You will be free to do whatever you wish,' she said, her voice serene.

I suddenly pulled her into a hug, and she squeaked with surprise. We held each other for a long moment, listening to the dulled sounds of the rain pouring down and the thunder crashing.

Then I pulled slightly away and looked up at her again. 'Thank you for this, Ceile. Thank you for everything,' I said. She smiled broadly, put her hand on my cheek, and then we both turned and walked into the airship, hand in hand.

The loading bay door closed silently behind us, shutting out the storm.

20

We didn't have to wander far to find the rest of the party. Bill had been right, the airship wasn't as big as I'd thought. The loading bay and a compact engine room were the only two chambers on this level. Taking the short flight of metal stairs to the upper level, we found a large crew station containing eight seats of various sizes, bordered by a small kitchen, one large washroom, one tiny washroom, a big bunk room at the back of the ship, five gun stations, and the pilot's cabin at the front. A wide glass windscreen ran from wall to wall and ceiling to floor in front of the pilot's chair, allowing the crew to also see outside the ship from their stations. Similar windows ran the length of the crew area.

Nox was already seated, or mostly. The station he had chosen was huge, but not quite huge enough for the big werewolf. I wasn't surprised. Ship builders didn't exactly take people his size into account when designing, well, anything, and in my two and a half centuries, I'd only ever encountered a handful of people that were larger than him, and almost all of them were larger therianthropes. A couple 'bears, a 'tiger or two, a 'lion, and one bizarre werefox that was downright gigantic.

My friend stretched the seat as far as he could, then gave up in irritation. He gave me a look that suggested I was to blame for his discomfort. I gave him a wink.

Petrel was also seated, though the chair was struggling to hold the dwarf's weight. Even if he wasn't restrained, I doubted he'd go far. Unless the airship spun right onto its side. Then he'd probably go out through the wall.

I shuddered a bit as I looked at the steel dwarf. I'd encountered similar creatures during the war. Like walking tanks. Usually carrying some dwarf heavy weapon, like a magma cannon or bolt thrower. Men and women had died around me, killed by these things. Even now, the hair on my arms stood up.

If he noticed me watching, he gave no sign. He stood completely still and silent, staring expressionlessly out the windscreen. I wondered if his builders had even given him the ability to show emotions. Then I wondered if there was enough dwarf left inside the armour for him to even have emotions.

On the opposite side of the room, Robin was stretched out and looked like she was ready for a nap. The dwarf woman had her seat completely reclined and her arms under her head. Her eyes were half-lidded, though she appeared to be watching Bill very closely.

I didn't get the same sense of discomfort with her as I did with her partner. She was very different from the dwarves I'd encountered in the war and in the skirmishes before and after it. Her clothing style was different, her runic tattoos were different, the way she carried herself was different. I suppose it shouldn't have been a surprise that two distant kingdoms would have distinctly different citizens.

Old habits die hard.

'I am going to go sit with her. You should see if you can get anything out of Petrel once you are done talking to Bill,' Ceile abruptly whispered in my ear. I thought about it, and then nodded. She smiled, squeezed my hand, and then walked over and dropped into the chair next to the dwarf woman. Robin looked surprised, then smiled and soon they were talking away.

'Martin! Come up here, my elderly friend. We're about to depart,' I heard Bill shout from the pilot's seat.

I navigated my way through the empty stations until I stood next to the wizard. Bill was already running through pre-flight checks and firing up the safeties. The quiet whine from the engine room rose to a gentle hum and the ship briefly shuddered.

As the engine warmed up, Bill turned away from the controls and gave me a smile. He gestured out the windscreen, though with the rain pounding against it and the general gloom outside, there wasn't much to see out there.

His face turned serious, and he said, 'Martin. Martin Tundra. I give you this last chance to abandon our quest. Once this airship sails, it will return with our prizes or it will not return at all. If you choose to quit after this point, you will have to find your own way home.'

I considered that, then shook my head. 'I'm not in a rush to meet Death. Get us on our way, Bill,' I said.

The wizard nodded gravely, then twisted around in his seat and said to the others, 'We're off! Please have your seat backs upright, your trays closed, and your seat belts engaged while the seat belt light is on! Keep your arms, legs, feet, nose, hands, ears, and perhaps your head inside the cabin at all times!' Then he looked at me and said, 'You may want to hang on tight for a moment. I imagine you want to see what we do to your car.'

I rolled my eyes and took hold of the back of Bill's chair. The wizard was an odd fellow.

There was a dull thump from below, and then the engines spooled rapidly up with a high pitched whine. Bill gave me a wink, and then gently pushed the throttle forward. The engine noise rose to a roar, and the Red Flag shuddered as it lifted slightly off the roof and began moving forward. Once we were free of the roof, the airship plunged into almost total darkness, disturbed only by the flashes of lightning that illuminated the City around us.

Bill flicked a switch on the control board, and suddenly powerful searchlights blazed out into the night. Slowly, they swung down, briefly revealing a naked man standing at his window and staring up at us. He fled in mortified terror.

Finally, the beams came to a stop, resting on my car four stories below. I frowned, but Bill gave me a quick squeeze on my arm and a gentle smile. 'She'll be safe. Watch,' he said. Then his eyes fell to the street and his hand shot to the ceiling.

At first, it didn't seem like the wizard was doing anything, but then my car rocked softly and lifted off the ground. As we watched, Bill's magic floated her past the front of the airship and then up onto the top, where she came to rest in between the three engines. The Red Flag shook briefly as she did, then the ship returned to smoothly hovering.

Bill cackled maniacally. 'Now, we shall take her back home and then we'll be on our way!' he shouted, voice rising with each word. He reached down for the controls and then paused. 'Oh, make sure no one uses the center gun, your car is right in front of it. Okay?' the wizard said, patting me on the hand. Then he gave a dramatic flourish, as best he could while belted into his seat, and yelled, 'To your seat, my elderly friend! It's stormy seas tonight!'

My watch pinged.

I picked a station next to Petrel and buckled in. The steel dwarf remained silent, though I thought I saw his head tilt slightly in my direction.

'Away we go!' Bill roared, jamming the throttle forward. The engines howled, there was a muffled crash from the loading bay, and then we rocketed forward into the rain and lightning.

21

It was odd, watching someone fly my car into my garage remotely. It hit me after Bill was finished and I'd closed the garage behind him that I was jealous. The wizard had put so little effort in to lift my car off the airship, carry it to ground level, and then gently put her into the garage. The skill required to shape nether into forms that intricate and powerful was immense, and I was pretty sure I didn't know anyone that could do what Bill had done without intense concentration.

The wizard had watched with an almost bored expression while simultaneously keeping the airship level in the storm.

And not only that, but he had also spent the additional effort to hide his work. Spells like that would broadcast across the City like an explosion, at least to anyone that could manipulate nether. Powerful wizards could reduce or completely shroud the fluctuating energies, but it took real talent to do what Bill had consistently done since I'd met him yesterday evening.

Along with the jealousy, there was frustration. The wizard was shaping forms of such complexity with so little effort that he was certainly stronger than me in telekinesis, but I had no way of getting a feel for just how strong he was in general while he operated behind the curtain. He was certainly, well, at wizard level, but could he be an archon?

Forgetting the possibility that he was more powerful than me, there was the frightening chance that there were two archons in such a close space. We were rare to start with. Two of us within a few Districts of each other was way, way rarer.

I wondered if the Government knew about Bill.

Neither of you are as powerful as me, Martin. And when he betrays us, you'll need my help.

I gave the Other a push back into the shadows, and whispered under my breath, 'Ceile trusts him, and we can trust Ceile. That's good enough for me, and that has to be good enough for you.' He laughed and vanished into the depths.

I suddenly realized that Bill was talking to me, and I shook my head and looked up at him. The wizard smiled gently, then said, 'I said, are you ready to go, Martin?'

I peered down at my house. I could see the glow of a wisp floating past the kitchen window, but the rest of the place was dark. It would keep.

One of my neighbours glared up at us from his living room, cellphone glued to his ear as he talked animatedly to someone while gesturing at the airship. Probably time to go. We didn't really want to get stopped by the Department of Enforcement to answer some questions about our adventure. I nodded at Bill, finally. 'Let's get this show on the road, shall we? Take us out, Bill,' I said and then headed back to my seat next to Petrel.

The dwarf remained silent, except for the gears ticking away beneath his metal skin.

Robin was watching me in what appeared to be amused confusion. Ceile patted her on the shoulder and then looked at me with a raised eyebrow. I winked at her, and she wrinkled her nose in return.

Nox was snoring loudly at the back of the room.

Bill turned back to the controls after making a quick check to make sure everyone was secured. 'Alright, hold on to your hats!' he yelled, one hand reaching toward the roof theatrically.

Just before he hit the throttle, it occurred to me that we hadn't righted whatever had been crashing around in the cargo hold, but then the airship was blazing through the storm in a wide arc and I couldn't do much beyond hold on.

Once we'd lifted free of the City's lower airspace, Bill brought the Red Flag onto a stable northward course, and we were free to get out of our seats and stretch. Not that there was much to see, but I snooped around anyway. I was impressed to find that three of the gun turrets were dragonfire, while the back two outwardly appeared to be traditional City-issue bolt cannons but actually fired some kind of dwarven shell.

'Thunder thumper. You'll love those,' I heard someone say from behind me.

I nearly jumped in shock. Instead, I spun, more or less gracefully, toward the door into the turret. Robin smiled at me, leaning against its frame. The dwarf woman's mechanic's uniform was cleaner than I thought, and I realized that what I'd taken for grease or oil stains were actually round holes with blackened edges. Noticing my look, she reached up and stuck a finger in one of the holes. I caught a glimpse of metal beneath.

'Krekt Thirteen. We fought with those bastards for decades before they wiped us out. One of their guys had a mini-gun, sprayed my unit. But, hey, it's all good. I got this neat chest piece out of it,' she said, dead pan. Then she pointed down at the ammo bay below the turret. 'Thunder thumper. Makes a hell of a thump. No, seriously. These things are loud!' she said, her face breaking into a wicked grin. 'The explosion itself is crazy, but the noise is brutal. Disorienting. Built them to take on underwyrms, but all they really do is bring the wyrm to you and drive them nuts.'

She laughed. 'So don't shoot the ground with it,' she said, wiggling her finger at me. Then, with a wave, the dwarf woman turned and wandered away.

I was again struck by how different Robin was from the dwarves I'd met in the past. She said her krekt had been wiped out. I wondered how many of her kin were left. Despite my prejudices, I was starting to like her. Ceile and I had talked to her on the flight over to my house, after I'd given up trying to get Petrel to chat.

The steel dwarf wasn't much for conversation. Every once and a while, I caught him nodding in agreement to something Robin had said, but he otherwise sat as still as a statue, his internals quietly clicking and hissing. I shivered as I thought about the dwarf. His kind didn't use constructs, as they shunned most magic and would have considered the idea an abomination. No, dwarves who wanted to prolong their lives in that way just kept cutting things off and replacing them with metal until they ran out of parts.

I wondered if Petrel had reached that point. I wondered what it would be like to go to sleep in my body and wake up in something else. To wake up after surgeons had cut open my skull, pulled out the important bits, and slapped them into a metal cage. To wake up and never feel the breeze across my skin again. I shook my head. That wasn't any less horrifying than transferring, even if it was still you in there.

Dragon!

The Other's yell nearly took me to my knees, and I put both hands to my head to try and steady myself. 'What?' I asked, weakly, trying to get my focus back.

Then the entire ship rocked. I heard a crash from the crew stations. Nox snarled.

'Dragon!' Bill yelled.

22

It was a dragon alright, and a big one. Jet black, I could only see it when lightning split the darkness. Erupting from the storm, the massive beast swiped at the airship with two legs' worth of gigantic talons and then vanished out into the night in a heartbeat.

Bill clutched the controls, and sweat was dripping from his forehead. The wizard's hat had disappeared. His face was a mask of concentration as he struggled to keep the ship out of the dragon's reach. 'Everyone grab a gun! Except you, Nox! Go out there and eat that thing, will you?' the wizard roared over his shoulder.

The werewolf growled in amusement as he leapt across the crew stations for one of the big thumper turrets. Slightly less gracefully, Petrel raced to the other, pistons whining with the strain.

The dragon materialized in a flash of lightning, all jagged ridges and horns and spikes, giving me just enough advance notice to brace myself as it struck the ship. This time, there was a shriek of metal from somewhere in the ship, and then I thought I could hear wind whistling from below decks. Bill cursed as the vessel listed sharply sideways.

I managed to get a hold of a crew station, and then spun and caught Robin as the dwarf woman tumbled past. Her face looked panicked as she clung to me, but quickly turned to exhilaration. With a sly smirk, she gave me a quick kiss on the cheek and then flung herself at the nearest turret station.

Breathing heavily from the exertion, I maneuvered my aching body toward the second turret once Bill had righted the ship. Ceile gave me a concerned look as she strapped herself into the third, but I waved her off. Staggering into the turret, I fell more than sat into the seat and buckled myself in.

I can take this thing. Let me out.

I shook my head, angrily. 'We can't survive the power you'd need to use against that thing. And we need to be alive to use the artifact. How did you know about the dragon, anyway?' I whispered at him.

Wouldn't you like to know?

Then he laughed and sunk into the depths.

'If you're all strapped in, I can be a little more active in evasion. I will try to keep her level as often as possible,' Bill howled from the controls. 'Oh, and if you wouldn't mind killing that thing, that'd be handy,' he said, sarcastically.

True to his word, the Red Flag suddenly spun and roared skyward. There were crashes and bangs from below and from the crew cabins. A roar of fury from somewhere out in the storm suggested that the dragon was less than impressed by our sudden mobility. The fact that

I could hear that roar over the howling engines and the crash of thunder and the whistling winds meant the dragon was even larger than I'd thought.

The controls on the console in front of me lit up and I unlocked the chair and loaded the chamber. I hadn't spent much time in this type of turret, but even the Arcane Corps trained on conventional weapons every once and a while. I wouldn't be nearly as effective as I would have been with my magic, but I could aim and shoot this thing.

There was a loud, angry buzz from Ceile's cannon, and then a brilliant dotted line blazed out into the storm. Dragonfire slugs, at that rate of fire, would carve through steel in short order. I wondered if that were also the case for dragon armour.

Now Robin's turret was blazing away as well. I shook my head as I scanned the darkness for the beast, wondering how the two women could see the damn thing out there. Sure enough, the dragon roared out of the storm, narrowly missing the airship. The brilliant lines pouring from the turrets danced across the black monster, at first leaving no mark, but then vivid orange blotches as the dragonfire gradually superheated the scales.

I laid on the trigger, hoping to add to the damage yet succeeding only in firing a large number of slugs into space as Bill rolled the ship to the side. Cursing beneath my breath, I rolled my turret, tracking the glowing orange patches in the darkness. Firing again, I sent a storm of destruction the dragon's way, feeling vindicated as I etched a line across its right wing. The beast drew its wings in and plummeted away, but not before Robin and Ceile burnt similar wounds across its back.

My cellphone toned. Somebody had just sent me a text. I burst into laughter, despite the somewhat dire circumstances I found myself in.

The turrets fell silent. 'Anyone see it?' Robin yelled from across the ship. No one answered.

I heard the thumper turrets finally come online. Nox was probably foaming at the mouth about the long start-up. Sure enough, shortly after the completion tone I heard the big 'wolf snarl, 'About time!'

Below, Martin!

'It's below us!' I roared, spinning the turret to bring one cannon to bear. Before I could get a clear picture through the screen, the entire ship lurched violently to one side and there was a tortured shriek as the dragon caught hold of the Flag and sunk its talons in.

Alarms started sounding from all around the ship. The monster roared, and the sound echoed impossibly loudly through the vessel. The wind and rain were now pouring in from a dozen rents in the hull.

I could hear the engines howling as Bill tried desperately to shake the dragon clear without sending us crashing to the ground.

'Say hello, dragon,' Nox snarled.

'Say goodbye, dragon,' growled a metallic voice from the other turret.

'Cover your ears!' Robin roared.

I barely managed to get my hands to my head when I heard two muffled whumps followed by an explosion of noise that robbed me of my hearing. In the eerie silence afterward, the ship rocked violently and spun away before finally coming to a shaky halt.

The dragon was gone.

23

When the dragon didn't immediately return after being hit with the thunder thumper rounds, we did some quick repair work to make sure the ship was at least flight-ready, and then Bill set us back on course. We couldn't risk staying in one spot while we worked on the Flag, not without knowing exactly where the beast was and if it were hurt.

Bill had made an effort to keep us flying toward Woodsholme as much as possible during the fight, and while we'd lost some time, we hadn't gotten completely turned around either. Ceile and the wizard had managed to get a good picture of where we were after going over some navigation data. The two were now deep into discussion over the geography of the area and our flight path as Bill flew the ship and my friend sat next to him.

The storm had died off, which made it easier for us to get the rest of the Red Flag sorted out. The dragon had done some pretty serious damage, particularly to the crew cabin which was, well, no longer attached to the ship. Instead it hung behind us, holding on by the twisted remains of its doorway.

Petrel, Robin, Nox, and I stood at the ruin, peering down at the swinging wreckage. 'We're gonna have to get rid of it. Petrel and I could probably slap the room back on if we had a proper dock and enough time, but we don't have either,' the dwarf woman yelled over the roar of the wind, shaking her head and turning away.

Petrel's head swiveled to look at Nox, then gestured at the torn remains of the door frame. The big 'wolf grinned toothily and the two lined up next to each other. With pistons and engine howling, the steel dwarf pulled one side of the tortured door free, just as Nox pulled the other side free with a terrifying snarl. A shrill shriek announced the departure of the crew cabin, which fell quickly away into the darkness below.

'Our friends are kind of scary,' Robin yelled from beside me, staring at the other two. I nodded with a slight smile.

While the crew cabin had been the worst of the damage, it was far from the only. The big black dragon had gouged huge holes into the engine room and cargo bay, and the outer armour was dented or scarred in a number of places. The aft drive had taken a pretty hard knock and was now spewing sparks, giving the Red Flag a sparkly tail and making the ship stand out against the night.

The dragon was a mystery. We'd been flying for hours, but we were still within City airspace. Enforcement usually swept for aggressives regularly, and put down any it did find. Intelligent dragons were sent on their way with a warning not to return and smaller feral dragons were captured and put to use as transport or weapon, but the larger ferals were considered too much of a risk and were generally killed.

And the black dragon was probably the largest feral I'd seen in decades.

I shrugged and turned my attention back to helping Robin collect debris from the kitchen floor. The Red Flag had an odd system that usually kept everything safe and proper inside the cabinets during flight, but it appeared to have malfunctioned and instead spewed silverware, aluminium foil, and dish cloths across the entire floor.

Once that was done, we headed down to the cargo bay. Oddly enough, it was exactly as I'd seen it when boarding the ship. There didn't seem to be anything that would have caused the crashing noises from earlier. Petrel stood in the middle of the bay, optic arrays scanning for trouble. Straightening up, he looked over at me, shrugged, and then headed back up to the main deck.

I hadn't heard the steel dwarf say anything since his brief outburst in the turret, but he did seem more animated. Maybe he was just shy.

'Everybody come here!' Bill's voice crackled from the comm system right by my ear.

Robin and I shared a curious look and then followed Petrel up. We found the others standing arrayed around the wizard, who was standing up in the pilot's chair, facing us. Nox looked surly. Ceile looked serene. Bill looked like he was dancing.

'Excellent! I wanted you all to see this, it's quite spectacular. Look! The first light of the day breaks to the north!' he flamboyantly yelled, spinning and pointing out the windscreen into the day slowly dawning beyond. 'Behold, the White Sun!' the wizard roared.

For a long moment, nothing happened. Then there was an explosion of light on the horizon to the north, and the White Sun lifted free of the distant mountain tops. I shielded my eyes from the stark glare of its light until Bill flicked a switch on the control panel that dimmed the front screen.

We all slid up against the windows and got our first good look at our location. A gigantic forest spread from horizon to horizon, punctuated with the occasional mountain. This was certainly not the wood that surrounded the City's northern borders.

'We're over the Locus Wood,' I said.

Bill clapped me roughly on the shoulder. 'We certainly are, my elderly friend! The great Locus Wood, a forest a thousand kilometres in all directions! Home to millions of species that exist nowhere else!' he said with a dramatic gesture. 'Including the elves! Woodsholme, our destination, may not be the largest of their cities, but it has a thriving black market. Likely caused by their proximity to our City, I imagine,' he said, winking.

'How far are we from Woodsholme, Bill? The Flag's a tough girl, but she's gonna need some work on her engines, sooner rather than later,' Robin asked. The dwarf woman's face looked calm, but there was a hint of unease in her voice, and I understood why. Her species and mine had very different societies, but we had much in common. The elves, well, the elves were almost alien.

The wizard clucked his tongue, then appeared to be making calculations on his hands. 'We should be there by nightfall. Seven hours under White, seven under Blue, perhaps a couple beneath the Moon. The Flag will hold until we arrive, we're making good time and nothing can surprise us under a cloudless morning sky,' he said.

Then the whole ship rocked violently, throwing everyone but Petrel and Bill to the ground.

24

'How does one not see a giant black dragon under a cloudless morning sky?' Robin screamed, scrambling across the ground toward the turret as she pointed at the massive black talon that had impaled the washroom.

'Get to the weapons! I'll try to shake her!' Bill yelled.

The beast bent forward around the ship, and its huge head lowered down in front of the screen, staring in at us upside down. Its jagged maw split open to show rows of vicious teeth, and more rows of shattered teeth. Black blood was seeping from its mouth, nostrils, and ears, and its glowing neon yellow eyes were terribly bloodshot.

It roared, and the ship shook.

'I think it's angry!' I shouted as I staggered toward my turret.

'It won't be so angry when I shoot it in the face again,' Nox snarled, darkly. The big 'wolf was up and across the room in a heartbeat, vanishing into the thumper turret.

The Red Flag rocked again, and it took all my strength to get up into the turret chair and buckle in. I heard either Ceile or Robin's cannons start firing, and a shriek of metal as the dragon moved across the hull. A loud whump announced Nox's return to the fight. I steeled myself for the thunderous result, and then frowned when nothing happened.

Nox cursed.

As I spun my cannons, the dragon came under my sights. It moved with startling speed for something so massive, managing to dodge first Nox's and then Petrel's first rounds. Now it was clawing at the starboard engine, just out of shot of the thumper turrets, trying to bring us down. I opened fire, the dragonfire slugs blazing across the ship to slam into the dragon's shoulder.

Roaring, the beast turned and lunged toward my cannon. I sprayed it with fiery agony, tracing lines across its face. In return, it slashed wildly at the shielding around the gun. All of the talons on its one leg were cracked and chipped. The thumpers had hit it pretty hard.

Across the hull, Ceile's cannon was still cooking the dragon's hide, a steady stream of light flashing between the two. I could vaguely hear the mechanical buzz from Robin's turret on the opposite side of the beast. It didn't even flinch, continuing to attack my gun. First one, then two long cracks worked their way down my view screen. Then the shielding shattered, and the dragon reached forward to destroy the cannon.

I heard two loud whumps, threw my hands up to my ears, and then there was no sound at all.

The black dragon slammed into the deck, prevented from going over the side only because its claws were still embedded in the armour around my cannon. The beast staggered dazedly to its feet, mouth open and tongue hanging out, eyes blinking rapidly.

In the silence after the dual thumper impacts, it was almost poetic watching the three dragonfire turrets lace the dragon with burns. It put its arms up weakly to block us, only to catch Petrel's next shot right in the chest. The violent shockwave from the thumper round sent the beast skidding backward past my gun, stopping only after it jammed all of its talons into any piece of the airship it could find.

Including my turret.

Two of the dragon's claws burst through the walls of my bay, one narrowly missing my chair. My hearing was starting to return, but now the only thing I could hear was the roar of the wind blowing in through the gaps. The turret shook as the dragon tried to get some leverage, and the bay twisted until I was almost sideways. Sparks erupted from the console and from the gun connections above and below me.

I wondered if my skill at conjuring a parachute had gotten any better.

The dragon's frantic movements pulled the gaps in the turret ever larger, and now I had a great view of the forest far below. I slowly checked my belts, and hoped Bill had thought to reinforce those. As if to mock me, one of the belts tore free and then whipped around the turret wildly. I dropped a couple inches toward death.

There was another blast of sound, and then I felt the dragon rip free of the ship and tumble past. The turret shuddered as its talons tore free, and the whole thing twisted even further. Another of my belts split. Now I was hanging in a very uncomfortable way by my waist.

The ship thankfully listed slightly to one side, allowing me to set a foot on solid ground but not much else. I could smell smoke, and there was an unhealthy vibration in the plating I was precariously balanced on. Then the ship listed violently the other direction and now I was hanging out over the precipice again.

I sighed. Well, at least falling to my death from a couple kilometres up was more exciting than rotting in some hospital.

Then the turret shook and the whole chair twisted backward away from the gap. I came to an undignified stop upside down, to find Nox clinging to the door frame with one hand and bending my throne toward him with the other. His teeth were bared with the effort, and I could see the claws on his feet had cut brutal rents in the flooring as he struggled to maintain footing.

When I was close enough to the edge, I gathered a small amount of nether from the air around me and severed my final belt with a slash of arcane energy. Nox caught me as I fell forward, and he leapt away from the tortured turret as it shrieked and tore free of the ship.

As we burst onto the main deck, I realized that my chest was tight and that my breath was ragged. My hearing had returned, but everything sounded far away. Nox was growling something at me, but I couldn't understand it. The big 'wolf dumped me into one of the larger crew stations.

I could see Bill frantically looking over his shoulder from the pilot's chair, his face desperate. He was yelling something at me, but it was lost in the white noise. The whole ship suddenly rocked, sending Nox skidding away and throwing me across the deck.

And as I staggered to my feet with the assistance of a wall, I looked over to find the big black dragon glaring in at me through the windscreen.

25

'I can't shake it off! That thing really doesn't like you, Martin!' Bill howled.

'What can we-' I paused and took a deep breath, 'what can we do, Bill?' I finished, staggering to my feet with the assistance of the now-tilted wall. Nox slid in next to me, jamming all of the claws on one of his hands into the bulkhead to steady himself.

'Both thumpers are gone, and two dragonfire turrets. It's just Robin left up there! That dragon is huge, the Flag was never meant to fight something that size!' the wizard roared, his voice shaky from the exertion of maintaining control of the airship.

I must have been hanging out in the wind for longer than I thought. 'Ceile? Petrel?' I demanded.

If Ceile was gone, I would erase the dragon from existence. I could feel the rot and decay of the mire of nether surrounding us. It whispered to me. All that power, just waiting for me to reach out and grab it.

Before I could move further along that suicidal path, I saw Ceile poke her head out from the far turret bay and give me a weak wave. There was blood on her face, and she hugged her chest with her right arm. I immediately pushed away from the wall to go to her, but Nox caught hold of my shoulder and pulled me back with a growl. As he did, the ship shuddered and rolled, and the only thing keeping me from rolling with it was the big 'wolf's grip.

The dragon had barely moved despite the airship's wild bucking. It still stared in at me, though I could hear its legs and tail doing horrible damage. The beast was completely ignoring the steady stream of fire that Robin was sending its way, even with a large patch on its chest dripping molten dragon scale onto the front of the ship.

I shook my head. This thing was really fixated on me all of a sudden.

A hideous shriek announced the end of Robin's turret, and shortly afterward the dwarf woman staggered out of her turret bay, pursued by black smoke. She coughed and fell to her knees, clutching desperately at the nearest crew station as the ship rolled again.

I scrambled for ideas. 'Bill, the missile launcher! Can't we use that? Point blank shot!' I yelled, gesturing at the launcher through the viewport above the deck.

The wizard laughed maniacally, and shouted back, 'Martin, my good friend, that weapon would do grievous damage to us if we were that close when one of its missiles exploded! And by grievous, I mean that the front half of the ship would likely be vaporized and all of us with it!'

The dragon lashed out at the view screen with its tail, and now there were long, slender cracks inching their way across the glass.

Now's the time. Let me loose.

I frowned and said beneath my breath, 'Having you loose aboard an out of control airship several kilometres in the air and crewed by my friends isn't a great idea on any day. Besides, we're weak. Something is wrong. You must feel it.'

The Other didn't reply, though I felt him lurking just below the surface.

'Lifeboats?' Robin asked in between coughs. Her question was punctuated by another massive tail strike against the windscreen, which rattled the ship and briefly deadened my hearing again.

Bill shook his head. 'The dragon's got two of them, and I am not sure the boats could outrun the blasted thing anyway. No, I've got something else in mind. Just hold on, my friends! We're almost there!' the wizard shouted over his shoulder.

The black dragon looked away for a second, and I caught a brief glance of one of its legs reaching forward to swipe at something before the ship shook violently, sending us all crashing to the floor. More alarms, more smoke, and now I could see a full blown inferno engulfing the port side of the Red Flag. The stricken ship began to slowly spin.

'Well, that's not good,' Bill said as the world drifted lazily past the windscreen.

'Wizard, if you've got something up your sleeve, now's the time to use it!' Nox snarled. The big 'wolf had latched on to the back of my jacket, and I found my feet floating free of the deck at regular intervals.

'Hey, where's Petrel?' Robin suddenly asked.

It's hard to tell who was more surprised, us or the dragon, but one instant the beast is staring in at me through the window and the next its face is covered with steel dwarf.

'Tah-dah!' Bill yelled with a flourish.

For a brief moment, the dragon didn't do anything, frozen in shock. Petrel appeared to use the time to get settled onto the beast's nose, then, before it could react, started punching it in the face.

It was mesmerizing. The steel dwarf started off slow, but with each strike he increased with speed until his fists were a blur. Quickly, he had pulverized the scales near the dragon's eyes and now blood and tissue were erupting from its skin with each thundering punch. The dragon tried to throw him off, but his legs were wrapped so tightly around its nose that some of the scales had cracked. Furious, the beast shook its head and roared. Abandoning stability, it let go of the airship with its front legs and started swatting at its face in fury.

Moving like a spider, Petrel stopped his attack and crawled away, each hand and foot hold sending showers of shattered scale flying. Before the dragon could get a solid hit in, the dwarf had skittered onto its back and resumed beating a hole into its hide.

A hint of desperation now spiked through the dragon's roar. It couldn't get at its prey while latched onto the ship. It gave me a dirty look and then flung itself free, spinning and rolling as it fell away, tumbling toward the forest below, leaving the after image of its blazing yellow eyes dancing across my own.

26

'Petrel!' Robin yelled, charging across the deck, heedless of the ship's motion, and planting her face against the windscreen to watch the beast plummet.

'He's resilient. Steeled for this, you might say! We have bigger fish to fry, Robin! Go for the lifeboats while the beast is occupied!' Bill shouted, pompously.

There was an explosion from the damaged engine, shaking the airship. The other two began to emit high-pitched whines as they struggled to keep us afloat. The spin increased. Debris began spilling out the battered turret bays, falling away in a shower of metal and plastic. A massive rift in the wall next to us appeared, and now Nox was trying to keep from getting blown out the side.

Ceile was clawing her way toward us, trying to use the crew stations alternatively as ladder and ramp. Robin was crouched against the pilot's chair, muscles straining against the bucking ship. Bill had managed to lose his robes and was now steering the ship in what looked like a t-shirt and jeans. I did what I could to hold tight to the wall and the counter nearby.

'The lifeboats!' Bill yelled. 'Hurry! If any of you are going to survive, go! I'll eject once you're all clear!'

Robin was already at the panel and sliding into the boat. She turned and put her hand out for Ceile. 'C'mon!' the dwarf yelled.

Ceile looked up at me, still ten metres away across a maze of debris and ruined crew stations. 'Go!' I shouted. 'Nox and I will take this one and meet up with you below!' I yelled, gesturing at the panel behind me. My friend shook her head stubbornly and started making her way toward me again.

Another violent explosion from below and now a jagged tear split the deck in half. 'Bill, what is this stupid thing made of, paper?' I yelled in frustration. The wizard snarled something about shoddy gnome construction.

Ceile and I stared at each other across the abyss. There was no way past the rift, not without going the long way around. Resignedly, my friend started to turn away, fear in her eyes. 'I will find you, Martin. Be safe! I will see you again! Be safe, Nox!' my friend shouted, then turned and headed for Robin. The dwarf caught hold of her hand and pulled her to safety.

The two women gave me a long glance as the boat's hatch closed. Then there was a dull thump and the lifeboat fell away.

'Didn't have the heart to tell them that our boat is destroyed, eh?' Nox shouted, nudging the sparking panel with his knee.

'That dragon was after me, Bill! Do you know something about that?' I snarled, ignoring the 'wolf.

Both Nox and the wizard looked surprised, but the latter shook his head. 'This isn't the time, Martin! Everything will be for naught if you die here. You two have to make it to the rear lifeboat, it's the only one left. Unless you want to try and get down to the cargo bay and throw on a parachute,' he said, loudly. Then he looked thoughtful, and said, 'I really should keep those things up here.'

There was a sharp bang from below decks, and the ship rocked violently. Nox lost hold of the wall and only barely managed to catch the edge of the hole in the side of the ship before being sucked out. I reached for his arm, knowing that there wasn't much I could do. The big 'wolf looked angry as he strained to pull himself back to safety. His claws slid slowly across the metal, leaving deep scars.

My friend looked up at me, and his eyes were sad. 'Aw, crap,' he said. And then the wind tore him from the airship and he vanished.

I screamed his name, then inched toward the gap, hoping to find him clinging to the side of the airship.

'Martin! No!' I heard Bill roar from behind me.

The Red Flag rocked again, and something smashed into me from behind, lifting me clear from the deck and throwing me toward the hole.

I heard the Other laugh maniacally.

And then there was nothing to see but sky and forest as I went out over the side.

27

This wasn't the first time I'd been in free fall, but I was an old man and I wasn't exactly at the top of my game. I flopped through the air wildly as I put my arms and legs out to try and stop my spin.

I heard the arrival of another text just before the wind ripped my jacket off and whisked it quickly out of eye sight, along with my cellphone. I sighed. As if I didn't have enough questions already.

Focusing on the task at hand, I managed to get straightened out. Now that I was falling in a slightly more controlled fashion, I looked around to get my bearings and then sighed again. 'Well, this adventure is starting off just great,' I snarled. The Other chuckled, idly floating beneath the surface.

Far to the east, the Red Flag spun toward the forest canopy at terrible speed. The damaged airship left a trail of flame and smoke and debris as it fell. I couldn't tell if Bill had ejected or not.

In the opposite direction, I could just make out the glint of a lifeboat falling away on the wind. Little more than a glider, the boat would carry its occupants away from its launch point but not necessarily to safety. I hoped Ceile and Robin would be okay.

Then I heard a roar from behind me, and a quick glance that way showed that our friend the black dragon hadn't met its end at Petrel's hands. And it appeared to still want to meet me. The big beast was getting closer by the second, its massive wings snapping violently as it strained to catch up.

Far below, spinning toward the canopy, was a big werewolf.

I cursed and pulled my arms in and straightened my legs out, and then I was rocketing downward. The dragon gave another roar as it adjusted its path to give chase.

As I flew toward my friend like a missile, I thought about what I was going to do. The only way out of this was going to require magic, not only to save Nox and me from an up close and personal introduction to the ground, but also to somehow fend off the dragon. When I had been healthy, I could have done all of that without too much trouble. When I'd been healthy.

I'd had a heart attack yesterday. I'd had good medical care since, but my body had been weak even before that. I hadn't used anywhere near my full power in ages. The Other had nearly knocked us unconscious, or worse, after twenty seconds of battering Cogs.

We're stronger now. Kill the dragon or let me do it.

I snorted. 'We haven't used that much power in decades. What makes you think we're suddenly able to do it again?' I growled. I felt him come right up to the surface.

You and your friend will die if you don't, unless the werewolf has a parachute in all that fur. You're wasting time.

I was surprised to find myself drawing nether from around me, feeling the ocean of rot stir and shift as I drank of it. I was surprised by how easily and how much I could pull from it.

I was surprised by how much I wanted to drain it all.

The Other's glee radiated from within my mind.

Excellent. Now do something with it.

It had been months, maybe years since I'd done anything particularly fancy, but my practiced hands wove the forms quickly and confidently. I started shaping and folding and shaping again the nether that oozed and dripped from my hands. The dragon roared toward me, mouth opened wide, front claws reaching for its prey. Somewhere below, the forest was reaching up to crush me. I laughed as I felt the form come together, the spell complete. It was exhilarating.

I missed this. So much.

The dragon was only metres away when I let the spell fly. There was a hideous sucking noise as a million motes of purple light burst into existence and then flew into the palms of my hands, gathering into a pulsing orb of sickly colour. With an evil grin, I threw my hands upward toward the beast, and howled an arcane command. For an instant, nothing happened, and the dragon roared in victory.

Then a beam of purple energy, as wide around as the orb, connected my hands to the back of the dragon's mouth. The beast made a garbled roar and a confused look crossed its face. Then there was a scarlet eruption behind the beast's head, and the beam burst through and out into space for a brief instant before I closed my palms, extinguishing the purple light.

The dead dragon fell limply past me.

The Other roared with laughter.

I flipped around and threw my arms and legs out completely to slow my fall. A quick glance showed that I'd caught up to Nox and now the big 'wolf was trying to match my speed, clumsily mimicking my position. The quick glance also showed that we were now a lot closer to the forest canopy than was healthy.

Having spent every drop of nether to kill the black dragon, I needed to grab more if I was going to try to save the 'wolf and me. As soon as I started to reach into the decay, there was a blast of pain, stars filled my vision, and everything got far away.

28

I guess my body wasn't quite ready after all.

Martin! Listen to me!

Even the Other's voice was murky and distant. I had to fight to keep my eyes open, and it took me a long while to realize that Nox had managed to close the distance between us and was now within a metre, trying to yell at me over the roar of the wind. His face was full of concern. I realized that my arms and legs were all over the place and that I was starting to spin.

I tried to correct, but my body refused to obey. I could make out the Other shouting at me as he thrashed just beneath the surface. Now I was rotating wildly, gaining speed. A sharp pain across my shoulders brought the world back into focus, barely, and then I was enfolded in blond fur.

Nox had caught hold of me and was trying to keep both of us level. I didn't know how much experience with free fall the 'wolf had, but he had the right idea. I was still weak, but I reached for nether anyway.

Again I felt pain and I started to black out and then the Other hammered through the surface

and then I shook my head to clear it as best possible, reached cautiously for the wind around me, hoping against hope that whatever was messing with Martin wasn't also going to be my problem. Even before I made contact, the aether was whistling around me, begging, no, demanding that I shape it and birth chaos across the world.

I was happy to oblige.

First, though, had to save myself. Oh, and I suppose I should save the 'wolf, too. Gathering aether to me, I pushed him away. He looked surprised for an instant, loosening his grip and then letting me go with a snarl when he realized what had happened. I gave him a wink.

I wanted to bait the 'wolf for longer, but time was getting short. I shaped the aether into forms of rushing and whirling air, vortexes that engulfed the two of us and sent us spinning lazily downward, slowing our fall. I felt sweat on my brow, and my shoulders and back began to ache. I had to be quick, Martin had done a number on our shared body and I wasn't much better off than he had been.

The trees rose up to greet us, and I kept folding and folding the forms, increasing the vortexes power and slowing us even more. Still, we were moving a lot quicker than I wanted. Out of the corner of my eye, I could see Nox alternating between glaring at the canopy and glaring at me. I made his ride a little rougher just for fun, and I thought I heard the big 'wolf snarl in anger as he somersaulted wildly.

Pleased with myself, I focused harder on the forms. I hadn't done anything this intricate in a long time. Usually, I just ripped things to shreds. This was actually pretty fun.

We burst through the canopy, and I did my best to keep either of us from smashing into the trees. I realized that Martin had been talking to me with increasing persistence during our descent, but I pushed him further into his cage. 'I'm busy, stay there and enjoy the view,' I said with a chuckle. The man swore at me and then fell silent, staring out through the bars.

Some of the trees we fell past were two hundred metres high, and that was good. If they'd been half that height, we probably would have had broken bones and nasty gashes when we hit the floor. As it was, I put a little more effort into my own landing, floating to the ground with my arms out and head raised to the heavens. Of course, that meant I had to pull some focus from Nox's landing, and the 'wolf slammed painfully into the floor.

I felt a little woozy, and I suddenly had trouble catching my breath. I sneered as I felt my body start to succumb to the exertion, frustrated with being hobbled by the ancient thing. I started to curse, but then I turned and almost jumped out of my skin.

I didn't wet myself around him like everyone else seemed to, but even I stepped back a couple inches when I suddenly found the 'wolf towering over me, teeth bared, claws out, eyes darkened to almost pitch black. Snarling, he leaned down until his nightmarish face was almost nose to nose with mine, and then jabbed a single claw into my chest painfully.

'When this is over, I'm going to find out how to rip you out of Martin's body, and then I'm going to tear your head and limbs off and make a fort with your parts,' he growled.

I wanted to make the comment that that wouldn't be much of a fort and that that wasn't much of a thank you for saving his life, when I felt the familiar tug and the bending of bars

and then I staggered and dropped to my knees. Nox watched me for a brief moment, suspicion clear on his face, until he knew it was me and not some trick by the Other and then caught my shoulder with one arm and hauled me up. Looking around us, the big 'wolf nodded and set me down gently on a fallen tree nearby. I thanked him as I sat there unsteadily.

'What was all that? You haven't used that kind of power in years. I didn't think you still could,' the big 'wolf said as he scanned my face. He hadn't let go of my arm. Shaking his head, the 'wolf said, 'And he did some pretty powerful stuff, too. You should be unconscious at best. Or dying at my feet.'

I shook my head slowly, trying to get enough air to answer. I didn't feel like I was on the verge of passing out anymore, but I did feel weak as a daigan kitten. 'I don't know. Something's changed. Last time I tried to do something like that, I ended up in the hospital,' I said, then paused a moment before continuing, 'Well, okay, not something like that, exactly. I've never tried to kill a dragon while I was in free fall.'

I fell silent and focused on getting my wits back. The werewolf watched me quietly. A couple minutes later, I nodded at him and he let my shoulder go.

I looked away from the big 'wolf, and then said to the Other, 'What about you? Did this feel strange to you? You did some powerful stuff, when was the last time you managed that?'

My questions echoed through my mind, deep beneath the surface and into the shadows far below. For a long moment nothing came back. Then I felt him stir in the depths.

Something's given us a bit of a boost.

I frowned. 'Something has given us a boost? Temporarily? How do you know that?' I asked. Nox stared at me intently.

Good questions. Maybe I'll answer them sometime. In the meantime, just enjoy it!

I felt him push out of the depths, floating slowly upward to hover just below the surface. I could feel his sneer.

I know you enjoyed it.

I snarled, frustrated. With Nox's help, I got to my feet. The big 'wolf started to say something when the Other spoke again.

Yes, you have good questions, Martin, but they aren't the questions you should be asking right now.

His voice rippled across my mind, and I put my hand to my head to steady myself. Rubbing my forehead, I asked, irritated, 'What question should I be asking right now, then?'

You should be asking why we're so popular with the dragons today.

With that, he cackled maniacally and then circled away. Nox was staring at me in frustration, having only been party to half the conversation. I shook my head.

'He says we should be wondering why we're so popular with the dragons today,' I said, wondering what the Other hoped to accomplish with these new games.

'Dragons? Plural? We've only seen one, what's he talking about?' Nox growled.

I didn't get a chance to answer. I heard an odd chirp over my shoulder and saw the big 'wolf's face flash from shock to anger. He grabbed hold of me and then I was spinning through the air and landing on my feet behind him.

'I hope you can do an encore of earlier,' he snarled. His claws clacked together in anticipation. I peered around him and then jerked back in fear.

Standing at the far end of the clearing we'd landed in, almost hidden by a group of thick bushes, was a green dragon.

29

The green dragon watched us carefully, then made that odd chirping sound again. Gingerly, it stepped free of the bushes, its lean form moving gracefully over the uneven forest floor.

Much smaller than the beast that had attacked us earlier, this dragon might have strained to carry me on its back in flight, and certainly would never have been able to do so for Nox. A closer look showed that its wings were stunted anyway. It likely had never flown in its life. Its eyes blazed neon green, bright enough to leave echoes when I closed my eyes.

It was an elegant creature. Where the black dragon had been a thing of nightmare, all spikes and jagged edges and raw sound, this beast was smooth, quiet, almost gentle as it crept over the leaves and branches and twigs that littered our landing area. I wondered if it were one of the intelligent species or not.

Nox moved us slowly away from it, trying to keep a rough orbit that would take us to the clearing's edge while keeping the dragon in front of us. In return, the beast circled slowly, watching us curiously.

'Maybe it's friendly?' I said. I heard the Other laugh at the back of my mind.

In answer, the dragon's mouth suddenly opened wide, showing rows upon rows of viciously pointed teeth, and it growled menacingly. It stopped circling and moved toward us, still making virtually no noise as it did.

Nox growled back, and he dropped into a crouch, teeth and claws bared and ready. 'I'll keep it distracted. Either you're going to have to kill it or you're going to have to run,' the big 'wolf snarled. Then he sniffed deeply. Looking over at me, he continued, 'I smell poison on it. Don't let it hit you.'

I nodded, then reached into the mire to draw some nether to me.

A blast of sound, a burst of light, and pain rippled through my mind. I collapsed to the ground.

Nox spun and lifted me. 'That went well. You're going to have to run! I'll keep it occupied, but you need to run, Martin!' the big 'wolf snarled.

I gasped for air. 'I don't understand. I've never had that happen before,' I said, trying to keep on my feet. The nether roiled around me, a landslide of decay and rot. The blood of a dying sun.

The dragon growled angrily at us. Nox set me gently down. 'Never mind that, just run. I'll find you!' he growled. The 'wolf turned away and stalked slowly toward the green dragon. The beast stopped moving, watching its prey. It clacked its jaws together, hissing in warning.

Nox finally came to a stop when he and the beast were only metres from each other. The massive werewolf crouched just outside of the dragon's reach, arms wide, hands out, claws arched in fury. He snarled with anger, then took a deep breath and howled. The few forest creatures that hadn't already fled the area now vanished in fear.

Again I reached for nether, and this time, I was able to dip a hand into the decay. I couldn't draw much, anything other than a steady drip threatened to send me to my knees. I moved slowly for some cover, hoping to gather nether while in relative safety. I grimaced as I felt the sickness and rot of the energy spin and ooze around my hands.

Let me out, Martin. You got the last one, this one's mine.

I shook my head at him, trying to keep my concentration. 'No. I'm not convinced you're in any better shape, and even if you are, I think you'd use the chance to butcher Nox. So, help me or shut up,' I said, under my breath.

Nox and the dragon continued to snarl at each other. Despite the size difference between the two, the beast didn't attack, instead watching my friend carefully.

Risking a quick glance, the big 'wolf saw me lurking behind him. Turning back to the dragon, he roared over his shoulder, 'Martin! Run, you moron!'

I guess we'll get to see if Nox really can take on a dragon.

I frowned at him, and the Other laughed and vanished into the depths. I just needed time. The trickle of nether continued. I wouldn't be able to gather enough to kill it, but I could wound it enough for Nox to do so.

I just needed time.

Of course, the green dragon's head suddenly swung to glare at me, and steam hissed from its mouth. Green ooze had started dripping from its teeth. Then it inhaled deeply and all three of us acted at once.

I threw myself sideways, crashing to the ground roughly, tearing my shirt and arms painfully. I rolled awkwardly, trying to put myself as far from where I had been as possible.

The green dragon spit a geyser of green liquid into the area I'd just been occupying, which burst and then sprayed in all directions. Where the fluid touched, the forest floor hissed and turned black.

And Nox launched himself forward, charged across the ground on all fours, and attacked the dragon.

30

The green dragon had been swinging back in anticipation of Nox's attack, but the big 'wolf's furious speed caught it unprepared. Before it could react, he leapt and raked all four sets of claws across its scaly hide in rapid succession.

The beast shrieked and lashed out with its tail, trying to crush the 'wolf as it spun to defend itself. Nox was quick, but it still managed to strike him hard enough to throw the big 'wolf into the bush. Without hesitating, the beast went after him, but only made it a few steps before the werewolf erupted out of the trees, impossibly fast.

Evading the dragon's claws, Nox slashed deep into its shoulder, using it to swing himself around and onto its back. Frenzied, the dragon's tall neck arced around, jaws snapping viciously at its attacker but missing by inches. The 'wolf cut at it again, but the dragon abruptly rolled onto its side, forcing my friend to leap away to narrowly avoid being crushed.

I struggled to get back to my feet, and winced in pain. I was in good shape for my age - though I suppose just being alive would be considered good shape for my age - but I hadn't done my own stunts in a long, long time. My arms were cut up pretty good, and the rest of me wasn't much better. I could feel the bruises forming on my legs, and I thought I'd rolled my ankle.

As the dragon and the werewolf fought, I reached out once more to the ocean of nether that surrounded me. What I'd managed to gather had been lost in my desperate escape from the dragon's poison, so I had to start again. This time, I wasn't immediately wracked with pain, but the flow was still little more than a drip.

I caught hold of a nearby tree and then focused on drawing more. Nox was as resilient as anything I'd ever encountered, but even he wouldn't last long if he got poisoned more than a couple times. I had to help him.

The big 'wolf circled the dragon, clacking his claws together loudly, snarling angrily. When the dragon lunged at him again, he darted past its deadly teeth and slashing talons, then carved another long crevice into the beast's side. Jerking to a halt, my friend then ducked underneath it faster than it could react and slashed the other side. The dragon spun violently, trying to crush the 'wolf with its bulk but succeeding only in giving him a platform to get at its neck again.

Latching on with the claws on his feet, Nox slashed the base of the dragon's neck before it could turn and attack. Then the big 'wolf opened wide and bit down deep into the green scales there. The beast shrieked, tried to shake him loose, and then snapped at the werewolf with brutally fast bites.

Green flecks dropped down all around him, and where they landed his fur darkened and smoked. Abandoning his perch, he leapt away, landing on his feet a few metres away. Spinning around, the big 'wolf was a blur as he charged back at the dragon, green scales falling from his teeth and claws.

The beast jerked its head around to meet him, and as its jaws shot downward to bite the 'wolf in two, I heard it inhale deep.

So did Nox, but instead of dodging away, he put on an even greater burst of speed.

The two met and I heard a rush of fluid as the dragon prepared to give my friend an acid bath. Before it could, Nox reached out, put a hand on the top and bottom of its jaws, and slammed them together violently.

The Other laughed maniacally.

The beast coughed raggedly, and its entire body shuddered. Steam and mucus sputtered from its nostrils, leaving black scars as the mess dripped down its nose. The beast tried to jerk away from its tormentor, but Nox was having none of it. The dragon could drag him around very slowly, but its neck wasn't strong enough to lift or throw nine hundred pounds of really angry werewolf.

Trying to get at the 'wolf with its front talons, the dragon lunged forward, but couldn't strike without hitting itself. It also bent the beast's neck at what looked like an incredibly painful angle.

Nox howled furiously as he strained to keep the dragon's jaws shut and to keep it from dragging him into reach of its legs. Despite having the beast trapped, he hadn't gained the upper hand. He couldn't attack either.

The 'wolf's almost black irises were locked with the dragon's neon green. He couldn't keep this up forever, and I could see that green ooze was still dripping from the beast's closed jaws. Puffs of smoke were rising from the big 'wolf's hands. I cursed and tried to pull more nether, succeeding only in giving myself a headache.

Suddenly, Nox let go and slashed fiercely at the green dragon's eyes. It roared and flinched away, avoiding the 'wolf's left claws but not his right. When the beast's head lifted high into the air, screaming so loud that it drowned out everything, it was missing its left eye.

Then it lashed out with its tail, faster than thought, and struck Nox full on the chest. The big 'wolf's face look surprised as the blow lifted him into the air and sent him crashing into the bush.

Rather than go after the 'wolf, the dragon instead turned to look at me. It shook its head, spraying gore in every direction, and hissed. The beast then stalked toward me, turning its neck just enough so that it could watch me entirely with its last eye. It was limping slightly, and I could see that the wounds Nox had given it were bleeding pretty badly.

I backed away slowly, glancing over at the trees where my friend had gone in but not come out. The nether I'd managed to gather still wasn't enough to do much more than tickle the dragon, and I neither had nor was proficient with any other weapon. I suddenly felt very squishy.

The beast closed until it was only metres away, looked me over carefully, then turned around and started moving cautiously back toward where it had last seen Nox.

I sat there, frozen in confusion, trying to figure out why it hadn't attacked.

The dragon reached the edge of the clearing and slowly circled as it tried to peer through the trees, searching for signs of the werewolf. It lumbered forward, then slashed at the trees to give it a clearer view.

Then a blonde, furry shape erupted out of the woods behind the dragon, charging on all fours. The beast heard the 'wolf coming, slashing wildly with its rear talons, but Nox was too fast. The big 'wolf cut massive gashes along the stunted wings, leapt sideways out of reach of the tail, and then jumped to its back.

The dragon twisted desperately to get the 'wolf, rolling across its back and lashing out with its legs. Nox dodged and then viciously slashed its tail, ducking beneath the beast's return strike, cutting deep rows along its other wing and then attacking its neck again. The dragon shrieked.

The battle was taking its toll on both combatants. Nox had brutally slashed and bitten the green dragon on almost every part of its body, but now he was limping and cut up pretty badly himself. Even the 'wolf wouldn't be able to keep this up for much longer.

The clearing was starting to look like a disaster zone. Most of the trees at the edge had been knocked over or shredded. The canopy above the clearing was almost devoid of leaves and branches, having been dislodged by the dragon and werewolf slamming into the few remaining trees. The ground was littered with foliage, Nox's black blood and the dragon's green, torn emerald scales, and the rapidly neutralizing acid.

Now Nox and the green dragon were circling each other warily in the center of the clearing, the beast staggering around on lacerated limbs, the 'wolf limping on bruised and cut legs. The dragon hissed angrily, glaring at my friend with its good eye. Nox snarled back, teeth bared, claws clicking together menacingly.

Uh oh. Better start running.

Before I could ask the Other what he was talking about, Nox burst forward, roaring. And then he collapsed, his right leg giving out beneath him. He recovered quickly, but it wasn't enough.

The dragon took a deep breath, and then bathed the big 'wolf in acid.

31

Nox screamed, dropping to his knees as smoke rose from all over his body. His hair was melting or falling off in bloody clumps. His whole body flailed, and then the 'wolf collapsed to the ground, convulsing violently.

And then he went still, his cries cutting off abruptly and his body going limp.

I stood there, frozen, staring at my friend in horror. We'd always considered Nox to be unstoppable. He took terrible wounds and just kept right on fighting. If you got into trouble, having the big 'wolf near made you feel invincible. Now, he was grievously wounded at best and dead at worst, and I didn't know what to do.

Running would be a good start.

The dragon had stepped cautiously forward, leaning down slowly to see if its foe was finished. With a rough push with one of its front legs, the beast rolled Nox over. The werewolf came to rest facing me, arms flung out at random angles like a rag doll. Black blood oozed from his nostrils and ears. His chest didn't rise.

His eyes were open and staring, bloodshot and unblinking.

I stood there, frozen, mouth agape. My heart beat in my ears. My vision swam with tears. 'Nox,' I whispered, raggedly. 'Nox, no.' My friend didn't answer, didn't get up, and now I was staring at the dragon. Horror, fear, sadness, all obliterated by something else.

Rage.

I didn't yet have enough nether gathered to do anything spectacular, so I reached out into that mire and breathed in the rot and decay. My whole body shook and pain threatened to knock me out, but I kept drawing energy, and all I needed was a few seconds more and then I'd erase the green dragon from existence.

Seconds it didn't give me. Despite its wounds, the beast burst forward, neon green eye blazing with fury. It hissed loudly as it came, mouth open, teeth bared. Poison dripped from its mouth and from its nostrils, and in between hisses, I could hear its tortured lungs working to expel fluid that was supposed to go out, not in.

As it charged toward me, I temporarily gave up preparing the forms and headed for the clearing's edge. The dragon was fast in straight lines over roughly flat ground, but it was wounded and the forest floor was uneven and littered with debris. The beast skidded wildly as I bolted to its side, running as hard as my bruised body would let me.

It crashed to the floor, but lurched to its feet quickly and was on me again before I made it into the bush. I cursed as I threw myself forward, narrowly avoiding the beast's wild swipe with its talons.

Every second I spent focused on something other than drawing nether meant some of the nether I'd already drawn would slip away.

The dragon didn't give me much of a chance to pout. I heard its jaws clack together noisily, and drops of acid sprinkled over the trees and bushes around me as I staggered to my feet. Another slash from a front leg split a tree near me into kindling, forcing me to fling myself away yet again.

I fell hard, rolling as soon as I hit the ground just as a massive, clawed foot slammed down where I had fallen. I managed to get to my feet and stumble drunkenly away. The dragon roared, and then I heard its jaws whip past just over my head, branches above erupting in a shower of twigs and leaves.

My rage was gone, and now shards of fear were spiking through me. My heart wasn't racing from emotion, it was because I was exhausted. My breath was just as ragged as the dragon's, my muscles ached, and I was soaked with sweat. Old people don't generally spend much time running from angry dragons.

I was starting to think that I might not make it two weeks after all.

I scrambled blindly through the trees, listening to the dragon crash along behind me. When it sounded like it was nearly on me, I shot off to the right, hearing it snarl angrily as the beast slid into the bush and lost sight of me with its good eye. Risking a quick glance, I saw that it had gotten tangled up and was now trying to break free.

Its eye glared at me as I put distance between us.

I laughed and began drawing nether. I could hear the dragon struggling to escape its cage of shattered tree and wicked brush. I could hear the Other yelling, but I was too occupied to hear about what.

Then I burst out of the trees and found nothing but air beneath my feet.

As shocked as I was by my second attempt at flight within as many hours, I still tried to reach out to slow my fall, but there was nothing to grab hold of. I crashed and tumbled down the slope, getting slashed and slammed by rocks and bristles. The nether I'd drawn leaked away, seeping back into the ocean of decay and rot. I hit my head on a flat rock, and stars bounced around my visions. I was abstractly aware that my fall had triggered an avalanche of debris that was now following me on my ungraceful descent.

Then the slope levelled out and I rolled roughly out into the corner of another clearing.

A dull rumble filled my ears, and I dazedly watched the storm of rock and dirt and brush roar toward me. I managed to prop my head and back up with my arms, but then time ran out and it was all I could do to keep from getting crushed.

It felt like minutes but was probably only seconds, and then the deluge stopped. I coughed, trying to peer through the haze of dust as I checked my parts to see how bad I was hurt.

Blood was dripping down my forehead, and a quick feel showed that I had a pretty nasty cut there. Maybe a concussion, too. My hair was caked in blood, and loaded with twigs and dirt. I was going to have to cut it, I'd never get all of that out. That was frustrating. I hadn't had short hair in over a century.

My arms were cut up and bruised, but nothing seemed broken. So there's that. All in all, it looked like I'd come out of my fall pretty well, considering. I smiled bitterly, reminded that my friend's body still lay somewhere back there.

Then I checked over my legs. After I'd pushed most of the debris off of them, I gave first the right and then the left a once over. The right was terribly bruised but bent fine and felt alright beyond the burn in the muscles. Then I tried to push the last of the debris off of the left.

I couldn't move it. My left leg was caught under the stones.

It didn't feel broken, and I wasn't losing feeling in it, but as much as I pushed and pulled I couldn't dislodge the two big stones lying across my calf and ankle. I snarled with frustration.

Just destroy them, idiot.

I frowned at the Other's rebuke, but mostly because I felt stupid. I was lucky that I hadn't broken anything or died when I blundered over the cliff above, and here I was struggling against a rock. I started to draw nether to me.

And then I snarled as that now familiar burst of pain wracked my body. 'Not now! What is going on?' I growled in frustration. The mire was once again out of reach, each attempt to draw from it sending sparks across my bones.

I sat there, angry. Had it even been a day since I'd gone into the hospital to be healed after the heart attack? I went to check my watch, only to find its face cracked from corner to corner and its display frozen at 1:78 White. I threw my hands up in the air in irritation, and asked, 'Great, how can this get any worse?'

The green dragon crashed down at the far end of the clearing, falling to its side facing away from me. It wheezed loudly, its breath haggard.

I froze, staring at the beast. Did it know I was here? Maybe it'd just die over there and I can get back to having a tantrum.

The dragon lifted its head slowly off the ground, then turned its neck to look directly at me.

32

The dragon got to its feet laboriously, never taking its eyes off of me. Once upright, it wobbled unsteadily, stumbling forward a few steps before collapsing with a weak shriek of pain. Steam hissed out of a nasty gash on the side of its face. Nox must have hurt it pretty bad.

Thinking about the 'wolf threatened to bring tears to my eyes again, and I glared at the dragon, which was glaring back from a hundred metres away. Without looking away, I tried a few more quick tugs at my leg. They proved as effective as the previous.

In the grand scheme of things, I supposed getting killed by a dragon was certainly an epic way to go. Unless you were run over by a dragon taxi. That was less heroic.

I knew I was out of range of the beast's acid spray, so there was that. For that matter, it hadn't moved far since its five point landing a few minutes ago, and it was really having trouble breathing.

We glared at each other from our corners of the clearing. The dragon sullenly clacked its jaws at me.

For the moment, neither of us was much a threat to the other. I could hit it with some sort of spell from here, if I could get the nether to do so. As that didn't appear to be an option, I needed to figure something out, and fast. Eventually the dragon would recover enough to drag itself over and then kill me.

I couldn't do much of anything with the trapped leg, and with it trapped the way it was, I couldn't do anything other than sit. First order of business was getting free. I looked around, searching the scattered debris for something to use as leverage. If I could find something that I could use to lift the stone, then I could hopefully slide my foot out. Alternatively, I might find something that I could use to cut my leg off.

Thankfully, I found a sizable and sturdy branch half buried in the mess that would probably work as a lever.

It was just a half metre out of reach.

The dragon had given up watching me, and was now licking its wounds. Nox had done horrific damage to it before the beast had killed him. It was still having difficulty breathing, and having seen what its poison could do, I wasn't surprised that even the dragon couldn't handle a lung full of it. It briefly looked up at me, hissed, and then went back to cleaning itself.

Focusing on the branch, I reached out - very carefully, very slowly - into the ocean of nether I was floating in, and drew some of it to me. An electric shock arced through my head, but it was dulled, nothing like it had been. Still, it was slow going. It could be an hour before I had enough to do any damage to the dragon.

It was significantly less than an hour when I took the small amount of energy I'd gathered and began to shape it. The dragon looked up at me suspiciously. I blew it a kiss, finished the arcane form, and reached out for the branch.

For a second, it did nothing but vibrate, creating a tiny dust cloud. Then it burst from the dirt and debris and hit me squarely in the shoulder. I cried out in victory. The dragon hissed.

Jamming the end of the branch in next to my leg, I gave it a few test lifts to make sure it wouldn't crush my foot. When it didn't immediately start breaking my bones, I took a breath, and then lifted with everything I had.

The stone moved an inch. I pulled the branch out and jammed it in deeper. A couple more of those would probably free my foot. I wrapped my hands around the end and started to pull.

A high pitched shriek echoed out of the forest from somewhere nearby.

The dragon's head shot up, and scanned the clearing's edges intently. I stopped and followed its gaze, listening. There were plenty of dangerous things out in the forest, but I'd considered the dragon as the only threat. Now that the dragon wasn't a threat at all, I was suddenly very aware that I was exposed and vulnerable.

Then a cacophony of yips and howls erupted from the forest not far to our east. A cacophony that was getting closer. The dragon began to drag itself slowly toward the west edge, never taking its eye off the bush in the opposite direction. There was just a hint of fear in its eye.

That took me aback. Green dragons are local to the Locus Wood. If it recognized those sounds and was trying to get away, then whatever produced them probably wasn't good. I immediately got back to trying to move the stone.

Another shriek, and this time it was much closer. Out ahead of the yips and howls to the east. I moved the stone another couple of inches. My foot was free enough to rotate it, but I was still caught.

Now the dragon looked a bit panicked. Despite its efforts, it hadn't moved much more than a couple metres, and now it looked completely exhausted. It was making erratic chirping noises as it clawed weakly at the ground.

'If you don't mind telling me what's coming to eat us, I'd appreciate it,' I said to it, sarcastically, as I struggled to finish freeing my leg. I frowned, and then asked someone else, 'I don't suppose you know what's coming?'

I'm amazed you've survived as long as you have, today. People are going to think you've been lying to them about being old and decrepit.

I cursed. 'Well, that's helpful,' I said. The Other laughed as he floated just beneath the surface, watching.

The noise was almost right on us, and this time I threw everything I had into lifting the stone. It shifted, grinding painfully across my calf, and then I was free. I got to my feet, crashed to the ground, and then crawled and crouched my way slowly toward the edge. I caught a rock and went down entirely, falling into the dirt. I managed to spin to face the east, but I was just too sore to get up.

The shrieks came, more frequently now, barely distinguishable from the storm of barks and yips and howls. I reached for the rotting mire once more, and as the slow trickle of nether came in, I suddenly wished I had at least brought the branch with me.

Then I could see a small dark shape charging through the brush toward us. It was the one making the shrieks, and with one last desperate cry the monster burst into the clearing.

33

If it wasn't for whatever was making the other noises, I might have laughed. The little creature that erupted out of the foliage slammed to a halt when confronted with the green dragon and me. Half my size, reptilian, wearing filthy clothes, and clutching some kind of package tightly in its arms, the newcomer was a kobold.

It stood there, twitching, looking rapidly between me and the dragon. The White Sun overhead glinted off of its bronze scales. The little beast looked terrified. Then it looked over its shoulder, shrieked in fear, and bolted toward me.

'Helllllp!' it yelled as it charged past without slowing, its draconic face continuing to look over its shoulder in terror, tail flicking around in a frenzy.

I watched the little thing disappear into the trees off to my right, and then turned back to the spot it had come out of. Both the green dragon and I were skidding ourselves away as best we could. We exchanged a glance. I wished I could interpret what I saw in its eye.

The howls and yips and barks converged into one massive cloud of noise, and then a swarm of gnolls erupted from the trees.

There were probably a hundred of them, all fur and stringy muscle and teeth, a werehyena in all but name. They loped at us, some on all fours, others striding on their lankly legs. Each one wore patchy armour and clothes, not a one of them looking the same in any way as their friends. All of them wore fury and frenzy on their faces, however.

Without slowing down, the pack diverged around us, some of them flashing past so close that I could have easily reached out and touched them. Whatever the kobold had done to them, it looked like they were angry enough about it to decide to ignore the dragon and me.

Well, most of them had decided that. As the pack thinned out, two dozen of them had decided they were hungry and were now circling both me and the dragon with ravenous looks on their faces.

If the green dragon had been hale and whole, the gnolls wouldn't have dared go anywhere near it, but the beasts could see that it was hurt, and badly. Now they were looking for meat, and the dragon had lots of it. Some of them got careless and lunged in, and caught the beast's tail in their teeth for their trouble, the vicious swing connecting with a sickening combination of crunch and squish. Three of those hit flew over my head to land lifelessly in the bush behind me.

Smartening up, the gnolls began alternating attacks. One group would dash in, slashing at the dragon's wounds, then another would do so from the opposite side when the beast tried to defend itself against the first. Soon it was bleeding heavily again.

If I hadn't been right in the thick of it, it would have been fascinating to watch the gnolls switch into working as a pack against the dragon. The few that had been circling me had joined the group, leaving me alone while they attacked the bigger prize. I used the opportunity to get shakily to my feet and back carefully away from the fray. Then I noticed something that almost made me stop.

The stagnant ocean of nether that I drew the energy from was bubbling and bursting and spewing as though superheated.

I'd felt it moving before, but nothing like this. This was different.

I reached slowly out into it, already anticipating the shock of pain I'd received earlier, but found only the familiar sickening feeling as nether flowed from the mire and into my hands. There was still some weakness there. It would take time to have enough energy to defend myself against everything in the clearing that wanted to eat me. I couldn't kill a few and then ask for a time out.

The fight against the green dragon wasn't going entirely the gnolls' way. The beast caught one of them in its mouth and bit it in half, then used the corpse to bludgeon another to death. A swipe of a leg sent a few of them falling away, their bodies slashed open to the bone. Still, there were a lot of them.

And if the dragon died, they'd all come for me.

So I just needed to kill all the gnolls, and then I'd have time to figure out my next move while the dragon and I glared at each other across the clearing. Then I'd decide just how badly I was going to hurt it for killing Nox.

Now you're talking. You're becoming more like me every day.

The Other's voice was full of dark glee, and I shook my head roughly. I was upset about Nox's death, but to the point of torturing his killer in revenge? That wasn't like me at all.

Before I could follow that thought any further down the path, there was a ragged howl from the trees the gnolls had entered the clearing from, and then a huge creature stepped out of the woods.

It was a gnoll, but it was massive, taller and thicker than Nox had been. Its claws and teeth were hooked and twisted in horrible ways. Its fur grew in haphazard clumps.

The dragon hissed at the gnoll, swiping its tail viciously into the cloud of smaller beasts, bashing a handful into a tree and crushing another to the floor. It dragged itself around until its head looked down at the newcomer. Steam had started to puff from its nostrils and the deep laceration across its cheek. Green ooze began to drip from its jaws.

Prepared to watch the dragon perform an encore of Nox's demise, I was shocked when the big gnoll leapt forward hideously quickly, hitting the beast hard on the side of the head. It reeled backward, and the gnoll hit it again, sending dragon teeth flying. Weakly, it tried to slash at its attacker with its claws, but the gnoll simply sidestepped and then kicked it in the face one last time.

The green dragon collapsed to the ground, wheezing and making quiet chirping noises. The gnolls burst into thunderous howls of victory, the big ugly one roared with laughter.

And then it saw me. As it slowly turned my way, the rest of the pack did too.

'Aw, crap,' I said.

34

I straightened up as best I could, letting my arms sit in a low casting position. The big gnoll watched me carefully then walked slowly forward, giggling in a deep, broken voice. Other gnolls tried to rush past it to come get me, but the monster snarled at them and they fled back to join the others ducking and swarming just behind the big one.

I tried to increase the flow of nether I was drawing, without success. I was exhausted, and it was amazing that I was able to draw at all, much less stand. My ability to gather energy was recovering, but my physical strength wasn't. Too much excitement for an old man.

I sighed. I was going to be eaten by gnolls. That's just embarrassing.

The big gnoll strode forward until it was just a few metres away and then stopped. The other gnolls danced back and forth, surging around their bigger cohort's feet and snarling and yipping at me. Finally, the big beast bellowed and all of the others went silent and still, twitching in place, some of them making small involuntary yips.

Once it had the floor, the monster burbled something at me, sounding like an idling car engine. The smaller ones burst into giggles and sharp yips. They returned to dancing around until the big one roared again. With the pack cowed once more, the gnoll walked toward me until it almost stood in arm's length, and then bent right down to breathe into my face.

Its breath was excruciatingly bad, and an ugly smirk creased its already ugly face. Some of the smaller gnolls had crept forward and were huddled around its knees in a twitching pile. Their eyes leapt between my face and my legs. One of them reached over and hesitantly poked my knee.

I was making one last frantic effort to pull more nether in when I noticed the dragon's head lift off the ground, poison dripping from its mouth, steam billowing from its nose. The big gnoll saw my gaze go over its shoulder, and spun incredibly fast to face the dragon. As one, the gnolls charged toward the scaly beast.

In a heartbeat, I shifted from shaping the energy into a killing rain to shaping the energy into a protective wall and dropped into a crouch as I unleashed the form. A shield of sickly light blazed into existence in front of me.

A wave of deadly acid spewed from the green dragon's maw, spraying across the gnolls. Those at the front dropped to the ground, killed in an instant as their heads and limbs were partially dissolved and their bodies hissed and spit as their fur, then flesh, then bone began to melt. The ones behind the leaders caught acid and poison in their eyes and mouths and across their torsos, and they fell to the ground to roll around screaming in agony and in the puddles that had once been their faster cohorts. The remainder immediately suffered burns across their heads, shoulders, and arms, burns that grew rapidly worse as the acid worked its magic, and then these too fell to the ground.

The big gnoll, standing in the middle of the pack and standing quite a bit taller than the others, took the brunt of the dragon's attack. The monster had enough forewarning that it managed to get one gnarled arm up in front of it. Instead of having its face and chest melt into a nasty gnoll pudding, its arm hissed and spit and dripped and then fell off.

What acid hadn't been soaked up by the gnolls splashed down harmlessly a foot or two in front of my shield.

Completely spent, the dragon's stream of poison cut off, it made a high pitched whining noise and then crashed to the ground. Most of the gnolls were dead, most of the rest were about to be, and a handful were fleeing in every direction without looking back.

Its energy spent, my shield dissipated. Its light slowly faded away.

The big gnoll was hurt badly but now it was really angry. It stepped up to the downed dragon, the twisted claws on its remaining hand clicking together in rage. Bending down, the monster scratched a long, deep line across the scaly beast's face. It burbled something in its odd language.

The dragon mewled quietly, breathing raggedly.

You'd better do something, or that gnoll will be all over you once the dragon is dead.

Looking inward, I found the Other floating just below the surface. 'Suggestions, maybe?' I said.

Let me out.

'I'm, I'm not sure if I can,' I stammered, searching the clearing for something I could use. 'I don't know how, we've never gone that direction before.'

You have to let go. Of everything.

My thoughts and my heart were racing. 'I'm not good at letting go of anything,' I said. I reached out into the mire of nether and began gathering it to me. Slow at first, then increasing speed until I felt the pain start to come. And then I kept going.

Impressive. You won't be able to keep that up long, though. Good luck.

Everything hurt, but I was drawing nether fast and soon I'd start shaping it into something unpleasant for the gnoll.

As if it had heard me, the monster turned and furiously charged, roaring as it came.

I guess being eaten by a big gnoll is a bit less embarrassing.

There wasn't going to be time to shape anything that could kill the beast, so I crouched down, ready to roll away. Again, I was out of time. That seemed to be happening quite a bit on this little holiday.

Before the gnoll got close enough, a blurred shape erupted from the trees, smashing into the beast and knocking it aside. The two rolled into a heap at the base of the cliff.

I cheered inside. This was going to distract the gnoll long enough for me to put something together. I just hoped I wouldn't have to kill both of them. That might be difficult in my current state.

The gnoll and the newcomer were locked together, the newcomer holding the gnoll's remaining wrist and its neck. Blood oozed from the spots it was being held. Both combatants were snarling and growling, occasionally trying to kick at each other with the razor claws on their feet.

They broke free, and the gnoll managed to slash the other across the face. The newcomer flew to the side, crashing to the ground and yelling in pain. The gnoll was on it quickly, claws slashing out, teeth gnashing in fury. The other shrieked and went to drag itself away, but the bigger monster was having none of it and pinned its foe to the ground with one massive foot. It raised its hand high over its head, prepared to crush the other with one brutal blow.

Then I cut its head off with a razor-thin line of arcane energy.

I hit the ground before the big gnoll did, the exertion finally catching up with me. The Other was saying something, but his voice was slurred and he sounded confused. The world went sideways, I saw the dragon bark at me from across the clearing, then a cracked and raw hand reach down to touch my face, then Ceile smiling gently while she sat next to me and Nox in the Electric Cat, and then a recovery room that I barely remember, and I heard my watch ping in reverse, and

?

'For the last time, Taylor, I'm not joining the damn army. I don't use the magic, I don't want it, and nobody's going to make me,' I said, quietly but forcefully. I wasn't looking at my companion, just staring out into the park, watching families lounging around in the White Sun's light. Cyclists and people using hover spells went past on the pathway. I realized I was gripping the arm rest of the bench quite tightly.

Taylor sighed, putting a hand up to his brow to wipe away some of the sweat. It was a particularly hot day. 'Listen, Edgar. I understand. It's good that you've hidden your power. You want to have a normal life,' he said, just as quietly. He too was gazing out into the City. The Moon lurked above, barely visible in the brilliant gleam of the Sun.

Turning to me, the man I considered my closest friend put a hand up on my shoulder. 'But understand this. This will be the last time the Government makes this optional. I had to fight hard to get the opportunity to offer you this opportunity. The next time, they will come, and they will take you away,' he said, and there was a hint of desperation on his voice.

I snarled, and the invisible storm of energy that always followed me roared into motion, prepared to answer my call. 'I won't let them take me. Maybe I don't know how to use it very well, but you - and they! - know what I can do. I won't let them come and hurt me or James or the kids,' I snarled, anger rising, and now I turned and looked into Taylor's eyes, and I was shocked to see there was fear there.

'Edgar, stop it, people will notice. You aren't incognito when you get riled up like that, you know. They can see it in your eyes, even if they can't put a name to it,' he said, quickly looking around us before continuing. 'Listen. The Department of Research haven't had their hands on a solaron in fourteen hundred years. And that was an elf! People like you are almost legendary, you're that rare,' he said, squeezing my shoulder.

'If the Government comes to take you away, you'll go to Research and they'll dissect you to try and figure out what makes you tick. And then they'll stitch you back up and you'll be their monster. James and your girls will never hear from you again, and they'll never know why you left.'

He shook his head, and said, 'But I have a better offer. Come and work for me at Operations. You'll report directly to me, that'll keep you out of Research's hands and out of the Arcane Corps.'

I shook my head, feeling helpless. 'And what will I do for you?' I asked, unhappily. Taylor chuckled.

'Whatever I need you to. Operations doesn't have a strict mandate. We do what needs doing, and usually without anyone knowing we're doing it,' he said, taking his hand from my shoulder and going back to looking out into the park.

Bitterly, I said, 'This is crazy. I'm a teacher, Taylor! I teach, I teach math and art to elementary students. It's me and James' anniversary next week.' I put my head in my hands. 'Hell, Katherine and Nala have their first magic lessons the day after. That's the life I want! The one I have.'

'They have lunarons,' Taylor abruptly said.

I fell silent in terror. For a long moment, neither of us said anything, then my friend spoke. 'They have a group of lunarons, and one that has taken them decades to build. When they come for you, the lunarons will be there. You might kill a few of them if you see them coming, but if one of them gets close enough, all of your power will mean nothing. It'll just be gone. You'll be just as powerless as the lunaron that took yours, but without the party trick that did so,' he whispered.

'They will take you, Edgar. They will find you, and they will take you. This is what the Government does. And even if you somehow managed to hold them off, they'd just kill you. You would be an incredibly valuable asset if you were under their control. You are a dire threat and a liability so long as you are not.'

I noticed that my friend was studiously avoiding lumping himself in with his overseers.

I stood roughly, and spun to face him. 'I don't understand, why me? Why all this effort for me? Why are solarons so special?' I demanded, heedless of the curious looks I was getting from the people around us. Taylor gave me a searching look.

'Edgar, do you remember when someone destroyed four whole Districts earlier this month? That was an archon, and by far the least powerful of the archons we're currently monitoring,' he said, waving at me to sit back down. I ignored it and started to say something, but my friend kept talking.

'Do you remember that elven city to the south that was completely razed last year?' he said, his voice rising slightly. I nodded slowly and started to answer but again he spoke over me.

'That was an aethon. An aethon of fire. A single woman. A powerful one, but again, not the most powerful on our lists.'

I was shocked. I'd heard that the city had been destroyed in some cataclysmic battle between rival elven factions. That there had been so few survivors and such total devastation had seemed odd but not enough for me to look into it.

Now Taylor stood and leaned in very, very close. 'You know that our world is sick, my friend? How the oceans are poison and the land seems to fall into oblivion beyond this continent? Do you know why this world is like that, Edgar?'

I frowned, and said, 'The Horsemen. They screwed up last time, the world never healed properly.' I shook my head, 'I don't need the history lesson, what does that have to do with anything?'

Now Taylor was shaking his head. 'No, Edgar, the Four Horsemen did not destroy the last world to usher in ours in such awful health. They never got the chance. It was a man, Edgar. A man who decided to kill the world himself,' he said, quietly.

'A solaron.'

I sat down painfully on the bench, disturbing a sylph that had landed on the back while I was standing. Taylor quickly sat down next to me, and he looked around to make sure no one was too close before continuing.

'Archons and aethons can cause terrifying devastation, but if the Government had a solaron under its control, nothing could stand against them. And that's what they want. They'll first try and make more of you, via Research's gentle ministrations. Then they'll make you an automaton that does only what it's told to,' he said.

'Don't let that happen. Join Operations with me. You're still going to be a weapon, but you're still going to be you.'

I looked out into the park again, my thoughts racing. My entire life had just gotten super complicated. The Yellow Dragon statue that loomed above the beach gleamed merrily in the sunlight. A girl that looked like my Nala darted across the grass, laughing and chased by a woman with a stern look on her face. I couldn't just vanish. My family didn't deserve that.

In the end, there was no choice at all.

'Alright. Tell me about Operations,' I said, quietly.

35

Dirt. Dirt in my nose, to be exact. I snorted the offending earth out, and then opened my eyes.

It was dirt alright, and I appeared to be lying face down in it. Grunting with the exertion, I twisted my head just enough to take in my immediate surroundings. There wasn't much to see. I was surrounded by gnoll corpses in varying states of disrepair. Just over one pair of bodies, I could see the broad, ravaged back of my saviour. It rose and fell raggedly, and twitched at each peak.

There wasn't much else to see from my vantage point, so I took stock of my situation. The cuts and bruises I'd picked up in my flight from the green dragon hurt and some were still bleeding slowly, but otherwise I seemed uninjured. Everything was really sore, but otherwise, physically, I was good.

I hesitantly reached out into the mire of rot and decay, and started to draw nether from it. I was pleased to find that my little dirt nap had given me enough rest that I could gather energy without the bursts of pain. As I felt the nether drip and flow around my hands, I got a shiver of pleasure. I didn't have a lot of energy gathered, but it would have been enough to do what took me ten minutes earlier.

Power.

I gave the dirt a wide smile. Alright, physically I was fine, my magic was in good shape, just one last thing to check.

'Are you there?' I whispered. When the Other didn't respond right away, I went looking for him in the depths of my mind. I finally sensed him, somewhere deeper than I could go, far beneath the shadows at the bottom. He didn't move. 'Are you alright?' I asked. When he finally answered, his voice was almost unrecognizable. There was fear there. But there was also wonder.

Martin. The dream. Did you see it, too?

The dream came crashing back, and I shivered again. It had been so real. 'I did. Do you know either of those two? Taylor and, what was his name, Edgar?' I whispered.

I don't know. They seem familiar. Did you notice the park?

I thought about it for a bit, then nodded. Which succeeded mostly in getting even more dirt in my hair. 'Yeah, that's Yellow Lake Park. But the dragon statue has been gone for over a hundred years, and it looked almost new,' I said.

Why would we see it from Edgar's eyes?

'I don't know,' I whispered. I had to wonder if we had seen the exact same thing, or if he'd picked up something from it that I hadn't and it had him worried. And I'd never seen him worried.

Then I froze when I felt movement over my right shoulder. Something small. And very close.

Whatever it was shuffled up next to me and stopped. It chittered something quietly, breathing very quickly.

Then it poked me in the butt and dashed away. I heard it yelp, 'hey hey hey hey hey,' growing quieter and quieter as it fled into the distance. Then the clearing was silent once more.

A few minutes passed and I was about to get semi-vertical when I heard it coming back, again yelping, 'hey hey hey hey hey,' getting louder and louder until I could feel the creature once again standing beside me. It chittered, shuffling in the dirt.

Then it poked me in the butt again.

'Excuse me,' I said, 'but that's kind of rude.'

I heard a terrified squeak and then the sound of small paws bolting for the trees. 'Helllllp,' it shrieked.

The damned kobold. What was it doing here?

I gathered my strength and rolled onto my back, then pushed myself upright. Now I had a decent view of the aftermath of the battle. Gnoll corpses were scattered all over the clearing. The big one's body was not far from the dragon. I couldn't see its head.

As for the dragon, it was huddled in a ball at the far end, its neck and head hidden beneath one of its stunted wings. The beast breathed rhythmically, much improved from earlier, which wasn't good news for me. Its scaly body looked terrible, cut and gouged and battered. I would have felt sorry for it, if, you know, it hadn't killed Nox and almost killed me. Yeah, it might not have spat acid at me earlier when it was killing the gnolls, but then, it might not have considered me a threat at that point.

A couple metres away was the beast that had saved my life. It was huddled and lying facing away from me so I couldn't get a good look at it. An odd creature, it was tall and lanky, with one long pointed ear and the other missing half its length. Its skin was covered in blisters where it wasn't pitch black and oozing. I could see claws on its feet that looked like they might have been sharp at one time but were now dull and chipped.

The clearing felt like a tomb. The wind was still. Any animals that might have been nearby had probably long ago fled at the start of the fight. Everything but me, the dragon, and the strange beast was dead.

Everything but us three and the kobold, that is. I looked over my shoulder in the direction the little creature had fled. At first, I thought it was gone for good, when I realized that what I'd thought was a knob on a tree was actually the tip of its scaly nose and what I'd thought were pinpricks of sunlight through the forest were actually its dimly glowing eyes in the shadows.

It stood, not moving, his eyes almost vibrating as it tried to watch me without giving itself away. It also appeared to be making involuntary pawing motions. I laughed, and it shrieked and vanished.

A cry of pain from the ragged beast interrupted my laughter and I turned back to it. Very cautiously, I circled around it, slowly navigating my way through the corpses. Sure, it might have come to my aid, but then again, it might have just been hungry. Or insane. Either way, it might be dangerous, especially in this much agony.

When I was a handful of metres away and in front of it, I leaned forward to get a better look at it, then gasped.

Wow. Tough bastard.

His face was horribly damaged. Here and there, tufts of blackened hair and blonde hair stuck out of the ruin. All of the jagged teeth sticking out of one side of his mouth were cracked, chipped, or otherwise gone. His features were burnt and seemed to have partially melted, but I knew him anyway.

'Nox,' I whispered, closing the distance quickly to kneel down beside him, tears in my eyes.

'Hello, Martin,' the werewolf growled, raggedly.

36

I carefully lowered myself to the ground in front of Nox, briefly thinking about putting my hand on his shoulder, then thought better of it. Instead I just smiled at him, eyes swimming.

'You, you look great, old friend,' I stammered. He smiled weakly, coughed, and winced. Blood was dripping from a gap where a fair chunk of his nose used to be, the black fluid falling through the cracked and stunned teeth on that side of his face.

'I told you it was a good thing I was coming with you,' the big 'wolf said. His eyes closed, and he shuddered with pain.

I had no idea what to do for him. My healing abilities amounted to being able to close a paper cut. If Ceile had been here, she might have been able to at least make him more comfortable, but the 'wolf was a mess and needed real healing, magical or otherwise.

'Can you sit up?' I asked him. He swallowed, wincing in pain even at that, and then rolled onto his back with a loud groan. With a great deal of effort he slowly got his back off the ground, leaving sticky bits of flesh behind. Once he was up, his half-lidded eyes looked me up and down.

'You're a mess. What did you do while I was trying to get down here?' the 'wolf growled quietly. He winced again, reaching a bloody paw up to his face, not quite touching the skin. One of his eyes was clouded and milky, and I wondered if he could see out of it.

'I took a bit of a tumble,' I answered, waving at the cliff over my shoulder. Nox snorted, then looked away from me and over at the dragon. It was still balled up under its wing, giving no sign it had heard us.

'Shame it didn't have the courtesy to die after I carved it up,' the big 'wolf snarled, pointing a cracked claw at the scaly beast.

'I don't think it's going to bother us anytime soon. You hurt it pretty bad, and then the gnolls did even worse,' I said, shaking my head. Then I turned back to my friend. 'How did you get down here, anyway? My entrance was almost an exit. It's probably twenty metres from the top.'

Nox shrugged. 'It took a while. I could stand, but I couldn't move very quickly. Took me hours to pick my way down from up there, by the time I got to the bottom, that big gnoll was coming over to eat you. How did it know you were going to cast something, anyway? It was all over the dragon and then just whipped around and went after you instead,' the 'wolf said, gruffly.

'No idea. It might have been an arcanist, I suppose. Then it would have seen me shaping,' I said, after thinking about it. Magic use wasn't limited to elves, dwarves, us, or dragons. Almost every intelligent species on the continent had arcanists and elementalists. That included gnolls, despite being near the bottom of the intelligence spectrum.

Nox barked a laugh, looking unconvinced. Then he shuddered and tucked in on himself, causing him even more pain. The 'wolf was shaking. He looked awful, and he was getting worse. I had to get him help, or he was going to die for real this time.

Something poked me in the butt.

I turned my head to glare down at the kobold, and it darted away, yelling, 'hey hey hey hey hey,' as it ran. It stopped ten metres away and then turned to watch me. It clutched its thin tail in its hands and stood there, quietly.

Whatever it had stolen from the gnolls was gone, though it now wore a pack strapped overly tightly to its back. It looked quite comical, though most kobolds were pretty funny looking. Even other kobolds thought they were funny looking. They were an odd bunch. This one was wearing particularly colourful clothing, or at least the small patches that stuck out from the dirt and grime were. A male, I could now see by the short crests along his snout.

I didn't have time to play games with him, and turned back to my friend. Nox had started making a keening noise, almost vibrating in agony. He watched me with wide eyes, shaking his head violently. Skin and fluids came off of him in a shower of gore. He lay slowly back.

I felt another prod in my posterior, and I turned around in a fury, prepared to terrify the little creature into fleeing for good. I figured he would have dashed a short distance away in fear.

Instead, he had remained next to me, though he cowered on the ground. He clutched something in one paw that was raised toward me. The other paw covered his face, though one eye looked at me through his scaly fingers.

It was my cellphone.

The kobold handed it gently to me, quickly snatching his hand back so that he could cover his face with both paws.

I sat there, dumbfounded. How the hell had he gotten my phone? Last I'd seen it, the gadget had been in my coat pocket, floating away on the wind. I looked back up at the kobold to ask, but he had vanished. I spun around, and found the little creature standing next to Nox. I shouted at the kobold hoping to scare him away, but he suddenly burst into flames. I stumbled back from the heat, but as I watched, the flaming figure reached down to touch my friend on the forehead.

Then I watched in horror as Nox was engulfed in flames as well. The big 'wolf screamed. I staggered forward, gathering nether without being sure of just how to use it to save him. Before I could begin to shape, there was a sharp crack and the flames vanished.

I stared at Nox in disbelief.

His body was healed.

The kobold looked over at me, tiredly. He twitched, then stuck a clawed finger out at the 'wolf, and barked, 'Helllllp.'

37

I stood there, staring down at Nox in shock. The werewolf was motionless except for the steady fall and rise of his chest. He was still caked in dead skin and dried blood, but the flesh beneath was pink and healthy.

The kobold's magic hadn't been perfect. The big 'wolf's claws were still dull and chipped, the teeth on one side of his face were still stunted and cracked, most of his fur was gone, he was still missing half an ear, and his body was covered in scar tissue. But what mattered was that he wasn't dying.

I looked back over at the little creature that had saved Nox's life, finding him once again crouched next to me, leaning as far away as he could without falling over. A fire elementalist, and one with some power, at least in healing. I had never met a kobold that had any idea how to use their magic. This one must have a hell of a story to tell.

Then I noticed the very ragged, very filthy, but very familiar jacket the kobold had wrapped around his small torso. Well, that would be where he got my cellphone, I suppose. Because today hadn't been strange enough already.

The little creature noticed me looking at the jacket, then started taking it off with a comically sad look on his face. I smiled and put a hand up. He gave me a suspicious look, then slowly put it back on.

At a loss as to what to do with the little beast, I turned back to Nox to find the 'wolf leaning up and looking at me. He raised one arm to look at it, rubbing off some of the mess. 'I'm a wreck. What happened?' the big 'wolf asked, glaring at the kobold, who darted behind me to chitter angrily at him. I chuckled at the little thing.

'He did,' I said, pointing down at the kobold. 'He's a fire elementalist, and I'm pretty sure he just saved your life,' I said as I knelt down next to my friend. 'And, let me tell you, fire healing is apparently pretty scary.'

Nox looked at me like I had told a pretty good joke, then turned to stare at the kobold curiously. 'How do you feel?' I asked.

The big 'wolf shook his head, putting both arms out in front of him so he could examine all his limbs. He stretched each, muscles rippling beneath the patchy hair and healthy skin. 'Well, I feel filthy and really need a bath. I'm weak, which isn't exactly surprising. And I should probably get a pair of pants or a loin cloth or something,' he quietly growled.

I laughed. The 'wolf didn't usually need anything to cover his fun bits. 'I don't think I can help you with the pants, but we can probably-' I started to say, when I suddenly burst into flames.

For a long moment, I thought I was dead as the fire roared around me, flowing up my arms and around my legs. The Other was shrieking at the back of my mind. Pain, and a lot of it. I howled as the inferno tried to devour me.

And then there was a sharp crack and I found myself lying on the ground, breathing quickly and blinking up at the sky. Then I sat up and dazedly looked over my body.

'Holy crap, that is scary!' Nox said from close by.

'Helllllp,' the kobold yelped, prodding my butt with a clawed foot. He looked quite proud of himself.

Sure enough, much like Nox I was almost fully healed. All the cuts and bruises were gone, the worst covered in thick scar tissue. Neither me nor the 'wolf were going to win any beauty pageants anytime soon, but I felt pretty good. Other than a bit of a headache, I was otherwise pain-free.

The Other was dead silent. I wondered what that had felt like for him. Then I wondered what healing had done to him. I shrugged without asking. He'd turn up eventually.

I stood slowly to my feet. Nox was staring at me in wonder. Things were looking up. Sure, we were hundreds of kilometres from home, had no airship, and had no idea if Ceile, the dwarves, and Bill were alive, but we were healthy and the 'wolf and I made a good team.

'That's pretty powerful healing magic you have there, my friend,' I said, turning to look down at the kobold. The little creature was gone. Nox and I gave each other a confused glance and then looked wildly around the clearing. And then we saw him.

The kobold stood next to the dragon, his scaly arms moving in an intricate dance that I didn't recognize but certainly knew.

'No!' both Nox and I yelled at once. I started to run, hoping to catch the little creature before he finished shaping, but went down with a crash as my weak body decided I wasn't quite up to running. The 'wolf made it to his knees, but no further. He was even weaker than I was.

We were too late. The kobold erupted into an inferno that whirled around him and shot flames into the sky. He leaned forward and put a hand on the sleeping dragon. With a roar that probably echoed for kilometres, the beast burst into flame.

For maybe a minute, the two figures were joined by a bridge of fire that spun and crackled and snarled. And then it was gone, extinguished with a thunderclap that knocked me flat, and nearly Nox too.

The kobold shuffled over to us, stopping a short distance away with a brilliant, ear-to-ear smile. He pointed over his shoulder, and barked, 'Helllllp.'

We looked past the little creature, and I sighed.

The dragon hissed angrily as it slowly got to its feet, neon emerald eye glaring at us.

38

I slowly got to my feet, helping Nox do the same. The kobold watched us curiously, still pointing at the green dragon and smiling proudly. The winged beast stood at the far end of the clearing, stretching its limbs and snapping its wings. It never took its eye off of us.

Much like Nox and me, the dragon's healing wasn't perfect. Its eye was still missing, though the damage to the eye socket and side of its head were gone. Most of the places Nox had gouged or cut it were missing large sections of scales, though the white flesh visible in the gaps was healthy and whole.

Nox and I were much better off than we were before the kobold's healing, but the green dragon looked like it had come out on top of us. It looked just as dangerous as it had before Nox and it had tangled.

We stood there, watching the dragon while the dragon watched us and the kobold confusedly watched everyone. Leaning against me, Nox was tensed up, though whether he was getting ready to fight or flee, I didn't know. I reached out into the ocean of nether around me and started gathering it. If it came to a fight, I was going to be a little more useful this time.

Then, with a final glare, the dragon bent its head down and snatched up a gnoll corpse, biting it in half and then swallowing one part and then the other. Then it reached over and repeated the trick, though this time it hacked up the gnoll's head and spat it into the bush.

'Maybe we should leave while it's busy,' I whispered. Nox growled quietly, but nodded. We turned and carefully made our way toward the edge of the clearing. The kobold remained where he had been standing, a terribly sad look on his face, still pointing at the dragon with one hand and clutching its tail with the other.

We hadn't made it ten metres when the dragon looked up at us and roared. It threw the gnoll it had been gnawing on off into the trees and marched toward us, quickly covering the distance and blocking our path. It stared down at Nox and me, head twisted to watch us with its good eye.

It wasn't going to let us leave. I didn't want to fight the beast, but there wasn't exactly help on the way. I motioned to Nox to go right while I went left, hoping we could confuse the dragon enough to get by.

Before we could give it a shot, the kobold dashed past us, his now familiar, 'hey hey hey hey hey,' following him along. I beckoned wildly to him, but he went straight up to the dragon. It watched him intently as he neared.

At the last moment, the dragon opened its mouth wide and darted down at the kobold, and I cringed as I prepared to watch the agonizing last seconds of the little creature's life.

Instead, the dragon bowed its head low enough so the kobold could get on, and then raised it high into the air, its little rider cackling with delight.

Nox and I looked at each other. The 'wolf gave me a bemused look and then said, 'What.'

The green dragon set the kobold on its back, and the little creature struck a pose, raising his arms to the sky in victory and barking, 'I win!' The dragon snorted, and gave Nox and me a dirty look before turning away and moving toward the opposite side of the clearing. Ten metres later, it stopped and looked back. The kobold turned to look back at us with a very irritated look on his face. He waved us vigorously toward him, yelling, 'I win!'

I looked at Nox again, and then I shrugged. 'This is too weird to not work,' I said. The 'wolf looked unconvinced, but when I walked toward the dragon, he followed, just over my shoulder.

'I'd just like to note that this idea is crazy, and not just because that thing tried to kill me earlier,' the big 'wolf growled quietly, waving a clawed hand at the dragon. Apparently the beast heard him, as its head spun around. The two monsters glared at each other for a long moment before the dragon snorted again and turned away.

'See? He likes you,' I joked. Nox snarled something under his breath.

The kobold jumped into the air a couple of times, then stopped and twitched. He quickly grabbed his tail in one hand and reached out to pat the dragon's neck with the other. 'I win!' he shouted, a massive grin on his face. The dragon twisted its head around to look at the little creature, then moved forward into the forest.

I reached over and put my hand on Nox's arm, and said, 'It's good to have you back, Nox.' The big 'wolf chuckled, and the two of us walked out into the forest in the wake of a dragon.

39

The green dragon and its unlikely rider moved through the forest, flowing gracefully around trees and through the bush. Nox and I trailed behind, close enough to make out the occasional, 'I win!' from ahead.

We were travelling east, roughly in the direction the airship had gone down. I would have rather gone west in search of Ceile and Robin's lifeboat, but Nox had surprisingly suggested we stay with our unlikely companions.

'Look, the lifeboat could have gone down anywhere, but at least it would have gone down safely. You know Ceile. She and Robin are probably already closer to the airship than we are,' the big 'wolf said, clapping me roughly on the back.

He had been watching the canopy above for threats, and as soon as he was done trying to knock me over, he laughed, pointing into a gap. 'Besides, we can track the ship,' he grinned. Sure enough, barely visible in the hole above and ahead of us was billowing black smoke.

I wondered if Bill had survived, and then I wondered what I would do if he hadn't. Petrel and Robin seemed like they knew some of the plan, but not all of it. My fate was tied to the wizard's now, and suddenly I wanted very much to get to the wreck and see for myself. It couldn't have been good. My last glimpse of the airship was of it spinning wildly out of control toward the forest canopy. I didn't catch the actual impact, but at that speed it wouldn't be pretty.

Other than our brief conversation earlier, Nox didn't have much to say. I wasn't surprised. I imagine taking a blast of dragon's acid in the teeth wasn't a pleasant experience and the brutal amount of pain he must have been in during the time between acid bath and being healed by the kobold - probably even including being healed by the kobold - must have been awful. Even with the worst of his wounds healed, he didn't look good. Where his fur hadn't completely fallen out it was mostly melted or blackened, with just a handful of patches of blonde remaining.

With so much fur missing, he didn't look much like a werewolf at all. He actually looked scarier like this, really, his ordinarily nightmarish appearance replaced with something almost alien. Something I'd never seen before. While I'm sure he would appreciate looking even more terrifying than he had, I'm sure he was probably a little preoccupied at the moment to think about that.

He'd have to wear clothing to keep himself warm now. I thought about that, and then shook my head. Maybe that was a ridiculous thing to think about right now, but something as mundane as clothing to me was foreign to my friend.

I wondered how much his brush with death had changed the 'wolf. He looked wary as he scanned the forest around us, maybe even afraid. It wasn't a look I'd ever seen on his face. It made my heart hurt.

Lost in my thoughts, I nearly jumped out of my skin when Nox reached out and put an arm on my chest, stopping me in my tracks. He was staring out into the woods. I realized that the dragon had also stopped just up ahead.

The kobold was gone.

I started to ask what was going on, but Nox shushed me quietly. He didn't seem concerned that the green dragon might not be as interested in tolerating him or me now that its strange rider was missing. Even so, I began to gather nether to me, prepared to turn the big beast to dust if it decided we might be tasty after all.

Abruptly, the kobold burst from the forest, charging toward us at full tilt. He kept looking over his shoulder, and as the little creature darted past us, he yelped, 'Helllllp!' And then he was gone again.

The green dragon, Nox, and I all shared a bemused look.

From the direction the kobold had appeared from came a dull chuffing noise, and it wasn't far away. The dragon hissed and lowered its head, moving to one side as it scanned the bush for the source. Nox looked like he'd rather run, but after a glance at me he moved away from our scaly cohort and settled into a fighting stance, low to the ground, one hand in the dirt, the other ready to strike.

I drifted back, nether flowing around my hands, the power whispering sickly words and promising terrible destruction. Then I wondered where the Other had gone.

Before I could ask him, a massive, black, tentacled horror burst out of the foliage and snapped Nox up into the air. A forest mrog, and a really big one.

I snarled and shaped the nether into forms of disintegration, but before I could unleash the spell, a slimy tentacle erupted from the trees near me and smashed into the side of my face, knocking me to the ground. As I dazedly tried to get to my feet, another caught me around my legs and lifted me into the air violently.

My vision was hazy, and I felt nauseous. The world refused to stand still. I could barely make out Nox snarling as he tried to slash at his attacker, but then he was carried out of my view. I'd lost the nether I'd drawn, and when I tried to gather more it felt like walking up a muddy slope. I couldn't focus.

As I swung around in the air wildly, I heard the chuffing noise again, and looking toward the ground - or the sky? It was hard to tell - I could see the mrog's hooked beak rising from the writhing tentacles, opened wide to have a Martin snack. I flung myself from side to side, trying to move far enough that the monster couldn't get a bite. I barely moved at all, and as the tentacle lowered me toward its mouth, I stuck my hands out into that ocean of rot and decay and power and tried desperately to gather enough nether to pull off one last spell.

Then the mrog was engulfed in a massive spray of acid and poison.

It screamed in agony, beak opening and closing in wild spasms as the tissue around it slowly melted away. Every one of its hundreds of tentacles flailed violently, and I found myself free and rolling roughly across the forest floor as mine let go, withering away.

The green dragon stood tall above me, steam billowing from its nostrils. I had to roll away to avoid the drops of acid that leaked from its mouth. Then the beast roared, turning toward the monster that had Nox and hissing furiously. The mrog swung to meet this threat, lowering the big 'wolf in front of it as a shield. My friend snarled, though his eyes were wide.

For an instant, as the dragon stalked toward the monster, I wondered if it was just going to kill Nox to get at the mrog. Then our big scaly companion stopped, angrily trying to shift its body and head to get around the 'wolf. Tentacles beat down on its body and head as it snarled in frustration. I had been forgotten in the chaos.

So I folded the nether I'd drawn in that time into forms of lines and annihilation and let the spell fly. A beam of pulsing purple light erupted from each of my hands, lancing forward to bore into the mrog. It roared in pain and slowly turned itself and Nox to face me. Before it could, the green dragon lunged forward and tore a massive chunk out of its side. The monster screamed again, spinning back to face the scaly beast.

I took my lines of arcane power and corkscrewed them, the beams disintegrating slimy flesh and tentacle and tissue and bone, and with a final shriek of agony from the mrog, burst out the far side and lanced into the trees beyond for an instant before I extinguished them.

As it died, the monster threw Nox away, and the big 'wolf burst free of the canopy. He spun wildly, trying to level out, and I watched him arc back toward the ground, unable to help. 'Save him!' I roared at the Other, trying desperately to figure out how to give my dark companion the reins.

There was no answer.

The green dragon was also watching the werewolf's flight, and out of the corner of my eye, I saw it move slightly to the side and then spit what remained of the acid out of its mouth. Lost in the horror of seeing my friend fall to his death, I barely registered the scaly beast rearing up to snag Nox out of the air.

I stood there, dumbfounded, as the 'wolf crashed into the dragon's chest, sending the two crashing to the ground. Quickly, the beast staggered to its feet and stepped away with an irritated look on its face. For his part, Nox lay there in stunned silence, staring up at the dragon in bemusement.

The beast gave us both dirty looks, and then turned away to start eating one of the dead mrogs.

'You have made some interesting friends, Martin,' a soft voice said from behind me. I spun around to find Ceile standing there, a happy smile on her face and tears in her eyes.

'Helllllp,' the kobold said, peeking out from behind her leg.

40

I held Ceile for a long time, and she stroked my hair gently. I had tried not to think about what might have happened to her, tried to keep myself busy thinking about anything but that. Because I knew as soon as I did, I'd think the worst and might have gotten lost in that despair.

I pulled away slightly so I could look up at her face, her light chocolate skin still glistening with tears. She smiled at me as I reached up to wipe away a tear. As my fingers brushed across her cheek, I was struck by the contrast between my wrinkled skin, all pale and blotchy, and hers.

I was so old.

Ceile must have seen something in my face, as she pulled me and kissed my forehead. 'How about we just stay together for now on?' she asked, quietly. I nodded into her chest. She lifted her head up, and then she gasped. I looked up and saw that she was looking away from me, and with a quick glance over my shoulder I understood why.

Nox stood near the green dragon, looking embarrassed and shuffling around slowly. Ceile gentle let go of me and walked toward the 'wolf.

'Nox?' she asked, shocked. He looked miserable, and as she got a better look at the naked 'wolf, Ceile put a hand up to her mouth in horror. 'What happened?' she asked, her voice barely a whisper.

The werewolf turned to glare up at the dragon beside him. 'This thing happened,' he snarled. The dragon clacked its jaws at him, and he jumped away, eyes wide.

Ceile looked stricken and moved toward the 'wolf, but Nox backed away quickly. 'I, uh, don't have any pants,' the wolf softly growled, looking in every direction but us.

There was a moment of silence, and then Ceile and I burst out laughing, much to the 'wolf's irritation. When she was finished, she came forward to take Nox's hand, smiling. 'Nox, you do not even have the right parts for me to be interested like that,' she said, looking up at him gently, and then finished, 'It is good to see you.'

Then she wrapped him in a hug. Nox looked like he didn't know what to do, finally settling on patting her awkwardly on the back. He let the hug go on for a bit and then broke gently away.

Returning to my side, she took my hand and gave it a squeeze. She gave the green dragon and the kobold an amused look, then shook her head and looked down at me. 'I was out looking for you two when this kobold appeared out of nowhere and tried to poke me. I tried to shoo him away but the little thing pulled your cellphone out of his pocket and then pointed into the woods behind him,' she said.

I started to tell her that the little creature had already given me my phone back, but it wasn't in my pocket. I turned to stare accusingly at him. Looking very guilty, he darted away to hide behind the dragon's legs, making a big show of examining its scales.

I shook my head and then turned back to Ceile. 'What about Robin, is she alright? How about Petrel or Bill, do you know what happened to them?' I asked. She looked thoughtful for a moment, and I thought I saw a shadow cross her eyes.

'Robin is okay. We had a rough landing northwest of here after we caught a draft that slammed us into the canopy. She had a broken leg, but I was able to heal it nicely. Once we took everything of use out of the lifeboat, we started following the smoke,' she said. 'I did not know what had happened to you both, or even Bill. The last Robin and I saw of any of you, you were all on the airship and it was crashing far to the east of us. The best we could hope to do was to find the wreck and then fan out from there.'

'You found the airship, did you find Bill there? We don't know if he managed to eject or not,' I said when she went silent. I gave her hand a squeeze. It probably hadn't been any easier on her than it had been on me, thinking about the other being lost or hurt. Or dead.

My friend shook her head and said, 'We found the airship, and Bill. But you will not believe what has happened to him. You will have to see it for yourself.' She did not sound pleased, but shook her head when I gave her a curious look.

I cocked an eyebrow but let it go. 'And Petrel? Unless he can fly, he had a hell of a fall,' I said. 'Nothing could have survived that, even wrapped in steel.' Then I paused for a bit, and asked, 'Could they?'

Ceile shook her head again. 'We did not find Petrel along our route, and he is not with Bill at the wreck. But I will say this much, neither of the dwarves are foolish. I do not believe he would have gone out on the airship hull to fight the dragon if he did not have some plan in mind,' she said. Her voice was certain, and her logic made sense.

I felt a bit better. The steel dwarf and I might not have been fast friends, but as odd as our little party was, we were on the same side, on the same mission. You never wanted to lose your allies so early on.

Ceile was giving the green dragon a dangerous look. 'You said that this creature hurt Nox. Why are you travelling with it?' she said, her voice very serious.

I looked at the scaly beast, and it cocked its head to watch me with its good eye. Then I shook my head and said, 'It and the kobold got us this far. I don't know if the little fellow has some kind of hold over it or if its injuries have affected it in some way, but it just saved Nox and me from these mrogs,' I paused to kick a partially melted tentacle, then continued, 'And we owe the kobold a lot, if he hadn't come along, Nox and I would both be dead.'

'It's true. Both of them saved my life. Which means I owe the kobold and more or less makes me and the dragon even,' Nox snarled, giving the dragon a glare. 'More or less,' he growled, jabbing a claw up at it. The dragon snorted.

Ceile laughed, looking back and forth between the four of us. I nodded at the kobold. 'He's a very odd fellow. A fire elementalist, a healer. And a good one! Though I don't recommend having him work on you unless absolutely necessary,' I said. My friend gave me a curious look, and I added, 'It, er, doesn't tickle.'

I didn't mention that it was the kobold that had brought the gnolls that had almost killed us down on our heads. The little beast gave me a petulant look from behind the dragon's leg.

I looked around, catching the eye of each member of our strange group, then I looked up through a couple holes in the canopy. The Blue Sun had risen and passed overhead on its steady fall toward the southern horizon. 'Alright, we should head for the airship. We don't have many hours left of daylight, and there are plenty of other things in the Locus Wood that would like to eat us.' Nox and Ceile nodded. The kobold danced around in excitement. The dragon just watched me, an unreadable look on its face.

In the distance, behind us in the forest, I heard a chuffing noise. Then another.

'Time to go!' I said, pulling Ceile around and heading toward the smoke. The dragon spun and then snaked forward into the forest, taking the lead. My friend raised an eyebrow but said nothing. We followed quickly in the beast's wake.

Nox walked a few metres off to my left, and his face was sullen. 'I need some pants, it's actually kind of cold,' he growled, quietly. As if he had willed them into existence, a pair of large trousers suddenly smacked him in the face, hanging there like some sort of strange mask.

'Helllllp,' the kobold giggled, closing his pack and darting away, tail twitching in amusement.

41

We travelled, mostly in silence, for a couple hours before we started finding signs of the crash. The airship had come in at a lean angle, scattering bits and pieces of itself across a wide swath of the forest, cutting the tops off trees and singeing parts of the canopy around them. I couldn't see anything blazing nearby as we followed the ragged line to the east, but the smoke ahead was getting thicker as the Blue Sun tumbled toward the horizon to the south.

I shivered as we trudged through the increasing shadow. The last thing we needed was to break out into open air and find the airship engulfed in a raging forest fire. Walking next to me, hand in mine, Ceile didn't seem overly concerned. She scanned around us, looking for trouble, but her face had only serenity in it. Noticing me looking at her, she gave me a wink and a smile. I smiled back.

It wasn't until another half hour had passed before we found the area where the ship had finally hit the earth. The green dragon broke free into a clearing, and came to an abrupt halt. The kobold, who had been riding on its shoulders flew forward and vanished into the underbrush. The rest of us came forward to stand beside the big beast.

Ceile looked over at Nox and me, and said, 'We are here.'

The big 'wolf shook his head slowly, and said, 'Wow.'

It's possible that the clearing hadn't existed until the airship had plowed through the trees, shredding both vessel and foliage. A quickly widening crater stretched for half a kilometre, not far from where we stood and continued out for half a klick, a wound of churned earth, torn trees, and battered metal.

At the far end was the Red Flag.

If I believed in luck, I'd probably say that Bill had been very, very lucky to have come out of that alive. The ship had lost both starboard and port engines, most of the turrets were torn free of the hull, hanging by twisted metal or missing altogether, and the missile launcher had somehow made its way into the cargo bay. The main deck itself was folded in half, and smoke billowed out of every hole, flames still flicking out across the wreck. I imagined that all of the ammunition had already lit off, or we'd be hearing regular explosive pops.

Ceile led us down into the crater, stepping carefully around the debris. 'Most of the explosions had stopped before Robin and I finally arrived, though a cask or two of dragonfire went off as we neared. We were sure that there were no survivors, and we had little hope that we would be able to salvage much from the airship proper,' she said.

I tripped and put a hand down to steady myself. The sides of the crater were still warm. Considering it had been more than a day since the ship had gone down, it must have put out some serious heat as it cut through the earth. Again I wondered how Bill had survived. We still weren't close enough to be sure, but it looked like the front view screen was scattered across the crater near the Flag and the pilot's seat crushed by the main deck.

When we were fifty metres from the wreck, Ceile waved for us to stop. Even out here, we could feel the heat pouring out of whatever was still burning inside the airship. Turning to us, my friend said, 'We have not been able to get much closer to this, most of what we have been picking up has been from the crater and the forest around it.'

'What she's saying is that we don't have any supplies,' a gruff voice shouted from the crater edge. We looked up to find Robin waving at us. The dwarf looked tired and her clothes were torn and filthy, but seemed otherwise okay. 'C'mon, we managed to find some water and some stuff that Ceile calls edible but I'm not sold on that,' she continued, reaching down to give Ceile a hand up the crater side.

Next she helped me up, and I gave her a smile that she readily returned. It was an odd feeling, being friendly with a dwarf. I'd only ever known a handful of them that hadn't been trying to kill me.

When she saw Nox, the dwarf's eyes widened and she peered at him searchingly. 'Nox? What the hell happened to you?' she asked, her voice an odd mix of concern and suspicion.

The big 'wolf waved absently over his shoulder at the dragon as he scrambled up the crater wall without help. 'This thing,' he said, sounding like he was sick of explaining it.

Robin looked confused, eyes moving back and forth between the almost hairless werewolf and his torn pants and the green dragon. For its part, the scaly beast just cocked its head sideways to look at the dwarf with its good eye.

'That must be a hell of a story. You trust this thing?' the dwarf chuckled, standing up and watching as the dragon clambered up the side with ease, looming over her.

I was surprised to hear Nox say, 'It's with me. Let it through.'

Robin looked even more confused, but I waved her off. 'It's an odd story, let's save it for once we've got everyone gathered up. Bill's over here somewhere? What about Petrel?' I said.

Robin looked a bit ill, and beckoned us to follow her into the wood. 'The ejection seat on the pilot's chair was damaged, so Bill went down with the ship. He survived the landing, but he was, er, hurt pretty bad getting out of the wreckage,' she said. Then she shook her head, and said, 'No one has any idea where Petrel ended up. Bill says that he had an escape plan in mind after his dust up with the dragon, but doesn't know what it was. None of us saw him after the dragon let go of the ship.' Her voice was quiet. I reached over and squeezed her shoulder softly. The dwarf gave me a grateful smile.

'Well, if anyone was going to fall that far and come out intact, it's your-' I paused, not knowing exactly what Petrel and Robin's relationship was, then chose a safe option, '-friend.'

The trees thinned out in front of us, and Robin said, 'We're here.'

We stepped out into another small clearing, to find a rough campsite set up. A fire had been started, and in the dimming light, I could see a figure sitting in front of it. I assumed it was Bill, so I stepped toward it, watching as details materialized out of the shadow, like its strange and tattered clothing, and something glinting around its legs. Something about it felt very wrong, and I stopped to stare at the wizard.

As I watched, the figure stood up and turned to face me slowly. It stepped toward me, and I could hear whirring and clicking noises as it did. Nox suddenly snarled in shock and anger, his eyes far better than mine in the dark, and I looked over my shoulder at him in confusion. Seeing the big 'wolf crouched and growling with teeth bared, I looked back at the wizard and then gasped.

It was Bill, or at least looked kind of like him. What I had thought was a jacket or shirt was skin. Torn skin. The wizard's upper half was naked, but every inch of it had been shredded, bits of flesh hanging off haphazardly. His face had escaped the grinder, but his brown hair and mustache were entirely gone, and several long, jagged slashes had cut him open to the bone.

Except he didn't have bones. Or blood.

Instead, beneath the torn skin was the shine of metal, slightly dulled where the worst gashes had been. And not an ounce of fluid dripped from the wounds. It was surreal.

Below his stomach, there was no flesh left at all. Scorch marks and ash covered much of his lower body. Where bone and flesh and tissue and organs would have been were steel and hydraulics and circuits.

'Hello, Martin!' Bill greeted me enthusiastically, and slightly electronically, as he reached forward to shake my hand.

42

'Don't be alarmed at my appearance, my friends! It may be a shocking sight, but I assure you that I am intact and in otherwise fine shape. If anything, the crash has improved my complexion,' Bill said, looking around at each of us, his hand still out, waiting to shake mine.

'You're a construct!' Nox snarled, coming to stand at my side and pointing a chipped claw at the wizard.

'Correct, my formerly hairy friend! In my line of work, you don't last long in an original model. Too much chance you'll die! Killed from wounds or damage taken that would have been survivable in a construct! No, I underwent the transfer rites nearly three centuries ago, and have no regrets,' Bill said, smiling and gesturing wildly with his other hand. 'Trust me, I have made very good use of disposable limbs, as I frequently come out of my adventures missing one or two.'

His tattered face made his smile slightly terrifying. Then he looked shocked as he did a double take at the sight of Nox. 'What has happened to you, Nox? You're naked!' he cried.

The 'wolf looked indignant. 'I have pants, thank you very much,' he growled, quietly.

Bill loudly laughed, and then said, 'A story for another time, then, as time waits for no man, werewolf, woman, or-' he paused, looking up at the green dragon, '-or miscellaneous!' he finished, pompously. 'Come! We shall discuss our new situation, refresh ourselves, and plan before we attempt some sleep. Most animals will stay far from the burning ship, but we'll stand watch while others sleep.'

The wizard gestured off to the water and food the ladies and he had rounded up, and - having forgotten about shaking my hand - turned and walked back to the fire, sitting down gingerly in his improvised chair. I heard motors whirring away underneath his metal surface as he moved.

I didn't know how to react to this revelation about the wizard. He was hardly the only construct wandering around making some attempt to appear human. Was it any of my business? Had it hurt the party, thinking Bill was an original model when he wasn't? The wizard hadn't ever specifically said he was.

Having taken my fill of water and some plants that Ceile claimed were good for us, I sat down across the fire from Bill. Ceile took the seat to my right, Robin that to my left. Nox was crouched between us and the wizard, and the green dragon was on the opposite, the scaly beast almost hidden in the darkness except for its glowing green eyes. The two monsters were glaring at each other through the flames.

Something bumped my leg, and I looked down to find the kobold peering around suspiciously. When I smiled and started to say something to him, he mashed a scaly finger against his mouth and shushed me loudly. Robin looked confused. Ceile looked amused. I just shook my head, and turned back to Bill.

Once everyone was paying attention, the wizard threw his hands into the air and began to speak. 'Listen, and listen well, my friends! The loss of the Red Flag is a grievous blow to our schedule. We were mere hours from Woodsholme before the fight with the black dragon, but now we are wingless, and are likely days from the city. Worse, we have drifted off course, and I'm no longer certain what direction we must be travel,' he said.

'Shortly after Martin was ripped from the ship, last of my companions, I discovered that the ejection seat had failed. I was forced to try and ride the crash out. With the immediate threat of the dragon gone, I was able to focus on bringing the ship down in a survivable way, but also to try and keep her on a northward heading toward our destination.'

He took a deep breath, which I thought was amusing as it wasn't likely he actually had lungs, and continued, 'My hope was that any survivors from among you would follow the smoke, and that we'd be that much closer to Woodsholme.'

Sweeping his arms over his body, he stared heroically off into space. 'Obviously I survived, though between the raging flames and the storm of sharp debris I am in slightly less pleasant condition. I salvaged what I could from the wreck, then made camp. I also prepared plans to go out in search of you all.'

Finally, he lifted a hand toward me and Nox. 'I admit, I was certain that you were both dead. I despaired of it. But you have miraculously proven more resilient than I'd expected. And brought some new members to our party! Quick, tell us what happened,' the wizard shouted, theatrically.

Nox snorted. I laughed and gave an abbreviated version of my and Nox's adventures. Bill and Robin looked enthralled, first staring at me with wide eyes, and then turning to look at the green dragon and the kobold in interest. Ceile smiled at their reactions, then spoke up.

'From what Martin has said, I believe the area where he landed is now closest to our original flight path. Robin and I came down to the west of there, we must have just missed the two - I mean four - of them as we travelled east toward the smoke. I think our best bet may be to back track to there and then head north,' my friend said, giving my hand a squeeze.

Bill was nodding, looking thoughtfully into the fire. 'The logic is sound, Ms. Angael. I'd agree that it's our best plan,' he said. Nox and I were both nodding, though the 'wolf looked uneasy.

'And Petrel?' I asked. 'Do we have any idea where he is?'

Robin looked sad and turned away. Bill shook his head slowly, and said, 'None. If he survived the fall, he'll come looking for us, but we have no way of figuring out where he might have come down or where he might have gone since.'

I felt a little angry suddenly. 'Shouldn't we at least make an effort to look? What if he's injured?' I said, loudly. I felt Robin put a hand on my shoulder and give it a tight squeeze.

Bill's face went livid, and he suddenly seemed to loom above the flames, looking down on us in almost godly fury. He pointed at me, and the metal beneath the ragged skin glinted angrily in the fire's light. I noticed that several of his rings were missing.

'The simple facts are these, Martin Tundra. Before the Red Flag went down, we had more than sufficient time to get you to the regeneration chamber. A week, eight or nine days maximum, to make the journey. Well within the two weeks you have of good health remaining,' the wizard roared.

'But the Red Flag is down and for the moment, we have no other ride. We are days from Woodsholme, and if we cannot secure transport from there, then we are days from our next destination. Suddenly, we are looking at three weeks. Maybe four. Long past the point where your doctor believed your health would begin deteriorating quickly, and charging toward your due date,' he continued, lifting one fist into the sky.

Suddenly, Bill went quiet, and he seemed to shrink down into himself until he was almost hidden behind the flames. He looked immensely sad, and when he spoke again, it was barely loud enough to hear. 'You. You have no time. We have to get you to the regeneration chamber before it's too late,' he whispered.

Then he fell silent, and for a few minutes, the clearing was silent other than the crackle of the fire.

Finally, the wizard spoke again. 'We cannot rest for long. I do not need sleep, so I will take watch. If there's trouble, I will wake you. If there is not, then I will allow you to sleep until shortly before the White Sun bursts from the horizon to the north, and we will begin the trek west soon after,' he said, staring into the flames.

As no one else had anything to say, we all moved off to find spots to sleep. Robin had found a battered container of somewhat singed bedding while searching through the wreckage, enough to provide a thin layer of padding between us and the ground. Ceile and I set up a few metres from the fire, and I was surprised to find Robin put her makeshift bed down next to mine as well.

The green dragon had retreated further into the woods, and I saw its neon green eye blazing in the shadows, staring back at me. The little kobold had curled up next to the fire in the chair I had vacated, and he was already snoring loudly. Nox had piled all of the remaining bedding down almost right next to the flames, heedless of the fire hazard. I could hear him muttering about the cold.

Bill stood at one end of the clearing, looking out into the forest. Through those trees, I could just make out the ethereal flicker of the Red Flag's wreck.

All talked out, the three of us settled in to sleep, and it wasn't long before Robin was joining the kobold in trying to warn away predators by noise, and Ceile was breathing slow and deep. I lay awake, struggling to shut my mind off and get to dreaming. When even Nox had drifted off, curled up next to the warmth of the flames, I heard something odd. Whispering.

I opened my eyes carefully, and found Bill staring at me from across the clearing. There was an odd expression on his face, and though he was pretty intently looking at me, I got the impression that he wasn't actually seeing me. Like he was staring through me. His lips moved in the wave and snap of the shadows, and I strained to make out what he was saying.

In a voice full of ice, I heard the wizard whisper, 'A world born in the ruin of the last. Too closely linked to the sins of the past.' And then he laughed quietly as he looked away.

43

When Bill woke us several hours later, I was fairly sure death would be preferable to being awake. Bizarre dreams of faceless shadows, portals to strange places, spiders that were spider but not, a tower built with some terrible purpose, and unicorns. Unicorns!

I resolved to avoid eating whatever those plants were before bed again.

Robin had moved in her sleep until her back was up against mine. She looked embarrassed when we woke up that close. I just smiled at her as I rolled up my bedding and then gathered with the others by the smoking remnants of the fire.

Bill looked none the worse for wear, beaming at the party and breathing deep of the early morning air. I chuckled and shook my head. I wondered if that was some odd holdover from his original model that he'd requested for his construct or just standard equipment for it. The wizard had found a pair of pants that more or less fit him, what might have been a table cloth to wear as a cloak, and his silly hat. Now he looked slightly less nightmarish.

Nox looked rough. I imagined that the few patches of fur left on his body didn't provide much comfort or warmth, and if he'd slept, it'd been poorly. The damage that had been done to his body stood out starkly with no fur to cover it. I resolved to get him a full set of clothing once we got to Woodsholme.

Then I remembered that even if my wallet had somehow stayed in my jacket long enough for the kobold to get his hands on it, I doubted the elves would accept City tender.

Ceile looked just as perfect as always, though she had some scrapes on her face and a nasty gash along her shoulder that had been hidden beneath her battered jacket. The wound had bled pretty badly, but thankfully didn't seem to affect her movement or strength in that arm. Flesh constructs were tougher than a normal human, but they could still be cut and bruised and hurt like one.

The green dragon sat across the clearing, watching us with its good eye. I wondered if it had slept. Then I wondered why it was here. Neither it nor the kobold had any reason to do so, though I knew at least the latter seemed to be interested in helping us. Maybe the dragon felt indebted to the little thing.

As for the kobold, he was dancing merrily around Nox's legs - much to the irritation of the big 'wolf - and shouting, 'I win!' repeatedly. I laughed, despite my friend's sudden glare.

'The White Sun will rise in an hour or so, and I hope to be well on our way to Martin's and Nox's landing spot by then. We should try to maintain a good pace, the sooner we get there, the sooner we can start heading north to Woodsholme,' Bill said once everyone was looking at him. 'Pack what you can, we can't spare the time to look through the wreckage again.'

Ceile and Robin had looted some survival backpacks from the lifeboat. Unfortunately, the packs were only partially prepared, so they'd be handy for carrying anything we came across, but had few items in them already. Loading up the food, water, bedding, and whatever else the party had found, we extinguished the fire and headed for the resting place of the Red Flag.

The airship was still burning, but many of the fires had died down and were mostly smoke and embers. Weeks from now, when everything had finally cooled, a good salvage crew could get a good haul out of it. Well, they could if they stumbled across it. I think there was a pretty good chance that no one but gnolls and kobolds would find this place again.

Paying attention to everything other than where my feet were going, I tripped and fell to my knees in the churned earth of the crater. Putting my arm out to stop my fall, my hand landed almost right on top of something solid in the dirt.

'Are you alright, Martin?' I heard Ceile ask. I waved her off, getting slowly to my feet with my prize. I brushed it off, and nearly jumped out of my skin once it had been revealed.

It was a thunder thumper round.

I was about to set it gently down when I thought about it. The round was completely intact. It would need serious trauma to set it off, so it wouldn't explode in my pack. And wouldn't that make for a nice surprise if we were attacked? I smiled and slid it into my bedding in my backpack. Looking around, no one else appeared to have noticed my find. Ceile had turned away and was walking a few metres ahead.

Soon, we'd left the crater behind, and as the White Sun lifted free of the horizon, we came across the remains of our battle with the mrogs. There was no sign of more of the monsters.

Not far from the clearing where the dragon and I had fought the gnolls, I was surprised to hear whirs and clicks close by and turned to find Bill falling into step beside me. He didn't look over at me, and when he spoke it was barely a whisper. 'Martin, is the Other there?'

I automatically peered into the murky places at the back of my mind and found no sign of my co-pilot. I looked away from the wizard, and said, 'I'm not sure. He's been quiet since early yesterday, when we were healed by the kobold, and I don't feel him nearby. He must be very deep down if I can't see him from here.'

It wasn't entirely accurate, but then, how I interacted with the Other was a mercurial thing anyway. Recently, it felt like peering down into a deep cave full of water, or at least that's how it was when I was running the show. The Other could come and go, sometimes near enough that I could almost feel our reality vibrating, and sometimes far enough that I couldn't find him, unless I went looking.

When my companion was at the helm, I was caged. Close enough to see and feel the outside world, but not close enough to do anything else.

'Martin, I need you to understand something about the regeneration chamber and the effects it may have on you. I haven't mentioned it yet, as I was unsure how the Other might take the information, and he is certainly by far the least reasonable of you,' Bill said, turning his head just enough to look at me out of the corner of his eye.

I frowned. 'What is it, Bill?' I asked, feeling some dread arc across my mind.

'The regeneration chamber will rejuvenate your body. And your mind. It will be as though your body and mind were that of your thirty year old self, with the added benefit of your current memories being intact,' the wizard quietly said.

I thought about that. 'I don't even remember that part of my life, or not clearly, anyway. I was in an accident when I was fifty-two that tore me up and did a number on my memory,' I said, thinking back to the murky years before my time in the hospital. It was like looking through smoked glass.

Bill nodded. 'Yes, I've read about that. Quite a few people died in that explosion. A renegade magic user of some kind gone mad, I believe. You're lucky to have survived,' he said.

'Yeah, I'd rather not talk about it. What does this have to do with anything?' I said, already imagining the dreams that would haunt me tonight.

Bill hesitated, looking around to see who might be listening, then leaned toward me, his eyes almost feverish. 'I can't know for sure, Martin, but if I'm correct, your psyche may have been shattered by that accident. Things may have been very different for you before,' he whispered.

'What are you saying, Bill? That I may not be who I think I am?' I said, grabbing hold of the wizard's arm roughly and pulling him closer. He looked sympathetic, and when he finally spoke again, his voice was soft.

'I'm saying that I don't know who will come out of the chamber. Things might be the same as they are now. Or the Other might be gone, and you might be the only one left,' he said, then shook his head slowly.

'Or you might be gone, and the Other might be the only one left.'

44

After that revelation, Bill gave me a sad smile and then moved to join the green dragon at the front of the pack. Ceile came over with a concerned look on her face, knowing that something had happened between the wizard and me, but I waved her off gently, wanting to be alone.

Nox, who had the best hearing of everyone here, had likely heard almost the entire conversation. He simply gave me a nod when I made eye contact. He knew I'd talk to him when I was ready, if ever.

My mind twisted and turned over Bill's words. Suddenly, the choice to use the artifact had become significantly more complex. I would die, and soon, if I didn't use the device. But it might not be me that steps out of it. If the wizard was right, and the accident had caused me and the Other to come into existence, then the chamber might heal that split.

And then I might die anyway, even with my mind and body regenerated. They'd just have a different pilot.

I frowned. It would be as though I'd undergone transfer into a construct.

The clearing where Nox and I had fought the gnolls came and went. Most of the corpses remained where they had been when we'd followed the dragon and kobold east, though the wildlife had been feasting while we were gone.

We climbed the rough slope that the big 'wolf had slid down to come help me, and finally came to a stop in the first clearing where we had fought the green dragon. The air felt stagnant here, and hot. Nobody spoke, though the dragon and Nox glared at each other the whole time we rested.

Bill finally nodded his head toward the north, and we started our march toward Woodsholme. It was rough going, and slow, as we picked our way through the tangled brush and forest. Even once we'd neared the city, we would likely find it no clearer. The elves had no need of vehicles, or at least not ground vehicles, and spent little time in the forest. They didn't have much use for roads or paths.

The party's silence continued in the oppressive heat. The dragon was still in the lead, the kobold still precariously balanced on its shoulders, the little creature looking around excitedly into the dense wood.

Bill was close behind, his arms behind his back, head bowed, body moving gracefully through the bush. I was amazed at how smooth his construct's movements were. It would have taken a very skilled engineer to build something so, well, life-like.

Robin walked next to me, her face staring forward. The dwarf was lost in thought, and I had to catch her arm to steady her more than once. She smiled gratefully and then returned to whatever she was thinking about.

Ceile and Nox walked together off to my left. They didn't speak, though the big 'wolf would occasionally pat the other on the head with a grin. Ceile would smile and give his arm a squeeze. I smiled at the two. They hadn't always been so friendly, understandably so given their lack of things in common beyond a dangerous job and me. Now they were almost as close with each other as they were with me.

It occurred to me that if any of us died on this trip, whoever survived would be the only ones to mourn.

With that cheerful thought, I returned to thinking about Bill's words, but finally gave up. There were no options that involved not using the regeneration chamber. It had to be done. And I could sit here and go over and over the possibility that I might not walk out of there the whole way to the artifact's lair, but what purpose would that serve? I was going to have to be focused and collected on the journey, or I'd get myself or someone else killed.

Other than the occasional, 'I win!' from the kobold, the party continued to move quietly through the forest for hours. I was again surprised by just how well my body stood up to the exertion. I'd gotten winded from walking only a couple blocks not so long ago. The Other's words about someone providing some kind of boost for my body resounded through my mind.

I had so many questions for my companion, but I was leery of telling him what Bill had told me. Would the Other try and break free, to prevent us from setting foot in the chamber? Would he be so afraid of his own demise that he would take us both to the grave?

'Where are you?' I snarled, under my breath. Turning my gaze inward, I dove into the murky waters, swimming into his domain. Peering into every nook and crevasse as I fell into the depths, I called for him. Finally, I floated at the bottom of the light and beyond was only darkness.

I had never gone below.

I'd never asked him what was down there, either. But I needed to find him, and he had to be in there somewhere. Steeling myself, I started to dive into the abyss.

Stop.

His voice echoed around me, and I slammed to a halt. I felt sick and exhausted and sad all at once. 'Where are you? Where have you been?' I said, angrily, forgetting that I would be talking to myself topside, probably giving my companions a bit of a surprise.

You should not be here.

I started to say something unpleasant and then shut up before I could. This was wrong. Something was wrong here, something was different. Then I realized. The feeling of his presence was wrong.

This wasn't his voice.

'Who are you?' I whispered. I felt the presence circle me slowly, just below the light. Like a shark.

Death lies below, Martin Tundra. Your path does not lie that way.

I feel terror ripple across my mind, and the whole cave trembles. The darkness begins to rise toward me, and I feel panic arc across my spine. 'Who are you? What have you done?' I shout in fear. The water has begun to spin around me, and as the shadows lift to devour, the vortex begins to draw me down.

Flee. He will return. Your path does not lie this way.

Without really knowing why, I suddenly turned and thrashed my way toward the surface. I only looked down once, and caught a glimpse of something monstrous in the darkness below before it is swallowed and disappears. I reached up and as I'm torn from this place at the back of my mind, I hear the stranger one last time.

They will all betray you. Do not forget.

And then I opened my eyes and found myself lying on the ground, surrounded by a sea of faces with very different looks on their faces.

45

'Well,' I said, 'that was weird.'

Ceile had hold of my hand and was squeezing it very tightly. 'What happened? You were quiet as we walked for a long while, but then you suddenly cried out, fell over, and screamed,' she said, her voice and face very concerned.

Nox was also very close, though he had settled on putting his hand on my shoulder. 'Was it the Other?' he asked, then suddenly leaned in even closer and snarled quietly, 'Is this the Other?' I shook away the smell of his breath and pushed my back up off the ground.

'No, it's me. And no, it wasn't the Other,' I said. I waved Ceile away, 'I'm alright. I just need some air.'

Everyone backed away, though Ceile and Nox were both well within easy reach. I breathed deep, and took the chance to look around. The woods around us looked very different than what I had just been walking through.

'Holy crap, the Sun is setting,' I said, on noticing the fading light.

Nox and Ceile exchanged concerned looks and the others looked confused. Well, the dragon didn't. It gazed down at me without expression.

I staggered to my feet, much to Ceile's dismay. 'How far have we come? How long was I under?' I said, looking around at each of my companions. When no one immediately answered, I turned to my friends and gently said, 'How far have we come, Ceile? How long was I out of it, Nox?'

'We walked all day. Hours. We weren't doing much talking, nobody noticed anything wrong. It wasn't until you started shouting that we got worried, and you weren't answering when we tried to talk to you. Then you collapsed. We carried you, Bill was concerned that you might be reacting to something and said we had to get you to Woodsholme, and fast,' the big 'wolf growled quietly. 'We put you down when you screamed, then we sat around until you finally opened your eyes.'

I felt weak, almost numb. 'Did you heal me?' I asked.

The kobold answered for everyone. 'Helllllp,' he said, poking me in the shoulder.

I smiled, then turned to Bill. 'Alright, we should probably make camp now. I can explain, as best I can, what happened as we do,' I said. The wizard nodded slowly, looking at me curiously.

'Yes, this will be a good spot. There are natural pools nearby, and we should be able to find food. If we're quick. I don't think we want to be foraging after night fall,' he said. 'We'll want to leave early once more, as well.'

As we set up the camp, I gave a brief version of my descent. 'I don't go in like that very often, and I go that deep even less often. I have so many questions, I had to find him,' I said as I helped the kobold get some wood set up for the fire. 'Whatever I found down there was definitely not him, and it definitely did not want me to try to go any deeper. And then my mind tried to eat me, I think.'

Robin shook her head, looking overwhelmed. 'What's it mean, then? Who was down there if it wasn't your buddy? And where's he, then?' she asked.

'I don't know. I think whoever was down there told me that the Other would be back, so I'll just have to wait to see if that happens,' I said, shrugging. 'In the meantime, I'm going to go get cleaned up, and then eat something.'

I headed for the pools, and Nox and Ceile joined me. The big 'wolf was still a little shy around Ceile, amusingly. He picked a pool a bit secluded from the others, and disappeared into the bush to get unpantsed. She chuckled quietly, not wanting to embarrass the werewolf, and then stripped out of her dirty clothes and slid into the nearest pool.

I'd known her for almost a century and a half, and she was my closest friend. Modesty wasn't really a problem between the two of us. I pulled off my clothes and hopped in with her.

It felt good to clean off the grime and as much of the dirt as possible without soap. It'd been days since I'd had a chance to do so. Of course, that meant I could now see every inch of wrinkled and scarred skin on my body. I looked terrible, and not just because of the scars. Two hundred and sixty-four years, I've lived. That's a lot of wear and tear for a human.

Ceile was running her fingers through her short brown hair, and I again admired the work that had gone into her construct. Her skin was flawless, other than the lacerations that she'd picked up on our trip. Healing didn't work the same on flesh constructs as it did for original models. A serious wound could be closed by a powerful healer, but it wouldn't be perfect and could easily be reopened if the patient wasn't careful. Only a proper necromancer could regenerate a flesh construct, and preferably the necromancer that made the construct.

The jagged gouge across her shoulder looked awful, even with the area cleaned.

We didn't speak much, with the two making sure I was okay and then letting it go. There wasn't much more I could tell them about my internal trip and the stranger waiting at the end of it. It felt odd to wish the Other would return, and even odder that my friends would also feel that way, if to a lesser extent and only because they felt that his disappearance was affecting me.

Once the three of us were all cleaned up, we returned to camp. Robin and Bill headed off to the ponds. Nox was freezing, not used to being damp without fur, so we left him to watch over the fire, and headed out into the forest to grab what we could for food.

We wandered the wood, gathering roots and leaves and whatever animals I could catch with a blast of magic. The light was almost gone, and my last attempt to take down a rabbit failed. We were about to turn around and head back when I caught the glint of metal in a thick strand of trees not far from us.

Cautiously, we closed in, Ceile drawing her pistol, me drawing nether. Metal was an odd thing to find, this deep in the middle of a forest. I didn't think it was a dragon. The colour didn't match up with any of the hues I knew of. But, just in case, I was already shaping the forms that would cut it into thin slices.

As we neared, the object stood out a bit more from the bush around it, and I shared a glance with Ceile. It was a ladder, covered in corrosion and overgrown with leaves. It had been sitting here a long time. We crouched down around its base, trying to see what might be up there.

Ceile pointed at herself and then at the ladder. I nodded, and stepped back. I couldn't cover her with this much foliage, I'd have to wait for her signal to follow her up. Holstering her pistol and pulling out her combat knife, she quietly and slowly climbed the ladder, testing each rung with her weight before moving to the next.

Then she reached the branches above and disappeared from sight.

I watched silently, crouched in the brush. It felt good to be doing this kind of thing with her again. It had been nearly thirty years since I'd been retired from Operations and she'd moved back to Enforcement.

I felt useful again.

I heard a series of quiet knocks somewhere above, and then reached out and followed Ceile up the ladder. Despite its appearance, each rung was strong and stable, and it took me almost no time to break through the leaves above.

Twenty metres above the ground, the ladder stopped at a platform shackled to the trees around it. Ceile stood there, offering me a hand and pulling me onto the metal deck with her.

It wasn't long or wide, and other than a box at the far end and a railing along one side, it was pretty simple. Made of the same metal as the ladder, the platform was completely still, despite the sway of the trees it was anchored to.

'It is a transport platform, I think,' Ceile whispered, walking slowly along the deck with her knife ready.

'True, but for what transport? It looks like this whole setup hasn't been used in decades. We're too far from the City for this to be one of ours, and from what I know, the elves don't come out here, either,' I said, cautiously following behind her, watching our rear.

When she reached the box, my friend crouched down to look it over, eventually tapping what looked like a clasp. Very carefully, she stuck the blade of her knife into a gap in the metal, and pried it open slowly. There was a quiet click, and then the box slid open with an electronic hiss.

'Oh, wow,' Ceile whispered, standing to look down at the contents. Inside the box was a panel, lit with brilliant coloured text. Text that displayed fluctuating numbers and other readings. An image and current status for a transport unit, listed as waiting and ready. Giving me an incredulous look, my friend reached down and touched the outline of the transport, which flashed red.

The platform hummed quietly, and a series of bright white lights burst into existence surrounding the deck, illuminating the forest for metres in every direction. I stared bemusedly as a metal cylinder materialized in thin air next to the side of the platform with no railing. Large smooth windows lined the sides of the cylinder, and a door slowly lowered to rest on the deck with a quiet thump. The inside was lit by similar lights to the ones around me.

Then a woman's voice with a familiar accent spoke. 'Green Line, Unit M online. Scientific Outpost 0504 direct to Woodsholme Main Entry Terminal. Transport is now ready, please board,' the voice crackled, with the same formal and long tone that Ceile used. My friend and I looked at each other in amazement.

Not only did the transport belong to the elves, but it also went straight to the city.

46

'An amazing find, you two. From what I can glean from the information panel, this transport was built to allow researchers quick access between here and Woodsholme. The outpost itself appears to have been removed years ago, stripped down for use somewhere in the city proper, but for whatever reason, the transport itself and its rails were not,' Bill said, his fingers tapping quickly over the console. He shook his head as he moved through screen after screen. 'The panel has no records at all after a point approximately thirty years ago, and has received no instructions or information since,' he continued, looking perplexed.

I watched him work as I leaned against the rail, my hand running through my beard. Night had fallen entirely, and we were lit only by the strange spheres of light. The Moon sailed past far overhead.

'Other than this weird corrosion on the metal, the platform's in great shape, and the interior of the transport isn't anything fancy but it's immaculate. I know enough about elven tech to know that's not exactly surprising, but still,' I said. 'It seems like this thing,' I pointed at the panel, 'was connected to at least a handful of other panels in different outposts nearby.'

I cocked my head to look at Bill. 'So why aren't they talking to each other now?' I asked.

The wizard thought about that for a moment, then shook his head again and said, 'I don't know for sure without venturing to another outpost, and I'm not sure we can take the time to get to the next one and risk finding the transport non-functional there.'

I narrowed my eyes at him. 'You want us to take this thing to the city,' I said, flatly.

Bill nodded, and said, 'Martin, we could be a week getting to Woodsholme on foot. Maybe longer! We don't know exactly where it is or how far we are from it right now. We're making poor time through the forest. You know elven technology, its quality. This transport will take us to the city safely.'

'It will, Martin. The elves, for all their faults, build things that last for centuries,' Ceile said as she stood in the doorway of the transport.

'Listen, I'm less concerned about this thing breaking down than I am rolling into the elves' city with three humans, a werewolf, a dwarf, a kobold, and a dragon. Without an elf to vouch for us, we might find ourselves spending the rest of my life, at least, in jail,' I said, tapping my fingers together. Then I frowned and turned to look down to the forest floor below. 'Speaking of dragon, I don't think it's going to be able to come. Not that I know why it's here anyway.'

Gesturing lazily at the transport, I said, 'There's room for all of us - though Nox may have an uncomfortable ride - except for the dragon.'

Bill looked thoughtful again as he closed the panel up. 'Hmm, yes, it won't be able to join us inside, and the rail system will keep it from riding on top. We'll have to ask what it'd like to do,' the wizard said, turning to brush gently past me toward the ladder.

Ceile raised an eyebrow at me with a smirk, then followed Bill down. I gave the transport a last glance, shook my head, and then joined everyone below. The wizard was giving the others a rundown of what we'd discovered. The kobold was bouncing around the prone dragon in excitement, yelping, 'hey!' with each jump. Robin looked uneasy, though I wasn't sure if it was the thought of taking the transport into Woodsholme or being left alone with the two.

If the green dragon was paying attention to the wizard's talk, it didn't give any sign.

'I can't know for sure how fast the transport goes. I know similar machines in the city could travel at speeds quicker than the Red Flag. Significantly quicker. This may get us back on track, schedule-wise!' Bill was saying, waving his arms theatrically, then dropping them to his sides and rolling his head back to look down his nose at all of us. 'There will be some danger! We know not what will await us when we arrive at the city. But the reward far, far outweighs the risk here,' he said, certainty in his voice.

Robin looked unconvinced, but after a quick look in my direction, nodded. The kobold had stopped jumping around and was now dancing at Bill's feet. The wizard smiled at the little beast.

Then he turned to look up at the green dragon, and quietly said, 'And now it appears that your part in this journey, whatever it may have been, has come to an end. I do not know what brought you along despite your early attempts to maim and murder the members of my little band, but you are a fascinating creature and I wish I had time to speak with you further.' Giving the dragon a grand bow, he winked at it, cried, 'Farewell, beast!' and then spun around and headed for the ladder.

The dragon cocked its head and watched him leave with a quizzical look on its face. Then it suddenly lunged to its feet and strode forward, nearly trampling the kobold and Robin, and finally came to a stop, looming over the wizard.

Ceile had her pistol out, trained on the dragon's face. I was drawing every ounce of nether I could get my hands on, ready to protect Bill. Oddly enough, I had the strange feeling that I should destroy the wizard rather than attack the dragon.

Bill stopped, then turned very slowly to look up at the dragon. 'What can I do for you?' he asked quietly, his voice full of menace. His rings were glowing molten red. The two glared at each other silently.

For a long moment, we all stood there, weapons trained on the scaly beast. Except for Nox. The 'wolf looked like he was torn with indecision.

Then he stepped forward, turned to look at everyone, and said, 'Wait! It didn't come all this way just to try and kill us.' Then he paused and looked away, and said, 'Well, again, anyway.' He didn't look completely convinced, but when he turned around to look up at the dragon, he said, 'I trust it.'

Before any of us could respond, the dragon started to shrink.

Wings folded into its back and vanished. Neck lowered into its shoulders, head coming to rest there. Tail curled up and melted into its rump. Scales lifted and then sunk into its skin. When the changes stopped, the dragon lay curled up in the deep grass in front of Bill.

'Yeah, because this adventure wasn't weird enough,' I heard Nox whisper from behind me.

A naked human woman stood up out of the grass. At least a foot taller than Ceile, she was incredibly pale, almost chalk white, and very thin. Long hair fell to just past her shoulders, hair that seemed white originally but resolved into a mint green once I'd gotten a better look at her.

One of her eyes was gone, leaving behind an empty socket shrouded in shadows. The other eye was black other than a blazing neon emerald iris.

She slowly turned her head to make eye contact with each of us, nodded at Nox, then walked past a shell shocked Bill, who - likely for the first time in his life - was speechless. The woman stopped when she was just behind the wizard, and she lowered her head.

'I am Vrarrs Kor,' she said, then headed for the ladder. She put a foot on the first rung, then stopped again. Looking back at us, she nodded at the kobold, who had stopped to stare at her, and then said, 'His name is Weezab.'

And then she climbed the ladder and vanished into the branches above.

'Weezab!' the kobold smiled gleefully, jabbing a scaly finger into his chest. Then he laughed so hard that he could barely stand and then bolted off to join the woman on the platform.

The five of us that remained were silent for a long moment. Then Bill said, 'Well, I'm glad that's settled. I think! Away we go!' and then followed the kobold up.

'We will have to figure out some clothing for her,' Ceile said, looking thoughtful. She reached over, gave my hand a squeeze, Nox a sympathetic smile, then she too was gone.

Robin looked uncomfortable, looking up into the branches above. I heard her whisper, 'I should have brought more firepower,' shake her head, and then hesitantly grab the ladder and head up.

That left Nox and me on forest floor. We looked at each other for a bit without saying anything, and then I shook my head. 'Sorry, Nox. I'm sorry for all this,' I said.

The big 'wolf shook his head, moved forward to drop a hand roughly on my head. 'Oh, I'm sure I'll have something to be sorry about by the end of this. How about we not keep score?' he grumbled quietly with a sad smile.

I nodded, and then the two of us joined the rest of the party in the transport.

47

The inside of the transport was fairly Spartan, with ten comfortable seats - five on each side - and a console in front of the chair closest to the front window and on the left. With everyone on board, Bill was going over whatever information he could get from the control panel. I watched over his shoulder.

'It looks like this and the platform console haven't, er, spoken with each other for a long time. Think no one's used it that entire time?' I quietly said to the wizard.

He shook his head slowly. 'It's possible. I've been trying to connect with the terminal at the city - just a weather check, I don't want them to know we're coming quite yet - but haven't managed to reach it,' he said, then looked up at me with a concerned look. 'I don't know what that means. The Main Entry Terminal is where all external traffic goes before heading into the city. I understand putting these outposts into standby, but I'd think they would go back to operating normally if they were activated.'

I frowned. 'They couldn't have just shut down the connection from the city to the outposts? Maybe they started decommissioning the platforms and transports and didn't quite finish up for some reason,' I said.

If anything, the wizard's face looked even more serious. 'If that's the case, then that would mean the elves got interrupted by something pretty major. Something that has kept them occupied for thirty years?' he said, shaking his head. Then he turned to face the others.

'Everything seems fine with the transport, but I can't connect with the home terminal. That could mean a lot of things, but what it primarily means for us is that we'll need to be ready for trouble. So make sure whatever weapons you have are good to go,' he said, then turned away. 'Settle in once you're ready, I'll send us on our way in a few minutes.'

Ceile and Robin were talking quietly while they cleaned up their pistols, the two weapons as different as their owners. The dwarf woman shook her hair as she suddenly laughed, a wave of crimson and curl flowing over her shoulders. My friend smiled at her, reaching out to pat her knee gently.

Nox was jammed into the seat with the most space, next to the doorway. The poor 'wolf had to hunch far over and stuck out into the aisle. He looked really uncomfortable as he sat there, sharpening the points on his claws that still had them. The elves were a very insular people, and their biology did not allow creatures like the big 'wolf to exist. There was no need, in their eyes, to build anything to handle his weight or size.

The kobold, who I now knew was Weezab, was asleep in his seat, tied up haphazardly in his safety belts. He snored loudly.

He had my cellphone tightly clutched in his hand.

I shook my head and smiled. Eventually, I should check to see what those messages had been. I wouldn't exactly have service way out here, but I could at least see who had tried to reach me before I fled the City. With Ceile and Nox on the airship with me, that had virtually eliminated the people who ever sent me texts or called.

Finally, my eyes fell on the human woman who wasn't a human at all and whose name was Vrarrs Kor. Much to the relief of Nox, Ceile and Robin had come up with enough material to make the dragon some rough clothing. It wasn't a modest outfit, but I had my suspicions that she had no need of protection from the elements or from damage that wouldn't harm her in her dragon form.

When the other women presented the clothing to her, she had looked it over coldly. But then, with a faint smile, she accepted the items and immediately put them on.

Kor lounged at the back of the transport alone. She had no weapon, but I was pretty sure she was dangerous even without one. Noticing me looking at her, the dragon cocked her head and smiled darkly. She nodded toward the empty seat beside her.

I raised an eyebrow, then shrugged and carefully navigated my way down the aisle, giving Ceile's shoulder a squeeze, Robin a smile, Nox a pat on the arm, and Weezab a grin as I passed. Finally, I sat down across from the dragon.

'Buckle up, my fabulous friends! I do not anticipate turbulence, but I'm pretty sure this thing goes like a rocket!' Bill shouted from up front. The doorway made a dull thump as it locked, reminding me of my car. The transport shook slightly, and I heard something latch somewhere outside and over my head. Two low-pitched hums burst into existence beneath my feet. Outside my window, the lights on the platform went out, and now the world was only lit by the lights on the transport.

'Here we go!' the wizard roared, lifting a hand theatrically and then jabbing it down onto the console. Everyone braced for departure, unsure of what kind of ride we were going to get.

Nothing happened.

Bill lifted the hand that he had covered his eyes with and looked around in confusion. Then he looked down at the console and cursed. 'Damned standby! Why do manufactures even do that?' he snarled over his shoulder. 'Here we go, take two!' he roared.

This time when he hit the button, there was a high pitched whine and then the low-pitched hums became low-pitched thrums. The transport shook again, and then we began moving forward, slowly at first but quickly building speed. The interior lights dimmed. Through the front window, I could just make out a rail that seemed to fade in and out of view.

And then the transport really wound up and now we were moving very, very fast.

It was a bit terrifying for the first few minutes. Besides the speed, the transport's path had become overgrown over the years, and we were blasting through leaves and branches and whole trees. At the rate we were moving and with our forward view only lit by the lights on the front of the transport, we didn't have time to see the impacts coming, either. It was silent in the cabin, all of us more than a little uncomfortable in the explosions of foliage and noise.

Gradually, I adapted to the cacophony, and though my body still tensed up with each hit, I found I could now do something other than cling to the arms of my seat painfully. I turned to look at Vrarrs Kor.

The dragon was already watching me with a strange look on her face. 'You have questions, Martin Tundra. Ask,' she said. Her voice was quiet, reptilian, and ice danced and hissed across her tongue. I wondered if she held us all in contempt or if that was just how she spoke.

'Why are you here? You almost killed Nox, and tried to kill me,' I said, leaning toward her. 'And then you saved our lives. Why?'

Out of the corner of my eye, I saw Ceile and Bill turn to look at the dragon and me, though between the racket outside and the snores coming from Nox, Robin, and Weezab, I doubted they'd hear much. Kor leaned in even closer, until we were almost nose to nose, and smiled evilly.

'I was but one test of many, Martin Tundra, and you won. You no longer have anything to fear from me,' she whispered. Then her eye narrowed and her smile faded. 'But other trials are coming. Before the end of this journey, you will win what you seek,' she said, shaking her head.

'But you will lose everything.'

48

My efforts to get more answers out of Vrarrs Kor were futile, and eventually I gave up. Whatever secrets she had, the dragon would tell us on her own time, if at all. She watched me quietly, her emerald eye glowing brightly in the dim light, a sad smile on her lips.

Frustrated, my questions echoed through my mind as the transport barrelled toward the elven city. Was the dragon telling the truth? If she had been a test, who had set her to it? Had I won purely by surviving, or was there more to it? And what point was there to putting me through them?

More importantly, for the moment at least, did that mean we could trust Kor to work with us, or could we end up having to fight her again? Nox seemed to have decided she was trustworthy. I wasn't quite that prepared to forgive her for almost killing the big 'wolf, but his word meant a lot. Really, though, should I trust anyone who wasn't Nox or Ceile?

I looked around at the others. Weezab was still snoring away, having managed to gradually worm his way from a seated position to being curled up on the seat. The little fellow had never given me a reason to mistrust him, though it wasn't like he and I could have a deep conversation. He seemed to be coming along because he thought it was fun. If only there was a way to find out what he was thinking.

Robin had also never seemed untrustworthy. Of any of the other party members, she would be the closest to being a friend. The dwarf and Ceile were definitely bonding, and it was interesting watching them interact. I didn't know if the dwarves of Krekt Fourteen had ever fought humans tooth and nail as their cousins below the City had, but it was certainly odd to be working alongside her.

The only dwarf I'd been remotely friendly with before Robin and Petrel was an engineer my unit had captured back in the war. Partridge, I think his name was. Spending time with him had been an eye opener, and I had talked with the dwarf for hundreds of hours over the years the City was locked in a brutal stalemate with Krekt Two.

Partridge had only wanted one thing. He wanted the war over and things to get back to normal so his children could have a chance to grow up as children rather than as future conscripts.

I shook my head as the memories came back. After the krekts had surrendered, we shipped most of their prisoners back to them. Despite being under Enforcement occupation, many of the prisoners went missing or were killed as traitors by their own kin. Partridge was among them.

I frowned sadly, then looked back at Robin. She was a lot like the engineer. I realized that I trusted her already, and I wondered how much of that was because of my time with Partridge. Then I wondered if I was being a bit reckless with my trust. Then I wondered if I was being a bit reckless with my trust because I was weeks from death.

I didn't know, and that made me shiver.

And then there was Bill. I shifted my gaze to look at the back of the wizard's head, the man sitting alone at the front of the transport, at the helm. Not just of the car, but also of our fates. Everything in this plan rested on his shoulders. Only he knew who or what we were picking up in Woodsholme. Only he knew the route and location of our entrance into the mountains, and then the location of our entrance into the krekt itself.

And only he knew what was waiting for us in the artifact vault.

No, there was an awful lot going on behind the scenes here, and I didn't think for a second that Bill had given any of us all the information. Even Petrel and Robin, who had been with him from the start, likely didn't have much of an idea beyond the rough layout of the descent from mountain side to the vault.

I needed the wizard, but I didn't trust him, and of everyone on this adventure, he was the most dangerous.

As if he had heard me thinking, Bill suddenly turned around to look directly at me. His mouth split into a massive toothy smile, and then he gave me an exaggerated wink before going back to looking out the front of the car. His fingers danced across the console.

I was surprised to find sunlight had started filtering through the trees above, having apparently spent hours lost in thought.

'Alright, everyone up. I still can't communicate with the terminal, but we're almost there and we should be ready to get out and fast when we arrive. I don't imagine the elves would just blow up their own transport without at least seeing who was in it, but better we get out onto the platform and then make for cover,' Bill suddenly said, loudly enough to carry easily to me and Vrarrs Kor.

On cue, the forest suddenly cut away and we were flying over open ground. Ahead, a thirty metre wide concrete wall stretched in both directions until the ends vanished in the distance. A vast platform perched on the wall in front, and our strange rail arced toward it. As we approached, I could see two other transport cars hanging from other rails running parallel to the edge of the platform. The thrum beneath my feet began to quiet, and we started slowing down at a pace that pushed me tight against my safety belts.

When we had slowed to a less precarious speed, Ceile was out of her belt and perched at the door in seconds. Nox struggled with his for a moment before snarling and cutting them off. Robin crouched just at the werewolf's knee, making a final check of her pistol before holstering it.

Weezab was still sleeping. Nox gave the little fellow a poke in the butt. The kobold leapt into the air with a shrieked, 'Helllllp!' before remembering where he was and settled at the foot of his seat while glaring at the big 'wolf.

For exercise's sake, I flicked a finger out into the rotting mire, feeling the decay and sickness creep up my arm, and drew, shaped, and folded a form that made my belts go away. Their dust slowly floated to the floor. I stood, straightening my arms and stretching.

Vrarrs Kor smirked at me.

As the transport slowly maneuvered into the platform, Bill turned and got to his feet. 'Be ready. The car will automatically open the door, we should make for the wall straight across from us. No shooting! If we fight back, they'll kill us all for sure,' the wizard said, emphasizing the no shooting part.

I tensed up. I'd definitely been getting stronger since I left the City, but a dash across an open platform with the potential for being shot at wasn't something I was sure my body could handle. Nox reached over and gave my arm a painful squeeze. I nodded at him.

'Just like old times, right?' the 'wolf said, quietly. I smiled at him and gave Ceile a wink. It's true, this was just like the trouble we used to get into decades ago.

The transport came to a stop and then went silent. The door made a dull thump, and then it pushed out and began to fold outward. The Sun beat down on the platform outside.

'Here we go,' Bill said, quietly.

49

The transport came to a stop and then went silent. The door slowly dropped, and as soon as she could fit out, Ceile leapt out the opening and darted forward, looking in every direction, trying to find targets. Nox was less graceful. The door hadn't opened enough to let him through, but the big 'wolf crashed through anyway, tearing the upper portion of the entrance clear off the transport car and flinging it to the side as he fell to all fours and loped across the platform.

'Subtle,' Robin said, nervously following the 'wolf out the door. Bill smirked and went out with her, the pair moving quickly. Ceile had reached the wall and was now crouching down, trying to watch every direction at once with a suspicious look on her face.

Weezab went out the door next, yelping, 'hey hey hey hey hey,' as he bounced across the platform with a grin on his scaly face. Nox reached the wall and tucked in to shield Ceile with some of his bulk as he joined her in looking around. He looked confused.

A hand fell on my shoulder, and I looked over to find Vrarrs Kor standing next to me. 'Do not forget, Martin Tundra,' she whispered, sadly. Then the dragon brushed past gently, stepped out onto the platform, and then slowly walked toward the wall. She looked around, arrogantly, as though whatever the elves could throw at her was inconsequential. Ceile and Nox both shook their heads at her.

Then there was me. I took a deep breath and then

Martin

The voice was the sound of the ocean crashing against the shore, and I fell to the side, reaching wildly for Nox's seat.

do not

I put my hands to my ears, trying to deaden some of the fury, knowing that it was inside and I couldn't shut it out. The water at the back of my mind was roiling, roaring with desperation.

go, city is

Ceile was racing toward me, concern on her face. I barely saw her. Dark spots danced across my vision. I felt a familiar presence just beneath the surface of the boiling water, thrashing violently as though trying to break free.

a trap

And then the Other was gone.

I fell to the ground, limbs shaking and numb, gasping for air. Ceile slid to a stop, reaching down and lifting me to my feet like I was nothing. I tried to help, but everything was far away, and then I felt my friend lift me into her arms and we were moving across the platform. She was saying something to me, alternating between looking down at me and staring nervously around the platform.

I wondered what could possibly rattle her, and as she carried me to the relative safety of the wall, I tried to get as good a look as possible at the platform. In the fog that was swirling around my head, I still registered that something was wrong here.

Dust and dirt whispered across the platform floor and the two transport cars. None of the consoles or panels were operating. One of the doors into the enclosed section of the terminal hung ajar, swinging mournfully in the wind. Weeds and trees had overgrown large parts of the platform.

This was the main point of entry and exit for external traffic, and from the looks of things, it hadn't been used in a long time. Hadn't been maintained in a long time. From what I knew of elves, that was severely out of character. They were clean and orderly to the point of sterility. This place was a mess and had been for a while.

As Ceile got me to the wall and set me down gently, I noticed that the display beside her was just barely illuminated. I could make out a bit of text scrolling along the bottom.

Evacuate, it read.

Evacuate immediately.

50

While I recovered from the reappearance of the Other and his warning, the party discussed our next step. From points on the outer platform, we could look down into Woodsholme, and what little we could see wasn't encouraging. Or rather, what we couldn't see. The city was big. Not on the same order as the City, but still massive. It spread out from the wall, all straight lines and white colour and pristine placement, and kept right on going until it touched the horizon and disappeared.

Nothing moved. The streets that we could see were deserted.

Even creepier, the only sounds we could hear from our spot were natural. The calls and cries of birds and other creatures in the distance. The wind whistling through the leaves and grass. The Locus Wood swayed and whispered from across the open area below the wall, but beyond that concrete border all was silent.

'We have a problem,' Bill said, crouched in front of me while the others stood or sat around us in a half circle. The wizard slowly looked at each of us while tapping his fingertips together. 'For those of you that don't know the elven people, this,' he said, waving at the debris and general disarray of the platform, 'is highly unusual. Abandoning a scientific outpost in the middle of nowhere, I can see, but abandoning a full blown terminal and then leaving it to rot suggests to me that they had to leave in a hurry.'

Nodding at me, he reached over and tapped the nearby display. 'Evacuate immediately is pretty good evidence that I'm right. Now, what were they evacuating from? And where did they evacuate to? Unfortunately, none of the consoles or panels up here are functioning other than this one, and it appears to have been damaged at one point. Other than the scrolling evacuation order, I cannot get any more information out of it,' he said, frustration lining his voice.

Turning back to me, the wizard continued, 'Your warning is equally troublesome. Your dark companion may be a monster, but I believe he is trying to prevent you from harm, at least in this case. If he says that the city is a trap, then I'm inclined to agree.'

'Maybe we should just move on, Bill. Can we complete our mission without whatever it is you needed from Woodsholme?' Ceile asked. Oddly enough, she sounded hopeful.

Bill shook his head. 'No. Our entrance into Krekt Twelve is from a number of ancient caverns above its western levels. Those caverns are a maze, and a treacherous one. My contact here has map data for almost the entire system, data that I have found only exists in his hands,' he said, quietly. 'I have done this elf a favour in return for the maps, and having delivered, I had planned for us to meet with him and collect our reward.'

Ceile looked crushed. I wondered what was going on with her.

'Now, obviously something has gone wrong in the city, and from the evidence, it may be affecting the entire city. If that is the case, then our mission here has become very complicated. We have no way of knowing what is out there. Fortunately, even if my contact is dead, I can still retrieve the information so long as we can get to his office, but that building is in the center of the city, and that means we have a lot of potentially dangerous ground to cover,' Bill said.

'How do you know the map will be there, wizard?' Nox growled quietly.

'Because, my mostly-furry friend, my contact is an elf, and elves are meticulous and obsessive. My deal with him was to provide a service in return for a map, a map that would be located in a drawer in his office and would be available to me, and me only, any time after I had paid my end of the bargain. Trust me, friends,' the wizard said with certainty, 'that data will be there waiting for us. We just need to get there.'

There was silence as we all looked at each other. Everything about this city felt wrong. It was empty. Dead. There was a brisk breeze, yet the air still felt still and stagnant. Smothering. It felt a lot like drawing nether.

Finally, I spoke up, my voice still a bit shaky, 'Alright, so we go get this thing. How do we get to it? How far?'

Bill thought for a moment, then replied, 'The center of the city is almost fifteen kilometres from us. That would be a sizable hike, even with the elves' penchant for straight roads, but I believe that we may be able to find either a working vehicle on the streets below or a working transport. If we can find either, then we can easily reach downtown before Sun down. If we cannot, I believe we will need to find shelter and hide somewhere. Whatever might be down there, we can't confront it during the night.'

I nodded at him, slowly. It was as good a plan as any for going down into the city.

The wizard smiled, and said, 'Our first order of business will be to check the opposing platform on the other side of the terminal. Those transports will be the ones that ferry people into and out of the city proper. If any of the consoles work in there, I may be able to summon us a ride. Otherwise, we'll take the stairs down to street level and start heading for the office on foot.'

The party nodded, and we carefully got to our feet. Ceile drew her pistol and took the lead, and Robin was right behind her. Cautiously, we pulled open one of the terminal doors and entered the windowed area.

The inside was as dishevelled as the platform, with rows upon rows of seats and benches slowly succumbing to the sun and rain and wind blowing in through some of the already open doors and several shattered panes of glass far over our heads. The carpet beneath us was no better off, the once intricate designs and patterns fading away, some ends and edges reduced to just long sections of twisted thread.

Ceile nodded back at us, and then headed for the doors. This level at least was clear.

The other platform was a mirror image to the one we'd arrived on, only there were no transport cars remaining. If there were any hanging out invisibly like the one at the research outpost, there didn't seem to be anyway to call them with all of the panels dead. While Bill marched around trying each console twice, the rest of us gathered quietly at the edge.

'Because the only way to make elves any creepier than they already are is to make them vanish, apparently,' Nox growled quietly. Robin giggled.

The silence was eerie, and from this platform, we could see hundreds of square kilometres of city. Nothing moved. No smoke or steam or anything rose above the concrete and steel and glass buildings.

Bill rejoined us, and he shook his head. 'We'll have to try our luck below. None of these panels are working,' he said, frustration rippling through his voice. Weezab reached up and clapped him on the side of the arm with a big grin. The wizard gave the kobold a dirty look and then headed for the door.

The little creature looked confused. 'Helllllp?' he asked, confusedly. I gave him a pat on the head as I followed Bill back to the terminal. The kobold gave me a smile and then skipped along beside me.

None of the elevators were working, but even if they had, I'm not sure we would have risked them. Each level lower than the top was in progressively better condition, insulated from the tender mercies of nature by each level above. We passed shops and security check points and luggage areas, all looking very similar and also very empty.

When we finally reached the bottom, it was if we'd stepped into a museum. This final level was almost pristine, give or take some dulling of the carpet, seats, and windows. The garbage disposals were empty, as though they had been replaced just hours ago.

Then Ceile slowly pushed open the big glass front doors and stepped out into the Sun, carefully scanning the neighbouring buildings and the street for danger. I slowly walked out behind her, searching the area for the feel of nether being manipulated. Bill was at my shoulder, and when I turned to look at him, he glanced back and then smiled sadly.

'Hello, Woodsholme,' he quietly said, throwing his arms wide in a flamboyant flourish.

Nothing but the wind answered.

51

Woodsholme was even more eerie at street level. Every building towered above us, with most rooftops reaching almost level with the transport platform, and with some soaring even higher. Every one of them had hundreds of windows, and even without the White Sun blazing down we would have had trouble seeing into any of them.

'I don't like this,' Nox growled, scanning the buildings around us, uneasily. 'There could be thousands of people watching us right now, and we'd never know.'

I agreed with him. It felt like I was being watched, though that was likely just my mind playing tricks. The city was a trap, the Other had told me. That wasn't helping my paranoia.

The streets themselves were barren, six lanes of empty pavement that split and spread at right angles, vanishing around the buildings and into the distance. The sidewalks that ringed each skyscraper had the same sense of having been abandoned as the terminal had. Dust and dirt blew over and around them, making small drifts at the edge of the street. Weeds and bushes had sprouted out of the cement, sometimes in large enough clumps that the sidewalk or street had been pushed away in inverted craters.

Though the streets themselves were empty, the parking areas were jammed, and I imagined that the underground lots would also be full if we went down to have a look. It could have been the middle of a business day, if it wasn't for the silence, the lack of people, and the dust all over the vehicles.

Ceile was also searching the windows above for signs of life. 'I agree with Nox. We do not know why the elves were evacuating the terminal. We should get two of these vehicles going, or, failing that, get moving on foot,' she said.

Bill nodded. 'We'll need at least two, I don't see any large enough to haul us all. Have any of you driven an elven vehicle before?' he asked, looking around at each of us. Weezab looked comically sad when he shook his head. Vrarrs Kor didn't reply.

Nox stretched and said, 'I don't need a vehicle. I'll keep up.' The wizard smirked as he nodded at the big 'wolf.

Robin looked uncertain, but she said, 'I won't know the mechanics of it without getting under the hood - if there is a hood - but I can probably drive it so long as it isn't completely different than dwarf or human stuff.'

I said roughly the same thing. 'Their tech might makes ours look silly, but unless they're operating by telepathy, it should be similar enough to operate.'

Bill nodded again, and said, 'Alright, that should be good enough. I'm fluent in piloting these things, and between Martin and Robin we should be able to operate a second. Let's get-'

Ceile interrupted him. 'I can drive any of these. Let us find two that work and then you and I can get us on our way,' she said to the wizard. I was surprised. I knew that she had done a lot of research to keep up her elven image, but not that she had gone to such lengths. The others gave her curious looks. Bill look unsure but nodded slowly at her.

'Alright, then. Let's check the closest ones and work our way along the sidewalk,' he said, turning away and beckoning everyone to follow.

The first two were indeed quite a bit like my car, at least from the outside. Unlike mine, however, neither of them had a hood. I wondered how they were serviced, then I remembered the door on the transport and its seamless connection to the body of the car.

'These are all unlocked,' Robin said, pausing to look up at the windows above us with nervousness etched on her face. I swiped some of the dust off of the opposing door's window and had a peek in. The interior was immaculate.

'And they look like they are freshly cleaned. Inside, at least,' I heard Ceile say from the other car. She popped the door and cautiously looked in, then said, 'The air is stale, and not just because of the heat.' She stood up so we could all see her, and continued, 'I am certain we can agree that these have not been used in some time, but there is something wrong beyond that.'

She shook her head. 'I do not know what,' she said, quietly.

An electronic hum suddenly burst from the car I was standing next to, and I saw Robin sitting in the driver's seat, looking very shocked. I opened my door to look in at her, and she said, 'It just started up when I put my hands on the wheel. If these things have keys, this one has them in the ignition.'

Sure enough, the other car did the same for Ceile. My friend shook her head slowly. 'The elves have very low crime rates, but this is still very strange for them,' she said after she let go of the wheel and stood up so we could all hear her. 'We must go. Now,' she finished, her voice insistent.

Bill nodded. 'You heard the lady, my friends. Three in each car, in you get. Drivers!' he shouted, pointing theatrically at Robin and Ceile, 'We are on one of the two major cross-city roads, Zero Street. We go north, right to the building. It is the Vernal Equinox building, and it is on the corner between Zero and Three Ave.' Seeing the pained look that Robin threw his way, the wizard laughed and waved her off. 'You'll see it! Trust me. Look to the left when you pass Two!'

Then his face went serious, and Bill said, 'If we are separated, continue to Vernal Equinox and hole up in the lobby. We'll meet there!' and then slid into the passenger seat of Ceile's car.

Weezab cheered, and after a few missed attempts, managed to open one of the rear doors and leap into the seat. Ceile and Robin exchanged a nod and a smile and then each driver was in and ready to roll. Vrarrs Kor opened the door behind mine and gave me an indecipherable look before getting in.

That left Nox and me outside. 'Keep close, Nox. We don't want to lose you,' I told him, reaching over to give his arm a squeeze. The big 'wolf smiled darkly. As I settled into the passenger seat, he leaned in close.

'You be careful,' he growled quietly, then shut my door.

52

Thankfully, our car had some sort of navigation package that accepted voice commands. Once the system had worked its way around our accents, it displayed the route to Vernal Equinox, including distance and directions. Which were thankfully limited to, 'go north on Zero Street.'

'What I wouldn't give to have this back home. I'm a dwarf and even I think dwarf addresses make zero sense. I mean, who names every street after something and then groups them in with other similar things? How does anyone new to a krekt have any idea where anything is? What the hell is wrong with a nice clean grid system?' Robin said, nose wrinkled in irritation.

I chuckled at her. Vrarrs Kor smirked.

With a bit of hesitation, the dwarf backed the car away from the curb, and then whipped around onto the street proper. Nox was close behind, just far enough away to avoid being run over if Robin had to swerve for some reason. Looking over my shoulder past Kor, I saw Ceile's car spin around and take up a position a few lengths behind.

Robin looked over at me suddenly, and her face was bright with excitement. I could understand. I might not be driving, but I could feel the power and handling this thing must have. I put a hand on her shoulder, and grinned. 'Might as well see what she can do. Just don't kill us,' I said.

Even before I had finished, the dwarf was walking on the accelerator. The engine howled like a banshee and we leapt forward with enough power to push me back into my seat. I couldn't quite see the entire instrument panel, but the speedometer was flashing red. I wondered if the elves had put a warning system in for when the car was exceeding a speed limit.

It was all very orderly.

'Whoa!' Robin was yelling, interspersed with mad cackling. I was surprised to find myself laughing along with her. A glance in the rear view showed Ceile's car far behind but slowly catching up. There was no sign of Nox.

I was just about to tell Robin to slow down when the werewolf blasted past us, teeth bared, eyes narrowed, ears back, arms scything through the air, the pavement cracking with each vicious step. Saliva oozed from his mouth. At first, it looked like he was yelling curses as he ran, but then I realized that he wasn't angry. He was laughing.

This was Nox blowing off some serious steam.

Our car began to slow down, and I looked over to find Robin staring incredulously at the big 'wolf. 'Holy crap,' she whispered.

Ceile pulled up beside us, and Bill waved us on before my friend jammed on the accelerator, launching her car forward and rapidly away. I had a quick glance of Weezab jumping around in the back seat, pointing at us and laughing, his scaly mouth yelling what I could only assume was, 'I win!' Robin growled and sped up.

We were almost flying along the empty street, and I searched the buildings we passed for signs of life or movement. Nothing. The parking areas continued to be full or almost full. It could have been a regular day if it weren't for the missing populace.

'I don't like this. Where the hell is everyone?' Robin said, her enthusiasm for driving waning in the face of the strange desolation outside the car. I nodded slowly. It was unnerving.

If Kor was uncomfortable, she hid it well. The dragon continued staring out the window listlessly, as silent as the streets.

Nox had slowed down considerably, falling behind us once again. Sweat dripped from his face, and I could see his chest rise and fall raggedly as he gulped in air. Robin let off the accelerator so we wouldn't leave the werewolf on his own, and soon Ceile had followed suit.

The change wasn't entirely just for Nox's benefit. Travelling at higher speeds meant we might miss something, and while we needed to get downtown and soon, finding additional clues might mean the difference between walking into danger and blundering into it.

We came up on a stretch of street lined with what might have been bus shelters. I'd been asking Robin some questions about her home when I saw something move out of the corner of my eye. I looked back toward the road and watched something step out from behind a bus shelter and into the road.

Right in front of us.

Robin had been fiddling with the navigation panel but reacted instantly to my sudden cry. Eyes widening, the dwarf jerked the wheel to the left, sending the car swerving hard and then toward the center median. All I could do was hang on and hope the elves' tech covered safety as well as power.

The dwarf tried to correct, but we were out of control and it was all she could do to keep us upright. With a violent smash, the nose of the car plowed into the median, which rippled oddly. Rather than shatter and twist into a million pieces, the front end remained relatively intact as the median absorbed the impact, slowing us down quickly without tearing the car completely apart.

We weren't coming out unscathed. As powerful as the science was behind the median's materials, it couldn't stop us altogether. Eventually, the collision overrode the absorber and then we slammed into the ground and flipped. Glass shattered and started raining through the cabin before suddenly disappearing. Air bags burst into existence, cushioning us from the final crash down, as our car landed on its roof, up against the median.

For a long moment, I hung there upside down as the bags around me deflated and slowly vanished. I was cut bad on my right arm, and I thought I might have banged my head against the window, but otherwise I was okay. 'The ridiculousness of coming all this way and then potentially dying in a car crash isn't lost on me,' I whispered with a sigh.

I looked over and found Robin groggily looking back. 'Are you alright, Martin?' she said, raggedly.

I nodded slowly, which made my head ache. 'I think so. At least, nothing that Ceile or Weezab can't handle. You?' I said. The dwarf nodded, rubbing her arms and wincing. I looked over my shoulder and said, 'Kor? Are you okay?'

The dragon hissed as she stretched against her seat belt and the remnants of the air bags. 'I am well, Martin Tundra,' she said.

'Alright, that's good. Let's get out of here,' I said. My belt was stuck tight, so I once again drew some nether, shaped the form, and then made them flash into ash. I was braced for the fall, but it still hurt when I plummeted to the shattered roof. Robin cut herself loose, and I helped her down. Kor was already climbing ungracefully out the window.

The werewolf was standing outside. He offered her a hand, which she looked at suspiciously before finally grabbing it with her own. The 'wolf lifted her gently to her feet. He didn't smile, but then, he didn't snarl at her, either.

After the big 'wolf had helped me and Robin out of the car, we all dusted ourselves down. Ceile, Bill, and Weezab were already running to us, having stopped their car nearby.

Even before my friend got to me, she was already making the gestures and saying the words I had seen hundreds of times before. A quiet rain suddenly formed above me, and I felt a cool and calming sensation trickle over me. My wounds closed and my headache faded. Shortly after, the rain dissipated without a trace.

Yeah, water healing is much, much nicer than fire healing.

Seeing that I was all patched up, Ceile immediately headed to Robin, performing an encore. As the dwarf slowly recovered from the effects of the spell, my friend put a hand on her shoulder and smiled at her. The dwarf looked none the worse for wear, other than her clothing being a bit more ragged.

Vrarrs Kor didn't have a scratch.

The four of us joined Bill, Nox, and Weezab, who were all looking back down the street. A couple hundred metres away, a tall, humanoid shape stood, facing away from us. The heated air billowing off of the pavement distorted most of its details.

Nox growled quietly. 'It's an elf,' he said, hesitantly.

As if the figure had heard the 'wolf, it abruptly spun on its heels, turning to face us with a jerky twist of its spine. I gasped as I caught a glimpse of ghastly white skin and a horrible, stretched grin, before the newcomer threw its hands into the air, and then vanished.

53

'What the hell was that?' Robin asked, pistol out and staring at the spot the twisted elf had been standing in.

Nox snorted, and then shook his head. 'Its smell was weird, and now it's gone. Whatever it was, it didn't move like an elf,' the 'wolf growled, quietly.

It seemed like a good idea to get off the street and out of the Sun, so we gathered what we could out of the wrecked car, Bill parked the intact one on the sidewalk in the shadow of the building next to us, and we gathered in the shade near the entrance.

If anything, the crashed vehicle made the street seem even more desolate. As far as the eye could see, it was the only thing on the street. If anything was looking for us, they'd have a pretty good idea where to start. Looking up at the thousands of windows looming above us and on the opposite side of the roadway, I felt something itch at the back of my shoulder blades.

The party was quiet, most of us unnerved by the appearance and then disappearance of the twisted elf. 'That was a handy trick it used,' Bill said as he scanned the buildings around us. 'Felt like magic, which isn't something the elves have much to do with these days.'

'Some sort of stealth tech?' I asked. The hairs on the back of my neck were all standing up.

'Maybe,' the mage said, but he didn't sound convinced. Finally, he shrugged and turned to look at the rest of us. 'We have to keep moving, we're vulnerable out here, especially with the incredible disappearing elf on the loose,' he said, and beckoned for us to follow. 'We need some rest, though. We'll raid some of the stores along the street and then hole up in a hotel while we regroup.'

Soon we were once again moving as a group, and I found the previous paranoia inching along the edge of my scalp. So many windows. Each building was identical to the last, just with different signs, and all of them with hundreds of windows. And the silence. Even the wind seemed to have vanished.

'I've seen this horror movie,' Nox whispered. Ceile looked over at him questioningly, but the big 'wolf just waved her off.

Our first stop was a grocery store, and I shook my head as we cautiously stepped through its doors. The shop was fully stocked, but there was no one at the till and no one wandering the aisles.

Nox growled softly. There was fresh cut meat and other perishables among the displays. 'This was done today,' he said, looking suspiciously around the elfless store. Tentatively, he reached out and skewered a cooked bird wing from a stand, sniffed his prize, and then dropped it into his mouth and ate it. 'It's clean. No poisons, fresh' the 'wolf said, shaking his head.

'Where is everyone?' Robin asked. There was a hint of fear on her voice.

Nobody had an answer, but it'd been a while since we'd eaten and with Nox's seal of approval, the party dug in. Having had our fill, we loaded up our bags with food and water and returned to the street. The door to the grocery store slid silently shut behind us.

The hotel was next up. Only a few blocks up the street from the grocery store, we came to a stop in front of a set of wide glass doors. An empty baggage cart blocked the sidewalk, as though someone had been wheeling it out to a waiting car and then vanished into thin air.

'Wait here, Ceile and I will have a look,' Nox growled quietly, skidding the cart out of the way and then following Ceile into the lobby. The doors slid open and closed with just a whisper.

I got the impression that even with all the elves here, Woodsholme would have been a very quiet city.

A few moments later, Ceile returned and waved us inside. 'It is just as empty in here as everywhere else. All the rooms' doors are unlocked, at least on the ground level. The panels behind the counter are working but have no records at all,' she said, shaking her head. As we followed her in, she continued, 'There is also a clothes dispensary here. Nox may have trouble finding something large enough, but the rest of us should be able to get clean outfits.'

The lobby was pretty small, but given the elves' love of efficiency and minimalism, that wasn't surprising. Much like the exterior of the building, the inside was a clean mix of concrete and glass. 'Dispensary? That sounds oddly vending machine like,' I said, looking around as we walked.

Ceile's face cracked into a big smile. 'It is exactly that. There is a holographic fitting room that you stand in and select items to view projected on yourself. It is fascinating.'

Robin frowned, and asked, 'Doesn't that mean we'll need some money? I haven't seen anyone's wallet kicking around.'

Ceile laughed, 'Money?' she asked. There was a thunderous crash from just down the hall. 'I believe Nox planned to just tear the unit open,' she said in amusement.

Sure enough, another set of doors beyond the lobby led to another room that I imagine had at one point been pristine but was now buried under an avalanche of clothing. Clothing that was still erupting from a demolished unit on the far wall. In the middle of the chaos was Nox, who was swatting angrily at the projectiles.

'I can't stop the stupid thing,' he snarled, in time to catch a pair of pants in the teeth. I heard Weezab burst into laughter behind me.

54

Everyone else laughed. As if on cue, the machine made a low-pitched groan and rattled to a halt. 'Alright, everybody grab what you can find that fits. Quickly! The White Sun is setting, and I want to get the map and get out of here before nightfall,' Bill said, already searching through the pile. 'Once we've got some clothes, we'll pair up and hit a room to get cleaned up.'

As most of the clothing was made of simple white fabric, it was a matter of finding something that fit. Most of us were close enough to elf shapes and sizes to find something, but finding an outfit that worked for Weezab, Nox, or even Robin, who was curvier and shorter than most elven adults, and Bill, who was just shorter, was going to be difficult.

All of the items were labelled, but the only one who understood the strange alphanumeric sizes was Ceile. While she could provide a rough conversion to the City's standardized sizes, it was a slow process as we tried to sort the mess into rough piles.

A few minutes later, almost everyone had found an outfit. Bill looked around, then nodded. 'Alright, group up. Splitting entirely up would be stupid, so this way we can maximize shower efficiency without leaving anyone alone,' the wizard said, winking. 'Ceile, Kor, Robin, suite 1. Nox, you're with me. Suite 2. Martin and Weezab, suite 3. Don't argue, Martin, the kobold probably doesn't know how plumbing works, and he likes you,' he said, then waved us into the hall. 'Go. Quick. I don't like this city and I'm liking it less every second we're in it,' he finished, gesturing for Nox to follow.

'I win!' Weezab yelped, leaping in the air in front of me with his arms raised to the air. I smirked at him. The little fellow's haul seemed to be a selection of completely random items.

Just as Ceile had said, suite 3's door was unlocked. I put a hand on the odd knob, which lit up softly and then the door slid open. The kobold bounced into the room, throwing his clothes on the floor and then darting around to look at everything. By the time he was jumping on the bed, I couldn't help but laugh.

'Alright, my friend. Hang out, I'm going to get cleaned up and then I'll show you how it works,' I told him. He gave me a big scaly grin before returning to trying to touch the light above the mattress. I shook my head, dumped my new clothes in the corner, and then went into the bathroom, chased by the strange ticking noise the bed was making with each bounce.

I shut the door just far enough to give me some privacy and stripped out of my beat up clothing. It felt good just having them off of my body, though now I was acutely aware of all the grease and grime on it. I stepped gingerly into the shower, and paused. Maybe I was going to need someone to show me how the plumbing worked, as the familiar taps and shower head were gone.

I fumbled with the strange bumps in the shower wall that had taken their place, and jumped in shock when I managed to activate the cold water, causing freezing rain to pour from the ceiling. Huddling in the one corner of the shower that wasn't getting rained on, I slowly got the hot water up until it was tolerable.

Now it was glorious. The elven shower appeared to have a large number of outlets on the ceiling, and using the knobs I could control how many were active and even what pattern the rain would fall in. Much like every hotel I'd ever been in, this bathroom had soaps and shampoos and I took advantage of them.

Over the sound of the shower, I could hear the tick of the bed and the kobold yelp, 'hey hey hey hey hey,' as the little creature bounced.

I laughed. I knew I had to be quick, but it was hard to want to give up the luxury of hot water after so long. Finally, I sighed and stepped out, grabbing a towel and began drying myself off. A look in the mirror made me a bit sad, seeing how white my hair and beard had gone, how faded my blue eyes were, the wrinkles and lines across my pale skin. I felt better than I had in years, but I looked worse than ever.

The other room had gone quiet, and I chuckled as I brushed my teeth with some hotel-provided toothpaste and my finger. The kobold had finally gotten bored. I wonder what trouble he'd be getting into while he waited.

I wrapped myself in my towel and slid the door open with my foot. 'Alright, Weezab. How about I show you-' I started to say before my words caught in my throat.

Weezab was gone. As was his pile of clothes. The bed looked like it had just been made.

'Weezab?' I asked quietly, as I inched around the corner to collect my own clothes. I reached out and drew nether to me, shaping forms of detection, looking for signs that something was wrong or magic being used nearby. I silently cursed my poor abilities with such spells.

I threw my clothes on as I listened for any sign of the kobold or the others, but I might as well have been deaf. The city was just as silent as it had been before we came into the hotel. I grabbed my bag, packed some of the hotel toiletries, and then slid the room door open.

And stepped out onto a sidewalk. To the north, I could see the Blue Sun rising over the mountains. To the south, the White Sun sinking beneath the forest. I looked around in apprehension, putting my arms out into the bubbling mire around me, and drank of the blood of the Blue. Nether dripped and oozed around my hands as I searched the desolation for signs of my friends, with the growing suspicion that I probably wouldn't find any.

Aside from the fact that my hotel room now opened up onto the sidewalk, it now also bordered on the outside of an entirely different building on an entirely different street. The pavement was just as empty as the one we'd been on, but now there were only four lanes, no median, and many areas for pedestrians to cross to the other side.

I couldn't see the walls that ringed the city. The street vanished into the distance at either end. I spun around, searching for one of the street signs that stretched down each corner of each building. When I found the nearest, I shook my head in disbelief.

I was in a completely different area of the city.

55

If I'd figured out my elven street numbering properly, I was now deep in the southeast quadrant of the city, twenty blocks east and nine south of the hotel. With each block a little under a kilometre long, I was easily twenty klicks from where I'd started.

I snarled a curse, but pushed down the urge to start carving a straight line to the center of the city. As much as I'd like to just start dropping buildings, something was at work here, something powerful, and I didn't want to start waking anything up. Not until I knew where my friends were, anyway.

Setting off at a light jog, I crossed the still deserted street and then headed up the block. I again marvelled at how uniform every building was, other than the occasional difference in height. They were all long and tall and white and covered with windows. There were no alleys, each one took up the entire block. If it hadn't been for the street signs at each intersection, I might have thought I was caught in some loop, running down the same block over and over.

I scanned around for trouble, but my eyes kept getting drawn up to those damn windows. If there was anything in these buildings, like our disappearing elf, they could follow me through the entire city and I'd never know. Then I smiled darkly. There could be thousands in each of these buildings, and I'd never know.

I wondered about where I should go. Would the others try and get back to the hotel, or would they head for the Vernal Equinox building? I was leaning toward the latter. There was no telling where they'd ended up, and if some of them had been dumped on the north end of the city, they'd be far closer to there than to where we'd started off.

So long as they were moved across the city and not just killed.

Shaking my head, I put that thought away. I couldn't start thinking about that. I had to assume the party was still here somewhere. I had to focus on keeping moving. I had a long way to go.

I passed grocery stores and electronic stores and clothing stores, all with the same exterior but slightly different signage. I ran past a hotel that was identical to the first, just with a different name. The deja vu was almost stifling, and between that and the oppressive silence, I felt like I hadn't moved in hours.

Martin.

I almost fell to the ground when he spoke. I had only heard his voice briefly in days, and that had been his brief and erratic warning. 'Where have you been?' I snarled, massaging my temples as I leaned against a column. 'And are you alright? Do you know what's going on here?'

Listen, we don't have much time. Keep moving. We can talk as you do.

Looking around quickly, I straightened up and started jogging again. 'Look, you've been gone for days, and that's never happened before. And then you come back with some vague message about the city. Please tell me you've got some answers,' I said, glad to have him back and glad to break the silence. I'd be talking to myself to bystanders, but then, there weren't any of those, now were there?

The kobold's healing. I don't completely understand why, but I was pulled far below and couldn't get free.

He sounded frustrated. 'What do you mean, you couldn't get free?' I said, shaking my head.

Martin, there's someone else in here with us. I don't know who it is. I'm not sure if it was keeping me locked down there, but I could feel it circling above. Like a shark!

That sounded familiar. I frowned, and said, 'Yeah, I met him. Or her. It was strange. I don't know who it is either, and it was more than a little weird hearing someone in my head who wasn't you.'

I don't feel it now, but we've got more important things to worry about right now.

I jumped off the curb and out into the street. The Sun's light blasting along the pavement made the air dance, and it was difficult to breathe as I crossed the roadway. 'I don't know, potentially having three of us juggling this body is a little concerning, but what else are you talking about?' I asked, getting up on the curb and into the relief of the building's shadow.

This city. I don't know what's wrong with it, but I know it's a trap and we have to get out of here. Now.

I shook my head and frowned, again. 'We can't leave. Bill's got something here that we absolutely need to get first. If we don't, we can't finish the journey. If we don't finish the journey, we die. Remember that part?' I asked, gloomily. Then I thought for a second, and asked, 'How do you know it's a trap? How do you always know these things?'

The Other was quiet for a moment, and I started to wonder if he had decided to retreat into the depths again. But then I felt his presence not far below, floating quietly.

Am I you, Martin? Are we one person, split into two personalities after the accident that neither of us remembers? What if we go into that machine and our body comes out but we don't?

There was fear in his voice, and that rattled me. I'd never heard him afraid before. It was disconcerting.

What if the real us is whoever is floating around down there with us?

'Look,' I said, trying to sound more sure than I was, 'we don't know who it is, but I don't get the feeling that it belongs in here,' tapping my head. 'As awful as you are, as dangerous and erratic as you are, you do. You were there when I woke up in the hospital, and you've been there for all two-hundred and two years since.'

I smiled, sadly. 'I don't know what's going to happen when we step out of the chamber, but I know we don't have a choice. Our body is getting stronger, I assume from whatever source it is that you mentioned, but we're still on track to die in the next few weeks. I think we have to hope that we'll come out of there with our personalities intact, because worrying about the opposite isn't going to help.'

The Other was quiet again, and I took the chance to pull a bottle of water from my bag and take a swig. Sweat was pretty much pouring down my head, and I was a bit sad that only managed to be shower fresh for such a short time.

I'm not good with hope. I'd always planned to kill us both one day.

I had to laugh at that. He said it in such a nonchalant way.

I turned the corner when I reached the next intersection, cutting diagonally across the street. 'Alright, I need you to tell me why you seem to know so much more about some things than I do. How do you know this is a trap? How do you know about the boost? About the dragons?' I asked, looking over my shoulder into traffic by habit.

I'm sorry, Martin, but you'll have to wait for those answers. Be careful.

I was about to get angry with him, but as I swung back to look where I was going, I saw a figure standing in the middle of the street not twenty metres away.

It was the strange elf from earlier.

I stumbled to a stop, and I shielded my eyes with a hand so I could get a better look at him. He certainly looked like an elf, but something was out of place. He was tall, but very lean, and paler than Vrarrs Kor. He was clothed in simple white clothes similar to mine, though he wasn't wearing shoes and had an unfamiliar short black cap on his head.

For a long moment, we stared at each other across the hot pavement. The Other's warning played through my mind, then I set off toward him.

The strange elf's face was almost skeletal, and he looked sad. As I neared, he cocked his head very slowly to the side. His eyes, which I originally had believed were emerald like Ceile's, actually seemed to be shifting colours.

I stopped once I was a handful of metres from him. I didn't start drawing nether quite yet, I wanted to surprise him if it looked like he was going to get angry. If he was an arcanist, he'd know the instant I started gathering energy.

We stood in silence for another long while, the elf kept his head cocked the whole time. He was almost perfectly still. He didn't even seem to breathe.

Finally, I said, 'I don't think you're from around here, are you, friend.'

The elf's mouth split into a massive smile, showing rows of very white perfect teeth. He never righted his head.

'I am Scayn. This city is mine. I will not let it go,' he said, and his strange, hissing voice seemed to come from every direction.

56

'You'll understand if I don't shake your hand,' I said, smiling slightly. 'And I appreciate peace and quiet, but I think you've taken it to extremes, friend.'

Scayn's mouth was still open, as though he had frozen in mid-sentence. Slowly, the elf returned his head to an upright position, and I heard quiet cracking noises as he did.

'It was too loud here. I made it quiet. Then people came and made it loud again. So I made them quiet, too,' he said, the words falling out in a jumble as he tried to speak without moving his mouth.

I looked up and around the area, in case he had others with him. 'If it was loud here, why did you come?' I asked.

The elf laughed, very loudly, and again the sound echoed wildly around the street. 'Built their home atop my head, now they're gone, now they're dead,' he sang, twisting his head awkwardly with each syllable. When he finally fell silent, his head was looking north, away from me. I cringed, thinking about what kind of torture his neck was going through.

'Party in the middle of the city. You should come. Other guests will be there. Varied varieties available at today's. I think you will enjoy it,' the elf babbled excitedly, his voice slightly muffled. Then, with a sickening crunch, his body spun on its feet, bringing his head around to face me once more.

'Big building right in the middle. Can't miss it. I am Scayn. Come visit me, come visit the others,' the elf said, giving me another wide smile. Then his eyes twitched, and he slowly winked as though he wasn't really sure how to. In a friendly voice, he finished, 'The city is mine. I will not let you go.'

Then he started running north, gaining speed until he was just a blur, before making an abrupt left turn a few blocks up and vanishing around the corner.

His head faced me the whole way.

Seems like a nice fellow. I'll bet his parties are spectacular.

I smirked. 'I'll bet. Well, we have to go. If the others are alive, then either Scayn has them or they'll be headed that way. I have no idea what he is, but if he had something to do with the elves' disappearance, then you and I are going to be the only ones that can do something about him,' I said as I started jogging again, following my original route and not the path taken by the bizarre elf.

So what's our plan, then? You know, if this thing killed all the elves through some sort of disease or something, we're already dead. Did I miss the meeting where that was brought up?

'Ceile would have said something. And the plan is to find the others, pick up what we came here for, and then get out. No problem,' I said. The Other chuckled.

And if you can't find them? If they're already dead?

I drew nether to me and shaped forms of light and lightness and sent purple spheres dancing around my hands. 'Then I start taking down the city building by building until there's nothing left.'

I love it when you get homicidal. Feels good, doesn't it? Power.

I sneered and gave him a push that sent him spinning slowly into the depths. He laughed the whole way.

He was right, though. Before my health had started to fade decades ago, I was the strongest archon working with the Department of Enforcement. The dwarves of the krekts below the City had feared me. Even my own people were afraid of what I could do.

I realized that I missed that. Being feared.

I was a little surprised with that epiphany. Maybe my dwindling power had tricked me into some level of humility, because it was a bit of a shock to realize just how much being normal - or as normal as a human with two pilots could be - sucked, to borrow one of Nox's favourite words. To realize just how much I wanted to reach my arms out into that rotting mire of decay, that ocean of the blood of Blue and let it pour into me like some waterfall of filth.

To realize just how much I wanted to use that river of nether to put my arms out and shatter every window to the left and right of me, and to keep blowing them out as I walked. To let the arcane energy whip and tear around me, every stride shredding the pavement at my feet, every step turning the air around me dark and angry. To walk surrounded by fury and rage and death.

Now you're talking.

I shook my head violently, though I didn't try and send him away again. Where had that come from? That wasn't like me at all. What was going on?

Caught up in my thoughts, I almost didn't register that there was someone in the middle of the street ahead, and it was limping toward me.

I slid to a stop, glad that I already had some nether to play with. The newcomer wasn't wearing any clothing, nothing but metal flesh and hydraulics and circuits. Sparks seemed to be shooting from one of its legs with each step, and one of its arms was bound in a make-shift sling.

'Holy crap,' I whispered as it neared.

It was made in the image of a dwarf, and it waved at me as it stumbled forward.

'Hello, Martin,' Petrel said, his voice electronic and full of static.

57

Petrel stumbled and fell to the ground, and I ran to him. Looking over the damage, I shook my head. It seemed pretty bad, but I wasn't an expert with cybernetics, especially not dwarven tech. Robin could probably patch him up, if I could get the steel dwarf to her.

'I figured you were dead. How did you survive the dragon?' I asked. I wondered if I could even support enough of his weight to help him move.

The dwarf slowly shook his head. 'I had a chute, which would have been great, except the damn dragon decided to get cute and jammed me through one of the Flag's engines,' he said. A burst of noise through his voice box made him put his free hand to his head. 'Fortunately, the blades were already damaged, so instead of taking my head off, they just crunched up around me. I wasn't badly hurt, but the bigger problem was that I was trapped on the ship.'

Then he reached up and caught my shoulder, pulling me toward him as he looked up at the buildings around us. 'Martin, I imagine you've noticed that the elves are all gone. But there's something else here. I haven't seen it up close, it just lurks around, watching, and then vanishes. There's something about it. I don't know, it feels magical but that's not exactly my area of expertise,' he whispered.

I nodded. 'Yeah, I just got to talk to him not twenty minutes ago. Calls himself Scayn, and, yeah, he's a real creepy guy,' I said, paranoia suddenly suggesting I also search the area. 'Look, we have to keep moving. Something big is going to happen in the middle of the city, and the thing Bill came here to get is not far from there. I don't know what Scayn is or what he has planned, but I'm thinking the quicker we get out of here, the better.'

Looking him over again, I said, 'Can you walk? I'm not sure how much help I can be, you're, no offence, probably pretty hefty.'

Petrel chuckled, which sounded awful in his damaged voice. 'I can walk, and probably better you not try and hold me up. I'd probably crush you if I fell.' With a metallic shriek, the steel dwarf braced himself and then slowly got to his feet. Looking around unsteadily, he said, 'I don't suppose you've seen any cars? When I got to the city and realized it was empty, I'd hoped to just take a vehicle out looking for you, but nothing.'

I frowned, then realized that I hadn't seen any cars since I'd stepped out of my hotel room. 'There were a ton of them when we first got here, we even crashed one of them when we almost ran over an elven girl, but I haven't seen any at all since the party got separated.' The look on Petrel's face shifted slightly from neutral to curious, and I chuckled. 'We've been busy since we got here. C'mon,

I want to hear what happened to you while we walk, then I can give you a rundown of what trouble we've been getting into,' I said, turning and gesturing in the direction I was headed.

'I was lucky. When the airship hit the ground, my engine tore free of the hull and slammed into the forest. Threw me pretty far when it did, tried to cut my arm off,' the dwarf said, pointing at the sling and some nasty gouging and scorch marks on the arm within. 'I have some ability to self-heal, but it's slow and can't regenerate some materials. Plus, I have to be asleep for it to do its work. So by the time I got myself in good enough shape to travel, you'd all left the crash site,' he continued as he turned to walk next to me down the street.

I looked over at him, and said, 'You really must have been thrown far if Robin and Ceile didn't find you. They were all over that crater, looking for salvage.'

The steel dwarf shrugged. 'I had to get under cover. While I produce almost no signature or noise while I'm asleep, I didn't want to risk having some animal come across me. Like a gnoll. Those things will steal whatever they can get their hands on,' he said, his words interspersed with bursts of quiet static.

Remembering the gnolls in the clearing, I nodded. I didn't imagine they left much of anything behind in their wake, especially not something as shiny as Petrel.

'Once I found the camp and none of you, I had to decide what to do next. Sadly, I have no ability to track distant targets, so attempting to follow you would have been foolish. Leaving me with attempting to trek across the wilderness to Woodsholme. I had a rough heading but no idea how far I had to go, and I was starting to believe I might never catch you,' the dwarf said, trudging mechanically along beside me.

'We'd still be walking, and for a long time, but we came across an old transport out there in the wood, and we were able to take it straight here. Did you find one as well?' I asked.

Petrel looked cagey, and waved me off. 'I'm not sure you'd believe me. Suffice it to say that I found transportation of my own,' he said in an odd tone. I gave him a questioning look, but he just shook his head, and said, 'Another time, maybe. Suffice it to say I arrived at the city sometime after you.'

The dwarf staggered, and I reflexively reached to help. He caught himself before I could, and hissed, 'No. Do not try and help me.' I pulled back and nodded at him.

We walked in silence for a while, before the dwarf once again started speaking. 'Listen, Martin. I have several enhancements, including a basic scan array. I am able to see various things with it, including a simple life form display. When I first arrived, I could see you all clustered in a single point, moving northward toward the center of the city,' he said. He turned to look at me out of the corner of his eye, and continued, 'I started to follow you, but you were some distance away. When you all stopped in a building, I thought you had stopped to rest.'

'But then you vanished. Where once there'd been life signs, there were none. I thought you'd all been killed, at least until I saw you all pop up in different spots. Yours was the closest, so I headed for you,' the dwarf said. Then he shivered. 'That's when I started seeing that strange elf. Scayn, you said.'

'You must have arrived at the south platform, just like us. But you said there were no cars? There were dozens when we arrived,' I said, abruptly.

Petrel looked at me, and said, 'I'm not sure what's going, but since I've been here, the streets and parking areas have been as empty and barren as the stores are.' Then he pointed at the bottle of water in my hand. 'Where did you find that, Martin?' he asked, suspiciously.

'In a grocery store after we crashed the car trying to avoid turning Scayn into jam. A store just like that one,' I said, pointing at the doors just off to my right. And then slammed to a stop to stare incredulously in the windows.

Leaving Petrel behind, I darted along the street, looking into each store, finding them all completely empty. Shelves, displays, counters, fridges, they were all barren. I looked at my water bottle, wondering if it wasn't real.

I walked slowly back to Petrel, who was slowly stomping his way toward me. 'What is going on? Were the stores full earlier like you said the streets were?' he asked as I got close.

I shook my head. 'Completely full. I don't know if the supplies we got from the stores were real and removed, or if they weren't real and just vanished. This city is messing with us,' I said, rummaging through my pack. The food I'd scavenged earlier was still there.

'What do we do?' the steel dwarf asked, staring suspiciously into the empty store.

I shook my head. 'We keep going,' I said after a long moment, dumping the food out of my pack and then continuing on down the sidewalk.

58

We walked for a while in silence, each of us lost in our thoughts. I had to wonder if Petrel thought I was crazy. I had to wonder if Petrel was real.

His story wasn't exactly air tight, especially the part where he wouldn't say how he managed to make it from the crash site to Woodsholme in such little time. And how did I know he actually could scan for life like he said? He was certainly more talkative than the dwarf I'd known back on the airship.

Maybe he had just been shy. Or maybe Scayn had made a poor copy of him.

The Blue Sun had sailed past overhead when we came around a corner and found ourselves on Zero Street. I'd purposefully overshot the hotel, preferring to get closer to the middle of the city before hitting the central road.

'That's quite the building,' Petrel said, his words bathed in static. As suspicious as I was about him, I had to agree.

What I'd thought was a mountain from further down the street was actually a monster of a building, roughly the shape of a sphere, which appeared to extend out in every direction for at least a block. Zero Street passed through it via two tunnels cut into its base. Much like the other buildings around me, it was covered in windows, looking out in every direction.

'Life signatures in that, another to the northwest that is headed toward the building, and one directly to the east that is headed that way as well,' Petrel said, then frowned. 'The reading for Scayn keeps appearing and reappearing around the outskirts of the city.'

'What's the sign in the building doing?' I asked, trying to keep my voice level.

'None of them are moving,' the steel dwarf said after a moment.

'Can you tell who's who?' I asked, looking over at him. I wanted to pick up the pace, but that would mean leaving the dwarf behind, and I wasn't certain that he was Scayn's toy yet.

Shaking his head, Petrel said, 'No, and to be fair I cannot tell you for sure that they're the party. Given the circumstances, it makes sense that they are, but we should prepare for the unlikely event that they aren't.'

Well, that's great news. I looked up at the sky, and said, 'We're pushing this pretty close. If Scayn is something ugly, I don't think we want to be fighting it in the dark, especially as we can't count on the street lights working. We didn't have any reason to go into that building, so we can probably assume they aren't in there to look around.'

Petrel nodded. 'Alright. I'm not sure how much use I'll be in a fight, but I can carry someone out if any of them are down. What about the map thing? Do you know where it is?' the steel dwarf asked. A burst of noise punctuated each question, and he swayed as he walked.

'In a building on the other side of that monster,' I said, gesturing at the central building ahead. 'Vernal Equinox. Bill didn't give us specific instructions, just said we'd all meet up in the lobby if we got separated.'

Petrel looked over at the median and then up at the windows above. 'Well, that's inconvenient. So we need Bill first,' he growled electronically.

I nodded. 'Yeah, we need Bill first. If he's in there, and he's down, you get him out and take him to the building. If we get pinned down, at least I can keep Scayn busy while you guys collect the map,' I said, and the steel dwarf nodded in agreement.

We kept walking, scanning the buildings around us for signs of life or trouble but finding, as usual, nothing. Soon, the central building loomed above us, and Petrel quietly said, 'This isn't going to be pretty.' Now it was my turn to nod in agreement.

The six lanes of Zero Street each abruptly descended into tunnels, and the sidewalks stretched up and over them, straightening into steps that ascended toward a large set of glass doors. A sign above them declared the building simply Woodsholme Central.

As we climbed the stairs, Petrel whispered, 'The signature to the northwest has stopped in an area that may be the building you were talking about. There are four signatures plus Scayn's strange one not far inside these doors. The final signature is to our northeast and closing quickly with the opposite end of the building from us.'

I sighed inside. I was going to have to decide, and quickly, if I was going to trust Petrel or not. Just to the side of our entrance, I dropped into a crouch, which the steel dwarf awkwardly emulated. I looked at him, and he looked steadily back.

Before I could say anything, I heard the Other stir in the depths, and suddenly I felt his presence floating just below the surface.

You have bigger fish to fry, and limited time to do so. Get moving.

I wanted to argue, but I knew he was right. I put a hand on Petrel's shoulder, and said, 'Follow me in, but not too close. If Bill isn't in there, get anyone who can't get out on their own and pull them out. Once everyone is free, head for the terminal. We've got a long walk, and I get the impression from Scayn that he doesn't let people leave.' When he nodded, I continued, 'I don't think we can risk trying to find the map without Bill. These buildings are huge, and if the city goes hostile. We'll get out, regroup, and then figure out how to go from there.'

I leaned in close. 'Listen, we picked up some hitchhikers along the way. A woman and a kobold. They're with us, help them if you can,' I said. The dwarf looked surprised, but nodded.

Then I ducked around the corner, slid the big glass door open, and darted inside.

Immediately beyond the doors was a long, wide, and incredibly tall corridor. It was bordered by buildings. Buildings the size of those outside towered over me, all glass and concrete. Elaborate signs pointed out floors and wings for various government agencies. The ceiling far above was composed entirely of windows, and the Blue Sun's light blazed in through its glass skin. Dust sparkled in the air above.

It was like being in a very weird snow globe.

Down the hall, I could make out five figures. Four of them were laid out on the floor in random directions. Nox, Weezab, Kor, and Robin. The fifth figure was Scayn.

The nether was already pulsing around my arms, the rotten mire boiling as I drained energy from it. If the strange elf put up a fight, I'd make him go away.

As I neared, Scayn jerked into a scarecrow position, and then sang, 'Come to join the party! That's excellent, that's great. We may feast tonight! It's been so long. This will be a tiny meal, but when one is famished, one does what one must.' With each word, he turned his head slightly, a giant smile on its face, until it had gone the whole way around his neck.

'What did you do to them, Scayn?' I asked, cringing and looking around at my companions arrayed on the floor. They all appeared awake, but only their eyes moved.

'They needed some quiet time. They were so loud! How would we enjoy the feast with all that racket?' Scayn giggled. His body was still in scarecrow form.

'Well, that's cute and all, but you're going to let them go now,' I said, shaping some forms of light and warning to spin wildly around my hands.

The smile vanished, and the strange elf dropped to a hunched stance, staring at me intently. 'Now, that's quite rude of you. Maybe I do not want to let them go. Maybe you cannot make me,' he snarled. And then went silent as Ceile put her pistol up against the back of his head.

'Well, unless there's more of you lurking around somewhere, either me or my friend will kill you if you don't let our companions go. And, trust me, you should let her shoot you in the back of the head, at least that will be quick,' I said nastily. I was only metres away now.

Scayn burst into laughter. 'Oh, this is funny. I'll need to keep both my eyes on you. But two eyes just won't do. You're too quick, too strong,' he said, amusedly. His eyes rolled in opposite directions. Ceile looked like she might pull the trigger just because.

'Two eyes just aren't enough. No, I think I shall introduce you to the Scayn. Its eyes are countless,' Scayn said, chuckling. His arms slowly rose toward the ceiling.

And then he vanished into thin air. Ceile nearly fell forward.

'That can't be good,' Nox hoarsely said as he shakily sat up.

59

'Where's Bill?' Robin groggily asked as the party left the building, headed south toward the terminal. 'And who the hell was that?' she said, waving weakly toward where Scayn had vanished. The dwarf leaned heavily on Ceile's arm. My friend had her pistol free and was scanning around us.

I shook my head, trying to keep pace with Weezab clinging to my leg. 'Petrel says Bill was near the building with the map. The wizard might have decided to get that and then meet up with us. If that's right, then that'll save us a lot of time,' I said, looking around for trouble. 'That elf thing was Scayn. He's a bit weird.'

Petrel, who was limping along next to me, suddenly hissed, 'Martin, the whole city just lit up. Life readings everywhere. Fluctuating, just like Scayn's was.' The steel dwarf was trying to watch everything at the same time. Oddly, he had taken Weezab and Vrarrs Kor's presence in stride.

'Yeah, I'm not going to tell anyone that this place's a good spot to vacation,' Nox growled. The big 'wolf was recovering quicker than the others, and I was surprised to find that he was helping keep Kor on her feet. The dragon had a neutral expression locked on her face. Well, that was a step up from total disdain. 'If that Scayn guy turned the whole population into zombies and now we have to fight them, I'm going home,' the werewolf said.

'Helllllp,' Weezab whined, quietly. He was looking up at all the windows, nervously. I patted him on the head.

'Just keep going. It's a long way to the wall from here, we'll have to-' I started to say, and then almost stopped in surprise.

The wall, which had been far enough in the distance that it could barely be seen in the dwindling light, was getting closer. Very quickly. I almost fell to my knees as my brain tried to tell me that we were actually moving toward the wall at high speed, and not the other way around. The party stumbled to a halt, just in time for the ground to start shaking.

'That can't be good,' Robin quietly said. 'Do we run?'

'Where would we run?' Ceile asked, standing tall despite the looming threat.

Only a handful of blocks away, we could see that the buildings along the street were being absorbed into the wall as it moved. I started gathering more nether, wondering if I could put enough of a dent in the wall to get past it.

And then it slammed to a halt, sending out a shock wave that knocked almost all of us to our feet and send webs of cracked windows down the block.

I looked around at everyone as we staggered to our feet, and said, 'Well, that's a little too convenient,' and then Bill darted past.

'Hello everyone! Petrel, you made it, excellent!' the wizard yelled. Then he waved a satchel over his head, and roared, 'Run, you idiots!' as he continued down the street, clutching his hat to his head.

There was a deep and loud groan that echoed through the city, and the ground shook again. I turned to look behind us, and this time did stop. 'Uh, holy crap,' I said. The group slowed to see what I was talking about, and looked up and up and up in shock.

Here was the Scayn.

The Central Building had lifted free of the ground, and was now looming over us on a strange, slender neck. It was like some weird insect's head. The building's doors slid open, revealing pointy teeth and writhing white tentacles. Saliva drooled from the gap. Each of the windows above suddenly blinked, and when each reopened, an insect eye stared down at us.

'Go go go!' I howled through the cacophony of the groans. As one, we all turned and started heading for the wall again.

Most everyone had recovered from their sedation, and were moving okay. Nox was down on all fours, running for all he was worth. I was shocked to see fear in his eyes. It was bizarre for him to leave us behind. Before this little adventure he would have stood and died to protect us. Vrarrs Kor was behind him, moving fast but looking like she was gliding along the ground. Elegant, even when running for her life.

The rest of us were in a rough cluster. Weezab could only move so quickly with his short legs, and he didn't look like he was happy about it. Ceile wouldn't leave my side, and Robin looked torn between staying and running. Both of the ladies had their pistols drawn, though I wondered what they could do to that thing.

Petrel was struggling and falling behind.

The Scayn's head moved above us, all of its thousand eyes following our every move. The groan just howled on and on as the surface of the building flexed and bent and melted to suit the creature's flesh.

Of course, I was so focused on what was going on above that I almost didn't see the massive white tentacle before it slammed down just behind Petrel, throwing the steel dwarf past me to collapse into a heap ahead. I spun to find a sliver of one of the buildings we were passing had come alive and was trying to crush us. Even as I watched, it lifted back into the air, looking like some abstract painting, all right angles but still arched and smooth.

Robin turned and opened fire on it, the dwarf woman howling with rage. Whatever slugs she had in that thing, they bit deep into concrete and blew big craters out of it. Ceile spun to join her, black lightning rounds peppering the tentacle even as it dropped toward them.

'No! Go, I've got it!' I was surprised to find myself yelling. Even before I'd stopped talking, I sent the nether spinning through shapes and folding into forms of explosive fury and roared out the words that made them reality.

A series of violent eruptions of violet energy burst on the tentacle's surface, sending it crashing into the building next to it with a violent roar of shattered glass and concrete and bent metal.

Ceile got up alongside Petrel and slowly lifted the dazed steel dwarf to his legs and started heading for the wall again. Robin moved alongside them, looking worried but unwilling to leave the two for safety. I moved along backward behind them, watching to make sure the tentacle didn't get back up.

Then the buildings next to us rose from the ground and arched over us, every one of their windows blinking and opening and staring down with those alien eyes. The edges of each building split away, forming new tentacles.

'Aw, c'mon!' I yelled as I reached out into the rot and decay and sickness of the oceans of nether and started pulling energy to me. A tinge of pain shot across my chest. I ignored it.

I spun the forms, falling easily back into a place that I excelled in, and howled into the noise. Stars of explosive acid shot out from my upraised hands, arced into the sky, and then rocketed into the tentacles around me. They erupted, sending fragments and debris into the eyes nearby, and what wasn't destroyed dissolved in the vicious acid I'd conjured for them. A new groan, slightly higher pitched, cut through the wave of sound already present.

New tentacles burst from the pavement, formed of tracks and tunnels. One was so close that the eruption of street threw me away, landing painfully on my side. I tried to get to my feet, but even as I did, a tower of metal and concrete dropped toward me. I began to shape forms of protection and shield, but I knew I wouldn't be fast enough.

I watched as my death approached, and wondered if anyone would be left to mourn me.

60

Before it could flatten me, the tentacle was struck with a giant beam of roaring flame that cut it in half and sent the pieces falling away, engulfed in fire.

I spun to find Weezab standing near me, scaly hands spinning and shaping, his mouth moving. I imagined him reaching into the raging inferno of fire aether and turning its energy into devastation. His face was twisted in anger and, in between words of power, savage laughter.

Getting to my feet, I nodded thanks to the kobold and then beckoned him to keep falling back. As we continued destroying tentacles, I had to marvel at the little fellow's strength. I knew he had power, as his healing abilities would have required it, but I had no idea that he could do this.

Pursued by the Central Building high above and the buildings to our sides and their thousands of eyes, I wondered if we would suddenly find ourselves crushed under the entire mass of a block's worth of stores. Did we have strength enough to fight back if the Scayn tried that?

I decided to find out. I sent my self deep into the ocean of nether, and started draining it. A river of decay roiled into my arms and I shaped it into forms of fury and reach, then yelled words of destruction. No build up this time, I loosed a beam of devastation from my palms, lancing out into the nearest building. Where it impacted, the surface caved in, sending shattered glass and crushed concrete and torn metal further and further in. I chanted, keeping the spell fresh, and swept the beam across the building's face, leaving a deep channel of ruin etched in it.

Smoking, and with all of its remaining eyes blinking furiously, the building collapsed to the ground, almost taking me down with its shock. I cackled, madly. Then my vision got far away and my chest tightened.

'No! Not yet!' I snarled. I was drowning in the nether pouring in from beyond and I was loving it. I didn't want to let go. I didn't ever want to let it go.

Weezab had seen what I'd done, and clearly liked the idea. When he was relatively clear of tentacles, he lifted a hand above his head and then chittered something. The earth shook again, and lava erupted from the neck of the building on his side of the road. Swirling his hand over his head, I watched as the lava spun and twisted, melting a hole through the bottom of the building until it finally keeled over with a huge crash.

Our victory was short-lived. Looking through the gaps left by the two dead buildings, I saw entire streets' worth of blocks rise from the ground and head for us, snaking along on their strange necks. My whole body ached, and my chest was tight. The Blue Sun was falling over the horizon.

We weren't going to win this.

'Weezab!' I roared. The kobold spared me a quick glance. 'Go! We can't take this thing!'

At first, I wondered if the little fellow would listen, but then he annihilated three tentacles with explosions that rocked the area and fled.

I was now very alone. Bill, Vrarrs Kor, and Nox were somewhere far behind. Ceile, Robin, and Petrel closer but gaining distance. Weezab closing on them. I faced an enemy that I couldn't do much more than delay, exhausted as I was.

As I sent blasts of energy out into the Scayn, watching concrete and steel come apart and explosions of glass burst across the street, I had a thought. Maybe I couldn't do this, but I knew someone that probably had a shot. If I could figure out how to get him here.

'Are you there?' I snarled as I watched the nearest tentacles smash their way toward me. I heard a dark laugh from somewhere at the back of my mind.

Yes.

'Can you kill this thing?' I asked, summoning a shield around me as the first tentacle slammed itself down. I wondered if it was surprised to find itself smashed to pieces rather than covered with Martin jelly.

Yes.

His voice was filled with anticipation, with longing. He floated at the very surface, and my body shook with his presence so near. We'd never done this before and I didn't know how it would end, but if I didn't try, everyone was going to die here and now.

I closed my eyes.

'Better hurry,' I said, and let go of everything.

61

I was surprised by the calm of it all. Usually when I breached the surface to throw Martin out of the pilot's chair, it was violent, agonizing. I'd be disoriented, trying to make sense of all of our body's senses as the information poured in in a different way than I did at the back of Martin's mind. Sometimes I was quick on the draw, and I could come out firing. Sometimes, not so much.

Martin always thought I had a death wish, that I wanted both me and him dead and gone, but the truth was much simpler. What I wanted was to see the world burn and its ashes scattered across the cosmos. He and I were just collateral damage.

This time, though, there's no transition. One instant I'm below, the next I'm above. I could hear the loud moan and groan as the Scayn grinded toward me and loomed above. I could feel the ground vibrating with the motion of the monster. I could see its shapes becoming more fluid and less angular as the night fell. And not only am I filled with wind aether, I am already drawing more. I'm a little confused as to how that happened, but I'm also a little busy to be thinking about it too much.

And I already knew that I was going to win. Because I knew something that the Scayn didn't.

There are two monsters in this city now.

Martin's shield was fading, but it didn't matter. I didn't need his parlour tricks. With a flick of my hand, I tore it to shreds and sent them flapping away like hundreds of purple rags. My other hand spun and whirled and a vortex of wind appeared at my center and grew to quickly surround me. I started using both hands, and the first tentacle that slammed down was simply deflected into the pavement next to me.

I didn't move an inch, but I didn't even feel the ground shake. Because I wasn't on the ground.

The vortex grew stronger and stronger, and I added a flicker of motion to the weaving. There's a sharp crack, and a burst of lighting tore its way through the whirlwind. Then another. And then another, and soon my personal storm was wreathed in electric fire. When the next tentacle crashed down on me, the wind caught it and then took it apart, piece by piece, the remains added to the wind.

My storm grew, and now it was a tornado, rising upward to touch a suddenly cloudy sky. I floated in its midst, right in the eye. I could barely see through the violence of it, but I didn't need to. The Scayn tried to reach me, but I started pulling its tentacles off and jamming them through its thousands of eyes, and when it finally tried to drop a building on me, it was too late. The edges of my vortex are already flashing along their faces, shredding the eyes and flesh and leaving only creaking towers of ruin.

I wondered if the monster could feel fear.

Now the storm reached out, but not toward the Scayn's head. No, I wanted it to die slowly. I floated forward until I hovered in front of its eye, and let it watch as I built even more storms. All over the city. Blocks on blocks of eyes and tentacles, shattered and torn in the wind. The monster tried to lunge at me, but I let it move only far enough to give it a better view of what I was doing.

I brought all of the tornadoes to me, and then I was the eye of a storm that almost covered the entire city. It's not enough. I reached out into the whirlwind of wind aether and pulled it into my arms, laughing.

I shaped and folded and shaped and folded the aether into forms of greater intensity and speed and the storm's walls writhed with lightning, its thunder louder than the Scayn's groans. The wind moved quicker and quicker. First small debris, then large, then tentacles, then shattered buildings began to lift free of the ground and floated upward. But not the head, no, the head would be last.

The Scayn watched me, and I imagined that if it wasn't afraid than it at least hated.

Far below, the city was washing away, the buildings and ruin that hadn't been carried up into the tornado are instead slowly annihilated in a blast of sand and small debris. In places, the city is completely gone, and I saw raw earth coming apart and joining the whirlwind of urban flotsam.

Then I saw a strange elf clinging to the base of the Scayn's head.

I laughed, and with barely an ounce of effort, I plucked him from his perch and brought him up to face me.

'What are you?' I asked. My storm had taken on a life of its own, and I barely needed to pay attention to keep it moving.

The elf smiled a huge smile of pristine teeth. 'I am ambassador to the elves! I take on their form to make the transition smoother. They never see what's coming that way,' he said, friendly. 'It was quite a party, friend. It's obvious we chose the wrong city.'

Then his eyes narrowed, and he said, 'There are others. They will come for you, now,' and winked at me.

'I certainly hope so. Goodbye to both of you,' I chuckled, and turned the elf into paste.

And now I revealed my masterpiece. From far above, I took hold of every piece of debris and formed a new vortex, one that brought its contents down like a drill. The Scayn never took its thousands of remaining eyes off me, even when I drove the drill down into its head, slowly at first, then with brutal force until every empty space in its skull is jammed with ruin.

I smiled, snapped my fingers, and then the vortex raging inside the Scayn's head pushed everything at once and the monster came apart in a billion pieces.

For fun, I jammed all that remained together repeatedly until there was nothing but dust in Woodsholme, the city that once belonged to the elves, then the Scayn, and now belonged to me.

I gently dropped to the ground, and made the storm vanish with a little push of aether. Surveying my damage, I nodded with pleasure. I couldn't remember the last time I got to erase a city. That was fun, I'd have to do it again sometime.

It occurred to me, as I stood alone in the devastation, that I hadn't heard Martin speak the entire time. And that I couldn't find him in the cage I usually stuck him in. In fact, the cage was completely gone, and there was just a cave full of deep water.

It also occurred to me, as I stood alone in the devastation, that I wasn't feeling very good. All of my limbs were shaking, and my chest was tight. I was having a lot of trouble breathing. Bursts of pain were rocketing up and down my spine. I was also on my knees and then on the ground and on my side. My vision was fading, and I tried to keep conscious but it was a losing battle.

The world went away, and then so did I.

?

'Do I really need to know how to use this?' I asked, waving the bolt pistol at Taylor, who smirked. 'My magic lessons are coming along very well, you know I make this rifle obsolete.'

'And if you get tired or hurt? What if you come up against a lunaron? Are you going to punch him to death?' my friend said, laughing. He shook his head, and continued, 'No, Edgar, you're going to need to have other weapons at your disposal. If your magic fails you - and make no mistake, it will fail you - you will need to be able to defend yourself or complete the mission without it.'

'Besides, I've seen you punch. You really, really need to know how to use a gun.'

I laughed and reloaded the firearm. 'Fair enough. Let's see if I can actually hit a target today,' I joked. Stepping into the firing box, I took the shooter's stance that Taylor had taught me, and then carefully emptied the clip at the foam target down the range.

I might have grazed its shoulder once.

'Well, how'd you do?' I heard Taylor ask from the benches behind me.

I drew energy to me, shaped it into a form that promptly blew the head off of the target, and then cleared my throat as bits and pieces of it floated down. 'Uh, great! I killed the target, one shot.' I said, trying to hide the smirk on my face.

Taylor snorted behind me. 'Sure you did. Well, just remember that the other Departments may call on you to do work for them, and if it looks like you aren't being used to the best of your abilities here, they might take you away,' he said, seriously. My smirk melted away, and my good cheer evaporated.

Noticing the gloom on my face, my friend got up and came over to clap me on the arm. 'Listen, I know this isn't exactly art class, but so long as you put the effort in this will be a good place for you to be. Research can't steal you away so long as I'm around, and I've put measures in place to make sure they can't if I go missing, too,' he said. Seeing the shocked look on my face, he laughed.

'Well, we're doing dangerous work, if you hadn't noticed. That first mission was a cakewalk, I'll be picking tougher ones as your training progresses. One or both of us might get killed, so there has to be some official orders in our files to make sure you and your family are taken care of. Anyway, as I don't think you're quite in the mindset for firearms today, let's go do some laps through the stealth courses and then you're free to head home for the rest of the day,' he said, holstering his pistol under his jacket.

Following suite, I returned the weapon to the training officer, who looked at me with veiled awe. Word travelled fast at base. Operations personnel were already a touch mythical among the far larger Department of Enforcement, and the rumour had already begun circulating that I was a solaron. That made me, just as Taylor had once said, a bit of a legend already.

'So, how's the family taking all this? I imagine it's been an awkward time,' Taylor gently said as I joined him.

'Well, the girls don't really understand, of course. They think I'll be doing secret agent work like they see on TV, so they think that's neat. I didn't go too much into the solaron stuff, I don't want them taking that particular information to class with them, at least not until they're older,' I said, remembering the two of them dancing around me excitedly, their daddy finally doing something fun.

Taylor watched me carefully. 'And James?'

I sighed, stretching my arms. 'He's always known what I am, but he'd never really thought about how it could affect our lives any more than I had. He's frustrated that we'll be moving into the base after we'd worked so hard to buy our place in the Haven. He's afraid that being so important to the Government means our lives are going to be under constant surveillance and even in danger,' I said, quietly. I pictured my husband with the stern look on his face as we talked about my news.

I shook my head. 'He's not a violent person, and he's particularly angry that I'm going to have to be. But he's a logical person, and he knows that we don't have a choice,' I said, then sighed again. 'Well, they have a choice, he could take the girls and leave. But he's not considering that an option, either.'

As Taylor and I headed for the exit, a man came in, dressed in a plain uniform with no Department insignia. He ran a hand through his hair and smiled at us as we approached. There was a mischievous air to him. He stuck his other hand out to shake mine, and then Taylor's.

'Ah, I wanted to introduce you two. Edgar, this is Peter. Peter, Edgar Lorn,' my friend said.

'What an excellent surprise! So glad to meet you, Edgar. Taylor will likely have us working together once you've had a chance to acclimatize yourself to Operations work,' the newcomer said, excitedly, then leaned in and conspiratorially said, 'But I've actually got a sense of humour, so you should enjoy my company over his.' Taylor smirked. I liked the man already. There was something familiar about him.

Peter followed us out the door, falling in beside me. The three of us talked about some recent intel, until a question came to mind for my new colleague.

'Tell me Peter, what magic affinity do you have?' I asked, curiously.

He laughed as though I'd just made a great joke, then reached out and squeezed my shoulder. 'Oh, my new friend. We are going to do great work together,' he said with a huge smile, and then he laughed even harder.

62

I floated, for what seemed like eternity, in oblivion. Darkness and silence. I felt pain, everything seemed to hurt. This seemed unfair to me. All my senses but pain were shut off? I decided to file a complaint.

'I'm sorry, Mr. Tundra,' Dr. Jacobs said from somewhere over my shoulder, 'but it appears that you are dead.'

'Well,' I replied, 'that sucks.'

I was surprised to find Jacobs here in oblivion with me, but when I turned to greet him, there was no one there. Well, if I was dead then I had best make the most of it. I settled back with my feet crossed, put my hands behind my head, and floated away.

'You were only dead for a few days, sir,' the emergency nurse told me. I felt her hand on my shoulder, and she gave it a friendly squeeze. 'No problem at all,' she said, and then I felt her hand slip away.

'Well,' I replied to thin air, 'that's a relief.'

Not that I expected to find anything there, but when I opened my eyes to look for the nurse, there was something else altogether sitting there.

Death. Horseman. Fourth of the Four and eldest.

He was ethereal and dark, shimmering like a mirage in the blackness of this place. Shrouded entirely in a thick, black cloak, with an abyss of darkness for a face. Behind him, reality seemed to hang in tatters, like he'd ripped his way through to get here. And though everything seemed to howl and rage around him - oblivion trying to mend the wound - the Horseman's cloak was still as stone.

If I'd thought that gazing into the void around me had been unsettling, attempting to look into Death's cowl left me cold with terror, and I felt every inch of my body rotting and fading to dust beneath the march of time.

As I cowered beneath the horrible emptiness of his cowl, the Horseman came forward until I was just metres from him. A single skeletal hand rose from his side, and I felt the creature's world-ending power rage inside his bones.

Then he was gone.

I spun frantically, trying to find him in the darkness, but there was nothing to see. Like the others, Death had vanished.

'I was never yours to have!' I screamed, surprised that I was screaming at all and not entirely sure why I'd screamed those words at all.

'But then you'd never hear the rest of it,' a voice said from behind me.

I twisted slowly around, and found Bill floating there. He smiled jovially, and gave me a theatrical bow. Clearing his throat - which still amused me as he still didn't have a throat - the wizard began to sing.

'A world born in the ruin of the last. Too closely linked to the sins of the past,' he said, his voice deep and clear. Then he went silent, and looked at me expectantly.

I frowned at him, and said, 'I know that part. You said it before.'

The wizard beamed excitedly. 'How wonderful, you were awake back in the camp!' he said, loudly. With a flourish, he raised his hands to the - well, sky, I suppose - and started to sing again, 'So Death went out to find a soul. So the next one would be whole.'

Then he went silent again, and this time, his smile was sad.

'There's more, isn't there?' I asked, 'I've heard it before, haven't I?'

Bill nodded, and said, 'You have. And you'll hear it again before the end comes.' And then he was gone, too.

'Aw, c'mon!' I shouted out into space. Floating as I was, it was hard to pitch a good fit. I did my best impression.

'This isn't like you at all,' another familiar voice said from behind me.

I spun slowly around, frowning, and stopped short. 'Martin,' I whispered in greeting.

Martin smiled and walked toward me until we were only a metre apart. 'I suppose we've never been formally introduced, have we?' he said, running a hand through his long grey hair. 'I'm Martin.' He stuck his other hand out, which I bemusedly shook. This was surreal.

'Hello Martin, I'm-' I started to say, then paused. 'I'm not sure I even have a name,' I said, frowning again. Martin chuckled gently.

'Have you ever chosen one?' he asked. When I looked askance at him, he shook his head and said, 'I don't imagine our mother thought to give us two names. Maybe we're both Martin.' He looked away for a moment, stroked his beard, and said, 'That would get confusing.'

'It's an awful name anyway. How about, hmm, Muz?' I said. That name sounded familiar, too, but I couldn't place it. Martin gave me a dubious look.

'Yeah, why don't you give it some more thought,' he said with a laugh.

I was surprised to find that light had started to invade my limbo, and Martin and I both turned to face it. 'Is that-' he said, voice full of awe. I nodded, very slowly.

As though we were floating amongst the stars themselves, we looked down on a massive sun that blazed with white light so pure that I wondered how my eyes could survive it. In the face of its brilliance, it would have been easy to overlook the far darker star that sailed through the cosmos with it, glowing with almost azure light, as though it consisted of blue embers.

Ancient siblings. Life and death. White and Blue.

A number of planets whirled and spun around them, and even as we looked down on the suns, a world barrelled past, blocking out everything before it continued on its path, a single moon caught in its grasp, orbiting impossibly fast.

'So. Are we dead, then?' I asked my companion without looking over.

'I don't know. You had control last, did you get us killed?' he said, dryly.

I struggled to remember what had happened before I'd awakened here, but it was murky. Trying to grasp those memories was like trying to hold onto a mrog tentacle. They just kept slipping away.

A brilliant light burst into existence out in the shadow, and suddenly a strong wind began to push me toward it. I reached out and caught Martin's arm to steady myself. We watched as moons, then planets, then even the suns swirled past us and into the light. My grip on my companion began to slip, and I looked over at him questioningly.

Martin smiled and shook his head. 'Looks like it's still your turn. I'll talk to you soon,' he said, and then I was lifted off my feet and thrown through the light.

63

For a long moment, I thought I'd fallen into the quite a bit brighter equivalent to the oblivion I had just left, as I couldn't see anything but pale greyness. Gradually, though, things start to resolve out of the mist, and soon I noticed that I was lying on my back.

With some effort, I sat up and blinked in confusion. I was on top of one of the walls that encircled Woodsholme.

I crawled to the edge of the wall and looked down into the remains. What little there were, anyway. The elves were meticulous and even obsessive in their planning. Every building had descended to almost the same level below ground. Now that there were no buildings - and there wasn't a single building intact - Woodsholme was a flat, white plain surrounded by walls and littered with the occasional small chunk of wreckage.

I'd been thorough.

I was surprised by how much staring down into that empty space echoed inside. Every last one of the elves that had live here were dead and gone, eaten by the Scayn or turned to dust in my storm. This place was hollow in every sense.

'That's a cheery thought,' I heard from beside me. I spun and almost reached out into the vortex of aether around me before I saw there was no one there. There was no one there, but I was surprised when I recognized the voice.

'Martin? What the hell is this?' I snarled, scanning around me. I heard a ghostly chuckle.

'Don't ask me, you're running the show. Something has definitely changed. Something to do with whatever was giving us the boost earlier?' he said, sounding thoughtful. 'Maybe you taking us to the edge of death again did something?' he asked, then he laughed again. 'Great work, by the way. Good thing I gave that to you to handle.'

He stopped short, and then he said, 'I gave you control. We've never done that before.'

I thought about that. 'Maybe. You're right that willingly giving me the pilot's chair was definitely different than when I'd take it. Our body was ready for me, rather than me having to fight it first,' I said, then paused. 'Martin, I can't feel you in my mind, where are you?' I asked, suspiciously.

He didn't respond for a long moment, then said, 'I think I'm still inside wherever we were earlier, but I can see and hear everything you can. That's really different from before.' Another pause, then he continued, 'Listen, do you remember the dream? Did you see it?'

Before I could answer him, I heard someone yell, 'Martin!' from nearby. I spun to find Ceile running toward me, a giant smile on her face.

'We'll talk later,' I whispered, then joked, 'Don't go far.' He laughed quietly.

Martin's friend charged up and lifted me into the air in a crushing hug. I patted her awkwardly on the back before she set me down and beamed at me. 'We thought you were dead. I am glad the Other was able to defeat that thing,' she said, gesturing down into the city, 'but we were afraid he might take it too far.'

I could see the others coming toward us across the wall. I looked at them, then turned back to Ceile, and chuckled, 'If I weren't a kinder, friendlier version of me, I might take offense to that, Ceile Angael.'

The woman frowned and stepped slowly away. 'You,' she whispered. 'You are still in control.'

I thought about that as the two of us stared at each other, and a wide smile slowly split my face. 'Yes,' I quietly said.

'Yes, I am.'

64

The party was a ragged bunch now. The nasty gash on Ceile's shoulder had reopened and torn further. I was surprised she could use the arm. There were cuts across her face and arms that looked like they might have been bad before someone had sent some healing her way. As it was, she was going to have some ugly scarring until she found a necromancer. Her new elven clothes were torn and filthy, probably worse than the ones she'd been wearing before. She walked close by, and kept sending me covert looks. Probably hoping each time to find Martin behind my eyes instead of me.

Nox was in the best shape of all of us, and it was probably because the 'wolf had inexplicably run off as fast as he could, leaving us all behind to die. As much as I'd disliked him, even I had to admit that was out of character. Sure, there was nothing he could have done but die if he'd stayed with us, but still. The outfit he'd managed to put together was intact and clean, though he had some cuts and bruises. The big 'wolf wasn't as close as Ceile, but he wasn't far, either. The looks he gave me were dark. Where Ceile disliked my presence in her best friend's mind, Nox hated me with a passion. His threat back in the Locus Wood was by no means idle.

I wasn't entirely alone. Weezab walked at my feet, but his usual amusing self was nowhere to be found. His outfit, formed mostly of elven children's clothing and my beat up old jacket, was ripped and shredded in a number of spots, and I could see his copper scales through them, which were mostly dulled and scuffed. He clutched his worn bag tightly in both of his hands, and twitched as we walked. I saw him cast a look of awe in my direction every few minutes.

Petrel walked just over my other shoulder, moving much better after Robin had had a chance to fix him up a bit. The damage to his left arm was still bad, and for the most part it hung limply at his side. He'd taken some time to try and clean himself up, but the steel dwarf was still covered in scorch and scratch marks. He didn't seem to care that Martin wasn't the one in charge, and we talked a bit about what had happened and where we were headed.

Walking with Ceile, Robin also didn't seem to be concerned with me. The two women talked as the party travelled through the forest to the west of Woodsholme. The dwarf wasn't much better off than Martin's friend was, and with her jacket so badly torn, you could make out a lot of her chest piece. Unlike Vrarrs Kor, though, Robin had put some effort into maintaining her modesty.

Speaking of the dragon, Kor walked next to Nox, which was about as weird a pairing as I could have imagined in the party. The big 'wolf seemed to have forgiven her, or at least put their battle aside, and now they were quietly talking. She didn't seem to have a scratch, though her clothes were mangled, and now, very revealing. I enjoyed the view, and when she caught me watching, Kor only gave me a slight smirk and went back to talking with Nox.

At the head of our party was Bill. He walked alone, following the information he'd found on the map. Interestingly, the elven map was an arm band that generated a holographic image that could be turned and manipulated, and showed map data for everything to the west of the elven city for hundreds of kilometres. My mind struggled to grasp the concept of that kind of tech. Sure, similar could be done through magic, but still. The elves were capable of some crazy stuff.

The wizard's hat was charred and torn, much like the head it was precariously perched on. His clothes were in better shape, probably because he'd run out ahead of everyone just like the werewolf had, and in that all-white outfit, he looked almost ghostly. If it hadn't been for the streaks of silver metal under his torn skin, anyway.

Petrel had given me a short version of what had happened to everyone else while I was busy tearing the city apart. Nox and Ceile had wanted to go back in to try and pull me out, but even they had to admit that going into that storm would have been suicidal. The whole group fled to the forest to wait it out. When the winds dissipated they returned to the wall, but couldn't find me. I'd somehow ended up on the west side of the city, so it had taken them some time to figure it out.

'Shall we talk now? No one seems to be talking to us,' Martin said. I frowned and massaged my temples. That was going to take some getting used to.

'Alright, where do we start?' I whispered beneath my breath. 'The instant we left the City, things have been different. I don't hate you as much, for one thing, and that's just strange.'

He laughed. 'I don't know about that, maybe you're just happy to be out of the box so often,' he said. 'You've been in control a lot more over the last week than you have in decades,' he continued, his voice serious.

'It's nice, sure. It's probably because we're both going to die in the next couple of weeks, I'm getting sentimental,' I said, quietly. I saw Nox prick his ears up at me, and I cursed. I have to be quieter.

Martin laughed again, then went silent. When he spoke again, his voice was troubled. 'Can you draw energy to you?' He asked, and there was worry in his words.

'Of course I can-' I started, reaching out into the cracks in reality for that tornado of aether, and then I fell silent.

It was gone. The winds were dead.

'That's what I thought. Well, my friend, we have a big problem, and I imagine you know what's causing it,' Martin said.

I nodded, and looked around carefully. 'There's a lunaron nearby. And close. How could that be? If something were tracking us in the woods, Nox would have picked it out by now. Or Ceile. And regardless, Ceile, Weezab, and Bill should have noticed that their magic was gone,' I whispered.

I barely heard Martin when he said, 'Unless the lunaron is one of them.'

I growled, and said, 'That can't be right. We've travelled with all of these people for days and been able to use magic. A lunaron doesn't get to turn its power on or off.'

'No, but if one of them had been replaced,' my companion whispered, trailing off.

I didn't respond. My mind was busy chewing through that thought. If one of them had been swapped out while I was occupied with destroying Woodsholme, then that could explain why the aether in the air around me had gone still, but it wouldn't explain why the other magic users in the group hadn't said anything.

But then I stopped short. No, there was a reason why all of this might be happening, and it made a lot of sense. I frowned and carefully looked each of them over.

I was the storm, and they were all afraid of me.

So they took the thunder and lightning away.

65

The Blue Sun was once again falling over the horizon when Bill had us stop to gather our bearings. With the map projecting onto the ground, we were all able to have a look at the coming terrain.

'The mountains to the south of us mark the eastern borders of Krekt Twelve. The artifact chamber is near its western,' the wizard said, spinning and zooming the image as he spoke. 'The caverns through which we'll enter the krekt lie almost directly above the vault. The map notes several entrances into the caverns, and has extensive layouts for the whole system,' he said, pointing at several triangles displayed along the mountain side.

'As exploring the entire set of caves would be time consuming, I've been working on several routes that take us into the deepest parts of the eastern cavern, and I think I've found two that should be fairly simple and a third that would be difficult but much better than any other option,' he continued. He looked very serious as he turned to look at each of us. 'I'm hoping that we don't have to use door number three, but it's passable as a last resort.'

The wizard stood, and the digital map vanished. 'Our next bit of this adventure has some complications. One is, of course, that we are over a hundred kilometres from the closest entrance into the caverns,' he said, then turned away from us and pointed out into the dwindling light and distance. 'The second is that.'

It was tough to see what he was pointing at. The Blue Sun's light wasn't nearly as strong as the White's, and it was gone over the edge of the world. I squinted my eyes and peered into the coming darkness.

'It's a mountain,' Nox growled. 'It stands out from the mountain range, though. It's a different colour.'

'Precisely, my furry friend! You all may have noticed that on the maps I had just shown you, that there was no such mountain,' Bill said with a flourish.

There was silence for a long moment as we all looked at the wizard in confusion. For his part, he stood tall, a mischievous smile on his face, his hands steepled at his chin.

'It's an aethon, isn't it.' I said after I'd thought about it. 'Somebody came out here and made themselves a mountain.'

'Almost, not-Martin! A dwarf, formerly of Krekt Thirteen. A renegade, who taught himself how to wield the power he'd been born with. Much like the elves, dwarves who pursue magic are exiled or killed, and in the end the renegade had to fight his way free of his home after he was discovered,' Bill said, clapping his hands and smiling. 'But this dwarf is no longer a mere aethon, my friends! No, he has become so immersed in his element that he is no longer a dwarf at all, having shed his flesh and bones for rock and stone.'

Robin interrupted him. 'You're talking about the Rook,' she snarled, coming forward to stand right in front of the wizard. 'Are you insane? You want us to go through its lands?'

Bill nodded, and leaned forward until he was almost nose to nose with her. 'I do, Robin. There is a reason these caverns have not been discovered or destroyed by the dwarves of Krekt Twelve. The elemental holds sway over that entire region, including our entrances,' he said, barely loudly enough for me to hear.

'How are we going to sneak past it? It'll know we're there as soon as we step onto its doorstep, and then it'll toy with us for days before killing us,' Robin said, an edge of fear in her voice.

The wizard burst into laughter, and said, 'Sneak past it? My dear Robin, that isn't our goal at all. No, I plan to ask for its assistance in return for some favour.'

'And if it doesn't need a favour?' the dwarf woman said, looking dubious.

Bill's face suddenly went dead serious, and he reared back until it seemed like he towered above us all. He pointed a finger at first Weezab, then me. 'If it will not help us, then we will let loose aggression and chaos and put our own aethons up against it.'

I wasn't entirely surprised to find out that the little kobold was an aethon, having seen some of what he could do back in Woodsholme against the Scayn. I didn't like the prospect of going up against a full-fledged earth elemental, but there probably wasn't much in this world that Weezab and I couldn't kill together.

'I win!' he giggled from next to my knee. I gave him a smile. It was mind boggling that something as simple as the little creature had somehow managed to not only survive but also to learn how to use his power. And to great effect! Especially as he was attuned to fire, which was by far the least forgiving of the elements.

'Wind isn't a whole lot better,' I heard Martin whisper. I smirked. Ceile gave me a suspicious look.

Bill, returned to looking like his battered self, put a hand on Robin's shoulder and nodded out at the rest of the party. 'Look, this wasn't ever going to be easy. We've encountered plenty of trouble already. The loss of the Red Flag. The desolation of Woodsholme. Both have cost us time and almost brought disaster down on our heads,' he said, dramatically. Throwing his other hand out, he continued, 'But we are nearing our goal! Once through the Rook's domain, a fairly short jaunt through the caverns, and then some breaking and entering on the outskirts of the krekt, we will arrive at the vault.'

He abruptly pointed at me, and the rings on that hand flared red. 'You will have the regeneration chamber. And your life renewed and restored!' He shouted. Then he pointed at the dwarves, and yelled, 'And you, your treasure and money for the rest of your life!' Then he looked at Vrarrs Kor and Weezab. 'Well, I'm not actually sure why you two are here, but I'm sure we can find something for you,' he said, waving dismissively.

'Now, let's set up camp and get some rest. We'll want to leave early tomorrow,' he finished, moving to start collecting some wood from the edge of the clearing.

Before he got far, I snarled, 'Which one of you is the lunaron?'

I might as well have announced that I was a gnome. Everyone looked confused.

'Aw, crap, that's not a good sign,' Martin said.

'Lunaron?' Ceile asked. 'What do you mean?'

Angrily, I glared at them all but a sickening sinking feeling wormed its way into my gut. 'Drop the act,' I snarled. 'Which one of you is it? You're so afraid of me that you'd cripple the greatest weapons this group has just to keep me caged?' I yelled, looking around at each of them. Turning back to Bill, I growled, 'And what happened to the original, then? Did they just head back to the City for cocktails?'

Now it wasn't confusion on their faces. 'You do not have your magic,' Ceile said, hesitantly, suspicion dawning on her face. Furious, I spun to face her, but before I could say anything, I felt the woman's healing magic flow over my body and I fell silent in shock.

Frozen, I saw concern and confusion, and relief, cross the group's faces as they realized what had happened. Ceile's spells took away some of my pain and fatigue, but there was no comfort in it. If a lunaron were nearby, her magic would be just as gone as my own.

To make matters worse, Weezab poked me in the knee and then summoned a candle's flame to his finger, the scaly creature gesturing encouragingly at the light. I stared into the tiny fire, watching its aether-born power flicker in the breeze.

'I cannot find any further injury,' Ceile said, quietly.

My mind raced. I looked down at my hands as I reached out, desperately searching for the vortex of wind aether that had always whirled and howled around me. Nothing. My connection to the Suns was gone.

'Curious,' Bill said. I looked up to find the man standing in front of me, a strange look on his face. 'Your little fireworks display back in Woodsholme might have put too much strain on your elderly body, my friend.' I frowned, but didn't respond. His tone suggested that he didn't think it was a bad thing. Finally, Bill shrugged and turned away.

'There's nothing we can do about it for now. Get some rest, perhaps you'll have your power back tomorrow.'

The others slowly turned away as well, and I tried to ignore the looks on their faces. Nox and Ceile both looked suspicious, and I wouldn't have been surprised to learn they both thought I was lying. The relief on Robin's face as the dwarf woman backed away didn't help things. Petrel and Kor's expressions were indecipherable.

I sat down heavily, and watched them all go about their tasks. I was irritated to find Weezab dragging his bed toward me, a big grin on his face. I sighed and lay down, not feeling particularly hungry, and listened to the little kobold noisily set up his nest of shredded bedding.

And just as I started to drift off, he leaned in very close and whispered, 'Don't trust Bill or the dwarves,' before subtly dropping my cellphone into my lap, flopping down with an exaggerated groan, and falling off to snoring sleep.

66

The next day was overcast and dreary, and we trudged through the forest in lightly falling rain. Our path, for what it was, had tightened considerably and now there wasn't room to spread out. I was sandwiched between Petrel and Vrarrs Kor, and Weezab walked along beside me. The little kobold looked miserable and wet, and he twitched as he held his tail in one hand and held his satchel tightly in the other.

Of course, now that I knew his simple exterior was an act, I had to figure out why. He had said not to trust Bill, Petrel, or Robin, but how did he know? And how many more dark warnings would I get before this adventure came to an end?

I hadn't had the opportunity to try and talk to the kobold alone, or have a look over my cellphone. The latter was for a more pragmatic reason, as I didn't exactly have a way to charge the stupid thing. I wasn't even sure it still had power, but something made me think Weezab wouldn't have given it back to me if it had become just a blunt, but fragile, object.

The Suns were still just as out of reach magically as they were physically. I felt blind. I kept unconsciously trying to draw aether to me, accustomed as I was to having the magic at my fingertips.

'This is unpleasant,' Martin whispered, 'but you have to stay focused. Nox and Ceile won't let anything happen to us, even if they don't particularly like you. Bill might be right, we weren't exactly in prime physical shape before you obliterated Woodsholme. You can't have burnt your magic out altogether. I've never heard of anyone managing that.'

I sighed. 'You're right, as much as I hate to say it,' I said, under my breath. I looked out into the woods and grimaced as I realized how hungry I was. 'Things were a lot simpler when you and I fought for control. Do you know how strange it is having to think about eating and drinking? If I'm in charge for much longer we might die of starvation,' I whispered. Petrel looked over his shoulder at me curiously. I gave him a slight smile and he shrugged and looked away.

'Well, don't do that,' Martin said with a chuckle. 'I don't want to die in here anymore than you do.'

I heard movement behind me, and then Nox was brushing past Kor to settle in just over my shoulder. I gave the big 'wolf a look, and was surprised to see concern on his wolfish face.

He studied me for a bit, and then said, 'So Martin's still in there? He can see and hear me?'

'Yes, but something's changed. We aren't separated in the same way. We're trying to figure it out,' I said, shaking my head.

He nodded, slowly. We walked on in silence for a while before the 'wolf spoke again. 'You're different. Maybe losing your magic will make you less of a wacko,' he said, though his tone was light rather than mocking.

I nearly stopped dead in my tracks. The werewolf almost sounded friendly.

Before I could respond, the path opened up into a clearing and Bill brought the party to a halt. 'This will be a good spot to rest up for a bit and have a chat about where we're going next,' the wizard said, beckoning for us to gather around. 'My friends! Much as we once faced with the trip to Woodsholme, our journey to the lands of the Rook will require many days. Though we will soon leave the Locus Wood behind in favour of the plains, the land is still rocky and uneven, and it will be slow going,' he said. Spinning to point a finger at me, he continued, 'And again, our elderly friend, despite his sudden youthful spirit, has only weeks left. His health is already on a sharp decline, though we've taken steps to steady that.'

I frowned. That sounded an awful lot like Bill admitting he was behind whatever was making Martin and I feel stronger.

'Fortunately, I have an equipment cache just beyond the edge of the forest, a cache that I've kept some party tricks in for decades. The particular piece that we are interested in is a portal generator. The exact mechanics of it are not easily explained and it's possible that you may not want to know just how it works, for your own sanity. What it does, my friends, is tear two holes in the fabric of reality and makes a bridge between them, and I'm hoping it can be used to cut a hundred kilometres off of our trip,' the engineer said.

I frowned. 'A portal generator? What are you talking about, Bill? There's no such animal,' I said.

'The elves don't even have that kind of tech, let alone us or the humans.' Robin quietly said in agreement.

'Portals, my friends! And you're correct, that tech is far above the engineers of this world. All but one, that is!' Bill said, throwing a finger into the air theatrically, a sly smile on his lips. Then he paused.

'Get on with it, wizard,' Nox snarled in irritation. 'If you're saying that you're the chosen one, I'm out of here.'

Bill suddenly snapped his fingers and then pointed at the 'wolf. 'You are partially correct, my fuzzy friend! I am indeed the maker of this device, and yes, it is indeed a portal generator. But I must admit I have misled you all, just a touch,' he said, grandiosely.

'You're a master wizard and a master engineer,' Nox said, incredulously.

'No, Nox. I'm not a magic user at all,' Bill said, his voice suddenly dead serious.

There was silence for a long moment, but then Bill suddenly burst into laughter and put a hand on my shoulder for support as he laughed. 'Oh ho, you should see your guys' faces. I wish I could make that reveal again just to have the repeat.' Wiping at his eyes, he straightened up and said, 'I say the truth, my friends! I am an arcanist, but one of the tortured few that can see the ocean around them but never touch it. Instead, I have learned the arts of engineering, and many of my greatest works can duplicate the effects of many spells. It is useful in my line of business to be believed one thing when you are truly another, and so I have fostered the belief that I have strength in the arcane.'

His gaze swept over the group. 'And yes, I am a great engineer. I have devoted my prodigious intellect toward designing and building machines that perform feats no other can match. The portal generator, my friends, is just such an animal, and it may be my finest work,' Bill said, throwing a hand in the air theatrically.

I frowned. 'Bill, if you have a functioning portal generator, why didn't we just use it to travel from the City directly to the caverns? Or to the vault?' I asked, shaking my head.

Bill suddenly looked cagey. 'Ah, well, there are some complications. I would not have chosen to use the device if we had other options, but time is short,' he said, and then looked into the sky. Turning back, he beckoned for us to follow. 'And indeed, so is the day. The Blue Sun will shortly take its leave, and we should be on our way.'

As we fell into line behind him, Bill continued explaining how the portal generator worked. 'A set of coordinates are selected, the machine warms up, and then the portal is opened. I won't bore you all with the technical stuff, but the main catch is that the user has to have already been to the destination, and left a marker device there for the generator to lock onto. As I did not have a device with me at the time, I was not able to leave one down in the vault,' the now-engineer said.

'Another catch is that the entire process is dreadfully unstable. Reality does not appreciate what the machine is doing to it, and therefore expends a large amount of energy trying to disrupt or destroy the portals. This generally causes bridge failure and other unpleasantries within ten minutes of portal generation,' he continued.

I raised an eyebrow at him. 'No return trips, then. Unless you leave someone behind to create a new one,' I said.

Bill shook his head, and said, 'Yet another catch is that once a set of coordinates has been used, it cannot be used again until reality has had a chance to heal. This can take anywhere from hours to days.'

I frowned. 'There are a lot of catches to this masterpiece of yours, Bill,' I said.

The engineer guffawed and then winked at me over his shoulder, 'This machine allows someone to cross the world in a matter of seconds, not-Martin. It is not perfect, but what it does is something that hasn't been seen on this world in millennia. When I have some spare time, I will refine the generator, and then think of what it can offer the nations of this continent,' he said, his voice hungry. 'Just think. Settlements thousands of kilometres away could communicate instantly. Resources could be shipped across the world with ease. Citizens could spend their down time in exotic locations whenever they wished,' he said, arms gesturing wildly.

'The gnomes could have rolled that bomb the elves dropped on them right back into their lap,' I said, sarcastically. Bill laughed even harder. Once he was quiet again, I asked, 'Alright, ignoring the terrible sales pitch you just gave us, why is the generator here? And why didn't we use it to get as close to the vault as possible?'

'Well, my misanthropic friend, I did mention that reality and the machine are not actually friends in any way. When it is active, the area around the generator is as unstable as the bridges. The Government would be less than thrilled to have my device inside the City limits, and I'm also not interested in letting the Department of Research get their hands on my work,' the engineer said.

'I don't know, Bill. The portals are only up for ten minutes, tops? What happens if you're in one when it collapses?' Robin said, nervously.

'I've added a safeguard of sorts by having it also build bridges to three other locations, so that losing one bridge simply dumps the user onto the next,' the engineer said, trailing off.

'That sounds foolproof,' I said with a smirk. 'So what happens if the bridge fails and there isn't one there to land on?'

Bill smiled sadly, and when he looked back at me this time he shrugged. 'Well, that's the last catch. If your points come unglued and there isn't another set to catch you, you fall into a place that I haven't figured out how to get to or get out of.'

'If you go in, you don't come out. Probably forever. I'm still working on that calculation.'

67

The Sun had almost set by the time the trees had diminished and then fallen away. The plains that ran from this edge of the Locus Wood to the West Barrier Mountains far to the west were rocky and hilly, and covered in waist-high grass for the entire length. At some point in the distant past, an attempt had been made to farm these lands, but all that remained of that valiant effort were some large piles of stone, some flattened sections, and the slowly decaying ghosts of equipment and buildings.

It was a particularly large example of rotting building that we were headed for, a ruin several hundred metres long and built into the side of a hill. The roof had collapsed along its entire length, and the wreckage jutted out from many of the walls. From a distance, it didn't look any different than the other ancient buildings, other than its size. As we neared, however, hints that something was out of place began to show up.

Bill took us right up to the building's side, and there in the midst of the desolation was an intact and reinforced door. The engineer put a single metal finger up against a flat portion on the frame, and we heard heavy locks disengage. With a flourish, Bill stepped slightly to the side as the door swung open of its own volition, and then stepped into the cold white light inside.

'A bit of camouflage and a bit of heavy security! I do not regularly come out to this workshop, but the generator, in the wrong hands, could cause terrible devastation. It's best that the number of people in the know about this place remain as low as possible,' he said as we filed in after him. Vrarrs Kor was last in, and I heard the door swing shut and the locks engage with a dull thump.

As we moved down the metal and cement passage way, I could feel a vibration in the floor, and a low and constant thrum. The portal generator, probably, and winding up.

After we had walked far enough that I was starting to wonder if we were going to come out the other side of the hill, the passage took a sharp turn and became a flight of stairs. Metal grating provided the flooring here, and looking down gave me an instant of vertigo as my eye sight sifted through the stairs and landings to the cement far below.

'I chose this location not only for its remoteness but also for its central location on our continent. Once I had completed my network of portal destinations, I'd be able to cross the world in a matter of seconds. Eventually I'd build another generator at each corner. It will be wonderful,' Bill excitedly said. 'Much of the raw materials I needed to build the machine was found on the plains, left behind by the failed settlers. The rest I brought in by airship. Not the Flag, obviously. She wasn't built to haul cargo.'

The thrum got louder and louder until we had to speak loudly to be heard over it. Finally, we arrived at the bottom of the stairs, met by a door identical to the one back at the entrance, which Bill popped open with an identical flourish.

And then we were introduced to the portal generator.

It was massive, alright. Taking up the entire cavernous room we stepped out into, the machine was all twisted cables and hoses wrapped around some sort of huge turbine connected to a hundred large boxy contraptions of some kind. The cables and such looked familiar, but the turbine didn't look like anything I'd ever seen. There was something very odd about it, and I felt a bit queasy every time I looked at it. If I paused to examine it for too long, I got chills. Cold sweat.

Something about that machine was very wrong.

Bill crossed the room to a control panel bolted haphazardly to the side of the generator, and his fingers immediately began darting across the keys. The display flashed from screen to screen quicker than I could follow, then the engineer turned to look at us over his shoulder.

'Excellent, it's still running! Well, my friends, tonight you will have a good meal, a hot shower, and a comfortable bed. This is our last glimpse of civilization until we return, so make the best of it. Tomorrow, I will tell you more about the portals and what is required of each of you to use them. Come, I will show you to the kitchen, showers, and bunks,' Bill said, gesturing theatrically. Beckoning us to follow, he continued along the chamber wall toward several doors.

I only half listened as the engineer gave us the tour of his strange workshop. While he talked, I searched the air around me invisibly for signs of aether. Frustratingly, I was still just as powerless as I had been since Woodsholme. I snarled something under my breath, which earned me some odd looks from Ceile and Robin.

'Maybe there's something else going on here,' Martin suggested. 'Usually if we overdo it, our physical health is affected, but you seem fine.'

'Well, it can't be a lunaron. What if it has something to do with how you gave me control?' I whispered, frowning out into space.

Martin was quiet for a moment, then he said, 'No, that doesn't feel right. Our connection is different, but if anything, your magic was stronger when you came out of the gate. Something else has changed. Could there be a nullifier around?'

I shook my head slightly. 'Even the dwarves haven't managed to make one small enough to hide yet, and definitely not accurate enough to just affect a single target. That'd take some serious engineering-' I trailed off, and slowly turned to look at Bill, a sneer slowly curling my lip.

My cellphone vibrated in my pocket.

I nearly jumped. I thought I'd left the damn thing shut down.

'The kobold,' Martin whispered. Nodding, I realized that I hadn't seen Weezab for hours.

Carefully, making sure no one was paying attention, I dug the phone out. Sure enough, the screen was lit up, and a single notification sparkled beneath the flat signal indicator. A reminder, set to go off at a specific time.

A reminder that I'd definitely not set myself.

A reminder with a single line of text.

It's your watch.

68

While I showered, I had a good look at my watch. I hadn't taken the damn thing off in decades, and was so used to its presence on my wrist that I rarely paid much attention to it. Especially after the face had gotten so scratched that it was nearly impossible to tell the time, other than the hourly pings it had made up until my first meeting with Vrarrs Kor.

Sure enough, while the gadget looked similar in almost every way, there was something just a little off about it. Not the fit or finish, those were familiar and comfortable, but looking the watch over gave me the creeps. It was almost identical to the feeling I got when I looked at Bill's portal generator.

I cursed silently as I scrubbed at the face. If the watch could have its black out effect turned on and off, then I could have been wearing Bill's little toy almost the entire trip and never known. And if it had only a short radius, then I could be wearing a shackle that wouldn't affect any of the others. Hell, it might only affect the person wearing it.

'If all that is true, then how did Bill get it onto our wrist? That's not something we'd likely overlook,' Martin said.

I shook my head. 'I don't know. He'd have to have done it when we were asleep or unconscious, and I don't know about you, but I hardly sleep. And I can't think of a time when we were out cold when Bill was close enough to do the swap,' I said, under my breath. 'The kobold could have after Nox and I fought the gnolls, but that means he's been working with Bill all along. Why would he go from being in Bill's pocket to trying to undermine Bill's efforts?'

Martin was quiet for a long moment, then he said, 'Pull the watch off. Break it. Even if Bill knows that we aren't contained, what's he going to do? If he tries to do it again, pull one of his arms off. He probably doesn't need two.'

I laughed, and said, 'You really are starting to sound like me. Maybe it's being cooped up at the back of our mind that makes me psychopathic.' I flipped the clasp on the watch's band.

And almost fell as a wave of dizziness and nausea rocked me. Only a violent grab at the edges of the shower kept me from going to my knees.

'What was that?' Martin said, concernedly. 'Are you alright?'

I shook my head and gasped for breath. When I'd somewhat recovered, I looked down at the watch to find its clasp once again shut. 'I think Bill's got a bit more than good will holding this thing on my arm,' I whispered. Reaching for it once again, very slowly, I felt queasier and queasier with each centimetre closer my hand got.

'See if you can shatter it, then,' Martin suggested.

The shower room was empty other than myself, so I wound up and bashed the watch face against the wall a few times, which resulted in me severely bruised and it only slightly more scuffed than it had been. Shutting the water off, I hopped out, towelled off, and then tried to crack the watch against the benches and anything with an edge.

After I'd spent five minutes ineffectively crashing my wrist into solid objects, I gave up. 'This thing's even more resilient than the original. Bill knows his stuff,' I cursed, quietly.

'Yes I do,' the engineer quietly said from behind me.

I jumped, then spun to face him, angrily. 'If you wanted me gone, why didn't you just use your little parlour trick to bring Martin out? And what if we'd gotten into serious trouble and you weren't able to shut this thing off?' I snarled.

Bill looked me up and down with a slight smile, and I realized my towel was somewhere near my feet. 'My friend, I have gone to enormous lengths to keep you and Martin alive so that we all arrive in the artifact vault in one piece. I have bent my limitless knowledge toward that task, including developing the device that is currently encouraging your body to ignore the effects of the cancer that is consuming it. You are stronger. You have more stamina. Your mind is clearer. I imagine you've noticed that,' he said.

Cocking his head, he continued, 'But keeping you healthy is not enough. I have spent years watching Martin, including studying how the two of you function.' He pointed a finger at me. 'You have wreaked havoc and chaos for your entire existence, and up until this adventure, it was fortuitous that you rarely held control for longer than an hour. You have proven time and time again that you have endangered your lives without any more reason than to cause devastation on a grand scale.'

The engineer dropped his arm to his side, looked down, and sighed. 'Unfortunately, my immediate line of defence against you doing so, the so called parlour trick, is no longer functioning. Either the device was damaged in the airship crash, or whatever happened to the two of you back in Woodsholme has changed the game,' he said.

'Martin gave me control rather than me taking it from him. That's never happened, and we're still trying to figure out how that's affecting us. I haven't been able to give it back to him,' I said, gruffly.

Bill nodded, then pointed at my watch. 'You saved our lives from the Scayn, and we're all grateful for that. But you have to admit, the level of power you and Martin have is terrifying. You erased Woodsholme. You didn't just defeat the monster, you took away every trace of both it and its victims. I've only seen that kind of devastation caused by a single person once before, and I can't take any chances with the lives of the party that you'll decide to turn us to dust,' he said, dead serious.

Shaking his head, he turned away. 'The watch only affects you, and I can turn it on and off almost instantly, from half a world away. Show me that I can trust you to behave, to be a valuable member of this group, and I'll give you back your watch,' he said, waving over his shoulder. 'In the meantime, put some clothes on, man, and go get something to eat.'

I stared at the doorway for a long time after he'd left, thinking. It made sense. I was their greatest weapon, but they didn't need what I could do unless we were up against something real powerful. I had to play nice, or I'd be magic-less for the rest of the trip.

Towelling off, I got into the new clothes the engineer had thoughtfully provided for all of us, and headed for the kitchen to eat. As I neared the portal generator, I felt that same sense of sickness and had to take my eyes off of it.

Thankfully, the kitchen door was nearby, and I turned away from the machine. When I'd stepped free of the generator chamber, I heard a whisper so quiet that a few minutes later I wasn't sure I had actually heard it.

They will all betray you. Do not forget.

69

The next morning, the group gathered near the portal generator, refreshed and equipped with clothing a little more sturdy than our elven casual outfits. Even our ratty bags had been replaced, the new ones complete with some basic survival gear. I had to admit, Bill was well prepared for almost everything. We probably could have survived the end of the world down here.

Bill stood in front of the control panel, facing the rest of us. The engineer's silly hat was gone, exchanged for a simple travel hat. The change was probably a utilitarian one, but had the added effect of revealing more of his face. It was a tossup as to who was more nightmarish at the moment, him or Nox, with the jagged gashes across Bill's face and the metal shining in their depths.

The werewolf stood next to me, having apparently decided that I was the next best thing to his best friend. He hadn't been much more then cordial this morning, but I was glad to have him there anyway. There was something comforting about having a massive therianthrope on hand. Even Bill's wide selection of clothing sizes had nothing that would fit the big 'wolf's torso, but a massive pair of pants had been doctored to fit his lower half. The lack of a jacket or shirt wasn't as big a deal now, though. Fur had started sprouting up on Nox's body, and though there were a lot of bare patches that didn't look like they were coming back, it was enough to help keep him warm.

Ceile had also decided to be close by, and she was just over my other shoulder, talking quietly with Robin. It was obvious that she was less than impressed with me running the show, but much like many times in the past, she had decided to protect me, if only so Martin would have a body to come back to. Dressed in the same boring earth tone outfits as the rest of us, she was idly checking over her arcane pistol.

Petrel was next to Bill near the control panel. The steel dwarf had gone back to being the strong, silent type, and hadn't said a word all morning. I wondered if it was because he'd been damaged that he had gotten talky with Martin back in Woodsholme. Between his own repair functions and Robin's work, he was almost back in the same shape as he'd been at the start of the journey. Almost. From what I'd heard Robin saying to Ceile, the steel dwarf needed a full blown repair station sooner rather than later.

As for Robin, whatever she and Ceile were talking about was making her smile. Unlike her taller companion, the dwarf had holstered her pistol and was now simply standing at ease, ready for anything. I shook my head and chuckled. If those two were getting more than friendly, that would really turn some heads back home.

I was surprised that somewhere along the way, my hatred for Robin and Petrel's species had apparently dissipated. Granted, before we set foot on the Red Flag, I'd hated pretty much everything. I was mellowing out, and I wasn't sure I liked it.

'Just look at it as if you're on vacation,' Martin chuckled. I snorted, which provoked some odd looks from those around me.

Next to the other ladies was Vrarrs Kor. The dragon was crouched down next to the control panel, and appeared to be talking to herself quietly. When she noticed me watching, she smiled darkly and then stood up and turned back to Bill.

There was no sign of Weezab.

Bill cleared his throat, and everyone turned their attention to him. 'Alright, everyone, here's what you need to know. When I enter the coordinates for the destination portal, the machine take a few minutes to wind up. The countdown is on. Once ready, the entrance portal is opened, then the exit, and finally the bridge between is created. The length of the bridge varies due to forces I haven't completely figured out, but usually it is between five metres and fifty. Sometimes it's shorter. Sometimes it's longer,' the engineer said, gesturing wildly.

'As soon as the bridge forms, we need to be on it and headed for the exit. Remember, we only get one shot at opening a portal at a location, and then we have to wait before we can do it again. And we don't have time for that, so we need to get it right the first time. Once through the portal, find cover nearby and get to it. When reality snaps back together, there's a bit of a bang on both ends. So, uh, don't be near it when it does,' he continued.

'You said we had ten minutes to get across, where's the problem?' I asked.

'Ah, but we do not have ten minutes, my friends, unless we are incredibly fortunate. The instant the generator starts powering up, the universe starts trying to power it down. I have had test runs where it succeeds and I have to wait some time to attempt starting the machine up again. And we cannot count on a very short bridge. I once opened a portal to the building next door and found myself standing on a bridge so long that I could not see the exit. Such things are rare, but we must be prepared for them,' Bill said, throwing a hand into the air theatrically.

Nox frowned. 'Alright, so what about the safety bridges you were talking about? What's it like in there if something goes wrong?' he growled.

'Excellent question, my furry friend! The environment the bridges pass through is a dangerous one. It is a place of infernos, of storms, of tsunamis, of shattered mountains, and of death, and it will try to hinder your crossing. If the bridge fails, you will fall to the next. The destination will have changed, but the goal is the same. Cross and exit as fast as you can. There are three such fail safes, and so long as the machine itself isn't powered down, those should be enough to escape,' Bill said, looking at each of us in turn.

I frowned. 'You're talking about the realm between. The realm of the blood of the Suns,' I said, shaking my head. 'You're talking about passing through the place where aether and nether are born.'

'Correct! That world and ours are intrinsically linked, but that place's distances are fluid and malleable. It is how we can travel so quickly across the continent. Yes, it is a desolate and terrible realm, but I've passed through it countless times in the decades since I first built it and I am intact,' the engineer said, giving us a twirl. I laughed. Nox looked unconvinced.

'Alright, fine. And what happens if we run out of bridges?' Robin asked. She sounded nervous.

Bill turned to look at her, and now his face was sober. 'Well, my dear Robin, as I said yesterday, then you fall into a place that I do not know how to rescue you from. I have sent probe machines into that realm, trying to map it, but distance and direction and depth spin and whirl in there. I can't create a portal that simply goes to a place in there. Leaving a marker behind and opening a bridge to it causes some devastating side effects,' he said.

'And those are?' Ceile asked.

The engineer turned slowly to look at her, and shook his head. There was dread in that look. 'Ms. Angael, when we build a bridge to another point in our world, the bridge passes through the realm I've been talking about. So if I open a bridge to that place, where does the bridge pass through? What lies beneath the two worlds we've seen?' he asked, and now his face was wild. 'What nightmares might live there?'

There was silence for a long moment, all of us exchanging glances. Bill was slumped forward, looking defeated. Finally, he straightened up.

'It's past time for us to be gone. Remember my instructions. Move quickly, then get away from the exit. Do not stop, do not slow,' he said quietly, and beckoned us toward a flat portion of the machine. 'Our first bridge will leave us on the very footsteps of the Rook's lands. The second is a few kilometres to the north, a sheltered area where I left a marker years ago while camping in the area. The third is east along the mountains and closer to where we are. That marker was left near an intake vent for Krekt Twelve, a location I'd hoped to use as a potential entrance but is too far from the vault and too near the active parts of the city.'

'The fourth is very far to the west, and the only reason I've chosen it at all is because it is closer than any other point I currently have marked and it's better than the alternative. A closer point would have been Woodsholme, but if that marker was still intact before we destroyed the city, it certainly isn't now. If you end up at this fourth point, there is a cache nearby to shelter in but you'll have a long walk back,' Bill continued.

'If all four fail, I have no words for you. Be quick, and we won't have to find out,' the engineer finished. He turned and walked to the control panel, and began entering commands. Then he left his hand hovering over the console, and looked over his shoulder at us. 'Prepare yourselves! Remember, move fast!'

And then he started the machine.

70

The constant thrum of the portal generator jumped an octave and the turbine at its heart began to spin. The barely perceptible vibration that had tickled our feet earlier ratcheted up violently until the chamber was shaking. Dust drifted down from the ceiling, and I heard something fall over with a crash somewhere behind the machine.

Bill now stood in front of the flat section, and he was opening and closing his hands repeatedly, slightly crouched. I heard him say, 'Bring me one who holds the stars. Bring me one who won't stray far,' and then fall silent. I was going to have to ask him about his little poem.

The rest of us stumbled in to crowd behind him in a rough line. My heart was beating in my ears, in time with the howl of the generator. I'd been alive for a long time, and I'd seen a lot. But this was something new. And that was exciting.

There was a blast of sound that briefly robbed me of my hearing, a shockwave that nearly took me off my feet, and then a blast of light that I struggled to block out with my hand. Through the shelter of my wrist, I saw a circle spinning slowly where the flat wall had been. A storm of energy raged around the edges, lightning crackling through its surface, and a furious wind whirled and roared from it.

Entrance portal open, check.

I couldn't see anything through it, just spinning clouds of wild energy. It was like looking into murky water as it circled a drain. Well, murky water that was also spitting lightning. I got ready, trying to keep myself steady on the shaking floor. Bill looked over his shoulder at me, and a dark smile split his face.

Then the chamber shook even harder, and this time I went to my knees. I heard a few of the others hit the ground as well. As we struggled to our feet, another explosion of light erupted from the portal, and now we could see the bridge and, some distance away, the exit.

Bill didn't hesitate. The engineer was into the portal seconds after the bridge had appeared. Petrel was close behind, the steel dwarf's legs pounding along the strange hazy surface, hydraulics whining. Then Robin and Ceile, the dwarf running for all she was worth, Martin's friend just over her shoulder. She threw a look my way as she went.

I was hot on their heels, when suddenly a big furry arm lifted me into the air. Then I was flying, tucked under Nox's arm.

We burst through the portal and into chaos. The bridge was flat and fairly wide, but there was nothing for hand rails and there were dunes of grey sand across it. A brutal wind pushed us toward the edge, and clouds of dust raged past, caught in its grasp. Lightning seemed to come from the sky and whatever lay below, crackling past mere metres away and vanishing with a blast of thunder. Dim lights whistled past on the wind and dust, illuminating just metres around them as they spun at the storm's will. Shadows danced in the murk beyond the bridge's edge, bits and pieces of darkness floating away from them, as though they were on fire.

If Nox was scared, he didn't show it. We shot past Ceile and Robin, eclipsed Petrel, and then Bill was falling behind us, a savage grin on the engineer's face. I could see just enough around the 'wolf's arm to see Vrarrs Kor hit the bridge running, the dragon leaping across the portal threshold with grace.

Nox was fast, but the winds made footing treacherous. Every powerful stride hit the bridge hard, every claw sinking into the surface, leaving ruin behind. I hoped that wouldn't slip up the others, but as we gained distance from them the clouds and storm moved in. Seconds after we'd gone by, everyone had vanished in the murk, and we couldn't see the entrance.

'Something's wrong,' Martin said, suspiciously. 'Can you feel it?'

'Something's wrong? Have you looked outside recently? This place is insane!' I said, laughing with the thunder. He was right, though. I felt strange. Feverish, almost. Fuzzy headed. A dull ache at the back of my head that increased with each step toward the exit.

A violent tremor shook the bridge, and Nox went down, sliding across the surface, blasting through deep dunes of sand. I went skidding away in the opposite direction, clawing at whatever I could reach to slow myself down. The bridge shook again, and it shimmered in the half light. For a second I could see through it, into the storm below.

I finally slid to a stop in a dune, and then searched the clouds for the others. The murk had closed in around me, and now I wasn't sure which direction was the edge and which was the exit. I thought I heard voices in between the roar of thunder and howl of wind, indistinct shouts somewhere in the distance.

The bridge jumped, throwing me in the air. As I slammed back to the ground, I saw the storm open up briefly, enough to see the exit portal only fifty metres away. It pulsed angrily, shooting sparks and roiling energy across the bridge. I struggled to get to my feet, and watched Kor appear out of the clouds ahead and leap through the opening, arms up to protect her head. Bill was right behind her, though he slowed and kept throwing glances over his back, looking for the rest of us.

A small shape appeared in the portal after the engineer had gone by. Sunlight was glinting off bronze scales, and the little creature was holding a tail in its hands. It was the kobold, and he was staring intently into the portal, searching. How had he ended up on that side?

I managed to get to my feet, but the shaking bridge kept me from moving forward. Weezab must have seen me moving, because in an instant he was through the portal and charging toward me. Before he arrived, the storm rolled over this side of the bridge again. I fell to my knees, cursing. The movement was too much, I was going to have to crawl.

Then pain blazed across my eyes, and I put my hands to my head as agony rippled through my mind.

'-have to-go-will tear us apart-run-' Martin said, brokenly. His voice was indistinct and echoed across my consciousness. My heart was thundering in my ears, fire ran along my spine, and I felt electricity rage across my skin.

'What the hell is going on?' I yelled through clenched teeth.

'The bridge is failing, idiot! Why are you lying here, we have to go!' a high-pitched voice shouted in my ear. Scaly hands gripped my wrists, and I opened my eyes to find Weezab standing in front of me, twitching. His tail flicked wildly in the wind as he tried to pull me to my feet.

'Something's wrong, Weezab. I'm being torn apart,' I snarled, shivering in the pain.

The kobold stopped pulling and leaned in close to look me over. 'It's this place! We're in the realm between, every ounce of aether and nether is here! It feels our strength, wants us to feed!' he shouted, and an exultant smile was on his face. He started trying to get me to my feet again. 'Listen, you and Martin are a one-off, you know? There isn't anything like you two out there. Your body is pulling both nether and aether toward you, unconsciously, and the combination probably isn't pleasant,' the kobold yelled over the roar of the storm. 'Now, c'mon, there isn't time!'

Taking a deep breath, I surged drunkenly to my feet. Weezab tried to help keep me up, though the little fellow wasn't big enough to do much more than push against my thigh. We started moving agonizingly slow in what I thought was the direction of the portal. It couldn't be much further. I fought the pain, tried to focus on walking in a straight line through the wind.

Ahead and to the left, the clouds swirled apart for a heartbeat, and I saw Nox. His back was to us, and he was searching the murk beyond. The big 'wolf seemed to be yelling, but the storm drowned him out. And then he was gone.

The bridge rocked again, and both the kobold and I went down. This time, the shaking didn't receded. Crawling forward so that his nose was almost level with mine, Weezab shouted, 'Hold on! The bridge is lost, we're going to fall to the next!'

The surface began to shimmer and then flash with each blast of lightning around it. The wind seemed to pick up, and for a long moment, the air was clear enough to see the bridge's entire length, and both portals. I saw Nox dive out the exit after giving us a look of regret. Over my shoulder, not halfway along the bridge, I saw Petrel carrying Ceile. Robin was holding on to the steel dwarf's shoulder, desperately trying to stay upright.

There was a brief instant where the portal seemed to stabilize, the bridge seemed to calm, and I could see mountainous terrain beyond the exit, trees and rocks bathing in the light of the White Sun. Then the opening flickered, collapsed in on itself with a burst of light and a roar that eclipsed the howl of the storm around us, and then a brutal shock wave hit all of us. Weezab and I were already on the ground, so we were simply carried backward a few metres. Petrel was thrown away, dropping Ceile and then crashing to the surface. Robin flew off into the suddenly encroaching clouds and vanished.

'Hold on!' I heard the kobold yell again.

There was a deep cracking noise, like the sound of a glacier calving or jagged cracks racing along a frozen lake. The bridge flashed and shook.

And then shattered.

71

There was a hideous feeling of not only falling down but also to the side, and I reached wildly for anything at all. The storm raged around me, as I fell or flew through it and its fury. This wasn't free fall, it was as though something had a hold of the back of my jacket and was flinging me around.

Then I slammed painfully down on the next bridge.

If anything, this one was even more desolate than the first. Almost its entire length was buried in the grey sand, and it looked like it was burning with the way the dust billowed off each dune in the wind. The exit was much further away, and a look over my shoulder suggested that the entrance was almost that far as well.

I sighed. I was back in the middle.

The dimensions of the bridge weren't the only thing that had changed. Weezab was lying face down in the sand only a few metres from the exit portal. Petrel was next to him, the steel dwarf struggling to his feet. Ceile was over my shoulder and a hundred metres back, pulling herself out of a waist-deep dune. I didn't see Robin immediately, until I saw a roughly dwarf-shaped crater in the sand near me.

The pain in my head had lessened, and the new bridge was stable, at least for now. I skidded over to Robin and helped her dig herself free. As soon as the dwarf could, she looked wildly around for Petrel and Ceile, and once she'd seen both, nodded thanks to me.

Leaning on each other for support, we started heading for the exit, but slowly. Ceile was nursing an injury of some sort. She was catching up, but not very fast. Ahead, Petrel pulled Weezab out of the dune and then bodily threw the kobold out the portal. The steel dwarf whipped around and started moving toward us, but before he could get much more than a metre or two, that deep, low cracking noise rippled along the bridge.

Where the last bridge had given us plenty of warning that it was going down, we were all unprepared when the surface of the new one rocked violently, flashed brilliantly, and then shattered terribly fast. I had a last glimpse of the portal distorting and then slamming shut as Robin and I were falling away.

The dwarf and I clung together, desperately holding on as we whirled through the storm. It tried to pull us apart, and it wasn't long before my muscles ached along with my head. Soon, a millimetre of air between us became a centimetre, and then we were at arm's length, holding each other's wrists painfully. Robin was screaming something, fear on her face, and I was surprised when I realized just how much I didn't want to let the dwarf woman go.

We slid slowly further and further apart, until it was only our fingers that were keeping us together. A sickly desperation had started to overcome the pain at the back of my head, and from the wild look in Robin's eyes, she felt it too. We weren't going to make it. We were lost, and we weren't going to make it.

I wondered where Martin had gone, and then Robin slipped away.

There was a peculiar tearing feeling as I watched the dwarf vanish into the storm, and something cold and horrible ran down my spine. I howled with loss, and at the same time marvelled at how much the thought of being alone had suddenly become so terrifying. My body shook as I spun uncontrollably through the wind, and I shut my eyes.

I felt fire rage along my veins, and I was wracked with pain and sickness and bent almost in half in agony. I felt like I was being raked over red hot nails, every inch of my skin howled. I spun uncontrollably, hugging myself as I fell. I closed my eyes against the assault, trying to force the pain away, but it was relentless.

It was in the middle of this struggle with some unseen enemy that I realized I was feeling despair for the first time in my existence.

And I suddenly understood that the reason I used to feel invincible was because in the past I would take the helm, destroy some things, bask in the destruction, and then go back into the safety of my box not long after. I was rarely in danger that I couldn't handle, and Martin took care of the rest.

I was the kingdom's greatest weapon, but I was also its spoiled king.

A king that suddenly found himself without his guards and authority in the middle of enemy territory. With no weapon. I was the spoiled king, and now, now I was afraid.

With that epiphany came something else - anger, rage, fury. I was angry that I felt fear. I raged that my power had been taken from me. And I was furious that this place, which had once been the source of my strength, would dare to try and destroy me.

I resolved to do something about it. Swallowing my fear, I took it and my despair and my pain and turned them into ash. I reached out into the winds and smiled as my mind cleared. Smiled as I felt the block trying to contain me, and the cracks in its defences. Energy began to seep through, slowly at first, then gaining speed as those cracks widened beneath the vortex of my will. I felt my watch begin to vibrate, then bounce on my wrist.

Then, with a flick of my fingers, an evil smile, and a mad grin, I turned the gadget to dust.

The effect was immediate. With my magic sight restored, this place hummed with energy, every cloud saturated with it. The power raged around me, begging me to take it and bore a hole to the next universe. To tear apart the foundations of this world and build a palace befitting my strength. To reach into the land of the dead and raise the spirits who dwell there.

Back on my world, I was a continent-shattering monster. Here, I was a world-eating god.

I took control of my flight, slowing my spin until I was falling slowly, arms out at a gentle angle. I laughed as the third bridge appeared below me, and I settled easily onto its surface.

This one wasn't long, and I saw that Petrel and Robin were already almost in the portal. Ceile was behind them, moving slowly backward toward the exit, searching the storm for me. Oddly, I was happy to see all three of them. I shrugged the feeling off and started heading for her almost at the same time she saw me.

The wind had ramped up, and so did the vibration of the bridge as Ceile and I met only twenty metres from the portal. She tried to yell something at me as we headed toward Petrel, who was standing just on the other side and waving us in, but it was lost in the storm.

We were almost there when the portal began to flicker and twitch, and the bridge shook violently. I cursed as the two of us went down, then struggled to our feet hand in hand and staggered along the wildly bucking surface toward the strangely dark and desolate location outside the exit. Petrel reached out through the increasingly distorted opening, caught hold of Ceile's other hand and started dragging us to freedom.

When she was almost all the way in and Petrel was reaching out to help me in too, something big launched itself out of the clouds to my right and crashed into me. I lost Ceile's hand in shock, and then I was skidding across the bridge, crashing through dunes wildly in the grasp of the beast. I clawed at the surface and clawed at the energy around me, and a few things happened in quick succession.

My attacker vanished as I tried to turn it to ash, leaving me sliding alone along the bridge. The edge of which came and went, and gravity caught hold of me. And I heard a low and echoing cracking noise from above as the portals slammed shut and the bridge shattered.

As I struggled to regain control with my magic, I wondered if falling off the bridge meant I had been pulled clear of the portal generator's influence altogether. If that was the case, then there would be no new bridge for me to land on. If that was the case, then I'd eventually hit a bottom, if there was a bottom.

If that was the case, then I was in a place that Bill said he could never reach and from which there was no escape.

I wasn't paying much attention to the storm around me, and it was only at the last second that I saw the creature erupt from the cloud and attack. I tried to defend myself, but it was fast and strong and I took two hard hits to my head that made everything far away and shot pain through my brain.

As I sank into unconsciousness, feeling the energy I'd gathered slip away, I had a bit of a shock. It wasn't wind aether that drifted away from my hands to be absorbed into the storm.

It was nether.

72

Sunlight. It was trying to melt through my eyelids, and I wasn't sure I wanted to find out what it would do to my corneas. Wherever I was, I'd fallen into a large dune face up and now sand was pooling inside the back of my shirt. The wind whistled around things I couldn't see, but the fury in it was gone. Now it only quietly ruffled my jacket as I lay there.

I sighed. It was going to have to be done. Gingerly, I reached up with an aching arm to shield my face, then slowly opened an eye. Even with the protection, the light tried to bore a hole into my brain, and I had to fight to keep my eyelid from slamming shut. Gradually the pain faded, and the world around me slowly slid into focus.

Amazingly, the light blazing down from far above was being filtered through thick cloud cover. I shuddered to think what it would be like to stand beneath a cloudless sky in this place, if its sun would light me on fire. I squinted into the lazily spinning clouds, wondering if night and day worked the same way in this realm as it did in mine. The White Sun had just been coming up as we stepped into the portal, had enough time passed since then to have our brighter star directly overhead?

I chuckled. If only I had a watch.

Slowly, I sat up and brushed the sand off of my face and chest as I looked around, and then sighed again. The dune I had made a crater in wasn't unique for anything other than its Martin content. Sand rose and fell in waves in every direction. The wind might not have been as strong as it was around the portals, but it still caught and lifted thick clouds of dust across the ground, giving that same impression of burning.

I frowned as I scanned the distance for anything other than hills of sand. If I waited long enough, the Sun would fall far enough for me to get an idea where south was, if this place followed the same path around the Suns that I was used to, but then what? Bill'd said that the realm between was fluid, shifting. His bridges constantly changed in size, even when going to the same location. There was nothing static about this place.

As I considered what my next move would be, I idly reached out and drew energy to me, shaping some simple forms and setting purple light dancing around my fingers. Even that beginner's skill felt good after the last few days. My body ached, but touching the source of my magic energized me. I marvelled at the ease of gathering power and the sheer amount that I could pull to me in this place. It was exhilarating.

I laughed, and noted the slightly hysterical tinge that arced across it.

Shaking my head, I turned my mind back to my bigger predicament. The Sun had passed its apex, and now I knew south was just over my shoulder. Theoretically, anyway. If I continued that line of thought, then Bill's workshop would be roughly to my right. The Rook's lands would be left. Neither of those made much sense. Bill had said that he hadn't discovered a way to get into this place with the generator, but what else was I going to do? Wait for someone else to fall in here with me?

I got to my feet and shook out my clothes. I was probably going to be sharing them with sand for the next century, but the worst of it drained into the dune at my feet. Turning right, I took a step and promptly sank to mid-calf. I shook my head. This was going to be slow going.

I trudged through the dunes for what seemed like hours. Oddly, neither sand nor air were hot. If anything, it felt a bit chilly, and I was glad I hadn't lost my jacket or my pack in the fall from the bridges.

I wondered how the others had made out. Vrarrs Kor, Bill, and Nox had escaped on the first bridge, Weezab had gone out the second thanks to Petrel, with the steel dwarf, Robin, and Ceile seemingly getting out on the third. Bill's lonely fourth point remained lonely. Then I wondered what that creature had been that had taken me over the edge and then attacked as I fell. Bill had neglected to mention that something might actually live in this place.

'What about you, are you alive?' I asked.

If the Other heard me, he didn't respond. I wasn't entirely surprised. Whatever happened to us on the bridge, it had felt like we were being pulled apart. Which probably meant I was going to go awhile before I heard from him again.

I shook my head. I was getting a very strange feeling when I thought about him. Like something was backward.

Putting the Other aside for the moment, I considered my destination. If my gamble paid out, there'd be some sort of connection between Bill's portal generator and this world in a spot that roughly corresponded to the workshop. Then I could try and break through myself or hope that someone else opening a portal would somehow let me escape. Of course, that would involve somebody going back to the generator and firing it up. Petrel, Ceile, and Robin were the closest to the workshop, but they were still closer to the Rook's lands. Would they think to come back, or regroup with the others?

Lost as I was in my thoughts, I got a bit of a shock when my foot came down on something solid beneath the sand. Instinctively, I threw myself backward as I wove a shield of energy around me, decades of warfare making mine the default answer. The expected blast didn't happen, and I cautiously inched forward to have a look, brushing lightly at the sand.

Pavement. There was a road under the dune, complete with street lines.

It was in rough shape, and ended in a crumbled mess not far from where I'd stepped. A large hill buried the other end, and I quickly scrambled my way up the sand to see where the road went. And then I fell to my knees in shock, looking down into the area below.

The wind had picked up and the horizon had gotten murky, so I hadn't really been able to see what was coming up. I was a little surprised when my road not only continued on after passing under the hill, but split into a number of others and in between the various branches were buildings.

They were ruined, all crushed stone and shattered glass. The drifting dust piled up against their sides, the wind carrying the rest through windows and along the streets. I couldn't see a block ahead with the world shrouded in it, and if Woodsholme had been desolation, this place was devastation. But at least it was something other than infinite dunes.

I kept the nether roiling around my arms and the shield intact as I slowly stepped and slid down the hill and onto the street. I walked carefully and quietly, though I knew anything in the closest buildings would have seen me coming the instant I hit the hill top, and that the wind was more than drowning out any noise I might have been making.

There was something familiar about the area as I made my way along the street. It was tough to get much of a feel for the crumbling buildings, but I couldn't shake the feeling I'd seen them before. Further down the block, more evidence of civilization appeared. The rusting, stripped down remains of cars, bent sign posts, twisted and dead trees.

A sudden urgency grabbed me, and I sprinted to the next corner for reasons I couldn't understand. At least, I didn't understand until I came around the block and then slid to a halt.

My brain tried very hard to twist itself into knots as it fought with what I knew and what I was seeing. I shook my head violently, trying to break whatever mirage was affecting me, but there wasn't any use.

'That's my house,' I said, though I didn't remember asking myself to say it.

The place was just as destroyed as the other houses on the block, but I would have recognized it anywhere. Most of the upper level was gone, but bits and pieces of my bedroom were intact enough to make out, and I could see through the stripped living room into the kitchen, where cabinets hung askew and ripped apart. My favourite painting, depicting a young family happily hanging out at the beach, had almost survived the devastation, having fallen from the wall and gotten jammed between the metal remnants of the couch and the broken drywall behind it. The two fathers waved, frozen in time, as they watched their girls running in the surf. It was an odd bit of colour in the midst of all the white and grey that had washed out my home.

Next to the living room window was the entrance. My hand painted front door was gone, and the hallway behind it filled with sand and debris. The garage door was bent in three and mostly ripped free from the rails. My car, once my most prized possession, had none of her pristine paint left, the once beautiful red wine colour sandblasted away, taking her down to the raw metal. She was askew in the garage, like a terrible wind had dragged her forward and to the side until she was partially outside and her front jammed roughly against the side of the door.

I'm not sure how long I stood there, staring into the ruins of my life, mouth agape, brain on overload. I tried to fathom which impossible situation had brought me here or brought my house to me.

'What are you doing here, fleshling?' a strange voice asked from right next to me. It was peculiarly crackly and seemed to get closer and further at the same time.

I spun to face the source, ready to fight and cursing myself for being so careless. And then, once again, I stopped in shock.

The newcomer seemed to wave in the wind, and when it moved, it crackled into its new position like electricity arcing between wires. It had a vague horse shape, but looked like it had no substance. Like an artist had sketched it with a blue pen, shading around the lines but given it next to no texture other than a flat grey colour. Much like the billowing dust clouds off of the dunes beyond the ruins, the beast's edges seemed to smoke and ripple.

A horn made of lightning crackled on its forehead.

I shook my head. I had to be dreaming, because this thing couldn't be real.

The creature was a unicorn.

73

Even in a world full of the bizarre, the magical, the horrific, there were beasts that were legends, the subject of tales to excite or to cause fear. Pegasi. Basilisks. Trolls. There were dozens of them, born of imagination or hallucination.

A soldier I'd fought with during the war swore on the White Sun that he'd actually met and spoken with a unicorn during a brutal thunderstorm he'd been trapped in while hiking the Barrier Mountains. He'd talked of violent rifts in mid-air that spat lightning and howled loud enough to shake the trees. He claimed the unicorn had appeared from the gap and led him to safety.

He also admitted later that he'd been heavily drinking at the time. Not that any of us had really believed him to start with.

'What are you doing here, fleshling?' the unicorn repeated in the exact same tone of voice. Its head flashed between looking my way and looking in other directions, snapping back and forth quicker than the eye could see. It was like watching a flip book that didn't have enough pages to properly animate the image.

My mind finally ticked into gear, and I got my senses back. Shaking my head to clear out the last of the shock, I said, 'I'm not here by choice, and I'm trying to escape.' My voice was hoarse and cracked. How long had I been wandering through this ruined mirror image of my District?

The unicorn stepped toward me, snapping from stride to stride with an electric crackle. I held my ground, and the beast came to a halt only a metre away. Its eyes watched me, flat grey other than a blazing blue pupil that twitched in time with the beast's distorting lines. 'Your very presence warps the fabric of this world, fleshling. Why are you here?' it said, then nodded toward the houses. 'You bring your nightmares to this world. Is it not enough that you and your ilk drain this place of the very energy that gives it life, you must unleash the storms on the few of us that are left?'

I looked at the beast, taken aback. 'I don't understand. What is this place?' I asked, gesturing at the ruins, 'And what do you mean I drain this place? I brought no storm with me, I was attempting to pass through and fell after I was attacked by something.'

The unicorn snorted, and its horn hissed and spit. 'This is your doing, fleshling. You are a locus of power, your presence alters everything around you as the energy that makes up this place is drawn to you,' it snarled, its whole body snapping closer and then cracking back to its original spot. 'This is not your home, nor is this your city. You must not rest here, you must move on.'

'This isn't real?' I asked, turning to look at the shattered remnants of my house.

The beast snorted again, shaking its head. 'Of course it is real. But it is not your home, it is a conjuration. No, those who would actually call this place home are long dead, and now there are only nomads passing through,' it said. 'Your powers are fed by stealing the energy from this world, faster than it can be made. We are born of that energy, our lives are made of it.'

This time, when the unicorn stepped toward me, it didn't retreat. Its head loomed over me, staring down. 'And without it, we die. You are killing us, fleshling. You have brought the storm. The elements are in chaos. Something has fractured the walls that contain this place, and we are dying,' it said, levelly.

For a long moment, I wondered if I was going to have to fight this creature, but then it crackled from right next to me to a few metres away, facing toward the street. A flash, and then it was looking over its shoulder at me. 'Others will be attracted to your conjuration, fleshling. I am the first but not the last, and I am likely the only one you will not have to fight. You must flee,' it said.

I stepped toward it. 'Wait, what is coming? Where should I run?' I asked, looking out into the clouds of dust.

The unicorn turned its head away and didn't answer. I took another step toward it when suddenly a mournful howl echoed through the dead city. I spun slowly, trying to find the cry's source, and when I came back around to my original spot, I found the unicorn standing right in front of me again.

'You must come with me, fleshling. They are coming, and if they kill you the destruction will break what little remains of reality here. I will carry you far enough to escape them, but we must go now,' it said, its head flashing back and forth, looking down the streets.

I frowned, but that howl probably didn't belong to anything good. Besides, the unicorn knew this world, maybe it also knew how to get out. I nodded at the beast, and said, 'Alright, thank you. How do I get on?'

Before I was finished asking the question, I felt a strange twisting and the whole world distorted. When everything snapped back to normal, I was sitting on the unicorn's back. 'You will not fall, and you may need to defend us. Be prepared,' the beast said, looking over its shoulder at me.

The howl sounded again, and this time it was very close. The unicorn snorted, the world shifted so we were facing the other direction, and then we were blazing through the ruins. The further we got from my house, the less familiar the buildings became. If this was a ruined version of the Upper River, then it was a poor rendition once we'd left my street behind.

'Do you have a name?' I asked the unicorn as I watched the wreckage flash and snap past us. 'Why are you helping me?'

'We are Imuren, and that shall suffice for a name. And I am helping you because you are a locus of power. If you were to die in this place, a reaction would chain through the energy, creating new holes and cracks. You were not meant to come to this world, fleshling, and you certainly cannot die here,' the unicorn said.

'Your power will slowly drain this world of life until it is just a dried corpse, but your destruction here would annihilate the structure that holds it together. My world would come apart at the seams, but yours would be exposed to energy that it was not meant to have. The devastation would be immense wherever our worlds converged,' it continued, then paused before adding, 'It would also allow passage to the realm beneath. And vice versa.'

I frowned, then asked, 'The realm beneath?'

The unicorn looked over its shoulder at me. 'The land of the dead. If your world was exposed to this place, the realm between, it would mean the deaths of millions. If your world was exposed to the realm beneath, there may not be survivors at all. The Horsemen would Ride, but the Purification would be meaningless,' it said.

'You know so much about my world, but we know so little about yours,' I said, shaking my head.

'Your species is young, as are the others on your world, and when the Four's work is done, you remember little and then go about trying again. My realm is apart from that great cycle, and so I have watched yours die and be reborn countless times. And I never forget,' the beast said, turning away.

I silently chewed on that for a bit. Everyone knew the tale that one day the Four would call the Ride and wipe most of us out, but when you start talking about stories that occur over millennia, most people tend not to believe there's much truth in them. Even with it being common knowledge that the Horsemen were out there and active in our world. I was guilty of believing the story but not concerning myself with it much, thinking the odds of the Ride happening in my life time were pretty slim.

Maybe those odds weren't so slim after all.

I started to ask Imuren another question, but the low howl sounded from behind us, and I turned to watch the roiling clouds behind us churn. In the murk, I could make out a big shadow charging along the street after us. 'Imuren, there's something back there!' I yelled to the unicorn. It snorted and we started moving even quicker.

The beast that erupted from the dust was big, fast, and looked like it was on fire. Where Imuren crackled with blue energy, this thing rippled and flowed like lava as it charged toward us on all fours. It looked vaguely like a lion, if lions had wings like a dragon's and a tail like a scorpion's. Magma seemed to ooze and spin lazily beneath its flesh, and as it ran it left after-images in my eyes. Every step it took shot embers out in all directions.

'Aw, crap,' I said. Looks like today was going to be a meet and greet with all the legends.

This ugly thing was a manticore.

74

If I wasn't already sure I was dreaming or dead, I was now. I was racing through a ruined effigy of my hometown, on the back of a unicorn, while being pursued by a manticore. A vivid picture of me and that soldier sitting in some awful bar, sharing a bottle of nasty liquor and swapping stories about our adventures snapped through my mind until I shook it away with a scowl.

Imuren was moving like a rocket, the pavement whistling past below us so quickly that it didn't even seem like the unicorn was touching the ground. Despite our speed, I didn't have to hold on at all, which was handy because the monster behind us was catching up fast, and I was going to have to discourage it.

I spun on Imuren's back until I was facing the manticore, and started drawing nether to me. Taking the energy and shaping it into forms of disruption and beam, I shouted a few arcane words and then a line of purple destruction lanced out toward the monster. It dodged away, but not before taking a hit that caused an explosion of burning embers and a furious roar. I snarled, trying to bring the beam to bear again, but the monster leapt, ducked, slid ridiculously fast.

Changing tactics, I let the beam dissipate and sent explosive spheres bouncing out into the street. When the monster neared, a line of destruction rocked the block, sending chunks of pavement flying and buildings collapsing. For a long moment, it looked like I had killed the beast, but then it burst from the smoke, its wings pumping as it flew a few metres above the road.

I snarled and then took every ounce of energy I had and started shaping and folding. I felt the power rage around my arms as I did, shaking in anticipation. I howled into the wind, and threw my hands into the air. There was a flash of light, then everything behind the unicorn and I vanished in a wave of energy wider than the street and higher than the buildings that bordered it. When it finally faded away, there was nothing but a flat stretch of sand between the curbs. There was even a rectangular path through the dust, until the wind closed back in with cloud.

There was no sign of the manticore.

As though it had been keeping the city together, the pavement suddenly got worse and worse until it vanished beneath the sand. Likewise, the buildings grew more and more demolished until they were nothing but foundations, and those were gone, too. Imuren galloped across the sand, snapping across the loose surface just as quickly as across the street. After minutes went by and the manticore hadn't returned, I swung back around on the unicorn's back.

'Imuren, you must have some sort of access to my world if you have watched it die. Can you get me back? Is there a way out?' I asked, leaning forward. The unicorn's skin hissed and crackled, and where I put my hands, tiny arcs of electricity ran along them. It was a bit disconcerting.

Imuren snorted. 'Your kind has used the realm between for many things, fleshling. You steal the blood of the Suns for your magicks. You tear holes in the walls between us to travel across your own realm faster. Each hole is a wound, and one that never fully heals. The storm rages around them, trying to seal them away, but they continue to come,' the unicorn said, each word punctuated with the snap of sparks.

Looking over his shoulder at me, it continued, 'One day, fleshling, a portal will open and the walls will shatter. The effect will be the same as though someone with your power had died in this place. The worlds will converge. Mine will die, yours will be in ruin.' Shaking its head slowly, it quietly said, 'And I do not know if the rebirth would include the realm between.'

'I don't understand, Imuren. If your world lies outside the cycle, why would the Four allow its destruction? Magic has always been a part of my world, and from what you've told me that's linked directly to this place,' I said, trying to wrap my head around everything that was going on.

'The Horsemen's hands are tied here, fleshling. Your world did not die, not completely, last time. The Ride was not finished. Purification was not completed. No, it was a human that destroyed it, not the Four, and so the realm above was reborn sickly and malformed. Poisons ravage its oceans. Storms savage its high mountain ranges. Deep wounds left over from the last world infect its poles,' Imuren said. 'Your world must be destroyed again, but the Four cannot call a new Ride. So your realm rots and carries us all into the depths.'

I'd heard all of that somewhere before, but I couldn't place it. Shaking the thought away, I frowned and said, 'So, the only way for all the planes to be saved is if my world is killed.' Imuren didn't respond.

We silently charged across the endless sand for a long time before the unicorn spoke again. 'I will help return you to the realm above, fleshling. It is too dangerous to allow you to wander this place, and you will not escape on your own. In return, you will help me,' it said.

'Alright, what do you want me to do?' I asked, cocking an eyebrow at the beast.

'Destroy the portal device. It is the only one of its kind. The slow decay of the realm between as her essence is stolen by you and your ilk cannot be slowed, but each time the portal machine is used it pushes this world, violently, toward its end. If it is stopped, then we may hold out long enough for the realm above to be killed, giving us time to heal before your species returns to trying to kill us,' Imuren said, flatly.

I almost laughed. The unicorn's matter-of-fact tone of voice while discussing the destruction of my world and almost everyone on it was pretty funny. Sobering, I considered what Imuren had told me, and just how big a gap there was in the knowledge of every magic user on the planet. In all of my years, I'd only ever heard that the realm between was simply a place where aether and nether were formed and then waited to be used by those with the strength to do so. If I hadn't been carried over the edge of that bridge, I would never have known any different, either.

Thinking about what the unicorn had told me back in the city, I suddenly asked, 'Imuren, if someone like me dying in the realm between would be so devastating, you'd have to be constantly looking for them. Something would have to get them out of here before something like that manticore got to them first.'

The unicorn didn't reply right away, just watched me quietly over its shoulder. When it finally spoke, its voice was sad. 'We Imuren, fleshling, have guarded this place against just such a thing for eons. We are quick, and only once have we failed to secure the locus in time.' It nodded out into the sands, and continued, 'The realm between was not always this way. The death of that fleshling did not destroy this world only because its strength was on an order lower than yours. It still stripped this realm of much of its life, and poisoned much of what remained.'

I frowned. 'But when you first encountered me, you almost left without taking me with you,' I hesitantly said.

Imuren went silent again, until we crested a rise and the land dropped steadily before us. When my eyes adjusted to the scale of it, I realized that we now racing down the side of a gargantuan crater. 'I am the last of the Imuren, fleshling. I am the last, and I am tired. I am old. I race with the wind but I am not as quick as I once was. I have fought creatures such as the one you call manticore for eons,' the unicorn said as we sped down the slope.

'Sometimes, I believe that it might be good to finally rest, and let this world end,' it whispered, just loud enough for me to hear.

Oh good, because as if I wasn't already screwed, the one hope I have of getting out of here is a passively suicidal mythological creature. I shook my head. 'Why are you helping me, then?' I asked, quietly.

The unicorn turned its head to look at me once again. 'Because that is the task we Imuren were given and, at least for now, duty wins out over exhaustion,' it said. Swinging back to looking forward, it went on, 'This crater is fresh, fleshling. One of the portals that was opened last night caused it. At the base we will find the wound, and my presence will allow you through.'

'Last night? I arrived with the White directly-' I said and then trailed off as I looked to the sky. Far above, not only was the White Sun overhead, but the Blue was skimming along the horizon, and the Moon sailed past, eclipsing both before vanishing to the south. My shock got even worse when another moon shot past shortly afterward.

'Time does not pass the same in this place, nor do the Suns and Moons follow the same paths. You likely do not recognize the Ash Moon, for it has met its end on your world, at the hands of the Horseman War. Its essence still wanders the realm between,' Imuren said. Then he nodded ahead. 'Look, fleshling, we have almost arrived.'

The ground had started to level out, and as we neared the center of the crater the wind and dust slowly opened around us. Then the portal appeared out of the murk - or what was left of it, anyway - and Imuren slowly came to a halt ten metres away.

It took a moment for my brain to understand what I was looking at. The air in front of us had gone opaque, in a column that reached far into the sky. Like stained glass, and glass that had vicious cracks that ran up and down its length. Each crack shimmered erratically, and pale purple light pulsed in the glass itself.

The world shifted, and I found myself standing in the sand next to the unicorn. I was immediately uncomfortable, as unlike what I'd walked in earlier this was pretty hot.

'Time passes quicker out there, fleshling, and I do not know where this will take you. Do you agree to destroy the machine that brought you here?' Imuren said, cocking its head to look at me.

I started to answer but caught a glimpse of something big and dark erupt from the clouds to my left. Throwing myself sideways, I started gathering energy to me, feeling the wind rage past as the manticore crashed into Imuren with a terribly loud snarl.

Imuren and the manticore slashed at each other savagely and then broke apart. They circled slowly, the unicorn keeping its back to me as best it could. The manticore's lion face snarled, showing off a mouth full of steaming black teeth. Its tail lashed out, tracing lines across my vision as fire seemed to dance beneath the chitin that armoured it. The sand beneath its cat feet sizzled and spat.

The unicorn crackled between stances, one instant rearing above its foe, the next on its feet. The lightning that formed its horn raged, shooting smaller bolts out in all directions. I felt the hair rise on my arms as it backed toward me.

'Imuren,' the manticore suddenly growled. Its voice snapped and cracked like a wood fire.

'Edros,' the unicorn snarled back. Its voice rose and fell like arcing electricity.

'Give me the fleshling, Imuren. I could taste its power from across this world. I could feast on that power for a thousand years, and never kill its host,' the manticore said. 'I could drag it to the west pole, where its death would cause less destruction.'

Imuren snorted. 'You are a fool if you believe you can drain this one without affecting the realm between, Edros, and even if you could do so, others will come for you. The Taavit will come in droves from below the earth. The Keila will flood the pole and attack in swarms,' the unicorn said, angrily. It danced back and forth toward the manticore. 'Other Edros will come. Will you convince all these foes to share the locus in such a way that it is not destroyed?'

Shaking its head slowly, the unicorn asked, 'What will you do if the Moerdrim come? Or the Zumitl? Will you stand your ground against either? Do you believe either will treat your prize with the same gentleness you claim to? Are you so willing to risk this entire world to sate your hunger, Edros?'

Edros hissed but said nothing, just flowed from one spot to the next. Imuren watched the manticore carefully. I crouched between the unicorn and the portal remnant, shaping and folding forms with the pool of nether I had oozing around my arms and hands.

When the beast abruptly lunged forward, I made it go away.

With its dust still floating away on the wind, Imuren spun and headed for the portal. 'Hurry, fleshling. You cannot destroy the creatures of this world. Your power is born of the same stuff that gives us life. You can but delay them for a time. We must get you out of here,' the unicorn said. As he did, his horn suddenly blazed so bright that I couldn't look at it. Energy began snapping back and forth between it and the glass.

I threw a shield up around us and the base of the portal remnant, and watched the unicorn's back as I spun and folded the nether. I wasn't happy to hear that I couldn't outright destroy the manticore, usually when I killed something it stayed dead. Behind me, I could hear sharp cracks as Imuren's power worked on the portal.

When Edros appeared again, bursting from the sand in an explosion of red flame, I hit it with a blast that lifted the monster into the air, then hit it again as it fell, slamming it deep into the sand. Erupting out, it dodged around my next attack with a flash, and lashed out with its tail.

The deadly barb on the end crashed violently against my shield, and the force of it drove me up to my knees in the sand. The manticore rolled away quicker than I could retaliate, and then leapt forward, swatting at me with the sharp claws on its front feet. This time I fell away, but not before I lashed out with a razor wire of energy that lopped off both of Edros' front legs. It screamed in agony, and with a powerful leap backward it snapped its wings out and lifted into the air. Lava dripped from the monster's wounds.

I watched it go, while I reinforced my shields. As I staggered back to their center, Edros vanished into the clouds above. I cursed. If it could attack from overhead, that would be a bit more difficult to deal with.

Sure enough, it fell from the sky, and it was only because I was waiting and ready with an armful of energy that I was able to swat the manticore out of the air and into the sand across from us. When it tumbled, smoking, into the dune, I hit it with another blast of purple light that took it apart at the seams and it vanished with a loud pop.

'Not long now, fleshling. When I tell you, turn and run for the portal. I will have to hold it open, so I will not be able to defend us,' Imuren said, its voice strained.

'What about you? Will you fight this thing after I've left?' I said, scanning the area for the manticore. 'Where do you go from here?'

'I cannot fight Edros for long. This one is young and I am old. There are others I will go to, allies. Others that will take up my duty if I am lost,' the unicorn said.

We were silent for a long moment, and in that quiet I started to wonder if the manticore had decided to find other prey. I took a few steps backward toward the portal, coming to stand beside Imuren's shoulder. 'I wish I had more time to learn about this world, Imuren. There's so much I didn't know. So much that none of us in the realm above know,' I said.

'And perhaps that is best. You have seen what devastation your kind have done to this world without knowing its true nature. Others would come here to see it. No, you should keep what you have learned to yourself, fleshling,' the unicorn scolded. There was an audible change in the sounds coming from its horn. 'It is ready, go fleshling,' it said.

'Thanks, Imuren. For everything. I hope you find the peace you're looking for,' I said, reaching out to put a hand on the unicorn's shoulder. Electricity danced around my arm. Then I turned and ran. I was determined to keep my shields intact until Imuren closed the door behind me, to keep Edros off of the unicorn for as long as possible.

Ahead, a jagged hole had appeared in the glass, held open by the energy snapping between the unicorn and it. Through it, I could see cement and lights and steam, some kind of passageway. I didn't recognize it, but anywhere on my world was better than being stuck here.

I was only a few metres from the portal when Edros slammed into the shield directly to my left at full speed, appearing out of the dust clouds faster than I could react. The impact threw me away as the shield shattered under the force of the monster's attack. Crashing down in the sand, I stumbled to my feet and summoned purple fire to my hands.

'Fleshling, go!' I heard Imuren scream.

The unicorn was maintaining the portal as it tried to dodge and move away from the manticore. For its part, Edros lashed out with its tail, striking Imuren's body viciously and sending sparks out in every direction. The monster leapt forward, slashing at the unicorn with its claws, and lightning erupted into both it and the ground.

Angry, I headed for Imuren, and I sent beams of energy lancing out toward its attacker. Edros dodged away before resuming its assault on the unicorn. I cursed, sending ever more power out, showering the area with destruction. The monster was fast, and it kept close enough to Imuren that I wasn't able to hit it with everything I had.

When a mournful howl sounded from somewhere in the storm behind me, I knew that this wasn't a fight I could win. I wasn't going to be able to hold off one manticore, much less two. I gave Imuren a final apologetic look, and then turned and leapt out the portal. Reality shifted around me, and I fell out the other side.

Right into the middle of a storm of gunfire.

76

I never had a chance to look back, as I had to roll for cover to avoid getting shot in the face. There was a violent cracking noise, and then I felt the portal slam shut behind me.

Bullets were whizzing past, slamming into the passage around me and skipping along as they ricocheted down the hall. I cursed as I had a look around. The architecture was definitely dwarven, all red metals and steam pipes and poorly lit, and a quick glance around the edge of my cover revealed that at least one side of the fight was as well.

I hoped Imuren had made it out, but there was no way for me to know and no way to find out. I drew energy to me, feeling the rot and decay drip into my arms. I wanted to shower the whole passageway with destruction, but I didn't know who was fighting who, and I couldn't risk accidentally killing people I might be able to work with. I also didn't want to end up with both forces attacking me. That'd be less than ideal.

Only one or two fighters were sending death my way, and they were both on one side. The others were firing at each other, everyone huddled in behind improvised barricades. Most of them were using pretty conventional sidearms that fired some kind of metal slug, with one side wielding a minigun and the other having a railgun and some kind of rifle.

Hearing the railgun fire made me want to crawl into the floor. A railgun slug could blow through a magic shield, and the metal crates I was hiding behind were a lot less sturdy. But they were slow to fire, and the side that had it didn't seem to be firing at me, so that was nice. The minigun, on the other hand, was alternating between spraying the other force and scything across my spot.

I cursed. Some days I wished my talents lent themselves to non-lethal abilities. If I could incapacitate at least one side, I could get this figured out.

'Crow, stop this and let's talk!' I heard someone's amplified voice say, booming over the cacophony of the gunfire. For a long moment, nothing changed and both forces continued battering each other's positions. Then, slowly, the roar of the guns quietened and then stopped.

A voice from the other side, which I assumed came from Crow, shouted, 'I know you have the outsiders, Penguin! I suppose the human that just appeared from that portal is one of yours, too! The whole platoon will be here soon enough, give them all up and I'll make sure you aren't executed when they arrive.'

There was a cold laugh from the one called Penguin. 'Like I'd trust a Mrek-Nine to offer that kind of mercy. No, Crow, you should go, let us leave the krekt. There doesn't need to be more dwarf blood spilt today.'

Crow's voice heated up. 'You know I can't do that. All three of them are wanted by the council. If I let you go, they'd put me on underwyrm duty for the rest of my days. Which would be short, because I'd be working with underwyrms!' he snarled.

'Martin, if that's you, could you do us a favour and kill Crow and his men?' I heard Robin's voice from Penguin's side of the hallway.

'Be silent, outsider, and be happy I have orders to take you alive!' Crow yelled. His squadmates roared with agreement.

I huddled there for a long moment. I still didn't know the whole story here. Peeking around my cover to have a look at Penguin's spot, I shook my head. There were a lot of dead dwarves at the foot of the barricades, and I couldn't see many live ones hiding behind them.

'Robin? Are Ceile and Petrel with you?' I said, loudly. There were some angry shouts from both sides, but thankfully no gunfire.

'Ceile is, Ceile is hurt, but she's alive. Petrel's here, too. We've been waiting for you!' Robin yelled before she was drowned out by the other dwarves.

Somewhere at the back of my mind, the desire to kill both groups whispered past. I shook my head to clear that odd bit of noise. As the two sides continued shouting each other down, I decided what I had to do, and started drawing energy to me. I shaped and folded and shaped again, and when I was ready I threw a shield around me and stood up.

Rather than kill everyone, I sent my magic ripping into the ceiling in wide arcs, letting the wreckage crash down around me. Protected by my shield, the concrete and metal and ceramics passed to either side, until, with a roar that echoed down the passageway, the ceiling collapsed entirely on Crow's end.

The hallway was completely silent, other than the sound of small debris falling and bouncing off the ruin. Dust had shrouded the passageway, and I quickly ducked up against the wall in case Penguin's squad got a little trigger happy. Fortunately, they either decided I was an ally or were too shocked to try and take me down, and no gunfire was sent my way.

'Penguin? I'm going to come over, can I ask that you and your friends not shoot me?' I asked, keeping cover.

There was some heated whispering between the leader and a few of the other dwarves, but finally he said, 'You're Martin Tundra? We've been waiting for you to show up. You'd best come here, your friends are going to want to chat with you, and it's past time for us to be moving on.' There was a pause, and then the dwarf continued, 'I, uh, ask that you not kill all of us, archon.'

I chuckled quietly, and then crept along the passageway wall until I found the barricades. 'I'm coming in, Penguin,' I said, and then stepped through a gap in the wall.

The dust was only slightly thinner on this side, but it was enough that I could make out the four dwarves that had their weapons trained on my head. They were dressed in non-combat clothing for the most part, and everything they had on was torn or damaged. One of the men looked like he was wearing a bathrobe that he had trimmed down to just the upper half.

They all looked terrified and exhausted.

I put my hands up and scanned the area for my friends. 'Alright, I have about a million questions, but it looks like we should be on our way,' I said. When Robin materialized out of the dust, railgun in hand, I smiled at her. 'Am I ever glad to see you.'

The dwarf woman smiled back, but before she could say anything, Mr. Bathrobe holstered his weapon and caught hold of my shoulder. 'I'm Penguin Mrek-Eight, and you and your friends picked a hell of a time to drop in on Krekt Twelve,' he said, quietly. Nodding at the other three, he whispered, 'Grab everything you can carry, and get the injured to the elf. Once everyone is able to at least stumble, we move out.' The dwarves nodded and moved quickly around the barricade to look for gear and survivors.

Giving me a gentle push, Penguin grabbed a discarded lightning rifle from the top of a crate next to us and started heading up the passageway. I gave Robin a hug and then we fell in behind the dwarf leader.

'How long have you been here? I can't have been more than half a day or so behind you,' I asked Robin, Imuren's warning suddenly whispering at the back of my head.

The dwarf woman looked at me funny, and then said, 'The portal dumped us out in this maintenance corridor over three days ago.'

Robin nodded her head at Penguin's back. 'We were lucky. Penguin's crew was holed up in the area, waiting for orders, when we crashed into their laps. Literally! Bill wasn't kidding about his portals going explosive when they closed.' A pained expression crossed her face briefly.

'Gave us a bit of a scare. The council is dead, replaced with a puppet group by Crow's faction. Nobody saw it coming, so there's no resistance. Not really. We've gotten in contact with and encountered small groups like ours, but nobody knows anything. We picked up some stragglers as we made our way here,' Penguin said, looking over his shoulder at me. 'There's an emergency line here that I could use to get in touch with the old council.'

Shaking his head and then running a hand through his scruffy black hair, the dwarf said, 'We managed to reach one of the councilwomen, who told us her security detail was taking her to a safe place and that she would contact us once she was there.'

He looked away. 'That was three days ago.'

He went silent, and Robin squeezed my arm. 'They weren't really excited to see us, but we convinced Penguin that we weren't here to fight them. We'd been resting up, deciding what we were going to do next, when the portal reappeared. Not in the same way, we couldn't see through it and the distortion was much slower,' the dwarf woman said, quietly. 'Ceile wanted to go back through it, to go looking for you, but we had no idea what might come out and what might be on the other side.'

Penguin spoke up again. 'Your friends convinced us that we should barricade ourselves away from the portal, in case something came through that wasn't quite as friendly as they are. We had to wait on the councilwoman's call anyway, so there wasn't any harm in it. The elf's healing had patched a few of us back up already, so I already owed them a favour,' he said. Then he cursed, and continued, 'One of my dwarves took exception to my decision to work with the outsiders, and last night he snuck away and reported our position and the identities of your friends to the rebels.'

We all crammed through another barricade as I tried to grasp the time gap, and then came to a stop in front of a set of doors. Penguin slapped a toggle on the frame, and then, with a squeal of tortured metal, they slid open.

The room on the other side looked like it had been some kind of control chamber that had been mothballed. A number of blocky computers sat on desks, covered in dust shrouds that were in return covered in dust. It was hot, and there were so many pipes running along the walls and ceiling that they might as well have been the walls and ceiling. If anything, the lights in here were even dimmer than they were in the hallway.

A couple dwarves were crouched around something on the ground, and as we got closer I could see it was a tall figure. Robin took my hand and gave it a tight squeeze. I gave her a curious glance and then frowned when I saw the terribly sad look on her face. 'She saved a few of Penguin's guys' lives, and mine. But you know that there's only so much she can do for herself, and not much we can do for her,' she said, quietly. Then she turned and wandered off toward a familiar metal dwarf in the corner next to a big control panel and display.

Seeing me coming, the two dwarves stood and stepped away. They looked at me suspiciously, but I barely noticed. Instead, I dropped to my knees in shock.

I'd found Ceile. And for the second time on this journey, I found myself kneeling before the terribly injured form of one of my best friends.

Her face and head were cut up in a horrific pattern that reminded me of Bill's damage, just with the white of bone peeking out in the gaps. Her right eye and ear were gone. Below her head hadn't fared any better. Her right arm was missing, just a short and rough stump. There were long slashes across her chest. Her left arm was intact but cut and bruised badly, as were her legs.

She'd obviously used her magic to clear up some of the damage, but even a powerful healer like her could only patch up a flesh construct. As much as her body looked like an original model, it was still just material animated by magic. She'd needed a visit with a necromancer for almost this entire trip, and more so than ever now.

Ceile was sitting cross-legged, her intact elbow on her knee, her chin resting on her fist. She breathed irregularly, and raggedly, as she stared at the metal flooring in front of her. The look on her face was one of indifference.

'Ceile?' I said, quietly. Tears were rolling down my cheeks. I'd gone to war with this woman, and yet I'd never seen her so hurt.

'Martin?' she asked, and her face brightened. She lifted her head and looked slowly around the room. 'Is that you, Martin?' she asked again, then she looked stricken and put her hand up to her face.

Her remaining eye was clouded over and scarred. My friend was blind.

I slid forward and gently wrapped my arms around her. 'I'm here, Ceile. It's me. Oh, my old friend, I'm sorry,' I whispered. She buried her face in my chest and shivered for a long moment, but when she pulled away, there was no weakness in her face. Despite everything, she was still the strongest person I knew.

'I am glad that you have returned to us. When the portal reappeared, I wished to go in search of you, but obviously I could not. Petrel had agreed to go and had been standing watch over the opening. Crow's unit ambushed us while we were waiting,' she quietly said as her eye wandered aimlessly.

Penguin knelt down next to us. 'Despite what that bastard was saying, I doubt he's bringing the whole legion down on our head. The krekt is in chaos, and I don't believe for an instant that the rebels are all that much more organized than we are. No, he knew about you three and came to collect you so he'd get the reward,' the dwarf said with a dark smile. 'We're on the outskirts, so there's no reason for the army to come get us until they've taken the krekt.'

Robin reappeared next to me and sat down next to Ceile, dropping a hand on her leg. 'We've got a lot to talk about, I imagine, but we'll have to do it on the move. Even if Crow gave up, which I doubt, others will eventually come and there's no reason for any of us to stay anyway. There's no order or help coming,' she said, shaking her head with a shiver. 'I've been here before. When Thirteen swooped down on us, we held out for day after bloody day, thinking the king would rally the krekt. Of course, he'd had his idiot head cut off and we were slaughtered while we waited.'

'We're going to head for an auxiliary transport centre not far from here. It's been decommissioned almost as long as this place has, but there are a number of transports that are still there, waiting to be scrapped. Me and my dwarves are going to grab a crawler and make our way to Eleven via some deep tunnels. We have a strong alliance with Eleven, they won't take kindly to revolution,' Penguin said. 'There's at least one airship down there, too. You and your friends can use it to get free of the krekt and then head wherever.'

Petrel appeared and loomed over us. 'Crow's unit has been moving back and forth between their barricade and Martin's work. I believe they're placing charges. We must go now,' the steel dwarf said.

'Right, everyone gather your stuff, help whoever needs it. We'll head for the service elevator and take that down to the transport level,' Penguin said, turning away from us and heading over to the console to give some of the others instructions.

I got to my feet, and reached down to help Ceile, but Robin gently pushed me away. 'If we run into trouble, we need you free to do your thing. I'll get one of Penguin's dwarves to help her, we're going to need my railgun, too,' the dwarf woman said.

I frowned, but nodded. When Ceile was on her feet, I gave her a quick hug that she returned gingerly. I turned to Petrel and gave the steel dwarf a friendly slap on the shoulder, which I almost immediately regretted. He smirked at me, clapped me on the arm - which almost took me to the ground - and then headed for the chamber exit.

A dwarf woman with short blond hair and subtle facial tattoos appeared next to us. She smiled shyly, throwing curious looks at me and Ceile, then took Robin's place at my friend's side. I got the impression that she had never actually seen a human or an elf in person, much less a human who looked like an elf. Ceile smiled when the dwarf took her arm gently and steered her toward the door.

'I'll take good care of her, archon,' the dwarf said, nodding at me.

That left Penguin, me, Robin, and one last dwarf who stood there looking nervously between the console and us. 'Stay together. We've rigged this room to blow, which should stop them from following us past this point. Like I said, we're on the outskirts. We shouldn't run into trouble once Crow's been stopped, but we'll still need to be careful,' Penguin said, and waved us toward the door.

I gave a last glance back at the console and then headed for the door. When I was in the hallway and Robin had fallen in next to me, I heard a familiar chuckle at the back of my mind.

Well now, isn't this an interesting turn of events?

His voice was darker than I'd ever heard, and when he finished, the Other burst into laughter that echoed across my consciousness and into the depths far below.

78

If Crow and his unit had hoped to find us sitting there waiting for them to break through the mess I'd made, they were going to be disappointed. By the time they made it to the control centre, only to have it blow up in their faces, we were well on our way down in the service elevator.

It was a big one, with more than enough room to fit the fourteen of us. Most of Penguin's dwarves were crowded into one half, throwing looks our way that were evenly divided between suspicion and fear. I imagined that our sudden appearance in their midst would have been difficult enough for them to take, but made worse by the fact that we were outsiders.

Ceile was crouched in a corner, her hand resting gently on Robin's shoulder. The dwarf woman idly checked and rechecked her weapons. I noticed that she had both her own and Ceile's pistols holstered at her hips, and my friend's combat knife tucked into the belt of her coveralls. Standing over them was Petrel, the steel dwarf staring at the elevator door. I knew he was probably watching his scanners, keeping tabs on anything that might be a threat.

The Other was silent, but I could feel his presence lurking just over my shoulder. Watching. Something about our connection had changed again, and I was a little worried that maybe some of the humanity my companion had developed over the last two weeks had gone away. I didn't really want the sociopath back.

I sighed. It was starting to get hard to keep track of everything that had happened to me and him over the last while. It felt like we were just making it up on the fly or something, choosing parts at random. Two hundred years our relationship hadn't changed, and then this adventure happened.

'I don't understand,' I said, quietly, 'That portal was supposed to dump us at ground level outside the access shaft. How did we end up half a klick underground?'

The others didn't offer an opinion. Why Bill would have neglected to mention that we might land in the middle of the krekt, I didn't know. I suppose his marker device might have somehow made its way down here, but that seemed unlikely. If the dwarves had found it, they probably would have destroyed it or sent the device down to one of their labs to be dissected.

Penguin interrupted my thoughts, coming to stand next to me. 'This entire section of the krekt has been locked down for ages, so long that it no longer even shows up on anything other than the most technical maps. They meant to repurpose it, but as is often the case with such projects, it was put on hold and then forgotten,' he said, standing at my side as he checked over his pistol. Holstering the weapon, he traced the single thick black line tattooed on his face, forehead to chin. 'One of the ladies came across the plans by accident, and when everything went to hell, it made a good spot to lie low,' he said, nodding over at one of his dwarves.

'We've got the elevator keyed to us, so we'll make it to the transport level unmolested. If anything, that level is even more remote than the control centre above us. A lot of this section isn't even powered anymore, so most of the doors between the active krekt and here won't open without some persuasion,' the dwarf said, looking at me out of the corner of his eye with a smirk.

Then his face sobered and he leaned in close. 'I don't want to pry, Martin, as your friend Ceile saved a few of our lives and that's a heavy debt. But you all came here by portal, and that's a technology that hasn't been seen in this world for millennia. A tech that lots of not very nice people would love to get their hands on. I said we'd get you and your friends to the airship and then let you be on your way, but I have to ask you to do something,' he whispered. 'I don't know if you're the one that built this new generator, but you have to destroy it. It's a powerful weapon in the wrong hands, and the damage it wreaks all on its own is too much.'

I almost laughed. 'Penguin, you aren't the first person who's asked me to do that recently. How do you know so much about the machine?' I said, very quietly.

'I think you know enough about us to know that we are always looking for pieces of the past to pour over. There are vaults full of them, far below us. We have a portal generator down there, a human device over two thousand years old. It doesn't work, but we know almost everything about it. I know almost everything about it,' he whispered. When he saw the surprised look on my face, he chuckled quietly. 'You don't get these soft hands as a mechanic or police officer, archon. I'm a scientist. We have more than enough documentation to suggest that our machine, at least, had a hand in the murder of millions and nearly tore the fabric of reality apart twice.'

That sounded familiar. 'You don't have to convince me, I've seen the damn thing in action,' I whispered, thinking about the desolation of the realm between. Then I frowned and said, 'Penguin, the vaults you mentioned, are they safe if the rebels find them?'

The dwarf closed his eyes and shook his head. 'I don't know. Most of the artifacts that actually function are pretty harmless, but there are a few particularly nasty items that are kept in the same vault. That one was keyed to our highest security level, so unless they've got someone with that clearance working with them, it's probably safe. There are only a handful of us,' he said.

'Nasty items? What kind of items?' I said, wondering if the regeneration chamber would fall under the nasty item umbrella, and just what terrible thing Bill might have his heart set on down there.

Penguin cocked his head and gave me a funny look. 'Martin, I owe your friend a debt, and so I am helping four outsiders travel through my krekt, a criminal act, and one that not all of my people here are happy committing with me. I will help you escape, but I'm not going to give you detailed information about Twelve's treasures,' he whispered, suspiciously.

I put my hands up and shook my head. 'Sorry, Penguin, I overstepped. I'm grateful for the help, and I'll do what I can to keep you and the others safe until we split up,' I said. The dwarf searched my face for a brief moment, then nodded.

'My men and women distrust you because you're human, and worse, a powerful magic user. But they do not hate you, as they are doctors and nurses and teachers and haven't been bred to do so. They fear your powers, yes. But they don't hate you,' Penguin whispered, gesturing at the other dwarves. 'They've never had to fight against the humans, as Twelve's last war with your kind was centuries ago. If anything, they dislike Ceile more than you, because they remember the war with the elves from only a handful of decades ago. Of course, your friend isn't really an elf, but judging a book by its cover isn't solely a human trait.'

He leaned in close again. 'My friends don't trust any of you, even the two exiles from Fourteen you picked up somewhere. But they trust me. And your friends have assured me that my krekt is not your destination, and so I have assured my friends of that. Don't make me a liar, archon,' he whispered.

I nodded, though I felt uncomfortable about it. Penguin and his friends should be long gone by the time we returned and made our descent to the vault, but still, I didn't feel great about lying to him. It'd be just my luck if we opened the door to the lab and found the scientist standing guard over its contents.

Giving the dwarf's shoulder a quick squeeze, I turned and headed for Ceile and Robin. Most of Penguin's dwarves watched me go. Petrel turned his head slightly as I approached, the steel dwarf still monitoring his scanners.

I sat down in front of Ceile, and gently put a hand on her leg. Her face brightened and she smiled, taking her hand off of Robin's shoulder and putting it on top of mine. When Petrel crouched down to join the three of us, I looked at them all and nodded. 'I'll give you a quick rundown of what happened to me, but you won't believe most of it. I still don't believe most of it,' I said.

As I gave them the short version of my time in the realm between, the three gave me very different reactions. Ceile's face was bright with wonder, fascinated by my encounter with the unicorn and the manticore, creatures of legend that were nonetheless different than their tales. Robin looked like she wanted to believe, but her brain wouldn't let her.

Petrel might as well have been asleep.

When I was finished, we were silent. Robin had slid down so that she was sitting leaned up against Ceile, the dwarf staring up at the ceiling and looking pensive. Ceile was smiling, her arm hanging over Robin's shoulder. I was still planted next to my friend's legs, resting my arm on her knees. Petrel loomed over all three of us, his silver eyes shifting slowly between the two women with an impenetrable look.

I looked away and wasn't surprised to find a number of the dwarves watching me intently. What I was surprised to find was a number of them watching with fascination and wonder, and it occurred to me that I hadn't been overly quiet while I was talking about my adventures in the portal. For the dwarves, a species who worshipped technology and rejected magic, hearing about a world that was entirely magic must be a very odd experience. A world that I had used technology to get into and then required the help of a magical creature to get out of. I gave them a friendly smile and then turned away.

Petrel abruptly straightened, his head ticking repeatedly. Then he shouted, his voice full of static, 'Hold on!'

Even before he finished his warning, the elevator shook violently and rocked. The outside of the car slammed up against the shaft's sides, and each brutal impact tried to throw everyone to the ground. Massive dents formed in the door and roof, and then with a final shriek of tortured metal, the car ground to a halt.

The lights flickered, then died.

79

For a long moment, no one moved. The elevator swayed slightly, which was particularly disconcerting in the dark. Finally, there was a loud snap and a brilliant red light burst into existence in the fist of one of the dwarves, followed by a second shortly after. I reached into the ocean of decay and used a tiny amount of the nether I pulled to create small lights of my own that hovered near the ceiling of the elevator.

'Is everyone alright?' Penguin asked. When he'd gotten confirmation from the other dwarves, he turned to Petrel. 'What's going on?' he asked the steel dwarf.

'The life readings went berserk, then vanished. The elevator shaft was full of them,' Petrel said, his voice cracking with static. 'Not much else I can tell you, Penguin. My scanners weren't designed for this. Best I can tell you is that we're going to want to be real careful once we get out of this box.'

Penguin cursed. For a long moment, he stood there silently, frowning, then he shook his head. 'Alright, everyone, here's what we're going to do. Elevator's out of commission, obviously. We're still ten levels above the transport facility, so we're going to have to do some climbing. None of the doors along the shaft will open, but each level will have a narrow platform we can rest on. We'll want to stagger the line, last thing we need is for someone near the top to fall and take out a bunch of everyone else,' the dwarf said, looking around at each of us in turn.

He turned to me and nodded. 'Archon, I'll need you near the front. If there's something nasty in here, the handguns aren't going to be enough, the railgun isn't great for this kind of thing, and the laser rifle is low on charge. We'll need your firepower,' he said. The dwarves around him looked unhappy.

I nodded. 'It's a good plan. Let's just make sure no one shoots me in the back of the head,' I joked. Penguin gave me a weak smile and then turned away.

'Alright, let's crack these doors and see what we've got. Petrel, if you don't mind?' he said.

Everyone moved as far away from the door as possible and took up firing positions. I was surprised when the blonde dwarf settled in beside Robin to cover Ceile. I was less surprised when I found myself given a wide berth by everyone else.

Petrel stepped in front of the doors, jammed his hands into the bent and dented seam between each, and then with an angry whine of hydraulics, pulled them open until even he could get through easily.

As soon as he was finished, I sent my lights out into the shaft so we could have a look at what we were facing.

We had come to a rest midway between floors, the car swinging just far enough on its cables to hit the wall with a dull thud every few seconds. The shaft was damaged, the metal scarred and dented in almost the same way as the elevator, and a quick flyby with one of my lights showed that it was like that for several levels above us. Below, strange grey plastic lines or cables crisscrossed the shaft until the sheer number of them blocked out what might wait lower down.

Standing with me and Petrel at the door, Penguin reached through and tapped one of the cables with the handle of his knife. It stuck there, and as he gave it a careful shake, I saw tendrils of the strange material gleam in the light. Shaking his head, Penguin pulled the weapon free with a sharp tug. The cables were webbing.

'Arakhin,' he hissed. There were gasps of dismay from the others.

I shared a glance with Petrel. This was very shallow for arakhin, a species of subterranean spider that had decided spiders weren't creepy enough and had evolved some pointy and very poisonous additions to their bodies. Usually they were found in huge caverns and tunnels deep enough that their lairs came into conflict with underwyrm passages, and that was a long way down, even from here.

For them to be this high up meant that something had opened a path between their caves and the transport level, because the arakhin don't dig. There were a few creatures that could carve through stone well enough for that task, but only one was common in this region.

'An errant underwyrm?' I asked, peering into the depths. Penguin sighed.

'I hope not, but I don't know how else they might have gotten up here. I'd like to think the krekt sensors would have picked up a wyrm moving so close to our boundaries, even this far out, but maybe that equipment is offline too,' he said, shaking his head slowly.

The underwyrms were a constant thorn in the dwarves' sides. Massive, blind worms with armoured plating and sharp hooked horns, the monsters burrowed mindlessly through the rock, dissolving it and devouring the slop left behind. They could be controlled, sort of, through sound and vibration, but from what I'd heard it was a never-ending battle to keep the things from carving up the krekts, too. They weren't particularly aggressive unless you really tried to make them mad, but they also didn't concern themselves with other people's property.

Penguin was silent for a moment, then shrugged. 'We don't have much choice. Even if we bailed out and got into one of the other landing's doors, the only thing waiting for us that way is the rebel forces. We aren't far from the transport level, and we know it's up and running. We keep together, move quickly, and keep our heads, we'll be fine,' the dwarf said. Gesturing to two dwarves behind him, who quickly moved to join us at the door, he pointed to me.

'So long as the shaft hasn't been breached, it should be fairly straightforward. We'll go down in threes. You two will go down with the archon. Keep your eyes open,' he said.

'Be careful, Martin,' I heard Robin say from behind me. I turned and gave her a smile.

'Take care of Ceile for me,' I told her, then nodded to the two dwarves.

They were out the doors and into the shaft quietly, carefully navigating the nest of webbing. I followed them out, slowly descending as I kept a steady stream of nether flowing in. It was tough going. Arakhin didn't use web to trap prey, but it was still sticky and they hadn't had the decency to build a proper ladder. I would drop a metre or two and then stop, free my hands, and kept the lights floating slowly downward.

Above me, I could see both Petrel and Ceile having trouble. The steel dwarf weighed enough to bow a strand of webbing, and so he had to climb with a buffer between him and anyone else. It looked frustrating, as he moved from one strand to the next, each bending and shaking with every centimetre he moved. Where possible, he would use the metal service ladder running along the shaft wall, but it was frequently shrouded in web.

Ceile was making slow progress, assisted by Robin on one side and the blonde dwarf on the other. I shook my head as I watched her climb, thinking that this would be so much worse without being able to see.

We'd managed to cover three levels without any problems when my light drifted past the jagged edge of a large chunk of wall that had been caved in from outside the shaft. The two dwarves running point with me carefully negotiated around the wreckage, and I saw both of them shake their heads and look back at the rest of us.

When I joined them, I understood why. The shaft wall below the damaged section was completely gone, opening up into a massive cavern that my light simply vanished into. Arakhin webbing shot out into the darkness, forming elaborate platforms before fading into the murk. I increased the light's strength and sent new ones out into the shadows, to be swallowed up in the maze of web strands.

Penguin climbed down to have a look. The dwarf was frowning as he peered into the cavern. He turned to me and his two dwarves, and whispered, 'Stay as close to the shaft as we can. Keep it quiet.'

Nodding, my companions started descending once again. I gave them a few metres and then followed them down. I heard Penguin whisper the command to the next group, go silent, and then did the same for the next group to pass by.

When he stopped whispering the second time, a quiet chittering sound floated out of the darkness below, and I stopped climbing to search the shadows for the source. There was a sudden flurry of motion and noise out into the cavern across from me, and I quickly spun to prepare a defence.

'There are dozens out there!' Petrel shouted, trying to swing himself close enough to fight.

The web strands out in the maze bent and shook violently, and I heard the sound of hundreds of legs skittering across them. But just when it seemed like the source was on us, the motion stopped and the cavern went silent. For a long moment, no one moved, all of us staring out into the cavern, looking for movement. When nothing presented itself, I shook my head and looked down at my dwarf companions, only to rear back in shock.

Both of them were gone.

Seconds later, we heard them scream in agony and terror and then there was nothing but silence once more.

80

For a moment, nobody did anything. Then, with angry and fearful shouts, three pistols and a laser rifle started spewing destruction wildly into the web. I threw a shield up and tucked in as tight to the shaft wall as possible as rounds bounced and ricocheted off of the arakhin's webbing.

'Archon, do something!' a furious voice yelled from somewhere above, which generated a few snarls of agreement. I frowned. I couldn't shield everyone, and sending magic blindly out into the maze could, at best, make our descent more difficult, or, at worst, bring the roof or car down on our heads.

'Cease fire!' Penguin was yelling, his own weapon out and searching the area for our attackers. Gradually, gunfire died off, leaving us in silence once more. 'The archon can't do much for us here. We need to count on our own weapons and wits!' he continued, then gestured downward. 'We need to move quickly, we'll be tougher prey once we get onto flat ground.'

I briefly made eye contact with Robin, and she nodded at me. She and Ceile were near the rear of the group, ahead of only a pair of dwarves that were watching for danger above. Penguin was right, I might be able to turn this facility to dust, but I couldn't protect the entire group. It was going to be messy. The best I was going to be able to do was make sure nothing killed me and nothing got by.

In the middle of the pack was Petrel, still descending slowly not far from Penguin, the steel dwarf relaying what information he could from his scanners. He was getting dark looks from the other dwarves. I frowned as I turned away and began climbing again. If Penguin's men and women started putting the blame for our situation on the steel dwarf, things would get even messier.

Whatever the arakhin were up to, they weren't in a hurry. We made it down another three levels without being attacked, and I paused on the door platform to watch the maze around us as the others descended toward me.

In the mess of webbing and shadow and metal, I almost didn't see the monster detach itself from the wall and skitter soundlessly at me. Out of the corner of my eye I caught the movement at the last second, and with a quick gesture and a shout, I hit the arakhin with a blast of energy that cut it in half and sent its remains spinning lazily down the shaft.

'They're all around us!' Petrel yelled electronically from overhead, and then they were all over us.

They were larger than the steel dwarf, and moved sickeningly fast, using their eight legs to navigate the web and get in close at horrible speed. Once they were within striking range, they used four limbs to keep themselves steady and lashed out with the jagged edges of the others.

The hollow boom of a railgun echoed from above, and almost at the same time one of the arakhin squealed and toppled out into the maze. I heard Robin jam another slug into the chamber and spin the rifle back over her shoulder as it recharged with a low-pitched whine. A hail of pistol fire erupted as she drew both her and Ceile's pistols, and then she was joined by the other dwarves.

One of the arakhin darted into the middle of our line and attacked one of the men. Despite taking a number of handgun rounds to the body, it reached out and caught the dwarf, jerking him sideways violently and then ripping his head off. Blood and gore sprayed down on us, and then the monster skittered away, dragging what remained.

Penguin snarled with frustration as he drained a clip into its armoured back, trying to shoot its eyes as it twitched in and out of the maze. When another arakhin suddenly burst from the web near him, he was surprised when Petrel caught hold of it by the abdomen and then bashed it into the shaft wall twice in very quick succession, hydraulics whining with the effort. Spider guts and pieces rained down around me, and then the steel dwarf launched the dying thing at another one, sending both arakhin crashing toward me.

When I went to turn them to dust, my chest got tight, everything got far away, and I staggered up against the wall.

The Other laughed.

The grisly projectiles toppled past as I felt my magic slip away. 'No! Not now!' I growled, trying to keep on my feet. I wavered against the shaft, fingers clawing for purchase, but fell to my knees anyway. I struggled to breathe, to bring my shields back up, but all I could do was keep the lights from dissipating, and I just swayed there drunkenly.

A dwarf dropped from a strand above onto the platform next to me, pistol firing as he knelt down. He leaned in, fear and concern wrinkling the green runes tattooed across one side of his face. He was yelling something, but it was like time had slowed way down and I couldn't make out what he was saying. He offered me his hand, but before I could take it a viciously spiked spider leg darted in and tore his arm off.

The dwarf pulled away in agony and terror, but the arakhin appeared from below and snapped him up, dragging him away as he screamed silently. His eyes watched me until he had vanished from sight, begging me to help.

'What is going on?' I snarled, bringing my shaking hands up to my face as I tried to shuffle into cover.

We've been too far from Bill and for too long, Martin. We didn't suddenly beat the cancer these last two weeks. You know that. His little toys were keeping us in good shape.

His voice was mocking, but there was also sadness there.

Doc said we'd start going downhill after two weeks, remember? We're dying.

I shook my head. 'Now's a real crappy time to start that again,' I whispered, angrily.

An arakhin leapt onto the platform, skittering out of the maze. If it made a sound, it was drowned out in the roar of weapon fire and the stupor my head was mired in. The monster charged toward me, rearing up on its back four legs, preparing to strike. Laser rifle fire lanced down from above, though, wildly spraying the platform near the arakhin, blue energy cutting into armour and then eyes in one brilliant flash after another. The creature shook violently with each hit, then collapsed to the ground as smoke poured from a messy hole where its eyes had just been.

'Can you fix this? If I give you control?' I asked, in between gasps of breath.

I cannot. We're too weak. You'll have to sit this one out. Don't get us killed.

I couldn't see what was going on above me, but everything was starting to close in again. I could hear the chittering of the arakhin, the shouts of the dwarves, the screams of the dying. I could hear the whine of machinery as Petrel fought the monsters somewhere overhead. I could hear Penguin giving commands. I could hear Robin yelling in anger and fear.

I heard Ceile yell my name.

My breathing was improving, and I was able to stop shaking enough to straighten against the wall. My legs hadn't quite gotten around to accepting orders, but with a huge amount of concentration I managed to gather a small amount of nether. It wasn't going to do much of anything, but it was a start. I felt better about myself.

And then another arakhin skittered out of the chaos to loom over me.

I thought about every form I could shape the nether into that might affect the monster, but the worst I could do to it was probably a sunburn. I sneered at it, skidding myself slowly along the side toward the open shaft. It chittered at me, jaws clicking together at high speed, twitching back and forth on its legs, its dozens of eyes watching. This wasn't looking good.

Just when I thought I was done for and starting to feel a little disappointed that I'd made it this far only to get eaten by a spider, Ceile crashed down from above, taking the arakhin flat to the floor.

Green blood oozed from around its eyes and mouth. Ceile's eye twitched sightlessly, her hand running across the monster's back and then over its face as it slowly recovered from its surprise.

Then, when it staggered to its feet and started flailing at its attacker, Ceile pulled her combat knife from her waist belt and jammed it into its eyes. The monster shrieked, bucked wildly, tried to lash out with its legs, but there was nothing it could do. With a cruel jerk, my friend shredded every black eye in its head, and then thrust the blade through the brain beneath.

The arakhin squealed one last time, a shriek that cut off suddenly, and then collapsed to the floor again. Ceile rolled off awkwardly, dropping her knife and scrabbling for a hand hold. I stumbled forward and caught her, wrapping my friend into a hug as I looked for more of the monsters.

Her breathing was ragged, but she was smiling gently. 'Maybe you should have Robin watch you, not me,' she whispered.

81

Even as Ceile's target shrieked its last, the other arakhin vanished back into their maze in a frenzied rush. I didn't have much hope that they were gone for good, and while we'd killed twenty or so, mostly thanks to Robin and whoever had the laser rifle, the damage was done. We'd had fourteen when we got in the elevator far above, but now we were only seven.

We gathered around the platform where I'd collapsed, regrouping as best possible. None of the survivors were badly hurt, mostly cuts and scrapes from the climb, and not much gear to be collected. Anyone that had gone toe to toe with an arakhin was dead and their body lost, other than me and Petrel. The steel dwarf had killed more than his fair share purely with his hands.

Ceile and I stood next to each other, arm in arm. Her crazy attack on that last arakhin had saved my life, and I still shook my head in disbelief any time I thought about it. She'd managed to get her knife back from Robin, climb down from a fair way above, in the middle of a firefight, and then drop onto my attacker's back, riding the damn thing while she killed it. All without her sight or right arm. Even with her training and finely-tuned senses, that was nothing short of epic.

Robin was standing on Ceile's other side, and she had a sour look on her face. She'd run out of ammo for the railgun during the fight, and had left it behind. The dwarf had plenty of rounds for her pistols, but the arakhin could take a handful of them before they went down, as the others had found out to their dismay.

She looked down at Ceile's waist and frowned. I got the impression that my friend hadn't run her heroics past the dwarf before she'd come to my aid, and Robin wasn't very impressed with that. She hadn't taken the knife back, though.

Petrel was close by, standing in front of the most open portion of our little stop and staring down into the web. The steel dwarf was covered in arakhin bits, and was now almost as camouflaged as the monsters were in the metal, concrete and webbing environment that we found ourselves in.

On the opposite end of the platform were Penguin and the last two dwarves of his unit. They were talking quietly while they watched for trouble. They were also throwing us dangerous looks, and I understood why. In the chaos since we'd left the elevator, seven dwarves had been killed, and all of them Krekt Twelve citizens. Penguin was probably angry at himself because this had been his plan, but I imagine all three of them were angry at me for my less than legendary performance and angry at all four of us for having survived when so many of them had not.

I breathed deep of the stale air, holding tight to Ceile's arm. My chest was sore, and I felt dizzy and nauseous. And afraid. If the Other was right, and Bill's booster had worn off, then I was in a lot of trouble. It'd been over two weeks since I'd gotten the news from Dr. Jacobs, and two weeks was all he'd given me for pleasant existence. That meant things were going to be very much unpleasant from here on in, and they were only going to get worse.

We need Bill.

I frowned, but he was right. If I was going to be anything other than dead weight, or just dead, I needed whatever it was the engineer had hit me with at the start of this adventure.

'We have to go. We're barely halfway, and who knows how long they're gone for. If they're gone at all,' Petrel said. 'My scanners are useless in here, something about the webbing is messing with them.'

Penguin gave the steel dwarf a searching look, but then nodded. 'We've wasted too much time already. We'll go down first, watch our backs,' the dwarf said, then turned away. 'If you think you can manage that,' he said, darkly. He nodded to his two companions, and then went over the edge.

The dwarf with the laser rifle was close behind him, but the blonde woman hesitated. She looked us all over before shaking her head and dropping in after the others. I wondered if she thought she might be safer with us despite Penguin's distrust. She'd seemed nice enough, and she'd watched Ceile for us. I hoped we could return the favour.

'Go. I should go in last, I can keep them off of our backs,' Petrel said, gesturing into the shaft.

Robin looked me over carefully, then leaned in close. 'You don't look great, old man. I'll go first, you take Ceile right after me,' she said, then frowned, and continued, 'Take care of her,' and then leapt into the gap.

Ceile took my hand, and asked, 'Are you ready, Martin? You will have to guide me, we will need to be swift.'

I squeezed her hand. 'You'll probably be faster than me. Let's go,' I said, then stretched up and gave her a kiss on the cheek. Her face lit up and she smiled, suddenly enfolding me in a tight hug.

Once we'd carefully climbed down off of the platform onto the first few strands, we made good time. Ceile moved with confidence, choosing foot and handholds with both my guidance and her own touch and feel. I admired her, more so than ever. Even with everything that had happened to her, she still soldiered on.

Robin moved at our pace, staying only five metres or so below us and watching every direction at once. Petrel kept a bit larger distance, though mostly because any strand he put his weight on bent precariously close to us if he didn't. The steel dwarf descended at an easy pace, stopping to keep an eye on everything and his scanners at once.

Penguin and the others were much quicker, and had soon vanished into the web below. I heard Robin hiss something into the maze after them, but shortly after, the dwarf woman looked up at me and shook her head with a frown. It looked like we were on our own after all.

Our descent toward the transport facility continued uncontested, despite the loss of the Twelve dwarves. Level after level passed with no sign of the arakhin, and though none of us said anything, the looks I exchanged with Robin and Petrel weren't optimistic. The sheer size of the maze meant there could be hundreds of the monsters somewhere out beyond the ruined wall of the elevator shaft. If it'd been an underwyrm that had carved out that space, then it could be massive.

A faint mechanical sound was growing louder as we dropped toward the base of the shaft. A soft thrum that danced along the web and through the walls. Penguin hadn't been lying, the transport facility was at least powered up. I hoped that he hadn't been lying about the airship, too.

I saw Robin wave in excitement and point silently through a gap in the web below her, and I breathed a sigh of relief when I saw a sliver of concrete there. Squeezing Ceile's hand, we slowly climbed down until we were crouched near the dwarf woman, and then felt the webbing around us shake as Petrel joined us.

There were two doors on the pad below us, one of which was open. Through it, we could see the facility. The four of us swung down onto the platform, and then we quietly crept up to the door to have a look. Robin gasped and I shook my head.

Penguin was lying on the floor a hundred metres away, his head a smoking ruin. The other two dwarves were not far from his body, on their stomachs, hands on their heads, weapons on the floor several metres away. Arrayed around them was a group of twenty dwarves, dressed in fatigues and carrying tempest rifles. A twenty first dwarf, dressed in a slightly different uniform, stood a little ways off, his pistol pointed at Penguin and still smoking.

All of them were casting nervous looks in all directions, and I could see why. The ceiling and floor of the facility had been carved up by the monster that had done the damage along the side of the elevator shaft, and from down here you could see just how massive the arakhin web had gotten. It ran the entire length of the chamber, probably five hundred metres, right up to the point where the facility opened up into the gigantic service shaft that ran to the surface.

Webs dangled from the ceiling, though the chamber itself was fairly clear. Penguin had been right, the facility looked like it had been mothballed, but there were three crawlers and an airship still docked among its eighteen stations. Robin caught my hand and squeezed it tightly, her face happy. All we had to do was get past the dwarves and then we'd be free.

It occurred to me that the nervous looks weren't entirely being cast toward the ceiling, and I followed some of the dwarves' gazes out toward the crawler tunnels to the south. Next to the passages was something that looked like the debris from the ceiling had fallen to form a huge pile of destroyed concrete and stone. I had to stifle a gasp when I saw the pile suddenly rise and fall in a familiar way.

No wonder the dwarves were antsy. The arakhin were a big threat, but hardly the only danger. The beast that had dug out their lair for them was still here. Sleeping.

The pile of debris was an underwyrm. And a really big one.

82

The underwyrm wasn't just big, it was old. I couldn't see its head, but its skin was buried under layers of gems and stones. Decades, maybe centuries of burrowing through the deep had given it an armour that wouldn't be easy to get through, at least not by any of the weapons anyone here in the facility currently had. I could, if I had my strength, but it would be tough, and I didn't think the wyrm would give me the time I'd need.

Thankfully, the monster didn't look like it was in any hurry to move from its position, curled up in front of the exit tunnels. Looking around, I could see that the passages the wyrm had dug were erratic and wildly curved, and I wondered if there was something wrong with it.

Maybe it's dying. Like us.

I frowned. The Other might be right, and if he was, then there was no way to know what the damn thing would do. If it hadn't reacted to the violence between the dwarves, then maybe it wouldn't be a problem.

Putting aside the underwyrm for the moment, I searched the web that crossed every inch of the ceiling above for any sign of the arakhin. I wanted to hope that they had been discouraged from attacking and were nursing their wounds in the maze over our heads, or that they were afraid of the wyrm, but I wasn't going to count on either.

And then there were the dwarves. All of them but the one that had killed Penguin had rifles of some kind. The clips looked like they just carried basic rounds, but you never knew with dwarves. They'd obviously not expected the underwyrm to be there, and as I watched, it was evident that this group wasn't any better trained than Penguin's had been. Better equipped, yes, but they stood awkwardly, not looking comfortable in their combat gear. Most of them looked like they'd rather be somewhere else.

Of course, regardless of how effective they were as fighters, there were still twenty of them.

The last one wasn't much better. He looked very angry, and his pistol hand shook with rage. We'd missed whatever had gone down between the two groups, but it had obviously not gone the way he'd wanted, and he'd killed Penguin. Spinning away and stomping over to the two dwarves that were on the ground, he grabbed hold of the blond woman's hair, pulled her up just enough so that she was looking into his eyes, and then put his pistol to the side of her head. They started shouting at each other, though it was lost in the hum of the transport facility's equipment.

I felt Robin settle in beside me and lean in close. 'Unless we want to climb back up the shaft and try to navigate through the arakhin web, the only way to the airship is right past all of the dwarves,' she whispered into my ear.

I nodded at her, and quietly said, 'There's enough debris on the north side of the chamber that we could sneak past. It's pretty close to them, but between the noise and worrying about the arakhin or that underwyrm, we might be able to slip by.'

Ceile gently pulled me back into the shadows of the shaft. 'Can we save the two that were with us? Neither of them have done us any harm, and Bluejay was kind to me,' my friend whispered.

I frowned, feeling bad that I'd never learnt anyone's name other than Penguin's, then said, 'I don't know if we can, Ceile. If my magic fails again, we might all be killed. Petrel's a force to be reckoned with, but I don't think he can take down all twenty one of them, not when they all have rifles. Robin's a good shot with the pistols, but there's just so many.' I sighed and shook my head. 'The airship looks like it has some weaponry, if we can make it there and get the ship running, we can cut the dwarves down and then pickup whoever's left.'

Petrel crouched down next to us. 'Martin is right, we can't risk the fight without his magic. There's a good chance that our trip to the airship is going to require some running as it is,' the steel dwarf said, quietly. Ceile looked sad, but nodded. Robin gave her shoulder a squeeze.

'Alright, here's what we'll do. Robin, you'll be first. You're quickest on your feet and we need you to get into the ship and get it started up as quick as possible. Ceile and I will follow from a fair distance back, then Petrel will come up last, a few bullets won't take you down and we might need that shield. If there's enough space between us, it'll be less likely that they'll know all four of us are here, and we can ambush them if one of us is seen,' I said, turning to look at each of my companions, who nodded. Robin looked a little green and Ceile, apprehensive. Petrel's face was emotionless.

We gathered at the doorway again, and I growled. The lead dwarf was still interrogating Bluejay, but now the blonde woman's face was cut and swollen. The handle of his pistol dripped her blood, and I thought I could see hair caught in the mess. I realized my hands were shaking, and Ceile took one of them in a tight grip.

I hoped the tremor was anger rather than my failing health.

'We have to go,' Petrel whispered from behind us.

Robin didn't hesitate. She darted from the doorway into the debris directly to our right and slid into cover. Much of the smooth floor was still clear behind the mess, though it was littered with rock and metal from the ceiling and walls. Looking back, the dwarf gave me a wink, then turned and clambered over some wreckage and vanished. None of the Twelve dwarves noticed, most of them had congregated into nervous groups and were quietly chatting, throwing the occasional glance toward the ceiling, the wyrm, and their other prisoner.

So far so good. No one was paying any attention to the doorway. I gave Ceile's hand another squeeze, and then the two of us quickly ducked into the debris. Again, no unwanted attention, though I had a brief moment of panic when the edge of my pack caught on an exposed pipe and nearly took me to my feet. It was only because Ceile was quick to steady me that it didn't.

As we moved slowly toward the airship and escape, my legs and arms began to shake, and I started feeling weaker and weaker. My breath was getting ragged, and now I was moving slower than Ceile was. She squeezed my hand in concern, but I kept us going. We had to make it to the airship.

A glance through one of the gaps in the debris pile showed that Bluejay was back to lying on the floor. There was a lot of blood around her, but I saw her breathing slowly, so she was at least alive. The leader of the other group had started working his magic on Bluejay's companion, and I wished I could hear what he wanted to know.

Shaking my head in anger, I felt rage ripple through my blood. I snarled and reached out into that ocean of rot and decay and let the nether ooze into my arms. The flow was slow, and the effort made my head hurt, but it was something. I couldn't murder the entire group, but if I kept it up I might at least get the leader.

Ahead, Robin vanished into the wreckage. I caught a glimpse of red hair and the back of her pack before she was completely gone. We were past the dwarves, now, and almost halfway to the airship. Unless something went really wrong, Robin should be able to make it without much trouble, and Ceile and I were just a couple tough gaps from that safety as well. I looked behind us, to see Petrel waiting patiently a few heaps back. The steel dwarf blended in pretty well, even with the added noise he was making he probably had the easiest time of the four of us.

Inching up to the gap, I checked on the Twelve dwarves. This was going to be a hard one for Ceile and me. We were further from the group than we had been the entire time, but a number of them were facing toward us and even in the dim lighting of the transport facility we were going to be pretty visible when we crossed.

I pulled Ceile to me, and whispered, 'When I squeeze your hand, I want you to keep low but move quick. There's a couple metres or so of open floor before it closes in again, so we need to be fast. This is the worst of them, there's only one more gap before we're in the clear,' in her ear. She nodded with a small smile.

The next pile of debris was ugly. The wall had caved in when the underwyrm had come through the roof near it, and the resulting hole was huge. Pipes poked out of the shadows, twisted and broken. Water poured out from one, pooling around the edges of the pile and then falling into cracks to tumble away into the depths far below. Steam billowed from another, adding even more noise to the racket blanketing the facility. It was going to be a messy landing.

When the coast looked clear, I surged forward and Ceile went with me, instinctively moving at my side. Chills surged down my spine, and I tried to keep my gaze forward so I wouldn't send both Ceile and I crashing into the debris by accident. As we reached the other side of the gap and continued into cover without anyone shooting at us, I let myself smile. We were almost home free, just a little bit more.

Then another chunk of rebar jutting out of the pile caught my pack, tearing it open and dumping its contents everywhere, throwing me violently to the ground, and bringing a sizable part of the wreckage around me crashing down. Ceile had gone into a crouch further in, her eye looking in all directions, her face full of concern. I struggled to get back to my feet, worried that the commotion would bring the dwarves down on our heads. I looked over my shoulder as I did, hoping I wouldn't see the group coming toward us, guns blazing.

When I looked back, I found myself face to ugly face with an arakhin.

83

The monster hissed angrily, and its jaws clicked wildly as all of its nightmare eyes twitched across my face. It was barely a metre from me, and must have been hiding in the debris I'd just unhelpfully scattered across the floor. It lifted itself free of the ground on its jagged and hooked legs, and stalked forward slowly. I backed away, acutely aware that there might be twenty one unfriendly dwarves approaching from that direction.

Ceile had somehow heard the arakhin's hiss through the noise, and now I saw her slowly coming toward me and the creature, her knife in hand and held out in front of her. She stalked along, carefully testing each step before moving, listening carefully. A few metres off to the arakhin's side, I wasn't sure if she'd get near enough to strike before I stumbled out into the open area.

I wondered which was preferable: death by arakhin or by a squad of dwarf civilians who probably barely knew how to shoot their guns.

Seemingly in answer my question, a hail of rifle rounds from somewhere behind me tore into the monster and then clipped Ceile, spinning my friend around and sending her sliding into the wreckage near the wall. The arakhin shrieked and crumpled as chitin and blood and gore spat off in every direction. As soon as it did, I went low and darted for Ceile, catching a bullet in the back for my trouble.

I went down in a heap, howling in agony as I tried to drag myself to my friend. My left arm refused to cooperate, and I ended up on my face in a pool of cold water and, increasingly, blood. I managed to roll over so I wasn't in danger of drowning, but that was it.

The lead dwarf stood over me, his smoking pistol half-aimed my way and looking down with a victorious smile. 'I've been looking for you, outsider,' he snarled with pleasure. 'You're going to make me a lot of money, you and your friend here, provided both of you don't die first. Medic!' he yelled over his shoulder, turning to look toward the group that had haphazardly gathered around the gap in the wall. Every one of them looked even more nervous than before.

Then one of them screamed, 'Crow!' and started bringing her rifle up.

Whether this Crow was the same as the one that had attacked Penguin's group far above us or not, I'd never know. Before the dwarf could react, Petrel burst from cover behind him, raced up, and promptly hit him so hard with both fists that his ribcage caved in. Without any of the others firing so much as a single shot, their leader flew backward into the twitching body of the arakhin and died.

The death of their leader spurred the group to action, and suddenly twenty rifles were firing wildly into the area around us. Their aim was terrible, but they were putting out a lot of rounds, and it wouldn't take long before someone got lucky enough to hit the three of us.

Petrel was already racing to fight back. With the steel dwarf baring down on them, half of the dwarves abruptly turned and fled. The others spread out, and I heard rounds rocket off of Petrel's armour. I knew he couldn't take too much of that. He had thick skin, but the hardware that operated his joints and whatnot was delicate, even when they were built with dwarf tech. An unlucky shot to his face could hurt him bad. Or kill him.

Whether or not the steel dwarf could take on twenty of his not so steel kin turned out to be irrelevant. With a shriek that drowned out the gunfire and the cries of the dwarves and the thrum of machinery, a host of arakhin dropped out of the web above, landing and attacking with horrible speed. The dwarves were almost immediately surrounded, there were so many of the monsters.

Two of Crow's dwarves went down without ever seeing who killed them. The others turned their fire away from Petrel, sending rounds blasting out into the ceiling, skipping across the floor, and hitting everything but arakhin. Another dwarf went down, a bullet from one of the others leaving an unsightly hole through his head.

The arakhin weren't getting it entirely their way. Petrel had changed targets to one of the monsters trying to attack him, catching its legs and tearing two of them free. As it screamed and reeled away, the steel dwarf spun and struck out at a second, sending a hand deep into the creature's eyes and then into its brain. That one dropped like a stone, its legs scrabbling mindlessly in death.

Several more fell to rifle fire, though not through any particular skill, and I heard the familiar blast of two pistols as Robin joined the fight from somewhere closer to the airship. A black lighting round slammed into an arakhin on the debris pile, and the monster burst in a shower of gore.

I turned my head when I saw movement nearby, and was happy to find Ceile crouching down next to me, without a wound. I saw her lips move and her hand move through a set of gestures, and then I felt the calm and comfort of her healing spell. Eerily, I felt the bullet push slowly out my back as the tissue regenerated itself. As the cooling rain faded away, I slowly pushed myself up until I could wrap her in a tight hug, which she returned with a smile.

'Are you hurt, Ceile? We have to get out of here, the arakhin have decided to come visit en masse,' I said to her, leaning in so she could hear me over the cacophony.

'I have healed what I can, but I need a necromancer. This body has sustained a large amount of damage, I do not know if it can be saved. I may need a new one,' Ceile said, shaking her head and faltering on that last. She knew what I thought of transfer, but we'd never really talked about it. I knew it was a discussion that we should have had decades ago, but how do you gently tell your best friend that you didn't think she was really who she thought she was?

We got to our feet, and I looked out into the chaos. None of the arakhin had decided to bother with us, and the dwarves were busy bothering themselves with the arakhin. Petrel was trying to edge away from his attackers, but they just kept coming. Ahead, I could hear Robin firing at something just out of sight.

The underwyrm went right on sleeping.

Bluejay and the other of Penguin's dwarves had dragged themselves out of the worst of the fray, and were huddling together near the debris wall. I made eye contact with the blonde dwarf, and she gave me a pleading look. She was hurt pretty bad, and her companion wasn't any better off. If they didn't get help, they were going to die here, and soon.

I sighed as I watched her burst into tears. I leaned in to Ceile again, and said, 'We're going to go get Bluejay and her friend. They're going to need healing. None of the arakhin are near them right now, I think they're tied up with Petrel and the other dwarves.' I squeezed her hand. 'I don't think I can protect us, but who knows how long they'll survive if we don't go get them.'

Ceile gently smiled, and then squeezed my hand back. 'The life of a hero,' she said with an exaggerated tone. 'Let us go get them.'

I was still a bit wobbly from getting shot in the back, and shaky besides, but I led Ceile to the gap and then out along the side toward Bluejay. The arakhin ignored us, concentrating their attacks on Petrel and the armed dwarves. Our greatest threat was being shot by one of them.

Bluejay was staring at me with gratitude and happiness etched on her face. When Ceile and I finally arrived at her side, she immediately started crying again as she brokenly tried to thank us. The other dwarf, a man with curly black hair and dark blue tattoos that crossed his face at right angles, was so overcome by our coming to their assistance that he wasn't able to talk. Once Ceile reached out and put her hand on each of their foreheads in turn, figuring out their wounds and then healing them, the two were much calmer.

'There's not much time. The arakhin just keep coming, and Crow's group is throwing enough death out into the air that we're more likely to catch a bullet than be eaten by a monster. We're going to head for the airship, you should come with us. Once we fire up its weapons, we can clear the facility and you can take the crawler like Penguin wanted,' I said, crouched down next to Bluejay.

The dwarves looked at each other, then back to me and nodded. 'We could try to grab one or two of the rifles out there,' Bluejay said, pointing out into the fray. 'That'd give us something to fight back with.'

I shook my head as I got to my feet, guiding Ceile to hers. 'You'd probably get shot in the face by one of school teachers or lifeguards that are firing the other rifles so accurately out there. The arakhin have been leaving us alone, and until they kill a few more of the more dangerous targets, maybe they'll keep doing so. Let's go,' I said.

When they nodded, I turned and the four of us slowly moved back toward the gap in the debris wall. More arakhin were falling from the ceiling, and now the whole facility seemed to be crawling with them. I shook my head as I looked west toward the airship and saw the sheer amount of them skittering around between it and us.

I gestured for everyone to crouch down after we'd gotten back into cover. 'I'm not sure we can make it. We need a distraction, there's just-' I started to say, then trailed off as I absently put my hand down on something in the wreckage under my feet.

The thunder thumper round. I'd carried the stupid thing all the way from the Red Flag's wreck, and forgotten I had it. When my bag had gotten shredded, I hadn't noticed it fall to the floor in the chaos.

'Where the hell did that come from?' Bluejay's friend asked in confusion. 'Those things are banned in the krekt, they make the wyrms crazy.'

I shared a glance with Bluejay, and she slowly nodded. 'Looks like we have our distraction,' I said, lifting the round up with a grin.

84

Before I could give myself time to think it over, I passed the round to Ceile. 'Ceile, my dear, when I ask you to, throw that thing out and as high as you can, please,' I said, gently turning her to face toward the underwyrm. My friend felt the thing carefully, getting a feel for its weight and dimensions and nodded.

'I'm going to ignite it once it's as far as possible from us. As soon as I do, start running. Don't stop if you can avoid it. I'm not sure what the wyrm will do, but I have a feeling the arakhin won't worry much about us once the round goes off,' I said, turning to look at the other two. 'Oh, and cover your ears, these things make a lot of noise,' I added.

When everyone was ready, I inched to the edge of the gap and looked for Petrel. The steel dwarf was still close by, fighting with several arakhin. He noticed me peeking out from the debris, and gave me a quizzical look as he spun around and swatted viciously at the monsters. I had Ceile hand me the thunder thumper and then lifted it enough so he could see it. He looked shocked initially, but it quickly changed to a wicked smile, and he nodded.

Getting quickly back under cover, I gave the round back to Ceile. 'Everyone ready?' I asked, and when everyone nodded, I started shaping the nether I'd been gathering and said, 'Now, Ceile!'

My friend wound up and launched the thunder thumper into the air, sending it arcing out over the horde of arakhin and steadily dwindling dwarves, and just as it was directly over the largest group, I folded the nether into a form of explosion and lit the round off.

The spell wasn't big, nor particularly powerful, but it was all I could do and it was enough. Bluejay and her friend were already running, their hands to their ears, and Ceile had tucked in with her good arm covering her good ear. I barely had enough time to throw my hands to my ears and then there was a brutal thump of sound and a shock wave that picked everyone and everything up and threw them around.

I struggled up off the ground, scrabbling toward Ceile, who had hit the deck a few metres away. An arakhin groggily swayed to its feet nearby, having been thrown over the debris pile and into the wall. Petrel had been pushed a couple metres, his metal feet carving channels in the concrete as he slid. I couldn't see Robin.

The dwarves and arakhin that had been closest to the thunder thumper when it went off were a messy pile of ragged tissue, shattered chitin and splintered bone, all crunched to the floor and mangled together. Everyone that had survived was slowly getting to their feet.

There were still a lot of arakhin, and I started to think we were going to get eaten after all.

Then the whole chamber shook, and the underwyrm lifted its head clear of the ground and into the web above. It paused for a long moment, making no sound, its head cloaked in the arakhin's maze. Webbing and stone and dust fell in a shower of debris that tumbled down its skin and out across the floor. Arakhin and dwarf froze as one, turning to stare at the wyrm in fear.

I wasn't waiting to see what it was going to do. 'Let's go,' I said, hoarsely. I gently pulled Ceile forward, and then helped Bluejay get unsteadily to her feet. The other dwarf had been thrown into a jagged mess of twisted metal and wasn't going anywhere ever again. The last of Penguin's dwarves shook her head sadly and then fell in beside Ceile. Together, we clambered over the last pile, and I felt my heart thunder in my chest as I saw the airship revealed far ahead and open concrete the whole way there.

We'd only made it a few steps when the underwyrm howled and went berserk.

It wasn't fast, but it was massive, and now it was really, really mad. High above us, the monster shook its head violently, tearing huge chunks of web free and sending the sticky cables sailing. Rock and stone fell, crashing down from the maze and crushing arakhin and dwarves. Panic broke fear, and now everyone was running or skittering in every direction, trying to stay upright as the whole chamber shook wildly.

I went down, almost taking Ceile with me. Before I hit the floor, Petrel caught hold of the back of my jacket and then we were all running again. A loud crash from behind us made me look over my shoulder in time to see the base of the elevator shaft collapse in on itself, sealing the transport facility away from the rest of the krekt. An arakhin shot past, its armoured legs clicking creepily along the concrete. The creature didn't even look at us as it went by with a hi-pitched keening sound.

One of Crow's men caught up with us, looking rapidly back and forth between me and the underwyrm. His rifle was nowhere to be found, and he settled in next to Petrel as our group fled for the distant ship. I exchanged a look with Bluejay, who looked simultaneously sad and angry.

With brutal force, the underwyrm suddenly lifted itself free of the ground and pulled its bulk into the ruin of the ceiling and the arakhin's web, vanishing with yet another howl that cut through the noise of the facility's machinery and echoed impossibly loudly around the chamber and then out into the service shaft. Between the noise of its movement and the constant rain of debris falling from above, we could track the monster's progress. My heart beat a little faster as I watched the stone and dust get closer and closer.

Ahead, I saw Robin watching us approach, her pistols drawn. She looked a little shell shocked, and I felt bad that I'd had no way to warn her. I waved her on, and the dwarf nodded and spun, headed for the airship. She was fast, ignoring the wave of arakhin fleeing around her, only taking time to point blank shoot one that got close enough to take a wild swipe at her.

Off to our left, a handful of Crow's group had decided the airship would be a good place to be, and suddenly my little party had grown to ten. A massive boulder that fell from the ceiling reduced that to nine, and then a terrified arakhin lashed out and cut another in half before it was crushed by debris.

When the underwyrm reappeared, it fell face first from the maze to our southwest, and crashed into the concrete with a thunderclap and a shock wave that threw everything on the ground to the ground. Nasty slurping sounds cut through the thrum of the facility, and then the wyrm sank into the floor like it was quicksand. Its body seemed to whistle past for an eternity before its segmented tail fell from above and vanished into the slowly-cooling hole the monster had made.

Robin was on her feet and already running. With the arakhin thinning out, the creatures scaling walls to find safety in the deeper stretches of their web or skittering into the older holes for solace in the depths far below, the dwarf was free to clamber up the maintenance ladder on the ship. With a quick glance our way, she slid into a hatch and vanished into the hull.

My group of eight fell apart as everyone but Petrel, me, Ceile, and Bluejay staggered to their feet and charged for the airship. I sighed as I watched them go. Three of them still had their rifles, and at least two of them gave me dark looks as they left. When the four of us were on our way once again, fighting the bucking floor, I started gathering nether once again.

The airship suddenly lit up, brilliant white lights flashing into existence along the outside of its hull. I heard a low pitched whine slowly build in intensity until it almost drowned out the facility's equipment. I cheered inside, and looked over to see Ceile smiling. If we can get free with the ship, we'll have a ride home once this adventure's finished. No brutal long walk, no trip through Bill's portals.

That thought made me frown. I needed to destroy Bill's machine. That was going to be an interesting day.

Back near the destroyed entrance, a circle of the concrete floor liquefied and then the underwyrm burst through it, howling through the mess. The chamber shook again, and I couldn't help but gasp when

I saw the monster crash down on the floor, buckling several sections and sending massive cracks shooting out in all directions. It paused for a moment, then it lurched forward on its multitude of legs.

Toward us.

The wyrm had no eyes, but even one as old as this monster could feel and hear, and it wanted to turn whatever had set it off into paste. Bluejay's eyes went wide when she looked back to see what I was looking at, and then she darted away with an apologetic look. Petrel looked over at me and shook his head. We weren't going to outrun the damn thing, and I was the only one that could fight it.

I snarled with frustration, acutely aware of just how slow the flow of energy was that seeped into my arms from the ocean on the other side of reality. Opening the gate wider made everything start to get far away, and I nearly fell to my knees when I tried. My body was having enough trouble keeping up with the others, and I knew they were all slowing their pace to match mine.

'I don't suppose you have another thunder thumper in your pocket?' Petrel said with an electronic laugh.

There was a shriek of stone scraping against concrete, and I looked back to see the underwyrm almost on us, its massive mouth open and acid glands spraying the fluid that would turn us into soup. As I gazed into the churning black hole that was the monster's throat, I shook my head and squeezed Ceile's hand. Not the most glamourous way to go out.

It took me a moment to realize that Petrel wasn't next to me anymore, and I looked wildly around for the steel dwarf. Over my shoulder, I found him standing on top of a chunk of fallen ceiling, facing the underwyrm, his arms wide, slightly crouched.

Before I could so much as yell his name, the dwarf ducked down and then threw himself at the monster.

85

Rather than fly directly into the underwyrm's mouth and certain doom, Petrel leapt into the air over it. I heard the hydraulics on his legs shriek with agony, undoubtedly not designed to be throwing the dwarf's bulk around. Smoke and sparks erupted from them as he tumbled through the tip of the spray splashing out of the wyrm's lips, rolled awkwardly across the top of its head and onto its back. Gems and rocks spewed out as the steel dwarf stopped his slide by jamming his hands hard into the monster's back.

He couldn't cut the whole way through it, but tearing some of the wyrm's armour up was enough for it to feel the attack. It spun abruptly away from me and Ceile and twirled itself violently into a coil, trying to shake Petrel off. When the steel dwarf didn't immediately fall off, the monster howled and then launched itself into the ceiling, crashing through what wreckage and arakhin webbing remained. In seconds, the underwyrm's head and the dwarf had vanished into the shadows overhead.

As Ceile and I put distance between us and its rapidly disappearing body, I hoped that Petrel would come out of his heroics alive, but there was no time to think about it. We didn't have any way to help the dwarf, and right now all we could do was get to the airship. The chamber was rocking as the underwyrm cut and carved its way through the stone somewhere overhead.

The ship was big, much larger than the Red Flag, some kind of cargo transport. Blocky and heavy, I doubted its five engines could get much speed out of her. There were no turrets, though I could see at least a few cannons nestled into spaces along the hull. They were probably guided by a couple security consoles near the pilot's station. Not powerful, but enough to keep the wildlife off of it.

There was a commotion around the ship, and as we neared I could see that Crow's dwarves were gathered below it in between the landing struts on this side of the ship and the closed entrance hatch, holding Bluejay at gunpoint and shouting. I sighed. As if we didn't all have enough to worry about. Slowing as we approached, two of the dwarves swung their weapons my direction. I pulled Ceile in behind me and put my hands up.

'Tell your friend to open this ship up, human, or we start killing all of you one at a time,' one of the dwarves snarled, loudly. His friends caught Bluejay's arms and threw her over to slide painfully into a heap next to Ceile. Now all the rifles were pointed our way.

'Now, there's no reason to get violent, friend. That wyrm is going to destroy this place, and we all need this ship to get to safety. We can all board, take it the surface, and then all of you can drop us off and take it wherever you need to go. Nobody else needs to get hurt,' I said, calmly. The loud mouth just looked angrier, though one of the others looked sympathetic and the others uncomfortable.

A voice suddenly cut through the cacophony of the underwyrm's passage. 'I'll tell you again. Any dwarves that would like safe passage out of here can drop their rifles and go stand over near my friends. Don't get cute with me,' Robin said, crackling through the speaker.

The lead dwarf looked increasingly livid, but two of the dwarves gave him apologetic glances, set their weapons down, and quietly walked over to stand near us. The other didn't look like he had any idea what to do, but kept his rifle pointing our way.

Furious, the first dwarf pointed his weapon at Bluejay, and started to yell, 'Fine, she's first, you should have-'

There was an explosion of noise and light, and the floor shook violently at my feet. When my senses gradually returned, I found that the only thing remaining of the lead dwarf was his lower legs, standing where he had been, the limbs smoking and ending just below the knees. A large, and also smoking, crater had appeared behind him.

A cannon, both barrels hissing with heat, was aimed down at him from the top of the ship. 'Sorry,' I heard Robin say over the speaker, 'The sights are low and she was set to fire both rounds.'

The last dwarf threw his rifle away while he stared in horror at the remains of his companion.

A new vibration shimmered along the concrete, and a personnel door slowly descended from the hull near us. Robin stood at the top, pistols out. She beckoned us all up, looking suspiciously at the surviving Crow's dwarves. 'C'mon, we need to get out of here before that damn wyrm destroys the ship or kills us all,' she shouted over the noise of the drive and the underwyrm's continued rampage around and above and below the facility.

We filed up, Bluejay first, followed by the other dwarves, then Ceile and me. Robin grabbed my arm as I reached her. 'Martin, I need you to stay here. I need to get the ship ready to go. Don't close the door until I tell you, I want to give Petrel a chance to catch the boat,' she whispered, nodding out into the chamber.

'Get Ceile comfortable, I'll be here,' I said, taking the dwarf's shoulder and giving it a squeeze. She smiled gratefully and took Ceile down the metal hall, where they vanished around a corner.

I turned and crouched down, searching the wreckage of the facility floor for Petrel. The whole place shook violently, and I wondered if the underwyrm had done enough damage to the structure of the rock around us to bring the whole mountain down on our heads. That would be problematic, and I grimaced as more and more stone plummeted to the ground out there.

Should leave the dwarf behind. He made his choice. If we all die, his sacrifice will have been a waste.

I shook the Other's voice away. Something was off about it. Something was off about everything about him, come to think of it. 'Why are you different?' I asked under my breath. He laughed but didn't answer.

The ship shuddered, and I heard the engines spool up outside. I cursed as I inched down the ramp to get a better view, hoping to find Petrel running for us.

At the far end of the chamber, the underwyrm slammed down from the ceiling and then sunk into the floor. When it had vanished once again, I saw a metal figure climb out of the new tunnel and start limping toward the ship. I jumped to my feet then spun back to the console near the door.

'It's Petrel! He's coming but he's hurt. Get the guns ready, they might not be enough to really hurt the wyrm, but maybe it'd be enough to make it think twice,' I shouted into the com. In answer, I heard the other cannons on this side hum to life and fold out to aim into the chamber. I turned and stepped down the ramp again. Nether oozed around my arms, but there was so little.

The steel dwarf came steadily toward me, and as he neared I saw just how much damage he'd taken. He dragged one of his feet behind him, walking on just the ankle. The parts of him that had been shiny were dull and pitted, courtesy of the small splash of acid he'd taken. Sparks shot from him with each step, and there was a trail of oil and grease behind the dwarf.

There was a crazed look on his face, and the mechanisms there were doing a pretty good job of giving him a wild smile.

Another violent tremor rocked the facility, and the underwyrm burst from the floor near the crawler tunnels. With an echoing howl, it crashed into the side of the chamber and then broke through into the stone alongside the elevator shaft. My brain tried hard to grasp the sight of seeing the massive monster swim up the side of the wall, swallowing the metal and stone as it did. Behind the wyrm, the floor had finally had enough and collapsed, a huge hole forming as the concrete and piping and cables plummeted into the depths.

As I watched, cracks shot out from the gap, and it slowly grew as more sections were defeated by gravity and fell away with sharp blasts of noise that ricocheted around the chamber. The abuse the monster had been wreaking on the area above had also taken its toll, and so much debris and wreckage was falling out of the sky that the transport facility was shrinking by the second.

My heart was roaring. If the underwyrm didn't get him, the collapsing chamber might.

As if it'd heard me, the monster crashed to the ground, almost toppling into the growing hole, and then twisted awkwardly in search of Petrel. The steel dwarf was close, if the wyrm didn't hear him right away, he might be safe. I was standing at the bottom of the ramp, and if I hadn't already been shaky, I would have been. I was holding my breath, and I wildly waved the dwarf to me, even though I knew he couldn't go any faster.

When he was twenty metres away, the underwyrm howled and then launched itself toward us. I gasped as I held the ramp strut hard to keep from falling. The steel dwarf was close enough that I didn't think the wyrm could catch him, but now the problem might be the monster catching the airship.

The cannons above me suddenly opened up, and slugs of brilliant light rocketed across the chamber to slam into the wyrm and into its mouth. It howled brokenly, and then shook violently, sending even more of the concrete around it tumbling into the abyss. It also slowed slightly down.

I felt the airship lift slightly off the ground, and I backed up the ramp as Petrel limped and fell roughly on its end. As he crawled toward me, I moved over far enough at the entrance that he could get by. The ship's cannons fired again, but this time the wyrm didn't slow, despite the burst of gems and stone that erupted from its skin as the round slammed into it. My eyes widened as the monster closed, blocking out the chamber as it did.

'Go, Robin, go!' I roared into the com, hammering the door close switch.

The engines shrieked with strain and the ship lifted entirely free of the platform. The door sealed shut, and Petrel and I stumbled to the small window near it. I gasped. The underwyrm was right on us, and all we could see was the chasm of its mouth. We were moving, but the monster was still gaining.

'Crap,' I said, but just as it looked like the wyrm might catch us, its mouth abruptly disappeared. As we watched, the monster rocketed off the side of the platform, plummeting into the service shaft. It never slowed or tried to stop.

The underwyrm howled one last time and then vanished into the darkness far below as the transport facility was erased in an explosion of dust and metal and stone.

86

Thankfully, the collapse of the transport facility didn't also bring down the service shaft, and the airship rose steadily toward the surface. We passed inert defence cannons, arrayed in regular patterns along the shaft's walls, then slid carefully through the defensive metal shield and out into open air.

The Blue Sun's light beat down on the ship's hull, and I stood next to the captain's station, looking out into the world with a hand shrouding my eyes. Along with maintaining them, Robin also had a strong knack for piloting them, and the dwarf held the monstrous craft steady as she ran through the diagnostics on the console in front of her. Just behind me and to my left, Ceile sat in front of one of the security consoles, eye wandering aimlessly around the compartment, her hand clutching her leg tightly.

Somewhere further back, I could hear the dwarves from Krekt Twelve talking quietly, Bluejay included. That wasn't surprising, really. The three dwarves that remained of Crow's group sounded like they had joined the rebellion largely because they'd seen what happened to people who refused, and were relieved to be free of the fighting. And regardless of what affiliation they had, they were Bluejay's kin, where my friends and I were strangers and outsiders. I caught the blonde dwarf looking my way every so often with an almost regretful look before returning to talking with the others.

Petrel had gone into self-healing mode, though I imagined he was also keeping half an eye on the chatters.

Finally, Robin looked up at me, and said, 'She's fully fuelled and in apparently pristine shape, though it's been decades since she flew anywhere. Slow and ugly, for sure. Not meant for hauling people around, but she'll get us to the Rook's location and then wherever we have to go once we're back from the vault.' She gave me a wink, 'A lot better than walking a couple thousand kilometres, eh?'

I smiled at her. 'Alright, let's get our guests to their destination and get on our way,' I said, reaching over to give her shoulder a squeeze. I turned away and found Bluejay and the other dwarves standing nervously behind me.

'There's a transfer station to the north of here, over top of an old mine that isn't being used. There'll be a crawler there that we can use to get to Eleven. They'll take us in, though we'll make sure not to mention our individual, er, affiliations during the chaos,' she said. Her kin looked embarrassed, looking every direction but at me.

I snorted, then leaned in close to her. 'Are you sure you can trust these guys?' I asked, nodding at the other three. 'We can drop you at different locations.'

The indignant looks on Crow's dwarves' faces made me snort again, and Bluejay laughed, surprising herself. 'None of us are soldiers, archon. We are safer as a group then we would be alone, and they have no reason to kill me now,' she said, then gestured out the window. 'We may only be a hundred metres from the edges of the krekt, but we may as well be a hundred kilometres. We're a long way from the rebellion.'

I nodded slowly, then looked over my shoulder at Robin. She had already turned away, and then the airship's engines howled and we were headed north.

The goodbyes were short, and for the most part it was just Bluejay that offered them. She looked grateful to be alive, but there were shadows in her eyes, and I imagined that this little adventure would stay with her long after she had settled into Eleven. I shook my head as the four of them vanished into the small metal building that capped the ladders that would take them down to the mine and its crawler. If I'd been a school teacher, the violence would have lurked at the back of my head.

I heard the Other chuckle, and his dark presence slid into the depths.

With the airship in the air once again, Robin set our course due west toward the Rook's mountain and, hopefully, the location of the other party members. Four days had passed since we'd ventured into the portals, and I hoped they were alright. Bill, Kor, Weezab, and Nox weren't defenceless by any means, but there had been a lot of time for things to go wrong.

The mountain was a couple hours away, and so Petrel shut down completely and Ceile and I moved to slightly more comfortable seating in the passenger area a few metres behind the pilot and security stations. As my friend and I lounged quietly, I could hear soft ticks and hisses as some of the metal components on the steel dwarf's body slowly knit themselves back together. It was fascinating but also a bit discomforting. Back in the war, we'd been surprised a few times when metal dwarves had seemingly come back to life after having been severely damaged and left for dead.

When I'd almost dozed off, lulled slowly toward sleep by the constant low-pitched hum of the engines and the drive, Ceile reached over and took my arm. I blinked and looked over at her.

'Martin, I have something to tell you. Something I have not told anyone. There are so many secrets at play in this journey, I want there to be little between us,' she said, very quietly.

I frowned, but reached over to give her hand a squeeze. 'You can tell me anything, Ceile. We've been together for almost two hundred years. You're my best friend,' I said, carefully. Then my mind raced as I realized she might be about to tell me about her early life, something I knew very little about.

For a long moment, she didn't say anything, staring sightlessly away from me. Then her face was stricken with sadness, and she lifted her arm up. 'Would you remove my bracer, please?' she asked, quietly. When I'd unlocked and pulled the ornate thing free, she reached over and drifted her fingers along its surface. She paused when she reached a small, straight section that consisted of a number of indented squares. A tear rolled down her cheek, and then she pressed one of the squares.

There was a high-pitched electronic whine, barely audible in the blanket of sound made by the airship's engines, and then an image flashed into existence in the air just over the bracer. I looked at the picture in wonder as it floated there steadily, marvelling over its clarity and colours. The bracer had to be elven tech, as sophisticated and graceful as the holograph and its projector were.

A smiling elven family was the subject of the image, a father and mother sitting in simple chairs at the center, three kids scattered haphazardly around their feet, two girls and a boy. Their brown skin and dark hair were a match for Ceile's, and the longer I stared at the picture, the more I realized that the similarities went beyond those. The mother had a striking resemblance to my friend, and the older child, a young woman, could have been Ceile's twin.

I looked up at her. 'Ceile, how do you know these people? Your construct looks like it was built in their image. The one daughter, give her a decade or two and you would look exactly like her,' I said, very quietly. My friend looked miserable, and her hand lifted from the surface of the bracer to float shakily inside the picture, as though reaching for the people inside it.

'I know them because they are my family, Martin,' she whispered as more tears wandered down her face.

'I am an elf.'

87

I stared at her in shock, nearly losing my grip on the bracer. I'd never heard of an elf undergoing the transfer rites, and hadn't even thought that was possible. It was human magic, and as far as I knew anytime it had been used on a non-human, it had failed catastrophically. Hell, even extra-humans like Nox couldn't use them. Therianthropes that tried to transfer ended up insane and shortly thereafter dead, as the big 'wolf had sadly told me.

But Ceile was my greatest friend, and if she said she'd been an elf at birth, then that was the truth.

Though she couldn't see me, she'd obviously noticed my bewilderment. Reaching down to squeeze my hand, she said, 'I was born in Woodsholme two-hundred and seventy-eight years ago. My family was caring and close, but the elves are not supportive of those who believe they were born in the wrong body, and life was getting more and more unbearable as I neared adulthood.'

I shook my head slowly, looking down to the smiling elves in the picture. The young boy in the middle, wrapped in his older sister's arm, looked happy but I could see sadness in his eyes. I couldn't imagine what it would have been like for Ceile at that age, knowing something was wrong but powerless to do anything about it. Bullied and hurt for something she had no control over.

That pain showed on my friend's face as she continued, 'I was brutally beaten by a group of bigots, a group that had harassed me and several friends before and were known to security. Charges were filed, but they were dropped when the indifferent officers chose to look the other way. My parents were furious, but after repeated calls for justice got my father put in jail and my mother threatened with her life, I knew there was nothing that could be done.'

Putting a hand over her face, Ceile fell silent for a long moment. 'I fled. Packed what I could and managed to get aboard a human transport destined for the City. I left a note, asking for forgiveness but saying it would be better for the family if I was gone,' she said, finally. 'I arrived with essentially nothing but a bit of money one of the women on the ship had given me, but I knew what I needed. I had heard of constructs, despite the elves' dislike of them, and I knew I needed the body that I should have been born with.'

When her hand dropped, her face was strong once again. 'I met a necromancer who was willing to make a flesh construct for me, in return for certain favours. It is a long process, the creation of a body, and the necromancer's tastes were not gentle, but months after I had arrived from Woodsholme, on my birthday, I underwent the transfer rites and left my old body behind.'

She looked up at me, and gently nodded. 'I had it made in her image. Sarahae, my older sister. We were the best of friends, and she was first to defend me against anyone. I loved her, more than anyone, and when she found out my plan to leave, her only response was that she wanted to come with me,' she quietly said. 'Of course, she could not. It was one thing for a troubled child who was unpopular with the authorities to go missing, it was another for someone as well liked as her to do so. They would have hunted us down within hours, if we had managed to leave the city at all.'

'Did you see any of them again?' I asked when she went quiet.

Ceile looked immensely sad again, then whispered, 'No. Elves are a very introverted species, so it is very difficult to leave the city to begin with, and my whereabouts and reason for fleeing were known and my family would have risked further misery if they had tried to contact me. Years after I had integrated into my new home, I received a message from Sarahae brought by a sailor whose ship had recently returned from Woodsholme.'

She smiled, sadly. 'She was pregnant. She hoped that I would one day meet my niece,' she said.

I gave her shoulder a squeeze and shook my head slowly. 'I'm sorry. Do you think they were both in the city when the Scayn arrived?' I asked.

Ceile was quiet for a moment, then shrugged. 'I do not know. We do not know how many fled when it became apparent the city was lost. Perhaps they escaped to Balespring, but I do not think so,' she said, then fell silent again.

'That must have been a hard thing for you to do, risking returning to Woodsholme. I wonder how Bill intended to get all of us supposed undesirables past the gates,' I said after a long moment.

My friend chuckled. 'Perhaps he hoped his garish robe would distract them,' she said as she slid her hand across the bracer's surface again, pressing a different button. The family picture flickered, and a new one appeared, this one with just her father and mother. Her dad looked serious but he was winking at the camera. Her mom had a wry smile on her face. They held hands tightly.

Another press and another picture, this time of the older sister. Sarahae. There were some fine details that were different, but otherwise she and Ceile definitely could have been twins. The girl had a brilliant smile, and she appeared to be laughing.

The bracer crackled, and the image changed again. The younger sister stared up at the camera, and she looked like she was having an epic pout. Her arms were crossed in front of her, and her bottom lip was stuck out. I laughed. No doubt she wasn't impressed with the picture taking. She might have been two decades younger than her sister, which wasn't a ton of time elf-wise. 'Leri,' Ceile whispered.

Finally, the picture flickered once more and now the young boy was featured. The sadness that had been hinted at in the family portrait was much more prominent here, and close up you could make out a number of half-healed bruises and half-hidden cuts scattered across his face. The gentle smile was also back, but I got the impression that without Sarahae near, it was only there for the camera's benefit.

'That must have been a horrible time for you,' I said, quietly. Ceile nodded.

'It was, but it is over. My home is in the City, as is my family. But I wanted you to know this last truth, as I have not told you before and it is perhaps the only secret you do not know,' she said. With one last button press, the images above the bracer vanished. I reattached it to her forearm, and she smiled at me before settling into her chair.

'Thank you for sharing it with me, my friend,' I said, settling in next to her. 'I love you.'

She suddenly beamed and a big smile split her face. 'I love you, too, Martin,' she said, reaching over to touch my cheek with a bit of guidance from me.

When Ceile was lightly snoring, I closed my eyes and leaned back. As the minutes passed, I fell in and out of sleep in time with the sound of the engines. When I woke up after a short nightmare in which I fought a red dragon with an underwyrm around the burning remains of my house, I felt someone standing behind me.

'Hey, we should talk,' a familiar voice said from just over my shoulder.

I scrambled to get free of my seat and spin to confront the newcomer, but all I managed to do before I suddenly faded into unconsciousness was turn in my chair so I could see who it was. I shook with disbelief as I caught a glimpse of him.

It was the Other, and he smiled sadly as the darkness took me away.

88

When I opened my eyes, I was standing on a beach, shoeless. The bone white sand covered my feet past my ankles. My torn jacket snapped back and forth lightly and my long hair floated gently in the brisk wind. Somewhere ahead, I could hear the quiet crash of waves, but the water was obscured by roiling purple cloud cover that kissed the ground and shot skyward until it met the grey blanket far overhead.

I'd never been here, but I knew where I was anyway. I was standing on the edge of the Reyan Desert, at the very southern tip of the continent, just metres from the deadly waters of the southern ocean. Looking over my shoulder, I saw an endless plain of sand, interrupted occasionally by a massive dune.

Nothing moved but sand and cloud.

When I looked back toward the ocean, he was standing there. Of course, he looked just like me, shaggy grey hair and beard, skin wrinkled and blotched, blue eyes that had faded to almost grey. It was eerie seeing him like this, just as it'd been after Woodsholme. We'd always shared the same space in reality before, so having him stand here in front of me like my identical twin was bizarre.

'Well, this is new. How did you put this together?' I asked him, gesturing out into the poison clouds beyond.

He shook his head, and said, 'I don't know, things keep changing. Look, we don't have much time, and with you running the show, you're the one that'll have to do something about it.' Taking a few steps toward me, he glanced around and then whispered, 'Bill. There's something wrong about him. Something familiar. He's kept us alive on this trip, sure, but I think he's linked to what's happening to us. You need to watch our back when you encounter him next, and maybe not mention that you plan to blow up his little toy when you get a chance.'

I frowned. 'We've never really trusted him anyway, have we? I don't know, he's definitely got some impressive tech, but something that inserts a third person into someone's mind? We're already pretty packed in here,' I said with a chuckle, tapping myself on the temple.

He smirked, then said, 'I don't know if he's directly responsible. Enough crap has happened to us since we boarded the Red Flag all those days back that could have set these changes off. I'm just saying that something doesn't sit right, I think we've got to worry about Bill.'

The world suddenly started to fade, and I looked around to see the sand grow indistinct and clouds hazy. Looking back, I found him standing twenty metres away and almost at the edge of the roiling clouds over the water. He waved, and looked sad.

'Time's up. It's up to you now, my friend. Keep us safe,' he shouted over the suddenly wilder winds.

I nodded, and said, 'I'll keep my eye out, Martin.' Something twisted violently inside when I did, and the whole world went upside down.

Then I opened my eyes and found myself inside the airship. Ceile was breathing gently in the seat next to me. Over my shoulder, Petrel leaned against the far wall, head bowed. Ahead, Robin flew the ship with skill from the pilot's station.

I extricated myself from Ceile's arm and got carefully up out of my chair. It was a little strange that she'd gotten that friendly, though maybe she'd simply forgotten in her sleep that I was in charge and not her friend. Leaving the passenger seats behind, I walked up the short ramp to the command level and stepped up next to Robin.

The dwarf looked up at me and smiled, then turned back. 'You aren't him, are you,' she said. It wasn't a question, and it surprised me.

'No. Martin is taking a nap,' I said after a long moment.

She looked at me out of the corner of her eye and shook her head. 'How do you live like that? Ceile told me that until we left the City, you hardly ever got out. You just lurked around, waiting for Martin to let his guard down,' she said, quietly. 'So much of your life was out of your control.'

I thought about that, what it had been like before everything started to change, and frowned. There was nothing but fog back there. I could see shadows and hints of images in the murk, but nothing solid. It felt like the fog that had blocked out me and Martin's first fifty years. Everything before the accident.

I hid my shock, and said, 'I haven't really thought about it. We've been busy.'

Robin nodded. We were silent for a while, then she spoke again. 'I think we should leave Ceile with the ship,' she whispered. 'When we get to the Rook, I mean.' She sounded like she felt guilty about suggesting it.

I stifled a laugh. 'That's probably the smart choice, but good luck getting her to stay. She and I might not exactly be close, but I know her pretty well.'

When the dwarf suddenly looked very sad, I wasn't surprised. She and Ceile were obviously pretty close. Maybe more than close, and now I was surprised by something. I actually felt kind of happy for them. So, that was pretty weird.

Abruptly, Robin reached out and caught my arm tightly. Her eyes were almost feverish as she stared up at me. 'Please. You and Martin have to convince her to stay. She can't come down into the vault with us. You're the one in danger, she doesn't have to be,' she said, hoarsely. I was happy that the ship didn't require constant supervision, as the dwarf wasn't exactly piloting.

Her face was almost pleading, and her grip on my arm was painful. 'Please,' she whispered.

I didn't really know what to say, so I just nodded carefully and patted her hand. She didn't look convinced, but she gave me a sad look and turned back to the helm. 'We shouldn't be much longer,' she said, pointing out the windscreen toward the rapidly growing mountain, then she fell silent. I nodded and walked away.

Feeling the need to be away from everyone, I ventured down to the cargo deck and wandered the empty passages. It felt like we were close to the finish line. Meet up with others. Convince the Rook to let us through. Descend to the artifact vault. Step into Bill's regeneration chamber and say hi to my younger self.

Then take this ship back to the City, I guess. And then what? Would the Government reinstate Martin's healthcare because we were no longer about to die? I wondered if there was a duration defined in the small print of his pension, as I didn't expect they would just go on paying us for the next several thousand years.

I scowled. Robin had been right. I'd piggybacked on Martin's life for as long as he'd lived. I'd never accomplished anything other than periods of short term devastation. Our body hadn't died yet because his healthcare and money and sense of self-preservation had kept us alive. Martin was a citizen and decorated war hero. An accomplished scholar and teacher, though that had been long ago. He was well liked and respected, even if he had few close friends. What was I?

I'd only ever been a monster.

I had no name, or at least, not one that I remembered and not one anyone else used. I had always been the Other. Did that mean I was a trespasser? Martin had once called me a disease. If that were true, then the regeneration chamber might just cut me out.

I shook the thoughts away, violently. None of this changed the fact that cancer was slowly turning our insides against us, and with the strange booster effect that was slowly wearing off, there was no way to know how far along it had gotten. This body was a time bomb. I felt weak and sore as I walked, my head ached and breathing was uncomfortable. I could feel the wind aether dancing and whirling around me, but putting a hand into it nearly brought me to my knees. Reaching between realms was hard on a healthy body, much less one as well used as ours.

Regardless of what happened, Martin and I needed to get to that regeneration chamber, and soon.

'We're here. You should see this,' Robin's voice crackled across the intercom, interrupting my thoughts. I dashed up the ramps and ladders and joined everyone at the front of the ship, and then we stood there in silence.

There wasn't a clear border between the plain and the Rook's land. Instead, what started off as streaks of grey popping out in the grasses beneath us grew until everything had been stripped of colour and nothing moved. If it wasn't for the wave and shimmer of the plain behind us, it would have looked like the wind had died altogether.

'It's turning everything to stone,' Robin whispered, hoarsely.

89

I nodded slowly. Robin was right. The grey plague stretched out from the monolith ahead, wrapping around it for as far as we could see. The mountains to the south seemed unaffected, covered in rust coloured earth and green trees, but it was difficult to tell for sure from this far.

Robin brought the airship in a bit lower and then to a stop, and we watched as the grey streaks in the grass slowly stole away the colour, turning the land to stone before our eyes.

Petrel shook his head. 'Maybe don't put us down in that,' the steel dwarf said, quietly. I silently nodded agreement. Turning to look at the rest of us in turn, he continued, 'What do we do now? We don't know where the portal opened, and if the stone has been progressing this quickly for four days, it might have already been overrun.'

I ran a hand through my beard, thoughtfully. 'Bill planned to bargain with the elemental and then kill it if it wasn't cooperative. He's certainly wily enough to do the first part, but just look at this thing,' I said, waving at the massive monolith ahead, 'Weezab is one of the most powerful elementalists that I've ever met, but even if he managed to meet up with them, I'm not sure he could take this thing alone. Hell, we don't even know what this thing is capable of.'

I looked up at Petrel. 'With that in mind, I don't think Bill would confront it without both me and the kobold present. Not right away, anyway. He'd hole up and wait for us or head to the mountains and look for a different way into the caverns. I think,' I said.

The steel dwarf nodded, and said, 'Bill's odd, but he's definitely not stupid. We should do a sweep of the edge of this mess, see if we can find a camp, then check the mountains for signs.'

Ceile spoke, for the first time in hours. 'And if we do not find any signs? We cannot afford to waste more time than necessary, Martin has little time left,' she said, giving my arm a squeeze.

I was surprised to find I didn't hate her touch. One more symptom of whatever was going on, I guess. I shrugged the thought aside and said, 'Then we go in and talk to the Rook ourselves. Carefully, of course. Petrel and I'll do it. Robin, you'll keep the ship running and ready if we have to bail. Ceile, you'll have to wait here with her.' Ceile squawked in protest, but I turned and gave her hand a squeeze. 'Listen, Martin would get really irritating if anything happened to you, and we might need to get out of there fast.'

A thought occurred to me. 'And we need you intact for the descent to the artifact vault. We'll need your healing,' I said. Ceile's frustrated expression slowly faded with the realization that she wasn't going to have to fight me to join the trip, replaced with the serene look that I hadn't seen in a long time.

Robin's face, however, soured and she gave me a dark look.

I gave her an apologetic look. As much as Ceile's blindness was going to make the descent harder, we were probably going to need her magic. Besides, Martin was the romantic, not me. 'Take us around the edge, if Bill's waiting near it, you can probably count on him having some flamboyantly visible signal ready,' I said. When the dwarf woman finally nodded, I looked over at Petrel. 'We should get up onto the observation decks so we can watch as much of the terrain as possible.' The steel dwarf nodded in agreement, and then he turned and headed for the starboard passages. I gave the two women a last look and then headed for the port ones.

The airship sailed for a couple hours, but by the time the White Sun had passed overhead, we had to acknowledge that if Bill and the others had been camped around the edge of the Rook's plague, they were long gone. The mountain loomed in the middle of the dead plain, towering into the sky, all right angles and flat rock. There were few shelves or plateaus that we could see, though the highest reaches of the monolith were out of sight in the clouds far above. It was an oppressive sight, made more so by the uncertainty of what waited for us up there.

We headed for the mountains to the south, but those were just as unhelpful. The land there was made up of deep crevices and narrow corridors that crisscrossed the rock, hidden beneath clumps of trees and bush. I wouldn't have put it past Bill to have climbed to the top of the foliage to put out a signal, but after another hour or two had passed without finding anything, we had to give up.

Which left us with one direction to go.

Gathered in the command area once again, we stood and watched as Robin took the airship up toward the clouds.

'Joke's on us if the Rook isn't up here,' I said with a chuckle. No one laughed, disappointingly.

Then we broke through the clouds and now we were all silent.

Where the lower portion of the mountain had almost been a column of uniform shape, its upper was a chaos of sharp ridges and jagged angles. Below had been a fortress, a monument to the agelessness of stone. Up here, the mountain was a weapon, an arrowhead.

Up here, the mountain was at war with the wind.

A single peak shot up into the sky, narrowing gradually until it came to a viciously pointed end another kilometre over our heads. At the peak's base, two massive ridges extended out toward us, like the arms of a throne, and below them, a long, flat plateau that stretched from cliff to mountain's edge, forming the seat.

In the middle of the plateau were a number of what looked like lumps of stone. They stood out against the flat ground, their colouring slightly off of the slate grey that covered the rest of the mountain. It was tough to get a good look at them, and when Robin tried to bring us closer, the airship rocked violently.

'The wind's crazy up here, I can't get us any closer. I might be able to drop you off back at the edge of the seat, but that's going to put us pretty far from the action,' the dwarf said, frustrated.

I looked at Petrel, and the steel dwarf cocked his head. 'As long as setting foot on the ground doesn't immediately turn us to stone, I think we have to,' he said with a shrug.

I nodded, and turned back to Robin. 'Drop us at the edge, then. Don't put the ship down, we'll throw something less essential out there first before we jump off,' I said. The dwarf woman looked unsure, but nodded. The airship spun away and out of the turbulence.

Petrel and I made our way down to the passenger ramp, and as Robin brought the ship to hover over the barren rock at the far end of the throne's seat, we lowered it and the steel dwarf carefully edged down until he sat at its edge. With a quick toss, he threw an old tool kit we'd found in the cargo area out onto the ground. When the kit and its contents weren't immediately turned to stone, he looked over his shoulder at me.

'I'd appreciate it if you could try and retrieve my head if this goes poorly. Preferably before it turns to rock,' he said, a slight edge in his voice. When I looked askance at him, the steel dwarf laughed. 'It comes off. If things go wrong, I can disconnect it, you'll just have to pull it off my body.'

I burst out laughing. 'That's a handy trick. I'll see what I can do,' I said.

Petrel chuckled, and then, with one last glance my way, he leaned out and put a foot on the ground.

90

For a long moment, we stood frozen in time, me kneeling on the upper half of the ramp, Petrel standing in the dust at its foot. I was holding my breath, watching the steel dwarf's feet for the grey streaks that were slowly killing the land far below us. For his part, the dwarf just stood there, eyes closed.

Finally, he turned to look at me with obvious relief on his face. 'Well, I'm glad you didn't have to come get my head. It's a very uncomfortable process,' the steel dwarf said, amused.

'Well, don't get too excited. Maybe it doesn't affect metal,' I said as I slowly moved down the ramp. When I reached the end, I crouched there, looking dubiously down at the stone below. With a sigh, I stepped down off the ramp and stood next to Petrel.

Fortunately, my feet didn't immediately start turning to rock, and I put a hand on the dwarf's shoulder. He smiled back, and gestured over his shoulder. 'Shall we go see what there is to be seen, my friend?' he asked. Giving the camera over the ramp a jovial wave, the steel dwarf turned and started heading further into the plateau, each step sending a small cloud of dust blasting in every direction.

I looked up at the camera, and nodded. 'Take the ship out a safe distance and watch for my signal. It's too risky to put her down here, but we still need you close enough that we get out fast if need be,' I said.

'Be careful,' Robin's voice crackled from the speaker, and then the ramp slowly closed and the airship lifted away.

I watched it go for a few seconds, then turned and followed the steel dwarf. It wasn't long before I caught up, and the two of us trudged toward the base of the peak and its strange lumps of stone.

Despite the raging wind above, only a small breeze whistled through this strange canyon, carrying the dust around in waves that shimmered in the light of the falling Sun. The ground was rough, broken up in random patterns and spider web cracks that shot out in every direction, making footing treacherous. Nothing grew. The cliff walls weren't much better, and after a large section collapsed nearby, Petrel and I kept our path as far from them as possible.

It wasn't a short walk, and we made it in silence. I didn't know what was waiting for us ahead, and I didn't imagine the dwarf did, either. I'd met hundreds of elementalists, and a handful of aethons, but elementals, well, they weren't common and every last one was different. They were people who had lost themselves to their element, and they could be everything from pathetic to very, very dangerous.

The Rook made this mountain. That likely put him in the latter category.

'Looks like we're here,' Petrel said, bringing me out of my thoughts.

Sure enough, we might have been over a kilometre from the far wall, but the nearest of the odd lumps wasn't far away at all. I heard several sharp clicks and whirring motors and looked over to see the dwarf's hands opening and closing sharply. Noticing my look, he raised an eyebrow and said, 'We should be ready to fight.'

I nodded, and hesitantly reached out for energy. I was surprised when it began flowing into my arms. Not very fast, but much better than before, and I didn't feel ill in the process. Smiling darkly, I let my hands gently weave the energy into simple forms, keeping it fresh. It wasn't going to be enough if I had to go toe to toe with the elemental. I'd probably get one good shot in, and then I'd be running for the airship.

As we closed on the nearest lump, something familiar caught my eye. Something about the way the rock sat on the ground and its shape. I started to speed up a touch so I could get a better look, but Petrel caught my arm and stopped me painfully. I turned to snarl angrily at him, but the steel dwarf waved me off and pointed at the base of the lump. I looked back suspiciously, and then gasped.

'Legs, Martin,' he whispered, and I nodded slowly. Legs, arms, and a stocky chest. We cautiously approached, and what had seemed like just a random chunk of stone was an almost perfect rendition of a dwarf.

'Statues,' I said hopefully and very slowly, ignoring for the moment that the dwarf had called me Martin, looking around at all of the nearby rocks. Dwarves, elves, a human or two, all facing toward the base of the peak. Most of them were posed in strange ways, as though the sculptor had caught his subjects by surprise. Petrel and I continued moving forward, turning to look at each new form as we passed.

Then the steel dwarf cursed, and growled, 'This is Nox.'

He was right, the larger statue to our left was the werewolf. Unlike the others we'd seen, he looked angry and on the attack. I was surprised to find anger rippling through my veins, my hands automatically preparing forms of destruction from the energy arcing around my arms.

I followed Nox's gaze out into the crowd of statues and found its target. A larger figure, mostly obscured by the army of stone around it, and the only thing facing this direction. I beckoned sharply to Petrel, and then started moving slowly toward it.

'That one's Kor,' the steel dwarf said, anger sparking in his voice. The dragon looked like she'd been firing an inferno rifle one handed and had a nasty looking knife at ready in her other. She also looked really mad.

My heart was thundering in my ears and I couldn't figure out why the possibility that these people were dead was bothering me so much. Hell, in the past I'd actively hoped Nox would be killed and planned to one day do it myself if no one else did. I'd hated Ceile almost as much. And I'd certainly not felt anything but indifference for our new companions. Something was really messing with me, and I didn't like it.

Those thoughts scattered as we left Kor behind and stepped around another group of stone dwarves to finally get our first good look at the big statue and the area around it. The thing was tall, humanoid, and looked like it was formed of the same grey rock that the other statues were. It was hunched over something in front of it, crouched low on its oddly indistinct legs and reaching for the object with its strangely shaped arms. Its head was a simple blob of stone, and its face was a mask, consisting of two empty eyes and a mouth stretched into a silent scream of despair. The whole thing was bizarre, like someone had started sculpting it from the stone and then forgotten it before adding any definition beyond the strange face.

The statue's simple hands were curled hungrily over, but not touching, the haft of a massive hammer.

The weapon was huge. Even with its head half buried in the dust and stone, it was still taller than me. I doubted Petrel could drag it, much less lift it. Oddly, it seemed to be a slightly different colour than the surrounding stone, and when I looked closer, I could see small veins of black creeping out from around the hammer and then vanishing into the mountain's flesh. Formed of straight lines and angles, the weapon was simple other than the viciously curled spike on the opposite end of the head. I imagined that anything hit by either end was probably in for a lot of hurt, but that spike looked like it would take a dragon apart without effort.

I shared a look with Petrel. The hammer didn't belong here, both of us could feel that. I felt like I had when I was standing near Bill's portal generator, not in horror but something like reverence. Something about the weapon felt not just old, but ancient. This thing was from a different time, and I stared at it in awe.

A light touch on my shoulder brought me back to the present, and I looked over to see Petrel point off to my right. 'Bill,' he whispered, and there was defeat in his voice. I shook my head slowly as I turned and saw the engineer, cut from stone, his ravaged face looking out from under the travel hat he'd switched to back at the generator outpost. Oddly, he didn't look particularly angry at all, but instead looked almost happy.

'What do we do now?' the steel dwarf hissed from next to me. He had turned to stare darkly at the large statue. 'Bill's the only one who knows how to get from here to the vault. Maybe you know something I don't, but as far as I know, you don't get healed out of being turned to stone.'

I frowned. 'No, but the elemental might be able to reverse this. We just need to wake it up,' I said, quietly. The steel dwarf looked over at me, unconvinced. 'Look, I have to try, I've only got a couple weeks, maybe days and-' I started to say, turning to the dwarf.

'Have you come to free me?' someone said in a voice that was the grinding and crashing of falling boulders. Petrel and I spun around, the steel dwarf dropping into an attack stance, me shaping and spinning the energy in my hands to prepare to defend.

Ahead, the statue's face had lifted up, and now its macabre mask with its empty eyes was staring at us. Where before it had looked miserable, now there was a glimmer of hope. When it spoke next, the words sounded like they were coming from somewhere inside its head, and its mouth didn't move quite in time with them.

'I am the Rook,' the giant rumbled. 'The hammer, strangers. You must destroy the hammer.'

91

The Rook stared down at us from its awkward pose, and despite its lack of eyes, I could feel its gaze shift between me and Petrel. The steel dwarf and I had moved away from each other, keeping a careful eye on the elemental and the other statues arrayed around it.

'Have you come to free me?' it asked again.

I ignored the question for the moment, and said, 'These statues, Rook. Did you make them?' I gestured out into the crowd of silent onlookers.

There was a series of loud cracking noises, and the elemental's head slowly turned to face me as I approached. 'I brought them here to help me, and they could not. So to stone they went,' it rumbled. 'Can you, human? Do you have the power? I do not believe your metal friend does.'

I frowned and sent a glance Petrel's way, only to find the dwarf vanished. I spun back to the elemental in anger, and nearly had a heart attack when I found a new statue standing only a few metres away. The steel dwarf, frozen in time, forever ready to attack.

'Do you have the power? I believe you do,' the Rook said.

'Can you bring them back, elemental?' I snarled, and now energy was snapping and hissing around my hands.

It looked at me silently for a long moment, then it nodded its head ever so slightly. 'I can, but you must help me first. The hammer, stranger. Destroy it, or remove it from here,' the elemental rumbled.

I shook my head. 'I don't know you, elemental. Give me one of my companions back first, show me you can be trusted, and I'll help you,' I said.

The Rook considered that for a few seconds, then nodded. 'Done. Choose,' it said, each word punctuated by a loud crack. Dust and debris tumbled over its shoulders and pooled near its feet.

I didn't hesitate. I turned and pointed back the way I'd come. 'Him. Give me the human construct that calls himself Bill,' I said.

'A treacherous game you play with that one, stranger. A creature of words behind words,' the elemental rumbled, leaning forward and giving me a dark look. When I didn't respond, it shrugged, causing even more stone to fall around it and shaking the ground, and shifted its gaze to the engineer.

Nothing happened right away, other than an odd vibration from the hammer, and I started to wonder if the elemental had been lying. Just as I was about to turn and call it out, though, Bill abruptly regained colour and flexibility and toppled to the ground with a shriek.

The engineer quickly forgotten, the Rook's head noisily turned back to me. 'Done. Destroy the hammer,' it said.

'What is it?' I asked after I made sure Bill had made it to his feet and was staggering toward me. His brief nap in the stone didn't look like it had agreed with him, and the engineer spent more time on all fours than he did on his legs.

The Rook looked down at the massive weapon in front of it, and the elemental grumbled. 'It is Tol'qor. Old. Older than this world. It was born of the element of earth and it stands with one foot in this realm and one foot in the one that lies between,' it said, and there was awe in its voice despite the anger on its face. 'I found it. Far below. I thought I could wield it, turn its ancient strength against my enemies.'

'I was wrong, stranger. The weapon is a cancer. I brought it here, to my throne, but I could not wield it. Instead, it leeches strength from me and leeches the life from the world around my land. It turns everything to stone, stranger! It must be destroyed,' the elemental finished.

The name was familiar, but I couldn't place it. I filed it away as Bill finally came to a stumbling halt next to me, the engineer breathing deeply and raggedly.

'Bill, you don't even have lungs,' I said with a smirk, not looking at him.

He gave me a crooked smile that didn't quite reach his eyes, and said, 'Am I ever glad to see you. Of all the people to almost lose in the portal lands, you would have been my last choice.'

'Enough talk. Destroy or move the hammer, stranger. If you do not have the power, then you will make a fine addition to my army,' the Rook rumbled, nodding slowly at the collection of statues.

I leaned in close to Bill, and whispered, 'The boost you gave me and Martin, it's worn off. Can you hit me with it again?'

The engineer smiled. 'Reactivated it as soon as this thing revived me,' he said, jerking his head at the elemental over his shoulder. Then he frowned, and whispered, 'But, aren't you Martin?'

Even before he finished his first sentence, I was reaching out into the air for energy, and smiled evilly as power came pouring in. Immersed in furious arcane light, Bill's last question didn't really register.

'Rook,' I loudly said as the magic howled around me, 'there are tunnels at the edge of your realm that we need access to. If I free you, you let everyone go and you let us into and out of those passages.'

The elemental nodded its head vigorously, shaking the ground and sending stone chips and rock flying into the air. 'Done. Hurry, stranger. The longer Tol'qor rests in my lands, the less my power will be to help you,' it rumbled.

I looked at Bill, and then engineer looked back with an impenetrable expression. 'Better go stand somewhere else,' I said with a smirk, then shaped and folded the energy in my hands into forms of force and destruction. With a savage cry, I sent a wave of power flashing out, slamming into the side of the hammer.

It barely moved.

Bill had fled, and out of the corner of my eye I saw him watching from behind the statue of a large dwarf, anticipation marking his face. The Rook had leaned ever further in, staring down at the hammer with hope.

I hit the weapon again, and this time, I saw tiny cracks form in the stone it lay in. Another strike sent shards of rock flying. Another tilted the hammer toward the ground. I was making progress, but something felt strange about my spells. They felt unfamiliar. Power raged through them, and I knew the shapes and forms without hesitation, but when the magic erupted from my fingers, it wasn't mine.

'Yes. Yes, stranger. Throw the weapon over the edge. When I am free, I will revive your friends and then dispose of the hammer,' the Rook rumbled. The mask was smiling now, its empty eyes staring down at me. Behind me, Bill was nodding in agreement.

With a howl of power, I sent energy ripping into the hammer, a brilliant flash of purple light that enveloped it and tore it free of the stone with a violent crack of breaking rock. I chased it, pushing the weapon across the ground with arcane force. Leaving a deep scar, the hammer moved slowly but steadily toward the cliff wall.

Lost in the exhilaration of the magic, I had no idea how much time had passed while I poured energy into Tol'qor. When I reached the face, I glanced back for a brief moment. The Rook hadn't moved, though it watched me expectantly from its position back at the center of the seat. Bill had followed me at a distance, standing out in the open with an evil grin.

I didn't know if the elemental could open me a path, and I didn't care. All that mattered was the magic and feeling it ripple furiously through my body. Turning back to my task, I gathered a huge amount of nether, shaped and folded it, and then unleashed a form of disintegration against the cliff face. Energy burst from my hands, sparks that crackled outward to slam into the wall in random places. With a thunderous explosion, my spell rocketed through every crack and weak spot and hole and then turned the stone to dust.

Instantly, wind roared in through the gap, and I had to struggle to stay upright. 'Push it clear, stranger. Free me,' I heard the Rook clearly say, despite the distance between us.

I spared him a glance, nodded, and then started gathering energy. One last push, and I was going to make it a good one. Light danced and whirled around me as I looked at the hammer and the edge not so far away. I smiled, and lifted my arms into the air.

'Martin! No!' Weezab yelled from somewhere nearby.

Before the kobold's yell fully penetrated my brain, I roared a word of power and sent Tol'qor crashing through the stone and out over the edge.

92

As the hammer toppled wildly out into space and then vanished into the clouds below, the elemental's throne shook violently, and I fell to my knees. When I managed to stumble back to my feet, and turned back toward the center, I found Weezab and Bill standing not far away, both of them staring at the Rook.

'Free,' the elemental roared.

'Crap,' the kobold said.

The Rook stretched free of its hunched over position, sending stone flying in every direction. At full height it towered over us, easily ten metres tall. With a thunderclap, the elemental stepped clear of its resting place, each footstep rocking the ground and drowning out everything with a violent boom. As it walked over the spot the hammer had been sitting in, the earth lifted into the air in chunks that spun and danced around it. By the time the Rook had stopped and turned to face us, the ground behind it was a completely flat light grey section of rock, and a halo of whirling stone whirled lazily around its head.

'And so it is done. For your help, I will allow you and your two friends to escape to your flying ship with your lives,' it rumbled, lifting one simple arm up to point back the way I'd come.

I snarled, and pushed forward past Bill and Weezab. 'That's not what we agreed on, elemental,' I growled. Nether was already oozing around my arms, and small motes of purple light drifted around my hands.

The macabre mask shifted to comedy, and the Rook's weirdly disembodied voice laughed. 'Take your small victory and leave, stranger. This realm is mine. All the magic in the world means nothing here,' it chuckled. The elemental then started walking toward us, and as it did, more stone lifted free of the ground and set to spinning around its arms. 'And with each second, my lands spread, even quicker now that the hammer is gone.'

Anger bubbled through my veins, and I started walking toward the Rook. 'You've made a mistake, Rook. Maybe you believe that no one can touch you,' I said, nastily. 'But you've never met anything like me.'

'Or me,' Weezab added, stepping in beside me. Fire crackled at his fingertips. I smiled grimly at him, and the little kobold gave me a dark look in return. Fury smoldered behind his eyes.

Another loud laugh from the Rook, and then it beckoned us toward it. 'We shall see, come and-' it started to say, and then I hit it in the teeth with a blast of energy. With a deep howl, the giant toppled slowly backward, smoke pouring from its mask.

Weezab and I fanned out, and I shouted, 'Just let everyone out of the stone and give us passage into the caverns, Rook, and we'll let you keep your little fortress.' I was already shaping and folding my next spell, and only distantly curious about the blood dripping from my nose.

Slowly, the elemental got to its feet. The stone that had fallen when it went down leapt back into the air to whirl around it, quicker than before. The mask was furious, and the Rook lifted its left hand to point at me. 'I know you, stranger. You wear a mask, but I know you. You lost everything, and you will lose everything again,' it rumbled. With a series of loud clunks, the stone circling its body suddenly encased the elemental, closing over everything but its face.

Then the new skin cracked and shifted, and now the Rook was covered in armour. Curved, bristling with spikes, and smooth. There didn't seem to be any seams, but the elemental resumed walking toward us without difficulty.

'Cute,' I heard Weezab snarl from nearby. Before the elemental had moved more than a few metres, the kobold chittered something vicious into the sky and then a fireball erupted from his hands, shrieked through the air, and slammed into a shield of rock that had suddenly burst up from the ground to block it. I sent a beam of destruction tearing into the air, rocketing past the shield and hammering into the Rook's legs. The elemental wavered but stayed upright.

A sharp whistle was all the warning I had before both Weezab and I were suddenly besieged by a swarm of rock shards the size of my head. I threw a shield over both of us while the kobold sent another fireball howling into the elemental's chest. The Rook barely moved.

'I don't suppose you can bring the Other out, eh? We could use that kind of firepower,' the kobold shouted between clenched teeth. A line of blazing flame appeared in the air above the elemental and then liquid fire rained down on its head. It tore the stone shield from the earth and held it over its head like an umbrella, and the fire hissed down the edge without causing damage.

'Why does everyone keep thinking I'm Martin, I'm-' I snarled as I lobbed a handful of explosive light toward the Rook, trailing off as I looked down and watched the nether oozing around my arms. That couldn't be right, but as I stopped and thought about the last few hours, I realized that I had been delving into the arcane all along. I fell to my knees, staring into the foreign energy that danced around my hands.

'I think we're in trouble,' I said, quietly.

'I think we're in trouble,' the Other whispered in my voice from over my shoulder.

'What the hell are you doing? Little help!' the kobold's voice shrieked across from me.

I snapped out of my little identity issue to find the Rook bearing down on us, the elemental thundering along the stone with massive strides. Snakes of rock writhed through the earth, slamming into my dwindling shield and skidding away. Boulders crashed down around us, sparking as they struck the shield and then bounced away.

Everything seemed to be happening in slow motion. I got to my feet drunkenly, mind full of fog. I noticed, not for the first time but for real this time, that blood dripped heavily from my nose, plummeting from my lips and chin to land in grisly patterns on my jacket and pants. I tried to shake the murk away, and felt rather than heard laughter echo through my brain.

When my entire vision was blocked out by flame, I blinked and reality slipped back into gear. Throwing new shields up, I gathered nether to me and then sent purple light blazing forward, smashing through a new stone barrier and hitting the Rook in the hip. The blast sent the elemental spinning away, crashing down in the group of statues off to the left. In return, a jagged missile of shattered rock shot through my own shield, deflected just enough that it rocketed out toward the edge of the throne instead of cutting me in half.

Weezab was on the move, summoning his own fiery shield as he left the safety of mine behind. The kobold suddenly burst into flame, and as I watched, the fire began to spin and grow. As the blaze writhed around him, the earth at his feet began to bubble and smoke. Soon the kobold is at the center of a vortex of flame that reaches high into the air, floating over an increasingly deep hole in the stone below him.

The Rook continued pelting the kobold with stone and rock, but anything that got close enough flared molten red briefly and then vanished in a cloud of smoke. Through a break in the column I saw exhilaration and mad laughter on Weezab's face as he sent two jets of crimson flame roaring out toward the elemental, who turned to face the kobold and raised his arms to avoid the blaze.

As soon as it turned away, I sent a lance of annihilating energy stabbing deep into its neck. The elemental tried to shift back, but I didn't let up, drawing every ounce of nether to me that I could and adding it to the beam. Reaching up to try and shield its face with an arm, the Rook howled in pain as my magic turned its fingers to dust and sent its hand flying away, smoking.

'Enough,' it roared, and hammered the ground with its other hand. With a low moan, the stone beneath my feet bucked upward, throwing me away to crash down painfully among the statues. Before I could get up, the stone around me cracked and spun upward to wrap around me. I heard a shriek, and then Weezab slammed down next to me.

The ground shuddered, and then the Rook popped up into my field of vision, looming above. The macabre mask looked irritated. 'I cannot kill you, though I could mash your little friend without consequence. You have freed me, which earns you your life. But I believe you would return to tempt your fate repeatedly if I do not give you what you have asked,' the elemental rumbled. 'I have no interest in seeing you again, human. Take your friends, fly to the tunnels, and do not come back.'

Then it straightened and turned away. The ground shook with each slow step, and with each tremor, and chunk of the rock holding me down cracked open and fell aside. I sat up at roughly the same time as Weezab, and then Bill was crouching down at our shoulders, and the three of us watched the Rook walk toward the center of the seat.

As it closed, the stone where it had been held by the hammer split and raised up into an actual throne. Slowly, the elemental climbed up into its new perch, then sat and leaned forward, resting its head on its intact hand.

'Go, strangers. Take your friends, and do not come back,' the elemental rumbled. Then the throne and its armour fused into one and the Rook had become part of the mountain once again.

93

The Rook hadn't been lying. Though he hadn't freed all of the statues, we found Petrel, Vrarrs Kor, and Nox waiting in various states of disorientation near where we'd left them. Bill suggested that we get everyone onto the airship before we started telling all of our stories, and so the seven of us headed to the edge of the elemental's throne to flag down Robin.

Once we were free of the stone, Bill got Robin on track for the entrance to the caverns and then the explanations began. The engineer and the other three that had made it into the first portal had almost immediately been set upon by the Rook, snatched from the ground near the portal exit and dragged through the rock until they found themselves deposited on the seat. The elemental had deemed them useless and turned them to statues.

Nox shivered when that part was mentioned. The big 'wolf was pale and shaky, and looked miserable sitting on the floor underneath a blanket he'd found in one of the cargo holds. Kor didn't look much better off, unsuccessfully hiding her discomfort as she lounged in a chair near the 'wolf.

Weezab, who had returned to his simple disguise, gave an exaggerated, wildly gesturing version of his journey from the second portal. With his limited vocabulary, it was hard to tell if he had been fairly close to the mountain when he fell out of the portal or if he'd somehow flown from a distance.

'I win!' the little fellow shouted, arms in the air, when he finished his story. Bill had been watching him curiously the whole time, and I wondered what the engineer was thinking about now that he knew the kobold wasn't exactly what he seemed to be.

Robin gave an abbreviated version of her, Petrel, and Ceile's exit from the third portal into the upper levels of Krekt Twelve. Bill didn't offer an opinion as to just why the portal had been inside the krekt rather than outside the service shaft, though he did look surprised. The engineer smiled when the dwarves mentioned that Twelve might be in full-fledged civil war.

'Good. The more they've got going on, the less we'll have to worry about on our way down,' he said with a tight smile.

Petrel hadn't enjoyed his stone experience any more than the others. The steel dwarf stood near Robin but hadn't said a word since we'd boarded the ship. He stared down at his hands, and I could hear something clicking and hissing quietly. I didn't know how the Rook's magic had worked, but I had to imagine that something as brutal as being turned to stone probably didn't play well with the dwarf's tech.

Ceile crouched on the floor next to Nox, her hand resting on the 'wolf's leg. Her injuries had provoked gasps from everyone other than Kor, though even the stoic dragon's eyes narrowed on seeing Ceile's missing arm and sight. Despite everything, Martin's - or my? - friend looked serene, a slight smile on her lips. She'd genuinely seemed happy just to have everyone here.

I'd found myself gravitating away from the group, coming to rest at the far corner of the deck, only half listening to the stories. For the thousandth time since we'd lifted off from the Rook's throne, I reached out into what should have been a vortex of wind aether, only to find the rotting quagmire of nether waiting. For the thousandth time, I reached out for my doppelganger's presence and found nothing.

But when I whispered, 'Where are you?' I heard it echo, from deep in my mind, in his - or my? - voice.

Lost in my thoughts, it took me a moment to realize that everyone was looking at me in silence. 'What?' I asked, a little rougher than I meant to.

'We want to hear about your escape from the portal lands,' Bill said, hesitantly. 'Robin says you fell from the bridge.' He was frowning suspiciously at me.

I shook my head and tried to remember what I'd told the dwarves. I cursed silently. I hadn't mentioned being asked to destroy Bill's machine, but I should have kept the story simpler. Giving that kind of information to the engineer could make my promise to Imuren null and void if Bill decided to go poking around. 'Sorry, I've got a lot on my mind. Yeah, something attacked me on the bridge, carried me off,' I said. I gave a lightly modified version of what had happened to me in the realm between, trying to emphasize that the way I'd escaped was probably a one shot deal and anyone else wouldn't be getting out.

Despite that, Bill looked fascinated, then excited. I sighed internally. So much for that.

When the questions stopped coming my way, the engineer nodded slowly and then turned to the group. 'And so here we are! Martin and Weezab's brute force solution saved us from a particularly stony fate, and gained us entry into the caverns we so direly needed to gain entry to. Our journey is almost over, my friends!' he loudly said, with a flamboyant bow. 'The passages will be difficult, but probably not dangerous, and if what our friends that visited the krekt have said is true, then the odds of us encountering much in the way of organized security on our way down to the vault should be very slim.'

He suddenly looked down, and began to pace around the command level. 'The entrances to the caverns will be our final crossroads. There will be no going back, only onward to the artifact,' he said. Without looking, he jabbed a hand out to point at Kor, Weezab, Ceile, and Nox. 'This is your last chance, and as I asked Martin those weeks ago as we prepared to leave the City, I ask you this. Are you prepared? Even if the descent goes without a hitch, chaos may ensue once we've breached the vault door. All of my planning can't foresee what waits for us after that.'

Kor didn't respond, just looked bored. Weezab nodded enthusiastically and cheered. Ceile smiled sadly and nodded slightly less enthusiastically.

Nox looked at me, but I couldn't read his expression, and when he looked away and up to Bill, the two shared another odd look. After a long moment, the big 'wolf nodded slowly, and hoarsely said, 'Let's get this over with.' Then he went back to staring at the floor.

'So be it,' the engineer said with a wild gesture. 'Pilot, take us down when you're ready, we should be overhead shortly.'

Through the tiny window near my spot, I watched the grey stone of the Rook's mountain pass by to our side. A part of me wondered if the elemental was powerful enough to swat us out of the air. It'd certainly been strong, and not for the first time since it'd let us go I wondered how I'd defeat it if I had to fight it again.

Staying off the floor, probably.

Minutes passed, and then I heard the sound of the engines lower in pitch as Robin brought the big ship into a slow descent. 'It's going to be a rough landing, the winds have picked up and the Rook didn't exactly build its mountain with landing pads in mind,' the dwarf woman said over her shoulder. I slid into the nearest seat as the cliff and the ground below rushed up to meet us. Luckily, our pilot was up to the task, and the ship touched down fairly gently.

'Rook Station, end of the line, all passengers disembark,' Bill said in an odd tone of voice. 'Mind the gap.'

94

When I got to the landing ramp, I found everyone had disembarked but Ceile and Robin, and the two women were heatedly arguing in hoarse whispers. When the dwarf saw me coming, she hurried toward me and then dragged me back.

'Tell her, Martin or not-Martin or whichever you are, tell her she should stay,' Robin hissed, desperation in her voice.

Ceile looked indignant. 'I am the strongest healer in this group, and Bill believes I will be able to navigate the caverns without too much difficulty, so long as I have someone to guide me. I had hoped you would be that someone,' she said, shaking her head. 'I will not stay behind while my greatest friend makes the greatest journey of his life.'

Robin was almost shaking. 'Listen, this is on his head,' the dwarf whispered, jerking a thumb in my direction. 'If you stay up here, it won't be on yours. If you stay up here, you won't be collateral, uh, damage.' She suddenly looked cagey and fell silent. After a long moment, she looked very sad and took Ceile's hands, before finishing, 'Please, Ceile. I don't want you to get hurt.'

My friend enfolded the dwarf in a hug, and whispered, 'Then you will have to watch my back, Robin. But I will not allow Martin to fall when he is so close to his goal.'

I frowned a little at all this talking about me like I wasn't in the room.

The dwarf shuddered violently, then sighed. She returned Ceile's hug, and though she looked sad, she nodded. 'Alright, Ceile. Alright. I'm sorry,' she whispered, resigned.

With that, the two women carefully stepped down the ramp. Nox, who was standing at its foot, watched them come down with a bewildered look on his face, then looked questioningly up at me. I shrugged, and the 'wolf shook his head and fell into step behind Ceile.

Once we had all gathered not far from the ship, Bill turned to us all. 'Unfortunately, we can't spare someone, or the time, to fly the ship back to Krekt Twelve. I have other plans for our return to the City, fear not!' the engineer said, with a flamboyant bow. 'Our entrance is just over the ridge. This will be your last glimpse of the Suns for a while, my friends, so take it in while you can,' he said. Beckoning to us, the engineer turned and started moving away.

Sure enough, when we crested the hill and started down into the shallow area beyond, I could see the spots where the Rook's land butted up against the mountain range, and the recesses in the cliffs that marked the caves we were looking for. As we approached, the stone in front of the entrances broke and rumbled away, boulders rolling as though they were caught in a massive wind.

I frowned. The elemental had a long reach.

Bill stopped at the foot of the cliffs and went over his maps, looking back and forth between the three caves that had opened up in front of us. I heard him say, 'Break their spirit, tempt their greed,' quietly as he did. I narrowed my eyes. Another line from his strange poem? I had to remember to ask him about it.

Before I could say anything, the engineer stood up straight and threw a hand into the air victoriously. 'This way, my friends!' he shouted, gesturing to the cave on the left. 'We are but hours from our destination! Come close, all.' Waving us all in, the engineer looked over his shoulder once and then leaned in conspiratorially.

'I have studied the cave maps extensively, and the passages we must take are winding and long, but not overly treacherous. Well, the first two passages are not overly treacherous. I'm hoping we don't need door number three. Unfortunately, I didn't have time to make a copy of the maps, so it's important that none of you let me die,' he said with a wink and a chuckle. 'I'll take the lead, Petrel will provide muscle, Weezab will back us up, preferably without setting us on fire. Robin and Ceile, you'll be next, and then Kor will go behind you. Our good friend Martin here will follow the dragon. Nox, you'll be last. Anything we might run into down there will think twice about taking something like you on, even if it has no clue what a werewolf is.'

When everyone had acknowledged him, Bill nodded and said, 'Make sure your weapons are handy. We probably won't see anything weird until we're really deep, but just in case.' The engineer looked up at me. 'I have a handful of flashlights, but if you could provide something a little stronger, that would be fantastic,' he said. I nodded, and he turned away to divide his lights up amongst the others.

When everyone that could use a light had one and I had summoned a couple floating lanterns, the engineer spun away with a flourish, and marched into the cave. The rest of us followed him, roughly in the order we were supposed to be in, and soon we'd left the Blue Sun and the Rook's lands behind.

It was humid inside, and somewhere ahead there was the sound of moving water. The surfaces of the tunnel around us had been worn smooth, and footing was treacherous in spots. Lichen and moss had managed to find enough of a hold in the stone to form large patches of bizarre colours in the otherwise sea of greys and browns.

The passage seemed to twist and turn at random, and it wasn't long before I'd lost track of what direction we were going. We passed several other tunnel openings as we walked, but Bill kept us moving without hesitation. From what I could see, the engineer was hardly consulting his maps at all, but still chose our path with confidence. It occurred to me, as we picked our way further and deeper into the mountain, that getting back out without the engineer would be next to impossible. I'd have to make us an exit, and that wouldn't be a quick process.

Lost in my thoughts, I didn't realize how far I'd fallen behind Kor when a massive furry hand dropped on my shoulder. I managed to stop from jumping out of my skin after a frenzied look over my shoulder revealed a grinning werewolf.

'Unless you want us to die in here, Martin, you should keep up with the others,' Nox chuckled. I laughed and nodded, but when I went to turn and catch up to Kor, the big 'wolf didn't let go. I looked back at my friend, curiously. He wasn't looking at me, just staring down the tunnel after the others. His face was bleak.

'Martin, how old am I?' he asked after a long moment.

I thought about that for a moment. 'You're somewhere around a hundred, I think,' I said, feeling bad that I didn't know for sure. The 'wolf never had much to say about his birthday, and he'd never done anything for it. Anytime I'd asked, I'd never gotten an exact answer.

When he didn't respond, I turned and put a hand on his arm. 'Nox, is something wrong?' I asked.

'I'm a hundred and four, Martin. Some 'thropes make it to a hundred and fifty, but it's rare. We don't get old, we burn out. Magic can't stop it. Medicine can't, either. We can't use constructs, transfer spells don't play nice with extra-humans,' Nox suddenly said, his voice hoarse. When he looked down at me, his face was desperate. 'They send us in, every once and a while, to clean up the mess, Martin. Usually we find everyone dead, therianthrope, construct, humans. Everybody but the 'thrope dismembered, and the poor bastard a twitching pile on the floor. Those are the easy ones. Sometimes we get there and both the 'thrope and construct are alive and pulling the limbs off of anyone they can find, minds completely gone.'

He closed his eyes and shook his head. 'Then we go in and erase everything. No trace of anyone that was there, whether they were dead or not. The Government wouldn't want anyone to discover a way to keep us alive after our best before date,' he whispered, then fell silent.

I didn't know what to say. I'd known the 'wolf for almost ninety years, and he'd never really talked about the end of his life.

'I've been looking for a long time for something that would give me more time, and I hadn't found anything. You must know what that's like! To see Death waiting. Until a couple weeks ago, I had given up. Now, though,' Nox said, opening his eyes to look down at me. His gaze was feverish. 'Bill's offered up a chance.'

'The regeneration chamber. I'm going to use it.'

Nox wasn't open to discussing it, and by then the others had gotten concerned and sent Vrarrs Kor back to collect us. The dragon gave us both a suspicious glance before taking my arm and gently pulling me away from the 'wolf and back on track. The 'wolf watched me go, a sad look and half smile on his face.

My insides were churning, but it wouldn't do us any good if I went back and tried to dissuade him. Not here. Once we were safely in the artifact vault, I'd get Bill's help to make the 'wolf see reason. I wasn't going to let him get into the regeneration chamber. Not without knowing for sure what it would do to him.

Shaking my head, I went back to scanning the tunnel for trouble. I'd tethered my conjured lights to the engineer and the big 'wolf, so the passage was well lit in both directions, but its path twisted and turned with such regularity that visibility wasn't much further than a few metres. I knew we'd travelled down and east, but couldn't begin to say how far. I also couldn't say how long we'd been travelling for. It felt like hours, but Petrel and Bill were the only ones with any way of keeping track of time and neither were saying.

'Martin, extinguish your lights, please, and then everyone gather as close as possible,' I heard the engineer call from somewhere up front.

With a whisper of power and a quick gesture, I made both lanterns vanish, leaving the passage lit only by the soft glow of Bill's, Robin's, and Kor's flashlights. Pushing in quietly, the party closed in behind the engineer as best possible, leaving me feeling more than a little claustrophobic, pressed between the tall dragon and the massive werewolf.

Bill put a finger to his lips, and then briefly shone his light ahead. As we watched, the shadows parted and so did the tunnel walls. A cavern up there, and now the sound of rushing water was much louder.

'The three passages that will take us to the edge of Krekt Twelve are all on the far end of this cavern. My contact marked this spot as requiring caution, though his notes make no mention of why, which is wonderfully handy. We should be able to hug the left wall, which will take us to door number one. That tunnel is easiest and shortest, maybe an hour at most. Door number three is at the center of the far wall. We don't want to take that unless the other two fail completely. It's short but it won't be a fun trip. Door number two is along the right wall, and it's a long passage. It looks easy, but it's long,' the engineer whispered, gesturing wildly.

Beckoning us to him as he turned toward the cavern opening. 'Stay close, keep your weapons ready. Martin, Weezab, keep the fireworks quiet unless we start getting overwhelmed. Then, light this damn place on fire,' he said. The little kobold grinned wickedly and chittered something unintelligible. I nodded.

Then we were in the cavern and moving quickly. The stone was still smooth, but was drier and easier to cross. The party's flashlights kept the floor illuminated, though they didn't penetrate far into the murk to our right. As my eyes adjusted to the dimmer lighting, I started to notice faint glimmers far across the cave, and along the ceiling. These lights weren't bright enough to do much more than show the most basic outlines and shapes, but it was enough.

The lights glinted off of water, and I could just make out a large pool that covered most of the middle of the chamber. At the far side, a different shade of black showed that a trail led along that wall to mirror ours. High overhead, shadow stalactites hung, dripping water that sparkled in the ethereal lighting.

There was a crash from ahead, and I heard quietly Robin curse. I hurried ahead, closing in behind Kor tightly to find the dwarf struggling to her feet with Ceile's help. 'I'm alright,' she hissed once she was upright. Looking down angrily, she said, 'I tripped on something, that's all. Something big-'

When she trailed off, I inched to Kor's side to see what the dwarf had seen.

'That's a bone,' I said in surprise.

'That's a huge bone,' Robin corrected.

If it hadn't been split in half, I doubted the dwarf would have tripped over it. The bone stretched out over the entire path, the end hanging out over the edge by a fair bit. Divided as it was, the narrow end was still five centimetres or so high off the floor.

There were teeth and claw marks all over it.

'Watch the floor. Keep moving, I've got a bad feeling about this,' Bill whispered harshly from ahead. I agreed with him, and the others obviously did as well, as we started moving again a fair bit quicker than before.

As we did, the sound of rushing water got louder and louder until suddenly the right edge of the path simply vanished below and we were moving above a narrow river. In the dim light of our flashlights, I could see the fast moving water was a cloudy grey, and I wondered how deep it was. The ceiling had also vanished into the shadows far above. I shook my head, slowly. The cavern was a lot bigger at this end.

'Hurry,' I heard Bill whisper as the group suddenly slowed to a crawl. I saw his back as he clambered over something, followed by Petrel.

'Helllllp,' Weezab said, fear in his voice.

My curiosity turned to shock as I watched Robin guide Ceile over the obstacle. It was a skull. A big one. A dragon of some kind, and it too had marks all over it.

Robin shone her flashlight out into the cavern as we got moving again, and now we could see that there were bones all over. A central platform across the river from us was blanketed in them, so thickly that I couldn't see the stone under them.

I made up my mind, and said, 'Weezab! Lights!' Gathering nether to me, I shaped and threw out forms of light and speed, sending balls of brilliant neon light flying out into the chamber. As I did, blazing spheres of red fire launched out into the corners I missed. The entire cavern flickered with light.

If Bill was ticked that I hadn't waited for his command, he didn't say anything. 'There!' he shouted, pointing ahead. Less than a hundred metres away was a gaping hole in the wall and floor that descended sharply before vanishing around a bend. I barely heard him over the roar of the water, the river slamming against the edges of the platform and then howling down a whirlpool beyond and sinking into the depths.

As distracted as I was by the appearance of our exit and the sheer size of the cavern, I didn't see the shape drop from the ceiling over door number one until it crashed to the ground with the sound of splintering bone and shattering glass. Bill had slammed to a halt and was now backing slowly away. Petrel stepped past him, snapping into a fighting stance. I saw fire burst into existence and spin wildly around Weezab's hands, the little kobold looking very serious.

'Why does it always have to be dragons?' I heard Nox whisper behind me.

The figure slowly lurched to its feet, leaning heavily on the cavern wall to do so. It was a dragon, or had been. The creature was all bone and sinew, flesh and scales virtually gone, nothing left for its massive ribcage to protect. Where it'd once had eyes, two raging spheres of blue lightning now crackled. Its massive wings dragged at its sides, nothing keeping them together but whatever magic it owed its existence to. Horns ringed its skull, and deadly looking claws still capped each foot.

It was huge, only able to stand on the trail because the path had widened quite a bit by the tunnel entrance. When its head rose drunkenly into the air, it glared balefully down on us from twice

Nox's height. The creature was easily taller than Kor, shoulders and head, and definitely a lot heavier.

'Well now, have you brought me something shiny?' the dragon suddenly rumbled, head jerking violently as it shifted its gaze between each of us. Its voice was hoarse, and faltered every few syllables. The creature stumbled forward a couple steps, the stone cracking loudly with each, and then came to a trembling stop up against the wall.

'We're just passing through, dragon! We didn't mean to disturb you!' Bill shouted over the raging water and from behind the safety of Petrel's back. The engineer was still moving away from the newcomer.

The dragon's head swung down, smacking against the rock with a cringe inducing crack. It sprung slightly back up, staring straight at the engineer. 'But you don't get to just pass through. This is my home, outsiders. You bring me something shiny and I let you pass through,' its ghostly voice said.

Then it turned to look at Ceile, and its head reared back. 'Elf!' it howled, 'You run with elves, outsider? Your kind put me here, elf! Five thousand years I've rotted in this place!' It stumbled forward again, and suddenly the blue lightning was crackling from inside its jaws. Bolts lanced into the walls around it, down its legs into the floor. 'Now, you all get to rot here with me!' the creature roared.

Bill bumped into me, having somehow navigated his way past the others while the dragon's ire was focused on Ceile. I frowned and started to say something when suddenly he spun and looked at me. His eyes were desperate, and the look on his face took away whatever it was I was going to say. 'Deep breath, Martin,' he whispered, harshly.

And then, before I could do anything, the engineer shoved me over the side and into the river.

96

I heard Nox snarl angrily and the bone dragon roar and then I hit the surface and went under. The water was brutally fast, and deep. I'd never been a strong swimmer, and these weren't exactly ideal swimming conditions. I hit bottom, then rolled roughly before being tossed back to the surface where I managed to suck in a ragged breath. The light of the flashlights was long gone, and now it was only the strange glimmering spots along the cavern walls and ceiling.

If anything the roar of the water got louder, and when the wall to my right suddenly shot away I remembered the whirlpool I'd seen the outline of earlier. With everything I had, I thrust my head out of the water, gasped in a few deep breaths, and steeled myself. An instant later, the water dropped out from under me and then I was falling again.

I tumbled and crashed down the steep tunnel, alternating between drowning and being battered to death. Spinning wildly, a sharp rock on the side of the tunnel carved a deep cut across my cheek, and it was only a desperate jerk that kept me from losing an eye. Even if I'd been capable of gathering energy to me, I had no idea what I'd do with it. I hit my head on outcrop and everything got far away.

As dazed as I was, I barely registered the tunnel levelling out and widening. The water slowed until I was just drifting lazily along in its clutches. When I ran aground, pushing an uncomfortable amount of sand down the back of my jacket and shirt, I lay there for a long while, the water lapping gently at my pants. I was cold and really wet.

Gradually, the blood dripping down my forehead and into my right eye to join the red stream pouring from my right cheek into the sand under my head convinced me it was probably time to be a little more proactive. With a groan, I turned over and pulled myself up the sand until I was out of the water and then sat down in the darkness.

Other than the sound of the water, I couldn't hear anything. What little light had peppered the walls and ceiling in the bone dragon's chamber was not present here. Even after all this time adjusting to the lack of light I couldn't see anything.

This must be what it was like for Ceile.

I sighed. At least I could conjure some lights. My friend wouldn't see again until a necromancer had done some work on her body. Or replaced her body. Shuddering, I let that thought fade. I didn't want to be dwelling on that when I was in the position I was in.

Reaching out, I grabbed a handful of energy and quickly shaped and summoned an ethereal light that slowly circled over my head, illuminating the new chamber I found myself in. It was much smaller than the earlier one, mainly consisting of two long and flat sandy sections bordering the river. At the far end, a couple holes in the wall marked new passages, and the water sank and vanished into another gap in the shadows there.

'Well, this isn't great,' I heard the Other say from just over my shoulder. I smirked.

'Glad to hear your voice. I was starting to think I'd gone a bit crazy there,' I said, staring off into the chamber.

'You are talking to yourself. I'd say that might mean you are a bit crazy,' he chuckled.

I snorted, then gestured toward the far end of the passage. 'Any suggestions? I could try to dig us out, but that could take days. And we don't, uh, have days. Hell, we could be anywhere,' I said, frustrated.

He didn't answer right away, and when he finally did his voice was odd. 'Bill put us down here for a reason, and I don't imagine it was for us to die of starvation. Can we freak out about the dragon now?' he asked. 'That thing wasn't just some bone construct, something reanimated it or is keeping it alive after its expiry date.'

'That's real necromancy, Martin,' he whispered.

The necromancers back in the City that built flesh constructs and toyed around with bodies - as long as they were licensed, of course - still couldn't bring the dead back to life. That was a magic that, as far as I knew, didn't exist or had been forgotten millennia ago. But the dragon back in the cavern somewhere far above had been alive, if barely. 'Alright, if it's been reanimated, then who could have done it and why do it here? The thing claimed the elves locked it up five thousand years ago. That far back, none of us were doing much more than crawling out of the dirt, much less testing the limits of necromancy,' I said as I scanned the chamber.

There was a wet cough from behind me, and then a ragged voice said, 'The dragon did it to itself.'

I spun around, summoning energy to me, and found Bill on his hands and knees at the edge of my sandy perch. The engineer was as soaked as I was, and there were new tears and cuts in his already battered skin. His expression was almost comically sad. Crawling forward until he was out of the water, he collapsed to the ground and trembled.

'Bill. Where are we, where is everyone else, and how do you know anything about the dragon?' I snarled quietly, looking down at him angrily. 'I could have drowned in that, Bill,' I said, pointing back at the river's entrance into the cavern.

The engineer coughed again, which was irritating as he still had no lungs, and said, 'Door number three, Martin. Door number three. I couldn't risk the fight, we were precariously balanced up there and the dragon had the upper hand, so I decided to get you to safety first and then bring as many people with me as I could.'

I shook my head. 'Dammit, Bill. I'm our most powerful weapon, why would you take me first? I could have at least held the thing off!' I said, loudly.

It was the engineer's turn to shake his head. 'I had to get you out first because I knew you'd try to go last. There was no way we could destroy that dragon, Martin, and going through it was the only way to get to the other two passages. I had no choice,' he said, sadly. 'The others may have had their reasons for wanting to get to the artifact vault, but when it comes down to it, it's just me and you that need to get there.'

He looked away. 'This passage will take us to a deeper cavern that runs up against the edges of Krekt Twelve. It's a tough trip, but the two of us should be able to make it without too much trouble,' he said as he slowly got to his knees.

I skidded across the sand toward him, which probably lacked the menace I was aiming for seeing as I was also on my knees and plowing slowly through the grit. 'Bill, we are not leaving the others behind. Didn't you tell them to follow you in?' I asked angrily as I got right in the engineer's face. 'Didn't you bring them all with you?'

If Bill was even remotely intimidated, he didn't show it. The engineer's brown eyes looked unflinchingly into mine, and a sad smile creased his face. 'There wasn't time, and even if they had all come most would have been left behind,' he said, and continued when I looked askance at him, 'I said that you and I would be able to make it through the passages without much trouble, but that isn't true for everyone else.' The engineer shook his head slowly. 'Robin and Weezab would probably be fine, but Nox, Kor, Petrel, and even Ceile wouldn't. There are tight sections ahead, which will be tough going for us, but the others?'

He looked away, and said, 'If they tried to follow us into the next tunnel, there would be no escape and nothing but death waiting in the passages beyond.'

97

Bill and I stared at each other for a long moment as I tried to piece together a reply. 'When were you planning to tell the group that door number three meant half of us were going home? Why would you even make it an option?' I finally managed to say, the words coming out in a rush. I struggled to my feet and stepped away from the engineer, rubbing my arms to try and warm them up.

'Martin, there were three passages in this entire cave system that passed close enough to the edges of the dwarves' tunnels to offer a reasonable chance of breaking through without requiring days to do so. If the dragon hadn't been quite so, well, animated, we would have gone into the other two passages first, and if both were impassable, then I would have sent the others back to the airship to wait for our return,' Bill said. I heard him get to his feet and brush himself off. When I turned around, he was watching me carefully. 'If the choice is you going on without your friends versus you not going at all, would you really choose to turn back? Knowing you've only got days left before even my little gizmo can't keep you on your feet?' he asked, doubt clear on his face.

I started to argue, but the words died in my throat. As much as I hated it, the engineer was right. If I refused to go on without the others, then this entire trip would have been for nothing, and all the pain and awfulness that my friends had gone through along the way would be meaningless. Nox had almost died, and had been terribly injured. Ceile had lost an arm and her sight. They were here because of me, so that my time wouldn't be coming to an end sometime in the next week or so.

There wasn't a choice at all.

I snarled something obscene and then shook my head. 'Alright, Bill. You're right. What do we do now?' I asked quietly as I turned back toward the tunnels at the far wall. I heard the engineer move to stand next to me, each step punctuated by a metallic click. He dropped a hand on my shoulder.

'If anyone else had followed me down here, they would have been here by now, so my best guess is that they all went after the dragon or fell back. I'm hoping that means that they aren't dead. Petrel had been mapping the caves as we descended, so he should be able to get everyone out or maybe even navigate their way down door number one. Either way, we can't get back up to them. We need to get moving, the last thing we want is to have to try and sleep in here,' Bill said.

I didn't say that, much like breathing, I didn't think the engineer needed to sleep. Instead, I nodded, and said, 'Lead the way, then.'

Bill squeezed my shoulder and then started walking further along the sandy edge. 'Stay close. We don't have far to go but it's going to get technical. I grabbed some climbing gear from the airship, but I lost a lot of it on my way down after you,' he said, beckoning for me to follow.

Just before we entered the new passage, I stopped and looked back thoughtfully. 'Bill, you said some of the party won't fit through after this tunnel, does that mean that they'd all manage to make it to the chamber we're in right now?' I asked. When the engineer answered in the affirmative, I said, 'Alright, so what happens if they did follow us this far, are they already screwed or is there a way out?'

I heard metal tapping on stone and looked over to find Bill pointing at the other tunnel entrance. 'That one goes back to the surface. It's a long way, though. But at least it's a way out and even the werewolf can get through,' he said.

I nodded slowly. Gathering energy to me, I began shaping and folding. 'We need to leave a marker, make sure they go the right way if they end up down here,' I whispered. With a snap of my fingers, I sent a ball of brilliant light slamming into the ceiling above each tunnel entrance. With a swipe of my fingers, the words 'do not enter' and 'this way' etched themselves into the lights, leaving blazing signs behind, signs that would last for days, hopefully.

It wasn't something I was particularly good at, and the effort left me breathing hard. It seemed like a simple enough task, but much like healing, I wasn't particularly skilled. There were plenty of mages back in the City that would probably mock me for the simple light show I could put out.

Well, mock me until I vaporized their house, anyway.

Bill gave my handiwork a look of approval and then turned around and headed into the passage. I gave a last look back and then followed him into the tunnel.

My lantern drifted into the tunnel with us, floating past my head and coming to a rest near Bill's. The passage very quickly closed in, though, and soon the light rested on the engineer's shoulder, providing what I hoped was decent visibility despite the once again twisting path we followed. I had to duck my head frequently, and I started to feel more than a little claustrophobic as Bill and I increasingly had to crouch or squirm around rock and stone to move on.

The engineer hadn't been lying. Robin and Weezab would have been able to negotiate the narrow and twisted stone of this tunnel, but Kor and Ceile would have had to break bones to squeeze through, much less Petrel or Nox. The steel dwarf would have had to come through in pieces, and the big 'wolf would have to have his body reduced to the consistency of jelly in order to come along.

The air felt stifling, completely still and getting hotter. It didn't help that other than our movements, the tunnel was almost completely silent. We'd left the water behind, its echo only distinguishable on the rare occasion both of us stopped. It was just the sound of our footsteps and harsh breaths that cut the silence, as neither me nor the engineer did much talking.

After a half hour of being left alone with my thoughts, I finally broke the silence. 'Bill, the dragon. Tell me about it,' I said, after worming my way under another nasty outcrop with the engineer's help.

He frowned. 'My contact neglected to mention that there was anything quite that dangerous in there. My assumption is that he was hoping I'd finally meet my end at its hands. He never did like me much,' the engineer said, his voice thoughtful.

'That thing was undead, Bill, and you thought it had brought it on itself,' I said.

The engineer nodded, and said, 'Yes. True necromancy is lost to the major four species, but not to a handful of the others. I don't know the dragon's whole story, obviously, but I'd guess the elves locked it down here as punishment and it cast some spell on itself that allowed it to rise from death.' Then he shook his head. 'Powerful magic, but not eternal. The dragon was still very dangerous, but another decade or two and it'll fall apart, joining all the other bones in its prison.'

'It's stuck up there, though? We aren't going to suddenly run into the damn thing somewhere between here and the artifact vault?' I asked. I noticed a breeze had appeared, whispering silently past, cooling me off as it did.

'You saw how big it was, Martin. The only way it'd get out of there is piece by piece,' Bill said, smiling nastily. Then the engineer frowned and turned to look at me. He leaned forward. 'Hmm, but you aren't Martin, are you? How curious,' he said, very quietly.

'Of course I'm Martin,' I said, and heard the same thing echoed from just over my shoulder. Confused and angry, I looked down at the ground and then my hands and stopped short.

The breeze was whirling gently around me, fed by the wind aether that spun and danced around my arms.

I gasped and the energy dissipated back into the air around me, and with it, the breeze. I stared down at my hands for a long moment, then looked up at Bill.

'Very curious, indeed,' the engineer said, with the barest hint of a smile on his face.

98

'You are a mystery, Martin. Or not-Martin. Whichever you are, you've been handling both nether and aether, and in my centuries of travel I've never heard of that. People are born with an affinity for one energy or none. You do not get to be both arcanist and elementalist. As far as I knew, the world doesn't allow that,' Bill said. He'd resumed moving down the passage, but at a slower pace so we could talk.

I barely heard the engineer speak. I was numb, completely thunderstruck. While I walked, I looked down at my hands. Nether oozed between the fingers of my left. Aether whistled around those on my right. When I looked out beyond the edges of reality, into the realm between, I could see the rotting ocean of the blood of the Blue Sun, and the howling vortex of the blood of the White.

'There are two of us, aren't there?' I asked under my breath.

'I don't know,' I heard my voice answer from somewhere else.

If there weren't two of us in here, then who was real? Was it Martin, whose second personality was a manifestation of his darkest side? Or was it the Other, who hid his true nature behind the Martin persona? More importantly, which one was I? Was I the original, or the illusion? Was I talking to myself, or was I the one looking out of the mirror?

Oblivious to my internal struggle, Bill had kept right on talking. Having been largely lost in my own world, I didn't immediately register him say, 'And once the horror has been done, the whole world ash beneath the Suns.'

When I did, it broke me free of my existential trouble. 'Bill. That poem, I've heard you speak verses from it ever since we left the City. What is it?' I asked.

The engineer stopped speaking and turned to look at me with a strange expression on his face. 'Something I learned from a client of mine. It's a children's song, long forgotten. It was catchy, I find it helps me think,' he said.

I frowned. 'It's a bit morbid for the kids. Which client taught it to you?' I asked.

A half smile marred the engineer's face, and he shook his head. 'A very, very important one, maybe-Martin,' he said with a wink, and then turned away. 'Speaking of that, have you figured out what you are, yet? Or who you are?' he asked, apparently not so oblivious to my identity crisis after all.

I didn't answer for a long moment. I really wasn't sure just how much I wanted Bill to know, but then, the engineer might be the only person I see before I set foot into the regeneration chamber. Maybe it made sense to talk to him about it. I sighed, and said, 'I don't know.

Things have completely changed over the last few weeks. The line between me and the Other, or me and Martin, used to be static. One of us was out, one of us was in. We could interact in a limited way, mostly through talking to each other, but nothing like what we started to have during this trip.'

'You said the kobold's heal affected you two in some way,' Bill said over his shoulder.

'It did. There was only one of us around for a long time after that, until someone else suddenly showed up,' I said, frowning. Bill looked back at me with an odd expression, and I shook my head. 'Another voice, and very peculiar. I wondered if it was a third entity, having revived courtesy of Weezab's heal or if my brain had just conjured it up. Just like the other,' I continued before slowly trailing off.

I rubbed a hand across my face, and said, very quietly, 'I'm both of us, aren't I?'

The engineer stopped and came over to stand in front of me. The light sway of the magical lantern gave his face a ghostly look. 'Yes, I think you are,' he said with a sad smile, 'but I don't have all the answers for you, I'm afraid. I studied you while I searched for the regeneration chamber, and learned enough about how Martin and the Other interacted to believe that you were not separate beings at all.' He paused for a moment, then continued, 'But I don't believe you are simply a case of multiple personalities, either. There's magic involved here.'

I shook my head. 'So, which am I, then? Was I born Martin Tundra, or the Other? I didn't come into life subconsciously telling myself to pretend to be two different people,' I said, bitterly.

Bill was silent for a while, looking at me sadly. When he spoke again, his voice was quiet. 'Martin - and that's what we'll call you because it's getting confusing - do you remember the accident that nearly killed you in your early fifties?' he asked.

I frowned. 'Not the accident itself. The first thing I remember is waking up in the hospital. Everything before that is a foggy mess,' I said, slowly.

'Two Districts were completely destroyed when a man lost his mind and murdered his husband, his children, and then everyone else within several kilometres, did you know that?' Bill asked.

I shook my head. I hadn't known much of anything about the mage that had caused the devastation, just that he and hundreds of others had died in it.

'He was a solaron, Martin. A being of unbelievable power. But he was also a tortured man who had been coerced into being a weapon, and as he slowly became more and more unhinged, he became arrogant and unable to control his temper. He was arguing with his husband that day, Martin,' the engineer said. 'An argument that finally pushed him over the edge. The magic he unleashed on the City that day wasn't simply destructive, my friend, it twisted and broke and reformed everything it touched. Hundreds died, but thousands more were affected in strange or terrifying ways.'

I looked at him, his meaning slowly dawning on me. 'You think it was this solaron's magic that made me into two? But would that mean that it had also given me the ability to see both nether and aether?' I asked, my voice ragged.

Bill shook his head, and answered, 'No, I think that particular little quirk is yours alone, Martin. As I said, I don't have the answers. I wish I'd had more time to look into those events and your past prior to them, but my priority was keeping you alive. If we survive this cheerful trek through the caves and then to the artifact vault, perhaps we'll go answer some of our questions some day after.'

The engineer reached up and squeezed my shoulder. 'Now, we've got to get moving. I don't know about you but I'm not used to these tight confines and I'm getting a little freaked out,' he said. Then he turned away. 'The regeneration chamber may give you some clarity as well as your health, Martin. Let's go put you in it, shall we?'

I didn't answer, but when he slid into the next section of the passage, I followed. Images from my time in the hospital cycled at the back of my head, interspersed with the broken memories that were all I had of my first fifty years. Something occurred to me as I thought about what Bill had said about the accident. 'Bill, did you know the solaron? What was his name?' I asked.

'Yes, I worked with him at the Department of Operations before the tragedy. Edgar Lorn was his name,' the engineer said, without looking back.

The name sent a shiver down my spine. 'He was a school teacher. Agent Taylor recruited him, and he joined Operations unwillingly. They turned him into a weapon. You're Peter,' I said, as the dreams suddenly burst to the front of my mind.

Now Bill stopped and looked back. He looked surprised. 'How do you know that?' he asked.

I shuddered. 'I've seen Edgar before. I dreamt of him. Watched him get recruited, then trained. I saw him meet you, though I didn't recognize you at the time,' I said, shaking my head slowly.

The engineer looked sad again, and said, 'It's true. I went by Peter back then. I was a contractor for Operations, and I worked with Taylor on a few nasty missions. While Edgar was training up. Watched them turn him into a monster. It was such a waste, though it probably would have been so much worse if Research had been allowed to take him apart.' He suddenly looked doubtful. 'You dreamt of him? But how would you know any of those details?'

He shook his head. 'I don't want to talk about Edgar anymore. Let's go, Martin,' he said turning away once more before I could respond.

When he started moving again, a sudden thought made me jerk forward and grab his arm. 'Bill. I'm not Edgar, am I?' I asked, dread turning my blood to ice.

He was silent for a long moment, then looked over his shoulder at me and sighed. 'No, Martin, you are not. I was one of the first responders, I found Edgar's body at the epicenter of the disaster, along with his family. My friend died in that mess. I don't know where they found you, I'm sorry. But you aren't Edgar Lorn,' he said, hoarsely.

Then the engineer looked thoughtful, and continued, 'As I said, though, Edgar's magic affected the very nature of reality around him. You aren't him, but some part of him might have imprinted on you. Memories. Bits and pieces of his psyche.' Now he seemed excited, and his eyes wandered aimlessly as he reached up and absently tried to stroke his missing mustache. 'That would explain your personality woes. Your brain trying to make sense of two different minds in your body!'

Now his eyes were feverish, and he spun around violently, ripping his arm from my grasp and grabbing hold of both of mine. 'Martin, have you seen any of his other memories? Anything at all?' he demanded.

I shook my head, taken aback by the engineer's sudden desperation. 'No, just the two dreams, sorry. Why?' I said. My arms ached in his grip.

'Because, my fascinating friend, it's possible that Edgar Lorn is, in a way, still alive,' he said, a mad smile twisting his face. Then he let go and reached up to tap my forehead gently.

'Right in here.'

99

The next hour of spelunking went quickly. Bill had fallen silent after his last declaration and hadn't said a word since. I had enough of my own to think about, so I wasn't any more talkative than he was. The engineer occasionally sent me strange glances as we travelled along the tunnel, but soon we were too busy climbing down slippery and wet stone for me to think about it. The passage had taken a sharp bend downward and merged with a small waterfall, and now we descended, precariously clambering and sliding, deeper and deeper.

'Are you still there?' I asked under my breath, and again my own voice echoed the question from the back of my mind. No other presence lurked in the shadows, watching. If Martin - or the Other - had ever been there, they were gone.

It was just me, now.

If Bill was right, and Edgar Lorn's madness had somehow warped my mind, then what had I been like before the accident? Who'd I been before the solaron made me something else?

Why didn't anyone come to collect me at the hospital?

I frowned. That was an old thought, one that had lurked around for the two centuries that had passed since I'd woken up, groggy and afraid, in an unfamiliar bed surrounded by medical equipment and being tended to by Dr. Jacobs. He and the other personnel there knew my name, even if I didn't. When they decided I was well enough to leave the facility, they gave me a comfortable set of clothes, instructions for getting new personal documents and signing up for temporary housing, and an appointment with a psychiatrist to help me deal with the accident. Dr. Jacobs also asked that I check in with him at his private clinic once I'd had a chance to get settled.

Those had been difficult days. All of my possessions had been destroyed along with my memories. I didn't know who I was, or what I was. Had I been a teacher? A security guard? The Government had a driver's license and a magic license in my name, but nothing else. No birth certificate, no records of employment. The clerk suggested that I'd only recently moved to the City, and that more information would have to be obtained from my place of residence.

That was a frustrating dead end. There were dozens of human settlements outside the City, but they were tiny, isolated, and unfriendly. Even if I had any idea where to start, the chances of finding anything out were pretty slim. Wherever I came from, it was going to remain a mystery. The best Records could tell me was that I'd applied for and received both driver's and magic licenses two years before the accident.

It'd been a lonely and dark time, those first few years. Not that I was entirely alone, what with the voice at the back of my head. Eventually I left the past behind, formed an uneasy partnership with that other part of me, and moved on. Worked some jobs, went to university, worked more jobs and then joined the Department of Enforcement.

'We're here,' Bill said, interrupting my walk down memory lane.

With a careful jump, the engineer dropped from a ledge at the bottom of our vertical passage down into a wide chamber and then vanished around a corner. I grimaced. The floor was at least a few metres below the ledge. Very carefully, I sat down on the stone and slowly slid over the side until I hung uncomfortably on the edge. I stole a glance over my shoulder, and sighed. This wasn't going to be graceful.

Fortunately, my landing spot consisted of more deep sand, and rather than the sharp pain in my ankles that I was expecting, I just sunk up to my knees in it. Bill gave me an amused look as he tossed his battered pack into a corner, and once I'd dug myself out I tossed him mine as well.

My lanterns drifted lazily around the ceiling of the chamber, illuminating almost the entire thing in pale light. It wasn't huge, though after the confined and unpleasant tunnels we'd just spent too much time in, it felt gigantic. Smooth stone made up the walls and ceiling, and the floor was entirely made up of the sand I'd landed in. At the far end of the chamber from us, a hole opened up in the wall and a new passage dropped away into the shadows.

Other than my breathing, it was completely silent.

Bill reached down to the elven gadget on his arm and pressed a couple buttons. With a high pitched whine, the map holograms flashed into existence over his hand and the engineer began zooming and panning a map after scrolling through a few to find the correct one. Without looking up, he suddenly pointed across the chamber, and said, 'There.'

We walked over to the target wall, and the engineer knocked against it. 'There are about twenty metres of stone between us and one of Krekt Twelve's service shafts. I need you to rectify that.' With two quick strikes, he scratched an x in the middle of the wall, and looked back at me. 'Keep it as level as you can. The shaft is pretty big, but I'd rather not have to make several tunnels to get into it.' Then the engineer gingerly pushed his way back through the sand and sat down next to his pack.

I stepped back a distance, reaching out into the rotting mire on the other side of reality, and began shaping the nether as it came pouring in.

'Oh, and be a little careful. I don't know for sure that there isn't an underground lake in between us and the krekt,' Bill said. When I looked back, the engineer was toying around with the maps again, unconcerned.

I chuckled as I folded the energy into forms of disintegration and drew my hands back to my sides. I started to chant the words that would bring the forms together, and as I did, brilliant motes of green light popped into existence around my hands and began drifting slowly toward my palms. When enough motes had gathered to form a sphere of light, so bright that I could no longer see through it, I howled the final command and shot my hands forward, slamming the two balls of energy together. A terribly loud roar of sound filled the chamber, and then a beam of power rocketed from my hands to the wall. Where it touched, the solid stone burst into fine grey powder.

It was slow going, and soon the chamber was hazy with drifting dust. I stopped briefly to tear a strip off of my shirt and wrap it around my nose and mouth. Bill didn't seem to notice, and when I looked over later I saw that he had gone so still that he'd been covered with a thin layer of powder.

Twice more I had to stop, once when water began pouring in from a small hole at the edge of my new passage, and once when the whole chamber began to rumble ominously. The first, I created a rough channel from the crater to the lower hole in the chamber, letting the slow flow of water pour - harmlessly, I hoped - down to a lower cave. The second, I turned and jumped out of the tunnel just as the floor a metre or so away cracked and tumbled into a lower cave. Gathering over the hole, Bill gave me an amused look as we saw the water I'd diverted had eroded through a few mud columns that had been holding a portion of the roof up. I gave him a dirty look and started carving again.

Then, just when I thought my arms were going to fall off, there was a sharp crack from the stone beneath my beam, and the wall exploded out into thin air and fell away. Quickly, I extinguished the beam, and Bill and I edged carefully up to the gap. The engineer clapped me painfully on the arm with a huge grin, and I smiled with him.

'Welcome to Krekt Twelve, my friend!' he said, as we looked out into the dimly lit depths of the service shaft.

100

I'd broken through about thirty metres above a maintenance ledge that ran the entire length of the shaft, and with the assistance of what remained of Bill's climbing gear the engineer and I climbed down to it and stopped to get our bearings. Much like the section of the krekt where the portal had left me, this place was silent. Dormant. Emergency lighting crisscrossed the walls, small boxes bolted into the concrete and metal that didn't quite manage to chase the shadows away with their pale red lights.

'The dwarves built this shaft to feed air and other utilities to dozens of levels. It was an ambitious plan, as Krekt Twelve's population had been in decline for years and couldn't support this kind of expansion. In the end, I think it was only the science and engineering labs that were built, and then even those were sealed up and abandoned,' the engineer said, quietly, as he gestured out into the murk. Leaning out over the edge, he pointed down into the abyss, and continued, 'The artifact vault should be about twenty levels below us, and of course, on the far side of the shaft. The elevators probably aren't running, and with the control panel's way up near the top, it doesn't make sense to take the stairs up there just to get them going again. We'll walk the service ledge around the shaft wall, and then walk down.'

I nodded. Somewhere above I could hear the deep thrum of some kind of machinery, and the clack of small rocks as they plummeted past, skidding and bouncing along the slightly angled sides. 'Do you think we'll run into any guards? Just how abandoned are we talking?' I asked, looking dubiously across at the service access door.

Bill sighed. 'This is why I brought the dwarves along. Petrel's scanners may be rudimentary, but they would have helped us avoid a patrol in the unlikely event there was one in this section. Worse come to worst, getting Robin into a maintenance uniform would have given us a bit of camouflage. Well, until the Twelve dwarves saw the rest of us,' he said with a chuckle.

Now I frowned. I'd thought we needed the dwarves to get the party down to the vault, but it didn't sound like the engineer considered their absence any more than an irritation. If Bill noticed my suspicious look, he chose to ignore it. Without fanfare, he slung his pack over his shoulder and started off along the narrow ledge toward the far side.

'Come, Martin! You may only have days left to you, and time waits for no man, woman, child, or other. We're almost done!' he shouted. I cringed as his voice echoed wildly around the service shaft. So much for a subtle entrance.

The ledge wasn't designed for casual walkers. Some sort of rail system along the wall had allowed a technician to connect a safety cable to it, giving them the ability to work on whatever they needed to with both hands while also being able to run along the edge with confidence. Without that equipment, I uncomfortably hugged the wall as I slowly walked in Bill's wake. The engineer, for his part, barely seemed to notice the bottomless pit to his right, moving steadily without slowing.

Fortunately, both of us made it to the platform in front of the access door. Bill reached for the handle, motioning for me to hug the wall out of sight, and then opened the portal with a quiet clunk. With the door out of the way, the engineer and I peeked carefully into the darkened stairwell. Nothing moved in the shadows, and a thick layer of dust coated the metal grating used for floor and stair. Other than that peculiar sound of machinery far above, nothing made a sound.

'Let your lights go, we should be able to navigate without them now,' Bill whispered, then hunched down and stepped through the door into the stairwell. I extinguished the lanterns and then followed him in.

The pale red lights spaced every ten metres didn't help make the stairs much less treacherous, and the fact that we could look through every surface into the depths made it even more dizzying. Each step sent a cloud of dust shooting out in every direction. No one had come this way in a long time. I hoped that the main corridors were just as deserted.

'Do you think that noise up there has gotten louder?' Bill suddenly asked, looking up into the shadows above.

I listened for a while, and then slowly nodded. 'Yeah, it has. Any idea what's making it?' I asked. The engineer didn't answer, just continued staring up for a long moment before resuming his descent.

My knees and hips were killing me by the time Bill stopped in front of a door on the opposite side of the stairwell from the service shaft. Crouching down, he beckoned for me to join him. 'The vault is on this level, just a few doors down on the right. Hopefully this section is just as empty as the maintenance side of it, but we need to be really quiet. If the coup is still in progress, there's a good chance that any patrol we run into will be disorganized and disconnected from the army, but we can't count on them being unable to send an alarm,' he whispered. 'And, trust me, once we break into the vault, someone in charge is going to know we're there. Regardless of who that is right now, they'll drop the army on our head.'

He leaned in close. 'We need to be in and out quick,' the engineer said.

I nodded, then asked, 'And if we have to fight?'

Bill grinned evilly. 'Then kill them all, and fast, so they don't have a chance to tattle on us,' he said.

I sighed and began drawing aether to me. Everything about this brought back memories of the assaults on Krekts One through Three, though it would have been Ceile crouched next to me, not the engineer. Thousands of dwarves had died at my hands over those decades of fighting, whether through Martin's arcane strength or the Other's elemental viciousness. I hadn't been much with weapons, much to my superiors' frustration. Fortunately, the few times I'd lost use of my magic, Ceile had been there to cut down whatever lunaron the dwarves had dug up.

The noise far over our heads suddenly stopped.

Both Bill and I looked up quickly, staring futilely through the dust and metal and shadow and distance. The eerie silence sent a chill down my spine.

'Maybe it was the fans,' the engineer quietly said. He didn't sound convinced.

Minutes passed and the silence continued. Finally, Bill shook his head. 'We can't wait any longer. We'll just have to be even more paranoid while we're out there,' he whispered. When I nodded, the engineer reached up and slowly pulled the exit lever until the lock opened with a clunk and the door swung open.

If anything, the hall was lit even more poorly than the stairwell. I breathed a sigh of relief when I saw the undisturbed layer of dust that coated the metal and concrete floor, and clapped Bill on the shoulder with a smile. The engineer returned the grin, and stepped out into the corridor. I was surprised when he pulled a battered shock rifle out of his pack, likely looted from the airship's stores. I couldn't remember him ever using a weapon on the trip.

Like most dwarven passageways, the hall was a chaotic mess of pipes and cables boxed in by smooth concrete slabs. Doors were regularly spaced along its length, marked by signage written in the dwarves' strange writing. The corridor shot off into the distance, eventually turning a corner and vanishing probably a kilometre away.

A hundred metres away on the right was the door Bill had been talking about. The artifact vault. This is where the journey would reach its end. I felt all the hairs on my arms and neck stand up.

Caught up in the anticipation, I snagged a foot on a loose line of cable and crashed to the floor, taking a couple of other bundles of cable off the wall and down with me as I did. The crash was brutally loud in the silence, and it echoed down the hall. Bill spun, his eyes wide. For a long moment, we were frozen, listening. At first there was nothing, and the engineer and I exchanged a relieved look.

Then a dull hum started coming from the big door on our left.

'Go go go, that's an elevator!' Bill whispered, catching hold of my arm and helping me to my feet. We turned and darted back toward the stairwell, just in time to watch the access door swing shut and lock with a loud thump. Frantically, the engineer hauled on the handle, but it was no use. The dwarves had obviously wanted to keep non-maintenance personnel out of that section, and an empty key card slot next to the lever suggested we weren't getting in without violence.

I stepped back, lifting my arm into the air as I began to shape the forms that would blow the door off of its frame. Before I could, Bill caught hold of my other arm and pulled me into the relative cover of the first entrance on the right side of the corridor. 'The noise!' the engineer hissed. 'They'll be all over us if they see the wreckage!'

We were out of time. The hum suddenly stopped, and there was a loud hiss as the elevator door rolled open. Bill tensed as he brought his rifle up, and I twisted the shapes I'd already made into slightly different forms.

A massive shape stepped cautiously out of the lift, shrouded in the dim light of the hallway. It was definitely not a dwarf, all jagged bone and horn and claw. Suddenly, the creature spun toward us, and it seemed to have two pairs of eyes. It snarled and then came charging forward. As prepared as I was to tear it apart, I was shocked when Bill laughed out loud and then brushed past me to walk toward the nightmare and the others stepping out of the elevator behind it. Then I recognized the creature as it moved through the light near me, and I let my magic fade and rushed out to join the engineer.

'Did you haul that thing the whole way here to gloat?' I asked with a chuckle.

Nox threw the bone dragon's head down on the floor in front of him with a toothy grin. 'Yes,' he growled.

101

'How did you find us?' Bill said, incredulously, as the entire party gathered in front of the open elevator. 'I'm amazed you managed to kill the dragon, but obviously you also managed to find your way down one of the first two passages I'd marked off.'

If I hadn't known better, I would've sworn the engineer sounded displeased.

Robin, a huge grin splitting her face, pointed at Nox and Petrel. 'You should have seen it, you guys. These two took that dragon apart, bone by bone. It was crazy,' she said, eyes wide with excitement.

The steel dwarf looked embarrassed, and quietly said, 'Well, the dragon was nearly dead already. Well, dead again, I mean. The 'wolf and I didn't have to do much, really.'

Nox snorted indignantly. 'We had to do plenty. I'm still putting dragonslayer on my resume,' he growled in mock seriousness.

This assessment of the bone dragon's danger didn't exactly mesh with what Bill had told me, and I gave the engineer a suspicious look. According to him, he'd separated the two of us because the party was likely doomed. When he noticed me looking at him, the engineer smiled darkly and then looked away.

I frowned, but when Nox dropped a furry hand roughly on my head, I couldn't help but smile as first him then Ceile wrapped me up in a big hug. My less monstrous friend carefully put her hand up to my cheek as she sent a scanning spell dancing across my body in search of injury. Whatever information her magic returned to her, it made her smile sadly and shake her head. Shifting the spell to heal rather than search, she gave my arm a squeeze as the elemental energy did what it could to fix me up.

'What did you see?' I asked her quietly.

'We must get you to the regeneration chamber,' she said, ignoring my question.

I sighed, then turned to the others. Weezab was hovering near the elevator door, looking nervously up and down the corridor. The kobold looked pale and unhappy, and when he met my eye, he shook his head slowly. I wondered if he had bitten off more than he could chew when he decided to tag along back in the Locus Wood. I wondered what had motivated him to come so far, hiding his true nature. And I wondered who he really was if not the simple kobold he appeared to be.

Next to him, Vrarrs Kor lazily leaned against the door frame, a shock rifle cradled in one arm, the barrel propped against her shoulder. The dragon seemed to be lost in her thoughts, staring aimlessly across the hallway at the wall. Even more so than the kobold, I wondered about her reasons for being here. She'd been an ally, if an aloof one, for almost the entire trip, but our less than friendly introduction to her made her motivations even more mysterious.

Bill and the dwarves were standing uneasily apart from us. The engineer and Petrel looked very unhappy with each other. I couldn't blame the steel dwarf. Bill had essentially abandoned everyone but me back in the bone dragon chamber, and while it didn't seem like the engineer had hoped they'd all died, he was certainly displeased that him and I had been found.

Robin, on the other hand, despite her earlier enthusiasm, was now staring miserably at Ceile.

I frowned. The dwarf woman had plenty of reason to not want my friend here, but I had a hard time believing that this is how she would act if she was unable to keep a loved one away from danger. Sure, Robin had been nervous when the group was knee deep in trouble before, but she'd never run or panicked.

Shaking my head, I took Ceile's hand. 'I have a bad feeling about this,' I whispered to her, for what was probably the fourteenth time since we left the City. Ceile just smiled sadly.

Petrel turned away from Bill and then smiled. 'It was lucky that I was paying attention while Bill was studying his elf maps, or we would have been completely screwed up there after he ran away,' he said. His grin got wider when the engineer threw him a very dirty look. 'As it was, I had enough of an idea of the layout to navigate passage number one once we'd taken care of the dragon. Our biggest problem once we reached the marked end was that the only thing we had to dig our way through to the upper service areas,' the steel dwarf gestured up the elevator shaft, 'was me. I'm surprised that you didn't hear the racket. But then, we're all a little surprised that the dwarves didn't hear the racket, but then, this place really has been abandoned, hasn't it.'

There were a lot of dark looks sent in Bill's direction, and I spoke up quickly before the group completely turned against the one person that knew what we were looking for. 'What matters is we're here. We've made it. Now let's go crack the safe, shall we?' I said, nodding toward the door just up the hall.

The engineer didn't hesitate. Spinning on his heel, he marched up the corridor without looking back. I was right behind him, Ceile's arm locked in mine. Just over my shoulder, I heard Nox's claws clacking against the metal floor, and then the quiet bustle of the other party members falling into line behind us.

And then we were there.

The door was nondescript, and looked identical to every one we'd encountered on this level. Simple text at head level next to the door labelled the room beyond as Room 1033, without elaborating further. The thick layer of dust on the floor was undisturbed at the entrance's feet.

'Bill, how long ago did you come here?' I asked.

The engineer gave me a crooked smile as he came to a stop next to the door. 'A long time ago, Martin Tundra,' he said in an odd tone. Turning to the others, he said, 'As soon as we open the vault, an alarm will go out. My hope is that either no one will answer it, or the response will be so slow that we'll have long been gone before it arrives.'

'Alright, stand back, Bill. Let's get this over with,' I said, disentangling myself from Ceile and reaching out for energy, prepared to turn the door into scrap.

Instead, Bill put a hand up, and smiled wider than ever. 'No need, my friend,' he said, then reached into his jacket and pulled out a card. I frowned and bent in to look closer at it.

It was marked 1033. Somebody behind me hissed in disbelief.

Without fanfare, the engineer slid the card into the lock, gave the handle a gentle pull, and then we all stepped back as the door rolled open. My heart was thundering in my chest as I tried to get my first glimpse of the chamber that held my salvation.

It was initially pitch black beyond the door, but a long moment later, brilliantly white lights began flashing into existence, one line of them at a time until the chamber was completely lit all the way to the back of the room. Even before the shadows were entirely gone, Bill was striding in, and once my eyes had adjusted to the harsh glare, I cautiously followed.

Row on row of empty lab benches filled the closest part of the room, their chairs tucked uniformly underneath. The walls they were bolted to were almost entirely storage space for equipment and monitoring gear. Oddly, the dust that coated everything outside the door was completely absent here, other than the wave that had flowed in at our heels.

Further to the back, the benches spread out, and the wall space began being occupied by lockers of various sizes and shapes. Readouts on the locker doors listed a bunch of different kinds of information, with some lockers apparently being maintained at sub-zero temperatures or at odd pressures.

Bill swept down the short set of stairs into the lab proper and didn't slow, leaving the benches behind. As I followed him into the locker area, I slowed enough to look at some of the displays as I passed.

Most of them were filled with technical data that I didn't understand, giving me no idea about what was actually contained within.

Then we passed a couple lockers whose displays were angrily flashing red. One of them had steam hissing out the top of the door.

If the engineer was concerned, he didn't show it. As he walked quickly past the increasingly common warning messages, he didn't acknowledge them with anything other than a disinterested glance. 'Don't open any doors,' he finally said over his shoulder.

'Yeah, because that's the first thing I do when a locker that's supposed to hold something potentially really dangerous is flashing danger signs,' Nox growled quietly from behind me.

Then we passed the last of the lockers, and the lab opened up into a wide flat area. Wires and cable were laid wildly around the floor, twisted and looped around several mobile benches covered in tools and gauges. Several work lights were set up at each corner of the room, shining their light into the center. Monitors hung from the ceiling, hooked to rails so they could be moved around the space.

Spread haphazardly across the floor were a number of bizarre looking objects that I couldn't begin to identify. One of them was almost as big as me, another was smaller than my head. They were all built with the same strange black metal, and I felt uneasy as I looked at them. I'd seen that metal somewhere before.

And then there was the regeneration chamber.

It looked like a cylindrical telephone booth, but was covered in weird circuitry and mechanisms. Much like the other things in this room, it felt alien, something not of this world. Or maybe not of this time. It stood in the very center of the room, bathed in the beams of every work light in the chamber, standing very much apart from the dwarven equipment arrayed around it.

I walked slowly toward the machine, passing Bill, who had stopped to watch my reaction. As I got closer, I could see it was actually pretty big, easily big enough to fit Nox in its weird glass chamber. There were sigils etched into places that made me think of warning and information signs, but all in a language and alphabet that had probably been dead for centuries.

Everything about it made me feel ill.

I turned back to my friends. Ceile's face was curious as she looked sightlessly around the room, clutching my hand tightly. Nox was staring at the regeneration chamber. He looked feverish. The others had fanned out around the room, oddly enough.

Out of the corner of my eye I saw something move, and I violently twisted around, pulling Ceile behind me. When I saw the twisted and tortured shape float out from behind the chamber to rise up above me, I gasped and recoiled in horror.

It had been a dwarf once, but its lower half had been removed, and now it leaned forward out of a cubic machine that had replaced abdomen, pelvis, and legs. Its arms were twisted and mutilated, all bone and sinew bolted together by metal and plastic, and its chest was no better off. I could see its heart beating erratically beneath a thin layer of black rubber. The whole monstrosity hung from the ceiling by cables and wires, much like the monitors.

I stared at it, trying to make sense of what it was, trying to grasp for energy to defend myself, and then I looked, really looked, into its butchered face.

And recognized it.

The dwarven engineer I'd met during the war, the one captured by my platoon. The one I'd eventually come to call my friend. 'Partridge?' I whispered, weakly. Beneath the ruin and metal, I saw the dwarf's mouth split open in a smile that did nothing to shake the terror in his eyes.

'Hello, Martin. I'm glad you've finally come,' he said, hoarsely, his voice full of pain and fear.

In the middle of my mounting horror, I realized that no aether or nether had come when I'd called. Nox was already moving to pull Ceile and me away from Partridge, and I stumbled back, wrestling with my once again sudden defencelessness. I heard Ceile cry out, recognizing the dwarf's voice and my terror but not knowing what was happening.

I heard the click of three shock rifles going live, and I whirled toward them to try and tell the others that it was alright, that this was my friend, but stopped with a shock when I found Bill's weapon pointed at my face.

'No more games, Martin,' Bill snarled, and now there was nothing friendly in his voice at all. 'And no more tests!' he shouted, oddly turning his head to stare at Vrarrs Kor.

Nox wasn't sure which way to look, and the big 'wolf was wildly looking back and forth between Partridge and the shock rifles pointed his way. Robin and Kor were both aiming at him, the dwarf woman looking very nervous and the dragon indifferent, and Petrel was watching the 'wolf very carefully, arms held ready at his sides.

Weezab had vanished.

'What the hell is this, Bill?' I yelled, sliding out from behind Nox so I could stand at the 'wolf's side. 'What have you done to Partridge?' I snarled, gesturing over at my tortured friend. I could hear the machines that made up most of his body whir and click quietly, briefly drowned out whenever he took a ragged breath.

The engineer smiled, and nodded at the regeneration chamber behind us. 'Partridge here has been an excellent resource! I brought him and a team of scientists and engineers here to study the artifacts the Krekt Twelve dwarves discovered in that ancient room. I needed to know what they all did and how they worked,' he said. His eyes flickered to one of the objects on the floor over by Partridge.

'Unfortunately, most of them died over the course of their studies. Partridge is the only one left! But imagine my joy when I discovered I wasn't going to have to learn to use these all by myself, after he figured out the basics. Granted, he did so under duress, and over the course of a couple decades, but figure it out, he did,' the engineer continued, nodding at the dwarf.

If looks could kill, Partridge's would have turned Bill into a ball of scrap metal.

'What have you done, Bill?' Ceile asked. There was anger in her voice.

'What I've had to do. Now, it's time to bring this sorry tale to a close. Martin, get in the chamber,' the engineer said, frostily. 'What you've searched for for over a century is right here. Get your life back. Life forever in a body that will never grow old.' His eyes were wild.

'It's time for this to end.'

Even before he finished talking, Nox was charging across the floor, snarling with rage. The big 'wolf didn't make it a handful of metres before Kor and Robin hit him with stun bolts that dropped him to the ground in a twitchy pile.

'Nox!' I roared and started forward, heedless of the fact that without my magic I was currently just an old man. I slowed to a stop when everyone's rifles suddenly pointed at me.

'So much work has gone into bringing you to this place. Decades of planning. We had to convince the entirety of Krekt Twelve that one of the artifacts had exploded so they'd think this entire section was teeming with fatal radiation. Now, we had to kill a few hundred of them and make it look like the artifact did it, but all in the name of science, right?' Bill said, walking toward me. 'All that dust out there? That was the vast majority of a full group of soldiers escorting engineers and scientists intending to get into this chamber and measure the devastation.'

He pointed at one of the objects in the corner of the room. 'That thing turns things into little bits. It's glorious. Amped up, it'll make a dwarf into a sizable pile of dust,' he cackled, then gave me a wink. 'I'm good at this, Martin. Or is it the Other? Have you decided which you are, yet?'

I felt Ceile take my hand, having navigated to me by the sound of my voice. Bill smirked at her.

'Now, I told Partridge I'd finally let him die if you get in there and get all regenerated. So don't leave him hanging. You don't want him to live like this, do you?' the engineer said, turning back to me and waving at Partridge.

'I'm not getting in there, Bill. What do you mean decades of work has gone into getting me here? Ceile only met you a few years ago,' I said, angrily.

The engineer sighed. He looked over his shoulder, and said, 'Kill Ms. Angael.' Kor's rifle came up, and Petrel started stomping toward us.

'No!' Robin yelled, dashing ahead of them to put herself square between us and the others. Furious, she screamed, 'She isn't part of the deal, Bill! The contract is for him! The client doesn't need her, she goes free!' The dwarf woman had her shock rifle trained on the engineer. 'Petrel, c'mon! We can take the contract ourselves, split the money half and half rather than by thirds,' she said to the steel dwarf without taking her eyes off of Bill.

The engineer shook his head. 'How dreadfully unprofessional of you, Robin. Of course she is part of the deal. As soon as her and this beast joined our little journey, they became part of the deal. Now, if Martin isn't going to get into the chamber, kill Ceile and see if that changes his mind,' he said, darkly. 'And now, you're going to do it, Robin, or we'll kill you too.'

Nervously, Robin was stepping slowly back, trying to keep in front of Ceile as best possible. Petrel marched steadily toward us, his face expressionless. Kor stood over Nox, rifle pointed lazily at me. Bill's weapon hung at his side arrogantly.

'Petrel?' Robin asked, quietly, as the steel dwarf came to stand before her. He looked at her silently for a long moment.

'Oh, to hell with it. Petrel, just kill both of them,' Bill snarled, rolling his eyes.

There wasn't any hesitation. With a savage swipe, the steel dwarf lunged forward and tore Robin's head clear of her shoulders.

I jerked back as the dwarf woman's blood splattered across me and Ceile. Robin's body collapsed noisily to the ground at my feet, and now I was face to face with Petrel and her head.

'Robin?' Ceile whispered in horror, reaching up to wipe the blood off of her face.

'Excellent, thank you, Petrel. You couldn't have killed her while you were following my directions through the caverns? You had plenty of time to kill any of them,' Bill said, clapping.

Petrel snarled over his shoulder as he stared at me, 'There wasn't an opportunity to kill any of them. As it was, I had to slow the group down so we wouldn't get here before you. I hope you got whatever you were hoping for when you separated from us.' His eyes narrowed. 'Now, Martin, unless you want Ceile to join Robin here,' he whispered, giving the dwarf woman's head a shake, 'I'd suggest you get in the chamber like our charismatic leader would like you to.'

I stared at Robin's head in horror. Blood and gore oozed from the torn remains of her neck, pooling around and on Petrel's feet. I imagined that it was Ceile's body lying at my feet, and I decided that wasn't going to happen if I could do anything about it.

'Alright. I'll get in the damn thing, just don't hurt her,' I said, putting my hands up in surrender. 'Just, tell me why we're here, Bill. Who's the client?'

Petrel nodded slowly and threw Robin's head across the room carelessly. Bill's evil smile returned. Partridge had lowered himself down in front of the control panel for the regeneration chamber.

'Excellent. Partridge get that thing fired up. Petrel, makes sure our friend Martin does as he's told. Kor, watch the werewolf. Kill him if he does anything other than lie there,' the engineer said, rifle still aimed at me. 'I've been watching you for a long time, Martin. Longer than you can remember. You're very important, though you probably will never remember why. My client has had me keeping tabs on you while I worked to find the regeneration chamber. Amusingly, I had already started preparations to come to you as a friend and bring you here when Ms. Angael gave me the perfect cover to do it,' he said.

'Why, Bill? Why does your client want me to use the chamber? And who are they?' I said. Petrel put a bloody hand on my shoulder and turned me gently toward the machine. Partridge began tapping buttons on the panel, and a high pitched whine blipped into existence.

Ceile squeezed my hand tight before letting go. There were tears dripping down her cheeks, and I watched her settle to the ground and reach hesitantly for Robin's body. My chest got tight with sympathy for my friend.

'My client needs you alive and healthy, Martin, something that you are only just barely. You probably actually have another year or so before the cancer kills you, but our time line got tighter so we had Jacobs give you less optimistic news,' Bill said, darkly.

I frowned. Jacobs had been working for someone? 'The client, Bill. Who?' I asked, heatedly.

The engineer burst into laughter, and then kicked Nox in the shoulder. 'Ask your friend. He brought them all the way here. Hell, in half an hour, you'll get to meet them anyway,' he chuckled.

Nox hadn't recovered enough from the stun bolt to do much more than snarl raggedly. The confusion on his face made me feel better, but there was also worry in his eyes. Bill leaned down and very slowly patted the 'wolf on the head.

'Oh, maybe he didn't know. All of the Government's assets have tracking spells on them. Enforcement and Operations have been following the 'wolf the whole way here,' the engineer said, quietly. Nox looked shocked. Bill looked back up at me with a huge grin. 'The client is your old employer, Martin.'

'And they're on their way down to see you, right now.'

The Department of Enforcement. Technically, I was a retired member, but really I'd been honourably discharged after I - or the Other - had gotten carried away in a mission and nearly wiped my own squad out. 'What would they want with me?' I said, confused. 'Why go through all this effort? Why didn't they just kidnap me and bring me here, if that was the whole plan? It's not like Operations doesn't do just that on a daily basis.'

'You needed a bit of an attitude adjustment, my friend. You also had to be tested to make sure you were still capable of what they want you for. And you are! You passed with mostly flying colours,' Bill said with a wink. 'I am a bit of a specialist, Martin. I do tasks that the Departments aren't equipped to do. They hired me and my associates,' he gestured at Petrel and then over at Robin's head, 'to take you on about as dangerous a trip as we could.'

I frowned, then nodded at Vrarrs Kor. 'What about her and Weezab? They aren't just along for the ride,' I said. Petrel brought me to a halt, and now I stood in front of the glass door to the regeneration chamber.

Bill's smile slipped slightly and he looked over his shoulder at the dragon, who looked back impassively. 'Insurance,' he sneered, before looking back at me. I noticed he never bothered searching for the missing kobold. Dismissing Kor with a wave, the engineer pointed his rifle at the machine.

'Can you feel it, Martin? The regeneration chamber shouldn't exist. This is an artifact built millennia ago in a time when humans built horrors every day without a thought. Think about it! They built a machine that killed anything that went into it except the tiniest fraction of a fraction of people. Can you imagine why, Martin?' Bill said, his voice quiet and full of wonder.

I wanted to curse at him, but my heart was slamming against my chest and I was having trouble breathing. My skin was crawling, and I felt like my body was leaning away from the machine of its own volition.

'It's an execution device!' Bill answered with a guffaw. 'An execution device with very peculiar side effects on the old, as you know. But do you know what the best part about this artifact is, Martin? The part that really shows you just what kind of monster we were all those years ago? When they discovered that their murder machine could be the fountain of youth? The engineers and scientists went out of their way to try and eliminate what they said was a flaw in their work.'

Green lights flared into existence along the edges of the regeneration chamber, and the high pitched whine was crushed by a wave of sound as the artifact roared to life. A constant deep and loud thrum pulsed out from somewhere inside the machine's guts, vibrating the floor of the lab. I could feel it buzzing in my ribcage, the sound penetrating my body and clutching my heart in its grip. I felt fainter than before, and Petrel's grasp on my shoulder tightened.

'The chamber is ready, Poe,' Partridge announced, watching Bill with baleful eyes. Slowly spinning on his rail to look at me, the mutilated dwarf shook his head, and sadness warred with the pain on his face. 'I am sorry, Martin. He told me he would finally kill me once this was done. I need him to kill me. I need this to end,' he said, and the longing in his voice sent a chill down my back.

The glass door beside me slid open with a hiss, and the hum of the machine got even louder. Inside, a vertical bed of sorts awaited a victim. There was a thin layer of red dust scattered across the inside of the chamber, and I morbidly wondered if it was all that remained of the younger people that had gone in and never come out.

'Make this easy, Martin. You'll thank us, later,' Petrel said. There was some sympathy on his face, which was mostly ruined by the gore dripping down his arms. With inexorable slowness, the steel dwarf guided me into the chamber.

I heard Ceile call my name in fear.

I heard an odd crash from the far end of the room.

I heard Bill shout in anger, and the sound of his rifle firing off.

I heard Petrel gasp, and suddenly I was falling to the ground.

Scrabbling to get up, and also to get the hell out of the regeneration chamber, I looked dazedly up to see a massive green form swiping furiously at the engineer, who rolled away awkwardly. Whatever the newcomer was, it didn't fit very well in the confines of the lab, and it had already slammed into the ceiling a few times, bringing chunks of concrete and cabling falling down around it. A cloud of dust was already shrouding the area, and I watched a green tail come scything out of it, narrowly missing Bill.

Then what I was seeing resolved itself, and I was looking at a green dragon. A green dragon with only one eye.

Vrarrs Kor.

I was wracked with confusion, but first thing was first. I had to get Ceile to safety. Using the chamber door frame, I managed to get to my feet, though every second I touched the machine made me feel nauseous. Stepping out into the lab proper, I found my friend already moving steadily away from the danger, guided by one of Partridge's twisted hands. When I made eye contact with him, he just shrugged.

Petrel was charging toward the fray, each step cracking the floor as the steel dwarf raced to attack the dragon. I growled and tore at the realm between, trying to gather energy to me. I didn't know if Kor could fight both Bill and the dwarf, and it seemed like she was trying to save my life. Or maybe she was just trying to increase her percentage. Whatever the case, I wanted the engineer brought down and I was going to help her.

I cursed. As before, neither of the Suns had anything for me. I felt blind. The ocean and the vortex were gone. I might as well have been a lunaron, stripped of my magic.

'Kor, look out!' I yelled, hoping the dragon would hear me and at least see the steel dwarf coming.

Whether she heard or not, it didn't matter. There was sudden movement along the floor in the dust cloud, and then there was a howl that shook the room and drowned out the machine. Petrel flinched away, but not quick enough. Nox erupted from the murk, lifting the steel dwarf clear of the floor and throwing him across the lab to crash ungracefully into a long, boxy looking artifact and its monitoring equipment. Before he could do much more than get to his feet, the dwarf found himself tackled by nine hundred pounds of werewolf, and the two crashed into the dust cloud and vanished.

Watching the shadows carefully, I reached down and gingerly pulled Robin's pistol from the dead woman's body, then slowly backed toward Partridge and Ceile. The machine hummed along, indifferent to the chaos around it. I heard Kor roar in anger and pain, and Nox snarl in fury.

I felt useless. I was a mediocre shot with the pistol, more likely to hit the two combatants that I didn't want to hit than Bill or Petrel. Something in this room had taken my power away. I needed to get it back. 'Ceile, your magic! Can you still use it?' I whispered once I was close enough for her to hear me. The look on her face answered my question. It wasn't just me, then, which might explain why Weezab had disappeared.

'Partridge, the artifacts in this lab, are any of them designed to prevent magic use?' I suddenly asked, spinning to look up at my old friend.

The dwarf twitched and closed his eyes in pain. 'Two, Martin. Poe has set them up on opposite sides of this section of the lab. I will disable them both, if you will destroy me when I am done,' he said, misery and terror rippling in his voice.

There was a violent crash from further into the lab, and now it wasn't just dust cloaking the area. Smoke billowed from somewhere beyond the cloud, floating along the ceiling before vanishing into ducts. I heard Petrel shout something and Nox roar a curse in response.

I shook my head at Partridge. 'No. I'm not going to kill you. Help us, and we'll take you with us when we go,' I said, heatedly. 'We can get you fixed up, Partridge.'

The dwarf was already shaking his head violently. 'You can't remove me from the equipment here without killing me, Martin, and regardless, Poe has wired me to explode if I leave the lab. He has gone through great pains to keep me here so that I could make his little toys,' he said, hoarsely. The dwarf suddenly slid down until I was nose to nose with him. 'You must beware, Martin and Ceile. The man you call Bill is no City mercenary. He has a dozen faces. He may proclaim to be working with your Government, but Poe only works for himself.'

Kor roared from somewhere in the smoke, and there was another thunderous crash. I didn't know how Bill was holding up against the dragon, but I couldn't count on either of the fights going the way I needed them to. Could I kill a friend, though? Even if it would be a mercy?

Something dark at the back of my mind whispered yes.

Before I could make the choice, Petrel emerged from the smoke, metal form battered, dragging a weakly struggling Nox behind him with one arm.

104

The werewolf was bloody, torn and bruised, and he looked dazed as he swatted weakly at the steel dwarf. The pair came to a stop twenty metres away, and Petrel gave me a dangerous look. Without saying anything, he lifted Nox over his head, and slammed the 'wolf into the floor. Then again.

'No!' I screamed in fury, breaking away from Ceile, who shouted in confusion, and charging at the steel dwarf, Robin's pistol blazing. I'm not sure what I hoped to accomplish, but I managed to spray the wall far behind the dwarf with destruction, and not the dwarf. I'd tried to stop out of arm's reach from him, but he threw Nox to the ground one last time and then lunged at me, sending the pistol flying. A second strike lifted me off the ground and threw me into the door frame of the regeneration chamber, where I slid painfully to the floor.

I coughed, feeling bone moving around in ways that bone should never move, and blood bubbled from my lips. That couldn't be good.

Leaving the unconscious 'wolf behind, Petrel stomped toward me, kicking debris out of his way. He hadn't gotten away without injury from his fight with Nox, each step sent sparks and oil spitting across the ground. 'You know, they say you're going to change the world. Promised us good money if we brought you here and then turned you over. Had to be dangerous, they said. Had to make sure you were up to it, or some such thing. I figured we should just dump you in the artifact and test you after, but hey, I don't get paid to come up with the big ideas, apparently,' the steel dwarf.

When he was standing over me, he leaned down with a concerned look. 'Dammit, I better not have broken you. Ceile! Heal him!' he snarled, looking first at her and then at Partridge.

Then Bill crashed down out of the smoke, rolling wildly before coming to a rest in a smoking, twisted wreck of metal and synthetic flesh. His head and face were relatively intact, but his arms and legs were wrapped tightly and very, very brokenly around his body, adorned with deep claw marks. Several spots on him were covered in a bubbling green liquid.

'Well, this is embarrassing,' the engineer growled, frowning up at the ceiling.

Kor loomed up out of the cloud, stepping slowly forward while watching Petrel carefully. Acid still frothed on her upper jaws, dripping down to hiss on the cracked flooring below her feet. 'Get away from the package, dwarf,' she snarled, her voice all ice. 'Unless you want me to destroy another machine today.'

The steel dwarf didn't move, only stared at the dragon in contempt. 'You and the kobold weren't supposed to interfere, dragon!

You were just supposed to watch and make sure the tests went as planned!' he shouted over the thrum of the regeneration chamber.

Kor took a lazy step toward the dwarf. 'That is my business. Now get away,' she said.

As she got closer, Petrel began to look increasingly uncomfortable. He looked back and forth between me, the dragon, and Bill. Finally, after staring for a long moment at the poison dripping from Kor's mouth, he slowly stepped away, watching her silently.

Barking a dark laugh, the dragon suddenly took a deep breath, turned to face the steel dwarf entirely, and then opened her mouth to douse him in acid. Instead, she burst into flames.

With a shriek, Kor stumbled and fell before wildly getting to her feet and crashing into the side of a storage locker, tearing it entirely free of the lab wall. The dragon rolled and flailed at herself, shattering walls and ceiling and anything else unfortunate enough to be within reach. The scream of pain went on and on until finally she went silent and collapsed in a smoking heap.

The fire immediately went out.

'It's about time you came back, kobold! That thing almost killed me!' Petrel shouted, angrily. Sure enough, Weezab stood in the hallway between lockers, one arm pointed at Kor, the other hanging at his side. The kobold gave the dwarf a dirty look, then looked down at Bill with a smirk.

'Petrel, bring Kor to me,' the engineer said, trying to twist his neck enough to see what was happening. The dwarf sneered at him, then walked across the floor to the dragon's side.

Before he could grab her, the dragon's blackened form slowly shrunk, taking on human form once again. The damage was still done, of course. Her body was just as horribly burnt as it had been as a beast. I could see her breathing raggedly, and her one eye opened and closed rapidly.

Heedless of her pain, Petrel caught hold of her arm and dragged the dragon across the floor until he dumped her unceremoniously in front of Bill. The engineer looked at her carefully, a searching look on his face. Suddenly, he nodded his head and smiled. 'Oh, Kor. I thought you might just be being overzealous in policing the client's conditions, but that's not it, is it? No, you're working for someone else altogether. Someone that would rather my goals not succeed, I imagine,' he said. I could barely hear him over the machine. 'Would you care to tell me who, before I kill you?'

Kor's eye opened, slowly, and she grimaced with pain. Silently, she stared at the engineer, and she carefully sat up so she was looking down at him. The dragon smiled, the gesture cracking the skin around her mouth and sending blood oozing down her face.

The engineer sighed, and looked over at Weezab. 'Kill her,' he said. The kobold grinned evilly.

A pillar of fire burst from the floor beneath Kor, almost obscuring the dragon and erupting up to the ceiling where it billowed out, scorching the panels and lapping around the cables and pipes. Soon, molten plastic and stone were raining down.

There was no shriek of pain or agony this time. The dragon's shape in the flame continued to look down on Bill, and then, just before she was nothing more than ash, she yelled, 'Pestilence sends you and your client her regards, Poe.'

And then she was gone.

Pestilence. The Third Horseman. Vrarrs Kor had been working for her? What stake did she have in all of this, and what had Bill done to earn her ire?

Weezab's eyes narrowed, but the engineer didn't react beyond a small smile. Shaking his head slowly, the kobold sent the flame away, leaving nothing but melted ruin behind. Once he was done, he turned to look curiously at Bill. 'So what are we going to do with you?' he said, irritated.

Petrel looked very confused, staring at the kobold. I almost laughed, remembering my own reaction to finding out the little fellow wasn't exactly ordinary.

Bill ignored the dwarf. 'There's a spare body in the lab somewhere, we should be able to pull my head off of this one and put it on there. I haven't tested it in a while, obviously, but Partridge does good work, so I assume he-' he started to say before suddenly cutting off, eyes widening.

I was almost as surprised as the engineer when I looked over and found Ceile wrapped around Petrel, Robin's pistol jammed into his eye. Without saying anything or hesitating at all, my friend pulled the trigger and blew a sizable hole in the steel dwarf's head.

'That was for Robin,' she said, as she pushed the body away from her with her shoulder. Streaming smoke from his face, Petrel toppled to the ground with a loud crash.

Nobody moved for a long moment. Weezab was shaking his head, still looking irritated. Bill actually burst into laughter. 'Oh, Ms. Angael, thank you. I needed that,' the engineer chuckled. Looking back at Weezab, he nodded. 'Take the gun from her and make sure she won't be a threat anymore,' he said to the kobold.

It wouldn't have mattered, as Robin's pistol had basically melted down after Ceile's point blank shot into the steel dwarf's skull, but regardless, the kobold pointed at her and I saw his mouth move. From nowhere, a storm of fiery energy erupted around my friend, and she screamed.

'Weezab! No!' I yelled, then coughed. Blood flecked the ground around me. 'Please!'

The vortex of red flame spun and weaved over her body, reducing the gun to slag and most of her clothing to ash. She shrieked as she fell to her knees, trying to protect her face from the fire. Soon her skin was bubbling in places, and I again tried to reach for energy of my own, to no avail.

I cursed. The kobold must be standing outside the influence of the artifacts, and that meant I had a long way to crawl if I hoped to counter him. Feeling the grinding bones in my chest, I didn't have much hope I'd make it that far, but I had to try. 'Bill, please!' I yelled as I reached out and tried to drag myself toward the storage lockers. If the engineer heard me, he didn't show it.

The pain was immense, and I only made it a few metres before I collapsed face first to the ground. Ceile was still shrieking, and I teared up as I yelled at Weezab again.

Before I could finish my shout, there was a sharp click over my shoulder. The roar of the kobold's flame suddenly vanished, and when I weakly raised my head to look at him, I saw both him and Bill staring in shock at something behind me. Rolling over painfully, I saw Ceile lying curled in a ball on the floor, smoke drifting off of her. But that's not what the other two were looking at. I twisted as best I could to look back at the regeneration chamber.

The door was closed. Inside the glass chamber, stretched out against the bed, was Nox.

Partridge looked down at me sadly, shrugged, and then pressed a button on the control panel.

105

A green gas quickly filled the glass chamber, and in seconds Nox had vanished. The continuous hum of the machine changed to a loud and steady pulse, matched by bursts of light from inside the cloud.

'This can't be good,' Weezab said.

There was a shriek of tortured metal from over my shoulder, and I hurriedly glanced back to see Bill's arms free of their undignified earlier position. Twisted and battered, they didn't look like they'd be of much use, but as I watched, the engineer reached out with them and started dragging his ruined body toward Petrel.

The howl of the regeneration chamber was getting louder, and I looked back to see the lights pulsing so quickly that it felt like the machine was moving in slow motion. Looking up at Partridge, I yelled, 'Please, Partridge, shut it down!'

The mutilated dwarf shook his head slowly. 'There's no shutting it down, Martin. This has to happen. It all has to happen so that I can finally meet Death,' he yelled back, and bloody tears poured down his ruined cheeks.

I stared in horror as the green gas spun like a tornado, whipping around the inside of the glass faster and faster until it was a blur. Exhausted, I finally fell onto my back.

Using his wrecked arms, Bill had managed to pull himself over to Petrel's body. With twisted fingers, the engineer seemed to be looking for something along the steel dwarf's neck. With a cry of triumph, he lifted his hands away as gas hissed out from the body, then the dwarf's head shook and came loose.

My eyes widened. The engineer was going to steal Petrel's body.

Sure enough, as I watched he pressed several buttons in the ruined flesh near his own neck, and with a series of loud clicks, pulled his head free of his body. Several thick cables ran between the underside of his now disconnected neck and his torso, and the engineer very carefully began pulling similar wires from Petrel's torso.

I was watching someone do their own head transplant. With slow, careful moves, Bill hooked his head up to both bodies' cables, his face a mask of concentration. Using all four arms, he lifted his head completely free of his original body and then set it down on Petrel's, disconnecting himself from the twisted ruin and then locking in to the dwarf's body.

'That was nasty,' Weezab said, and I looked up to find the kobold crouched down near me. The little creature jerked his head at the engineer, who had gone completely still. 'We can always hope Petrel's body rejects Bill's swollen head,' the kobold laughed, darkly.

'Why did you warn me?' I asked, angry. 'I thought I could trust you.'

Weezab sobered, and he watched me for a moment, then shook his head. 'Sorry, Martin. You and I have a lot in common. Or the other you and I. You'll have to choose, soon. We could probably be friends, if things were different,' he said, leaning in close. 'But do you know what's better than friendship, Martin?'

I frowned at him, and his mouth split into a vicious grin. 'Power,' he said, 'And that's what I'll be getting once we put you in there and then get you to the client.'

'Why would you work for the City? Why would you trust them?' I snarled. I could taste more blood in my throat.

The kobold burst into laughter. 'Oh, Martin. The City sure isn't my client, friend,' he chuckled, and then stood up and headed for Bill.

The engineer was still crouched over, kneeling awkwardly next to his fallen body. His eyes seemed to be moving very quickly behind their lids, and his fingers, that used to be Petrel's fingers, twitched restlessly. Weezab came to a stop a respectful distance away, and I saw his lips moving.

Looking away from the two, my eyes fell on Ceile, who hadn't moved. She was breathing, at least, but either she was unconscious or in horrific pain. I hoped it was the former, but unless the kobold healed her, she was going to wake up to whatever agony she had been in originally.

The regeneration chamber suddenly shut down.

Weezab abandoned Bill's side and headed outside the magic nullifying artifacts' effect, turning to stare suspiciously at the chamber. The engineer still hadn't moved, though now his eyes were flickering open and closed. I propped myself up on my elbows, and watched the green gas inside the glass slow its spin until it simply drifted lazily along the walls.

There was a loud thump from inside.

Then another.

Then a massive, furry, blond, and clawed hand smashed into the glass from out of the cloud. There was a hiss of escaping air, and then the door slid open, the gas rapidly dissipating as it rose into the lab.

And then Nox stepped out.

Three metres and nine hundred pounds of thickly furred, razor clawed, razor toothed, brutally vicious werewolf. He was whole once more, or maybe even better than whole. He looked thicker and more muscled than he had been before we'd left the City.

After he'd moved a few metres, the big 'wolf stopped and slowly looked himself over. A frenzied grin split his face. He threw his head back and howled, arms spread wide, fingers curved, then returned to examining his pristine claws and shaggy fur.

'Yesssss,' the big 'wolf hissed.

'Nox?' I said, 'Are you alright?'

He very slowly raised his head to look at me. 'Look at me. Look at what it did to me, Martin,' he said. His eyes were feverish. 'I'm perfect.'

'Well now, isn't this fascinating?' I heard Bill say from off to my side.

I looked over at him, and watched as the engineer, on Petrel's body, slowly stood and twisted to face Nox and I. Steadily raising his arms toward the sky, a huge smile split his face. 'Can you imagine? Here I was, thinking it was good that I had a prototype body or two kicking around down here, and then Ms. Angael goes and gives me this gift! Of course, the specs aren't exactly the same, but the hardware is close enough,' he said, loudly.

Shaking his head, he slowly lowered his hands. Looking over at Nox, the engineer cocked his head. 'Now you, my furry friend, are even crazier than me. I wouldn't get in there! Especially knowing that humans don't exactly do well in there. And you are, at a base level, human, 'wolf,' he said with a sneer. With a chuckle, he turned to look down at me. 'Now, if you'd be so kind, help Martin into the chamber before he does something stupid like die.'

Over his shoulder, he said, 'Weezab, light him on fire if he doesn't play nice.' When the kobold didn't respond, the engineer looked back at the storage lockers in irritation.

The little fellow was gone.

Bill cursed. 'Damned kobold, should have left you as stupid as the rest of your moronic species,' he snarled, then turned back in time to get a face full of angry werewolf.

106

The engineer crashed across the floor, sending equipment and artifacts spinning and rolling away. He managed to get to his feet in time to catch Nox's hands in his own, and then I heard the hydraulics and motors in his arms howl in protest as he struggled to keep the 'wolf's claws from tearing him apart. Frenzied, the werewolf snapped at the engineer's face with his teeth, showering the man with saliva. Both of their feet dug deep into the concrete as they each tried to push the other.

Bill did not look pleased.

There was a hollow thud that I felt vibrate through the floor, and then the engineer ducked down and caught hold of Nox's waist. With a shriek of metallic effort, he managed to lift the big 'wolf into the air, and then tried to throw him. The strength was there, but Nox wasn't letting it happen. As soon as the engineer got him into the air, the 'wolf jammed all of his claws into the ceiling and then brought a whole slab of it down on their heads.

'I never liked you, Bill. And now, now I'm going to eat you,' he growled as he clambered up out of the debris.

'You should be happy, 'wolf. You've been a big help, betraying your friend and all,' the engineer mocked as he pushed himself clear of the ruin.

With a furious snarl, Nox charged, and raising his arms high in anticipation of crushing Bill down into a second ball of scrap metal.

And then, with a sickening sucking noise, first his right arm, then his left tore free of his shoulders, showering the big 'wolf and the engineer with gore.

The two limbs fell to the ground next to the engineer and then burst in nasty explosions of blood and tissue and shattered bone. Nox stared confusedly down at the blood remains, and then turned his head to look at the equally bloody holes where his shoulders had once been. Bill stared at the 'wolf in fascinated horror.

'Nox!' I screamed, rolling on my side and trying to drag myself toward him. He looked slowly over at me, and as I watched, red spots began to appear all over his body. Several of them grew and then burst, sending brilliant red blood to drip down through his fur.

He looked so sad.

'Looks like I was right, Martin. I told you I'd have something to be sorry for. The tracker,' he said, collapsing to his knees as his legs caved in on themselves and then split open as the bones inside tore the weakening flesh.

I was so far away, and tears were falling easily from my eyes. I wanted to touch him, to tell him it'd be okay. But then, it was never going to be okay ever again.

Then Nox smiled sadly at me, and his head made a hideous slurping sound and fell free of his torso.

I sat there for a long time, trembling, arm still reaching for my friend, staring as what remained of his torso bubbled and burst. Everything but his bones liquefied over the course of a few seconds, and then it was just his skeleton in a puddle of gore. Then even that cracked and crumbled to dust, leaving only a ghastly imprint of 'wolf's figure on the floor to mark his passing.

I gradually let my arm fall until it hung limply at my side, my hand cracking painfully against the lab floor. I couldn't look at my friend's body anymore, so I stared blankly at the concrete below me instead. I was so numb, even the tears couldn't fall.

Metal feet clacked loudly on the concrete, stepping into my field of vision and coming to a halt. 'This was always about you and me, Martin. Ceile still lives, and her life is in your hands. Will you let me get you into the regeneration chamber?' Bill asked, gently. 'Please?'

Looking slowly over at the motionless figure of my other friend, I watched her for a while. Her chest rose and fell raggedly, but at least she was breathing. She looked horrible, and I shook my head. 'No more, Bill. Don't hurt her anymore,' I whispered without looking at the engineer.

I felt a metal hand rest on my shoulder, and I heard him say, almost too quiet to hear, 'You don't even know what you are.' When I looked up at him, I was surprised to see the engineer's face was sad. Gently, he crouched down and then lifted me off the ground in his arms. I cried out in pain, and the engineer looked apologetic.

'It's almost over, my friend. Two hundred and sixty four years of planning, finally come to fruition. A glorious day!' he said, quietly, slowly carrying me back to the chamber. I wanted to respond, but I was gritting my teeth against the pain and I was so disconnected from everything.

In the end, the only thing I found myself caring about was Ceile.

Distantly, I heard the artifact firing up again, Partridge's hollow eyes watching me as the engineer set me gently into the glass chamber, hooking my arms into the supports. I barely noticed the pain this time.

'The final part of your tale begins now, Martin,' Bill said. He looked at me for a long moment and then turned and left the chamber.

The machine was humming once more, the deep thrum pulsing through every centimetre of my body. With a loud hiss, the door slid shut, blocking out everything but Bill and Weezab, the engineer

watching me from a short distance away, the kobold peeking inquisitively in through the lower part of the glass.

I couldn't see Ceile.

There was a sharp pop, and the green gas began spewing into the chamber from vents at my feet. Weezab looked oddly concerned as the cloud quickly filled past his sight. Bill locked eyes with me and then nodded slowly. And then the gas was all I could see.

Alone in the verdant haze with only the pulse of the machine to keep me company, vertigo threatened to knock me out. My brain struggled to make sense of up and down, hurt as I was and unable to see. I reached out to try and grasp anything with my hands, but the wrist straps didn't allow me to move far enough.

The sound in the chamber suddenly increased in volume and speed, and I ducked my head against the noise, trying to block some of it out with my shoulder. Instantly, I began to ache from head to toe on top of the pain I was already in. My joints felt like they were on fire, and I felt blood begin dripping from my ears and nose. My already bloody jacket quickly got even more so. I blinked against the pain, head swaying uncontrollably.

Then the lights started. The first flash slammed me into the bed, holding me in place. I screamed in agony as my injuries twisted in the light's grasp. My head was jammed into my shoulder, and as I watched, droplets of blood lifted free of my face and slowly floated away to splash against the glass wall. It felt like I was coming apart at the seams. My fingers were clenched tight, though I didn't remember telling them to. My feet shook violently, adding even more vibration to the bed. My heart thrashed against my broken ribs.

Then the second flash turned everything white and the whole world went away.

?

My boots were comfortably propped up on the airship controls as I watched the gnome city pass by far below. Already, the gnomes' defences were on their way, airships and antiaircraft spells rising from the spiralling towers and erratic shapes of Kastrin's buildings to fight me and my tiny fleet off.

I grinned evilly. My tiny fleet of elven ships, I should add.

A multi-coloured ball of raging fire slammed into my ship's reactive shielding, just to starboard of the control deck. My chair shook lightly, but the impact was mostly absorbed by the elves' wonderful toys. Sure, the gnomes would burn through the ship's armour and turn it into a flaming cloud of scrap metal, but I didn't need my ride to last all that long anyway.

I just needed enough time to drop my package into Kastrin's heart and wipe the gnome city clean off the map.

There was an explosion somewhere overhead as another spell went off, showering my windscreen with sparks and embers. I had a quick glance over my readouts, and was pleased to see that the city was definitely unprepared. Not even ten ships were on their way up, and maybe a single squad of magic defence had been roused from sleep. Too long, the gnomes had been at peace, avoiding the wars that the other three routinely had, bashing each other's faces in with enthusiasm over some stupid thing or another.

The Government, or rather the Department of Operations, had decided the gnomes needed to be bloodied a bit to bring them down to our level. Of course, we didn't want them at war with us. The elves, on the other hand, particularly their city to the south of the City, were starting to get bold along our boundaries. It would be very convenient if the two countries were at each other's throats.

So here I was, at the controls of one of the elves' greatest ships, leading three other ships into battle. Well, a fantastic replica of one of the elves' greatest ships, of course. We wouldn't want the elves to have forewarning of the attack by stealing their ships.

Now the sky was filled with destruction, lines and waves of deadly fire rocketing out in wide patterns as the defenders tried to hit us from so far down. In the midst of the storm of energy rose two gnome airships, all strange shapes and magic sails. Above decks, I could see the gunners, hands flaring with power, ready to send even more damage my way.

I laughed. The gnomes were in for a surprise.

'Edgar!' someone yelled from behind me.

I frowned, and looked over my shoulder to find Taylor standing at the other end of the empty command deck. My old commander looked furious, but he kept a respectful distance. He still wasn't sure if I held enough loyalty to not turn him into kindling.

'End this, Edgar! This is insane! Do you know what you have in these ships? Do you even know what you're doing?' the man shouted, pointing a finger angrily at me.

I yawned. 'Of course I know, Taylor. It was my idea,' I said. Without much effort, I called down the Suns and tore the first gnome airship into a million pieces. The astral energy raged around my arm, my hand so bright it threatened to blind me.

Taylor cursed and then came forward into the room. The ship shook as another arcane missile slammed into her from below, and he had to reach out to steady himself on one of the crew stations. 'This is his doing, isn't it? Peter's tricked you into this. You'd never have obeyed this order before you met him,' he snarled, shaking his head. 'Edgar, don't do this. The Department is going far over the line this time.'

I clucked my tongue, and then spun my chair around and settled my boots onto the deck. Slowly, I stood up, looking down at him, letting a slight smile play across my face. 'So I should disobey a direct order from Operations, Taylor? You know what they'd do. They'd kill Martin, and Katherine, and Nala, and hell, probably even the poor grincat. Then they'd wipe my brain and let Research tinker with it.'

Stepping toward me, Taylor put his hands up pleadingly. 'Please Edgar. There are over a hundred million gnomes down there, and however many other creatures in the land around us. You know damn well the Scayn won't stop once the city has been converted. If all four of the seeds you and your fleet are carrying land, this entire region will be uninhabitable for centuries. We'll end up having to come back to kill the damn things ourselves,' he said.

He was right, of course. If even one of the seeds dropped from my airships managed to touch down, the gnomes were doomed. The Scayn was a nightmare creature, spreading from surface to surface, making everything in its grasp a part of it. The towers and buildings below would go silent, and then they would rise up against anything living. They'd strip the city of life, not as quickly as, say, a dwarven nuclear storm bomb, but far more effective psychologically.

At least, far more effective if your goal is to provoke your target into mindless retaliation.

I shrugged the thoughts away. I didn't care how many died. In the end, my family was all that mattered, and I would trade a billion lives for theirs any day. As Taylor stepped up onto the pilot's platform with me, I shook my head. 'I can't stop it now, Taylor,' I said, as the ship rocked violently again, 'The Government needs the elves and the gnomes killing each other, and that's what's going to happen.'

A gentle tone sounded and then began repeating every few seconds. I looked over my shoulder at the readouts and saw that the fleet was almost over the target. 'Looks like it's time for us to get out of here-' I started to say, and then Taylor hit me so hard in the chest that I crumpled to the ground in a daze.

I coughed as fury boiled the blood in my veins. I howled for the Suns, planning to cut the man into strips, when I realized that they were gone. Struggling to sit up, I felt a sharp pain on the right side of my chest. Some sort of metal half-sphere, and judging by the agony I got hit with every time I moved, currently stapled or embedded in my flesh.

Taylor crouched down in front of me. 'Research came up with it. Had to strip the tech from some old human artifact. Does a lunaron's work without having to feed it. Very expensive!' he said. His tone was jovial, but he looked sad. I threw a wild punch at him, but the man just blocked it and casually hit me in the face, dazing me even further. 'You're the greatest threat the City has ever had, Edgar, and you're too unpredictable. Operations decided that it was time that you be handed over to Research so you can be properly re-educated.'

He looked up through the windscreen. Magical fire was flashing across the shields, cutting slowly through. 'You were my friend, and because I still have some respect for the school teacher that used to routinely beat me at darts, I intend to kill you rather than let Research have their way,' the man said, turning to look back at me. 'They'll be unhappy, but everyone else will be pleased that you're no longer a concern, and the Government will still get its war.'

I was feeling almost drunk, and when I tried to raise an arm again, I couldn't do much more than skid it across the deck. Taylor looked sympathetic. 'Had to tranq you, sorry. The only way to get you back to the City safely. If you were going back to the City.'

Taylor stood up and backed away slightly. 'I am sorry, old friend. I should be grateful that you let me get that close to you, though I imagine it was because of arrogance rather than friendship.' The ship rocked again, and this time there was an explosion from somewhere below the command deck.

Looking around as a high pitched alarm began to howl from the console next to him, Taylor sighed. Pulling his pistol out, he put the barrel against my forehead, pushing until I was up against the rail behind me. 'Our time's up. Goodbye, Edgar Lorn,' he said, and then pulled the trigger.

There was an explosion, and I shut my eyes in anticipation of my old commander's bullet adding a hole to my skull. A shockwave pushed me further into the seat, and heat washed over my face and chest. I felt flecks of blood and skin and bone and metal splash across me.

When I didn't immediately die, I slowly opened my eyes and found Taylor on the floor across from me, leaning up against the wall. His eyes were wide, and he was saying something over and over but too quietly for me to hear.

Both of his hands, and his pistol, were missing.

Peter leapt up onto the command deck and raced to my side. Looking nervously out the windscreen, he said, 'Good thing I came to check on you!' Throwing his smoking chimaera gun away, he bent down, gathered me up in his arms, and then lifted me up. Savagely kicking Taylor in the face as we passed the dying man, Peter laughed. 'Did you know his name is actually Bill? I might use that someday,' he said with a chuckle.

The ship had begun to list hard to one side, but we were done here anyway. Peter quickly navigated the main deck and into the ordnance bay without trouble. Arrayed over the drop pad was a pulsing Scayn seed, and next to it, the modified missiles we'd use to get off the ship. With a loud pop and then a hiss, the drop pad slid open as the timer hit zero and sent the seed plummeting toward its destiny.

The howl of the wind made it next to impossible to hear each other, but the pad soon slid back into place and the room was quiet except for the distant sound of explosions and gunfire. Peter smiled and shook his head, then dumped me more or less gently into one of the missiles. 'Thanks for the rescue,' I wearily said, 'I owe you.'

He laughed. 'More than you know. I'll pull that thing off of you when we land,' he said with a bow. Then, just as I hit the start-up switch, I heard him whisper, 'Go on and give to Death his due. And let the game begin anew.'

Then the launch bay vanished as the deck dropped away and my missile carried me out into the night.

107

I opened my eyes, and found myself floating above the Suns, watching the planets spin and twirl around them, watching the moons spin and twirl around the planets. A comet flashed past, falling around the White Sun and vanishing into the distance. An asteroid the size of the City appeared from the darkness at the edge of the system, heading toward the Suns on a path that would take it straight through the orbits of most of the interior worlds.

Over my shoulder, I could see clear to the center of the galaxy.

Then the images started erupting from the back of my mind and I put my hands to my ears and threw my head back and screamed. Memories, both mine and not, flooded through the depths, and my brain struggled to bear the load. Sights and sounds flickered past, attached to emotions that turned me inside out.

I stood on a park bench in a park I couldn't put a name to, in a city that wasn't the City. I was just a child, and I turned and jumped off. Someone squawked, 'Careful!' at me, and I spun with a giggle to glare balefully at the man sitting on the other side of the table. My father, the memory told me. His close-cropped black hair and green eyes looked very familiar. He gave me a wink and roguish grin.

The scene flickered, and now I was sitting in bed. Outside a large window, I could see the City stretching to the horizon and then disappearing beyond. I slowly got up, feeling weak and sick, and stumbled to the dresser and looked into the mirror. One part of me was surprised to find that I had black hair and green eyes to match my dad's. I could see I was a teenager, and in between the angst and sickness that marred my face, I looked sad.

Your mother, the memory told me. She's sick, too.

'Edgar,' someone said. When I turned to see who it was, I wasn't in the bedroom anymore. Instead, I was standing over a fresh grave. I was surprised I could hear whoever it was, as the wind was howling. Flowers and trinkets were caught in the gusts and carried away. 'Edgar, you have to calm down, the wind is impolite,' the newcomer said. I didn't recognize him then, but he knew my name better than I seemed to.

I nodded, and let the magic disappear. 'Sorry,' I whispered, though not to the man.

He didn't seem to take offence, and came to stand at my side. We looked down at my mom's grave silently for a while, then he said, 'You can learn to control this, Edgar. Your ability to use any magical energy you like is a very valuable thing. I can help.'

I looked up at him, and through the tears I asked, 'Who are you?'

He smiled, and stuck out his hand. A gentle smile stretched beneath his moustache. 'My name is Poe,' he said.

Now I walked in a crowded hall, bordered by legions of lockers and classroom doors. I was heading for a biology course that I couldn't bring myself to care about, and I was angry that the curriculum for my choice of degree required the damn class. Maybe angrier than the situation warranted, really. I shook my head, trying to break the black mood, but it had been getting harder and harder to do so these days.

Caught up in my thoughts, I promptly walked right into another man who was coming the other direction, talking animatedly with a woman next to him. We both went down in a heap, to the protests of the other students trying to get down the hall. I struggled to get to my knees, and I felt the astral energy around me flare with anticipation.

Before I got overwhelmed, I felt a hand come to rest on my shoulder. Looking up, I found the other man standing over me, a friendly smile on his bearded face. 'Wow, sorry about that!' he laughed. 'Are you alright?'

My discomfort evaporated. I liked polite, attractive men. 'I think so,' I said, smiling shyly.

His smile got even bigger, and he stood up and offered his hand. When I took it, he hefted me up. 'I'm James,' he said, giving my hand a shake.

'Edgar,' I offered.

His companion giggled, and she said, 'C'mon, James, we're going to be late.' She gave me a smile and then started to pull Martin away.

Laughing, James tucked a strand of his long hair behind his ear. 'Duty calls. Hey, how'd you like to go for coffee this afternoon?' he suddenly asked.

The memory told me that I accepted, but the images flickered again and now I lounged on a park bench, looking out over a beach. 'Daddy, can I go play in the sand?' a small voice said from next to me. I looked over with a smile to find a young girl standing on the bench with a big grin on her light-brown skinned face. Nala, this new memory said, my youngest daughter.

'Don't go too far, little one. And don't jump off,' I said, with mock seriousness. She giggled and jumped anyway, charging across the grass and leaping out into the sand, crashing down messily next to another young woman that was sitting there on a towel reading.

Katherine, daughter number two. She swatted at her sister in irritation, and Nala darted away with a laugh. They were very different, the girls, and not just in looks. Katherine's skin was almost as pale as James', but she had my temperament. She was prone to black moods, whereas Nala took after her bearded father, mischievous and fun-loving. James and I had adopted them, orphaned refugees that had come in from a human settlement that had been destroyed in a skirmish with a kobold tribe.

Nala eventually tired of bothering her older sister and went dancing off toward the water. Katherine watched her go and then lay back contentedly to go back to her book. I smiled, and turned my head to look idly elsewhere down the beach.

When I looked back, there were three young men standing over her.

I slowly stood up. The stars whispered my name.

At first, Katherine didn't have anything to say to them, trying to read her book without looking up. When one of them reached down to pull back her book, she snarled something and jerked it back.

I started walking toward them. Energy spun around me, small suns caught in my orbit.

Whatever she'd said to them, the first boy's face got really ugly and he lunged out and slapped her.

The urge to turn the kid inside out rippled violently out from the back of my mind. The Suns waited at my fingertips, ready to make him disappear, or to throw him far out into the lake, or to remove his limbs and beat him to death with them. The desire to hurt the kid was so strong that I fell to my knees, faint, feeling sick to my stomach. Putting a shaking hand up to my forehead, I wondered what was happening to me, and my gaze settled on my daughter and her antagonists.

Katherine cocked her head at the boy, snarled something familiar, and then he vanished in a puff of red mist.

'No!' I roared, scrambling to my feet and sprinting for my daughter even as the other two boys were sprinting the away from her, screaming in terror.

And then the memory changed again, each flash of sight and sound and feeling adding substance to the fog that had once filled that space. Forward and backward in time, seemingly at random, I rocketed through my past, seeing my life for the first time but, of course, not the first time.

My name is Edgar Lorn.

I saw a sister and her husband, the three of us talking quietly. The words were friendly and pleasant, but there was something not quite right in the looks the husband and I were exchanging. There was hatred there. Hatred that my sister cried about when her husband wasn't there, knowing he was a bigot and would forever want me hurt for who I chose to love.

I saw me and James' wedding, in the forests of the Treed Lands District. The wedding commissioner, a steam construct dressed in a very dapper suit, ran the event with a tight fist. Or would have, but other than the two of us, there were only a handful of James' friends there to watch us tie the knot. It was a quiet and beautiful time, a happy one.

I saw me struggle to keep the darkness contained, the shadows that lurked in the depths, even as my strength with the astral magic grew, despite my ignorance. I saw my temper get me into trouble a hundred times. I saw me hit James, shocking my poor husband with the unprovoked violence, and saw him struggle to deal with his loved one's troubled mind.

I saw Peter become my confidant, my best friend. When James and I had a huge fight, Peter was there to help me through it, to agree that my husband had been wrong, that I was justified in being angry. When my work with Operations got dangerous, Peter was there to back me up, to help me make the hard choice, to sacrifice whatever needed to be in order to finish the mission. I saw Peter nod as I told him I was going home to end my marriage and to take my girls away, heard him tell me not to take no for an answer, to be strong.

I saw James standing shell shocked in the living room as I declared us dead. I felt my anger boil the blood in my veins, felt my heart thunder with fury as the argument progressed. And then I felt the fear as I raised my hands and called the energy into them.

My name is Edgar Lorn, and I killed them all.

?

I was cold hearted when the argument began. I asked James to sit with me on the couch, hoping that he'd agree that it would be best if we separated, that I take the girls with me. It should have been fairly simple, just like Peter had said.

By the time we'd been arguing for half an hour, both of us were furious. James wasn't on the couch anymore, having gotten up and was pacing the living room angrily as we yelled at each other.

'I don't get you, Edgar. You're gone for days on whatever horrible thing the Department wants you to do, and then you have the nerve to come back and call me distant? To say that the girls will be better living with you? How are you possibly going to take care of them? You come back, and take them on fun trips. You don't have the first idea how to care for them,' my husband said, sounding incredulous. 'Do you even know where they go to school? What classes they take? What they do for fun?'

I frowned at him. 'I'm sure they'll tell me those things once I've had a chance to spend more time with them. I know you've been trying to keep them away from me,' I said, frustration rippling through my voice.

James looked embarrassed, but held his ground. 'You're not well, Edgar. These missions, and spending all this time with that Peter, they're changing you. Nala isn't old enough to see what's going on, but Katherine is, and she's always been closer to you than me. She's picking up on your moods, how you act, Edgar!' he said, coming closer and whispering hoarsely. 'Being a teenage girl is hard enough, but you've gotten so dark and she's emulating it.'

He paused, then looked scared. 'She's getting dangerous, Edgar, and she's way more powerful than her classmates. Her instructors tell me that there's a strong chance she'll reach archon levels in the next few years. That's crazy, Edgar! An archon by twenty?' he said.

For a moment, my anger took a back seat to admiration, and I understood why James was afraid. He barely made arcanist, himself. I'd probably be a bit scared, too, if one of the girls had more power than me.

'All the more reason for her to come with me, then. At least I can teach her something about her magic,' I said. It came out as mocking, though it felt strange for it to be.

In fact, nothing about this argument felt right.

James sighed, and hung his head with his face in his hands. When he looked up, there were tears in his eyes and on his cheeks. 'What happened to you, Edgar? What happened to us? I love you!' he said, raggedly. Shaking his head, he closed his eyes again, and whispered, 'When did you stop loving me?'

I suddenly felt like I was falling. The world had flipped and was going the other way. Everything seemed to come from a distance. Misery rolled over me in waves, and I wanted to reach out to the man I loved.

Still loved.

Instead, I slapped him. 'When you decided to be a coward and tried to cut me out of this family,' I snarled, but I wasn't sure why.

James reeled from my strike, shocked by the sudden violence and the strength of it. He fell to the ground, sitting there with one hand over the growing red mark on his cheek. For a long moment he didn't do anything, just stared into the distance, his face blank.

I stared at my hand in confusion. It felt unfamiliar. Alien. Why'd I hit him?

When I stood up from the couch, James looked up at me, and then he stood too. He came forward until we were nose to nose, and he said, 'Get out.' His voice was dead serious. His eyes were dry.

My mind suddenly roiled with thoughts and feelings, and not all of them felt like mine. In the depths, rage bubbled out, and my mind hissed with it. In contrast, beneath that fury was misery, misery that felt familiar. It was rapidly drowned in the anger that slowly began crawling across my face.

'I'm going to take the girls to Becca's place for a few days. When I get back from dropping them off, you and I can talk about how we're going to move on from here. If we can move on from here,' James said, his voice getting less steady as he saw my anger build. 'If you have a mission, I'll be here when you get back, and we can talk. But the girls, Edgar, the girls can't be here while we're like this.'

He shook his head, and he looked very tired. 'While you're like this,' he said, sadly. Seconds went by, where we stood staring at each other, James trying to maintain a brave face, me trying to calm myself down. Rage oozed through my veins like magma.

Suddenly I hated James, but I didn't know why.

'No,' I said, and now my voice was ice. 'No, you are not.' I was surprised by just how much I meant those words, by the amount of menace in them. I was also surprised to find my hands blanketed in astral energy.

James must have seen something in my face, and he started to back away, his hands up. 'What are you doing, Edgar? Stop this,' he said, and I sneered at the fear on his face.

I desperately tried to stop the building storm of astral fury, but I might as well have tried to stop a tornado with my bare hands. The energy quickly spread out, a million tiny stars spinning and flaring around me, and though James couldn't see them, he could feel the slow shift of reality as the sheer potential power whirled around me. My eyes blazed with it, and then the air began to brighten as the blood of the Suns poured into me.

The furniture began to shake and dance, and the light fixture overhead exploded and showered me with fragments of metal and plastic. James tripped and fell at the edge of the living room, collapsing against the wall painfully. His eyes were wide, and his mouth was moving, though I couldn't hear him.

Nala suddenly appeared, dashing out from down the hall to slide to a halt next to James. Her brown eyes turned to look up at me, and the confusion and hurt on her face made my heart want to crawl out of my chest. She was trying to cover him with her body.

I saw something move out of the corner of my eye, and I looked over to the kitchen to find Katherine standing there. Astonishingly, she glowed with the sickly light of nether, and with a howl, I felt her magic slam into mine. She looked angry, and sad.

'I'm sorry,' I said, and I meant it.

I let the stars loose, and I felt a smile split my face but there was nothing but horror inside. Then there was nothing left to do but watch my spell unmake my husband, my children, my home, and then reality itself as the world screamed around me.

108

The thrum of the regeneration chamber slowed, and with it the painful thump of my heart. There was a quiet pop, and then I heard the door open behind the green gas that was slowly vanishing up the strange vents above me.

A pair of metal hands attached to metal arms materialized out of the cloud, carefully releasing the bands that held me to the bed. Free, I toppled forward, and Bill appeared instantly to catch me.

'You're beautiful,' he said, and there was awe in his voice.

I felt completely discombobulated, so I didn't have a response. My mind wasn't awash in suddenly unearthed memories, but everything felt raw. It hurt just to think.

With the engineer's assistance, I stepped out of the artifact. Ceile sat on the floor not far away, anxiousness and concern on her face as she looked sightlessly around the room. Weezab stood not far from her, and when he saw me, his jaw dropped.

'Holy crap,' he said, 'It worked.'

Dazedly, I looked down at my hands, and I nearly fell in shock. They were young hands, with smooth and unblemished skin. The hair that fell into my face as I stumbled was sand rather than snow. All of my senses felt stronger. I could hear the subtle difference between the thrum of the regeneration chamber and that of the lab's ventilation system. The various coloured lights on each of the artifacts were brighter.

'Martin?' Ceile asked.

I looked up at her, and gasped. While it was obvious that either she or the kobold had healed her burns, my friend was still very hurt. I glared at Weezab, who looked back impassively. He was probably hoping to keep her pacified so the scaly bastard could keep an eye on me. 'I'm here, Ceile. It worked,' I said. Pushing Bill lightly away, I walked, slowly at first but building strength, over to her side and crouched down. 'How are you, old friend?' I asked her, taking her hand gently.

She grimaced, and shook her head. 'I am hurt. I need a necromancer, and soon,' she said. Then her face lightened, and she let go of my hand and reached gingerly up to my face. 'Oh, Martin,' she whispered as she softly touched my cheek, running her fingers over the newly smooth skin. 'Oh, Martin, you are whole again.'

'Good and bad, I think,' I whispered. I took her hand briefly and gave it a squeeze, then slowly got to my feet. I turned to look at Bill. 'Is it true, then? Am I Edgar Lorn?' I asked the engineer. Ceile's face looked confused, but she stayed silent.

A slight smile bent Bill's lips, and he came forward while searching my face. 'Yes. You are Edgar Lorn,' he said after a long moment.

I shook my head. 'How is that possible? I don't look like him. Hell, if anything I look more like his husband, James. And I'm not a solaron! I'm an arcanist, and apparently also a wind elementalist,' I said, not pleased with the hint of panic in my voice. 'You pulled me out of the fire, and the next thing I remember I'm waking up in a hospital and I look very different and the staff are calling me Martin Tundra.'

I gave a strangled cry, and horror almost took me to my knees. 'I killed them all,' I said, hoarsely, staring down at my hands.

Bill stepped close, and grabbed hold of my shoulder tightly. 'I'll give you the abbreviated version, as our time is coming to a close and I'm expecting visitors. Listen closely, Ms. Angael, as I'm certain you'd like to know what our good friend Martin is talking about,' he said, looking down at Ceile and then back up to me. 'Yes, Martin Tundra, you are Edgar Lorn. You are a man who has struggled with a personal darkness that had gotten stronger and stronger until one day, you suffered a psychotic break and used the power of the Suns to annihilate several Districts' worth of people.'

He suddenly looked excited. 'But you didn't do it with fire, Martin, despite the memory you have of your burning home. No, your magic did some terrible things to reality in that area, shifting buildings and people and objects in ways they weren't meant to be shifted. It was terrible,' the engineer said, though he didn't look like he actually thought it was terrible, 'and wild. That level of chaos, of randomness, I'd never seen before. You would have made a fabulous wind aethon, my friend.'

I frowned and shook my head at him. 'But I am a wind aethon, Bill. I used that power to kill the Scayn, right?' I asked, and when the engineer smirked at me, said, 'Didn't I?'

Bill let go of my shoulder and stepped back a metre or so. He fiddled with something on his arm, and then nodded at me. 'Reach for your magic, my not-so-elderly friend,' he said, anticipation dripping from his voice.

I was immediately suspicious, wondering why the two would suddenly give me access to my greatest weapon, but I cautiously reached out anyway. And then gasped and snapped back from the realm between.

The mire and the vortex were gone.

When I'd reached through the cracks, the only things waiting for me were the Suns.

Bill was grinning widely at me, and he said, 'I haven't let you entirely off the leash, but go on. See what it feels like.'

Carefully, knowing what was there, I opened the door and basked in the light. 'Holy crap,' I whispered, feeling the energy raging around me, jaw slack in the face of the power just waiting for me to let loose. It was an immensely strange feeling, like I was just a conduit for the Suns to erupt down onto my world and cause havoc. Oddly - or maybe not so oddly, I suppose - it was a very familiar feeling.

Slowly, I stuck my hand into all that energy, and drew some to me. It wasn't much, thanks to whatever Bill had blocking me off, but as soon as the power passed through the cracks in reality between this realm and that in between, I felt it gather into a sphere and begin to orbit me. I had my own star.

'You are a solaron, Martin, and you have performed a very unique trick for more than two hundred years of your life. Astral energy, a particularly ungainly term for something so awesome, is the purest of magic. Nether, all the forms of aether, they're all distilled from it,' Bill said, leaning in. 'You, my friend, have been distilling them yourself.'

I must have looked really confused, as the engineer burst into laughter. 'Oh, Martin, you should see your face! It's a great trick, really. You've got yourself so convinced that you draw your power from arcane or elemental sources, and everyone else thinks you just make the effort to mask your spells. And they'd never know different, unless you ran into another solaron, the odds of which are, ha, astronomical,' he said, chuckling.

Then he sobered and shook his head. 'No, Martin, much like the being you called the Other, your abilities and where they come from are elaborate lies, lies born when your magic ran wild all those years ago, and changed every survivor forever,' he said. 'Everything you were was twisted, right down to your appearance.'

I thought about the man with the short black hair, and shook my head. 'I don't understand. You rescued me from the house, why didn't you turn me in? How many people died because I lost control that day? My whole family,' I choked up, pausing for a moment and then continuing, 'My whole family was killed,' I said, hoarsely.

Suddenly buried in a loss I hadn't known about only minutes ago, I screamed, 'Why didn't you kill me?!' Ceile and Nox had been my only family for over two centuries, and it was bad enough I had to mourn the big 'wolf. Now I had other ghosts, and that pain was sharp and raw. Whatever had happened had prevented me from ever putting them to bed, and now the faces of a husband and two daughters lurked at the back of my mind.

Bill shook his head and he again fiddled with something on his arm. 'Because my client didn't want you dead, Martin,' he said, simply, then turned and walked toward Partridge, who had been silently hovering nearby.

109

The tormented dwarf's hollow eyes stared sadly at me, 'I am sorry, Martin. I have done terrible things in the name of bringing you to this place and beyond,' he said, raggedly. Then he looked down at Bill. 'Is it time? Will you finally keep your end of the bargain?' There was longing in his voice. Anticipation.

'Yes,' was all Bill said, before shooting him in the head with Robin's pistol.

The dwarf's death was quiet, sad. Much like he had been in life, back when I'd met him. He made no noise, and the round that killed him made only a quiet thud as it went through his forehead and into his poisoned brain. Then he slumped forward in his prison, and black ichor dripped slowly out of the hole.

I was rapidly becoming overwhelmed with everything that was happening. Fury bubbled through my veins, and I took a few angry steps toward Bill. 'Bill, you bastard. Why did you do this to him?' I demanded, gesturing at the lab and Patridge's platform. 'Why did you bring him here?' Now I was right in front of him, almost nose to nose.

Bill's face went dark, and he suddenly moved slowly forward, forcing me to step back. 'I needed an engineer to work with me on several important projects. Work that I couldn't trust to a large team, but couldn't do entirely on my own. And when he developed terminal cancer, much like yourself, I did what I had to do to keep him working,' the engineer snarled, waving the still hissing pistol around.

'Now, have a seat next to Ms. Angael and relax. Operations should be here soon enough,' he said, pointing at Ceile. When I didn't move, he aimed the pistol at my head.

I laughed, cruelly. 'I doubt you'll kill me now, Bill, seeing as you seem to have gone to a lot of effort to get me here,' I growled.

The engineer smirked. 'Kill you? No. But I can remove a few of your limbs, cut you into shreds, and have Weezab put you back together again in roughly the same shape as your friend, here. And repeat, if I have time and you continue being cute,' he said.

I decided I'd rather not lose a few limbs, so I sat down gently next to Ceile and took her hand.

'Good,' Bill said, then looked over at Weezab. 'Watch the door, I want some advance notice of their arrival.' The kobold looked back suspiciously, then turned and scampered away.

The engineer watched him go, then quickly darted over to one corner of the artifact area, snatching up one small object before crossing the room to stand in front of a large item that was surrounded by strangely glowing lines. Bill's fingers danced across a touchpad on the item's side, and colours being dancing up and down its length.

With a grim smile, the engineer threw a dust shroud over the thing and then came back over to join us.

'What was that, Bill?' I asked, frowning over at the artifact.

'A clean up,' he answered, without elaborating.

I watched the dimmed lights flowing along under the shroud for a while, then turned to look up at the engineer, who was jamming the first object into the remains of someone's pack. 'And that?' I asked.

'Something unpleasant. Now sit there and be quiet,' he answered, absently.

We fell silent, and I leaned my head over on Ceile's shoulder. 'What has happened, Martin? What has happened to all of us?' she asked, quietly.

I shook my head slowly, and said, 'I don't know.' I eyed the engineer again. 'Bill, what does Operations want me for?'

At first, I didn't think he'd heard me, as he continued securing his prize. Then he slowly turned to look over his shoulder at me, and smiled. 'You're a weapon, Martin. A flawed one, but also one of the most powerful on the continent. Do you think the Government would let that kind of power just blunder around? They want you back under their lock and key, where they can pull you out when they need entire armies annihilated,' the engineer said.

'And why does Pestilence want to prevent that?' I asked, remembering Kor's final words.

Bill's smile slipped, and his eyes narrowed as he looked at me. 'Who knows what her motivations are. The Third Horseman is just as liable to meddle in our affairs as the others,' he said, but something told me that once again, he was lying to us.

Having secured his pack, Bill walked back over and crouched down a few metres away, watching us quietly. I heard him whispering the lines of his poem, and his eyes were almost feverish as his gaze darted around my face. I stared back, darkly, and in return he smiled.

Then the whole room shook violently, sending dust falling from the ceiling and lab equipment crashing from the shelves.

Bill was on his feet in an instant, pulling the pistol from his jacket and throwing it across the room. Moving past us to stand in the hallway between the storage lockers, he scooped a pair of shock rifles off the ground and readied one in each arm. 'I've always wanted to do that,' he whispered with a grin. Looking over his shoulder at us, the engineer said, 'Be ready, I don't think these are our visitors.'

On cue, Weezab came darting back. 'Dwarves. Lots of them,' he said, his voice even more high pitched than usual.

The engineer cursed. 'I thought I had those alarms disabled. Where the hell are they?' he snarled to himself. Shaking his head, he looked at the kobold and said, 'You'll have to melt that service door, we'll take the stairs to the top level and head for the surface from there.'

Weezab looked dubious. 'It'll take some time, and that hallway is filling up fast. Might have to kill some of them off first,' he said.

Bill nodded. Turning to me and Ceile, the engineer said, 'We can't wait for Operations to get here, even Weezab can't hold off the entire army in these tunnels, and I'm not giving you back your magic. Take cover near the doorway, and head for the service stairwell when I tell you.' Then he stepped in close to me, and leaned forward. 'Just in case you want to get cute, keep in mind the dwarves will kill you if you're caught, and I will torture you if you don't obey,' he growled.

I glared at him, but I stood and helped Ceile to her feet. My friend linked her arm in mine, and she looked apprehensive. Despite everything that had happened to her, the injuries and then Robin's murder at the hands of the now deceased Petrel, she was still strong. I couldn't imagine what it would be like to be in this situation without my sight. I would be huddled in a corner crying.

'C'mon,' Bill said, beckoning for us to follow. Weezab made a gesture, and his hands burst into red flame, then he fell into step beside the engineer. I guided Ceile after them, briefly considering trying to grab something for use as a weapon, then thought better of it.

Watching the kobold walk along, obviously in control of his power, I looked at the engineer's arm, searching for the device that was blocking me from mine. I frowned. Before I'd started this journey, I'd only thought that the rumoured lunarons were capable of stripping my magic from me. I knew the elves and dwarves had developed tech that could defend against spells, but Bill had come into at least two items that did so, both of which affected a single person. Artifacts like the regeneration chamber, maybe.

As we neared the doorway, I could hear movement in the hallway. Weezab popped his head out and then turned back with an evil smile on his face. Bill nodded at him. 'We have fourteen minutes, and then it's going to get a little uncomfortable on this level. Kill as many as you have to, but I need you working on that door,' the engineer said.

The flames raging around the kobold's hands got brighter, and the little creature nodded. He suddenly darted out into the hallway, and I heard shouts and the sound of a lot of people coming abruptly to a halt. Before they could react, I heard a loud whooshing sound, and then I watched Weezab's fire grow until it spread out across the ceiling.

Over the roar of the flames I heard the kobold laugh, impossibly loud, and then he vanished in an eruption of red flame and dwarven gunfire.

'Go!' Bill yelled, roughly shoving Ceile and me out the door and down the hall toward the service door. 'Hug the wall,' he hissed, then spun and dropped to the floor, both shock rifles roaring.

I pulled Ceile gently around so she was closest to the corridor wall and then we got moving. I kept my head down, hoping that Weezab's flames were giving us some protection from the dwarves' weapons as we stumbled toward the end of the hall. My friend was breathing raggedly, her injuries at the hands of the kobold still causing her misery. I still felt woozy from my adventure in the regeneration chamber.

A handful of rounds ricocheted off the wall to my left, and we instinctively hit the deck. Looking back, I saw Bill and Weezab backing slowly toward us, the kobold generating a cone of flame from his scaly hands that flowed like water along the walls and ceiling and floor, the engineer's rifles thumping loudly as they shot their shock pulses down the corridor into the storm of fire.

I frowned as Ceile and I regained our feet and started moving again. The kobold's attack was powerful, but it had to reduce his visibility to almost none, and even if Bill had inherited Petrel's life scanners, they weren't precise enough to help here. If the dwarves had heavy weapons set up or coming, we wouldn't know until the splitter rounds started tearing us apart.

Sure enough, something massive flashed past, slamming into the wall twenty metres away and erupting with enough force that it knocked me to my knees and pushed Ceile into the wall. The explosion rippled out, sending shards of concrete and metal whistling in every direction. Slowly, I gathered my wits and drunkenly got to my feet, nothing but a high pitched whine in my ears. Ceile helped me up, and we both tucked in tight against the side of the corridor, somewhat covered by a column of pipe and cable.

The elevator door hissed open behind me.

I was so surprised that the lift was still working that I stared blankly at the empty car for a long moment. I looked over at Ceile, who was looking in my direction worriedly, up the corridor to Bill and Weezab, who were still holding the dwarves off, and then back into the car. Gently, I pulled my friend into the elevator and then hammered the highest button. We crouched down in the corner, and I watched the doors, willing them to shut and get us moving.

Another heavy round shot past, and my gradually returning hearing registered it impacting with a violent explosion. Shrapnel clinked across the walls, some pieces even bouncing into the lift. I tried to shield Ceile as best I could, but even with my posture direly improved thanks to the artifact, she was still a larger figure than me.

The doors began to shut, and I wanted to cheer. But I knew our escape had been a little too easy. Bill had masterminded almost the entirety of this adventure, it seemed pretty sloppy for him to let us get away that easily. I was waiting for the other shoe to drop as the gap between the doors slowly slid to nothing.

Just before it did, something blocked out the light from the hallway, and then a metal hand slammed through, denting the doors and sending them retreating toward the frame. Bill strode through, then spun and hit the same button I had. He sneered at me over his shoulder.

The roar and howl of fire got louder and louder, and now the hallway outside was lit by Weezab's magic. I saw the kobold step into view, face masked with concentration, flame bursting from his palms. With one last flare of crimson destruction, he let the jet of fire vanish and headed for the elevator.

He didn't quite make it two steps into the lift when Bill kicked him in the chest and sent the kobold flying across the hall to slam painfully against the wall. Furiously, he leapt to his feet as gunfire began raining down around him. The elevator door was closing fast, and there was no way the scaly creature was going to make it. Sliding to a stop, he burst into flame, and just before the doors hissed shut, a jet of fire burst through the closing gap.

Bathing Bill in red fire that briefly enveloped him. The engineer shrieked, arms coming up to protect his face an instant too late, his shock rifles dropping to the ground, forgotten. With the flame's source left behind as the elevator suddenly leapt upward, the fire faded away, leaving the engineer to collapse smoking in the corner.

His eyes were fluttering wildly, snapping open and shut at high speed. Large patches of the synthetic flesh on his face were melting and oozing off, leaving large gaps of dulled metal. His hat was just a lump of ash, and I could see titanium skull under it. The engineer's body, built of strong dwarven alloys, seemed mostly intact, though a number of small hoses were hanging loose, dripping some kind of chemical.

The kobold's work hadn't agreed with him any more than it had Ceile.

My eyes fell on the discarded weapons, lying at Bill's feet. I wondered if he was hurt enough that I could get my hands on one of them before he could do something about it. Squeezing Ceile's hand, I slowly got to my feet, looking back and forth between the engineer and the rifles. When he didn't immediately react, I inched toward him, holding my breath. He had gone completely still by the time I was almost within reach of my prize.

Then the elevator rocked violently, throwing me across the car, the rifles in the opposite direction, and Ceile flat to the ground. The lift continued ascending, but there was a not so comforting grinding noise coming from its exterior, and the whole thing shook as we passed each floor. From somewhere below, I could hear a loud, dull thumping.

'Do you hear that?' Bill said, and I looked over to find him staring at me from his position slumped against the wall. Smoke still rose lazily from his face and body. 'The dwarves are throwing around some serious hardware. Whoever sent them in didn't want us captured, they wanted the whole lab destroyed.'

My eyes flickered to the rifles across the car. The engineer was closer, but if his body was still functional, he hardly needed a weapon to kill me. Noticing my glance, he smirked. 'Now, now, Martin. You didn't think I let you get into the elevator by accident, did you?' With a groan, he stood and stretched. 'I just had to get rid of the kobold.'

'Greedy bastard,' I said, shaking my head. 'Won't Operations be less than impressed that you've managed to lose so much of your team?'

Bill burst into laughter. 'Oh, Martin, you should see your face. No, they won't be very upset to see the dwarves gone. They might be a little less pleased that their little babysitters are dead, but it'll go down easier when I tell them both were working with the Horsemen,' he said. Walking over to the rifles, the engineer looked pointedly at me then crushed them with a metal foot.

I sighed. This week was not going my way.

The elevator shook again, and this time it slowed almost to a crawl as the side of the car dragged against the shaft wall. Now, the lift greeted each floor by smashing into the platform, making it next to impossible to stay on my feet. Then we'd hit an open section and the elevator would jump up, and soon I was bruised all over.

'Speaking of Operations, they should be waiting for us at the top, unless the plan has completely gone off the rails. I'm going to hand you off to them, or they'll make a nuisance of themselves. Play along, and you'll both get proper care and treated well,' Bill said, having to space his sentences out in between each jolt from the elevator. Giving me a meaningful look, he continued, 'Resist, and they'll cut Ceile up in front of you and then leave you drugged and lying in a puddle of your own filth until they get around to doing whatever it is they want you to do. They won't have my fancy tech, but they'll have other things to keep you under their thumb.' He patted the object attached to his arm that he'd been fiddling with down in the lab.

A sizable amount of it fell away in a small shower of ash and then the entire thing hit the floor.

There was a long moment, where he and I stared at the remains, me crouched next to Ceile, him standing above it, arm still outstretched. Then we slowly met each other's eyes.

'Crap,' he said, then turned and threw himself through the elevator doors in a crash of tortured metal and shattered concrete.

Bill's violent exit from the elevator sent the car spinning around, crashing hard against the side of the shaft and plowing into a service platform as it continued its tortured ascent. The wreckage of the door gave me a dizzying view into the passage, and Ceile and I struggled to stay safely huddled in our corner of the lift.

I silently cursed. If I'd been faster on the draw, I might have captured or killed the engineer. As it was, I was blazing with energy, orbited by a thousand roaring stars. I just had no idea how to use it to get Ceile and me off the damn elevator and onto some forgotten level without destroying the lift and us with it.

My friend was hunched in on herself, shivering, and I glanced over at her worriedly. Her health was getting worse by the minute. I shook my head. Even if I managed to get us off this elevator, we wouldn't make it far. Ceile's body had taken too much punishment, so much so that I wondered if even her personal necromancer could fix the damage. She might need a brand new construct.

A chill rippled down my spine. That would mean my friend was just as dead as I would be without the regeneration chamber.

The explosions below were much louder with the destroyed doors, and I tried to ignore the possibility that some enterprising member of the dwarven cleaner force would think to break into the elevator shaft and then put a rocket directly into our underside.

Then I frowned. Bill had said something about fourteen minutes. Something bad. How long had it been?

For that matter, how high did this elevator go?

In answer to my first question, the explosions echoing up the shaft from the lab level were interrupted by a brutally loud whump, and then they went silent. The whole lift began to vibrate. When we slowed as the car rammed another platform, a wave of dust shot past, headed up. The vibration got stronger, and I found myself leaning forward, listening. Something far below was making a high pitched shriek, and it was getting louder. And closer.

Ceile took hold of my hand. 'Martin, what is making that sound?' she asked, her face sightlessly searching the air for the source.

'Something nasty of Bill's, I think. He said it was clean up,' I answered.

I wished I could see what was coming, but the idea of trying to get across the bucking elevator and then sticking my head out the wrecked door seemed a bit silly. The noise got closer, and now I could hear a loud hiss beneath the shriek. I called the astral energy around me into my free hand, and I prepared to find out just what I could do with its power.

Without warning, the lift erupted through a floor, then a pair of doors, and then came to a rumbling halt embedded at an angle in the wall between the elevator shaft and whatever level we'd just arrived on. Quickly getting to my feet, I whispered, 'Let's go,' in Ceile's ear and then guided her carefully out onto the intact floor of a very wide hallway.

And right into the sights of twenty elite Operations soldiers.

I put Ceile behind me, and raised my hands. We backed slowly away, my eyes dancing back and forth between the ruined elevator shaft and the soldiers, but a quick glance behind showed that there wasn't a point. The corridor stretched for another couple hundred metres and then came to an abrupt halt. We were trapped.

The shriek had gotten loud to the point where my head was pounding from it. If the cacophony bothered the newcomers, they didn't show it. The lead ranks dropped to a knee, those behind split apart, and then three cloaked figures stepped forward, hands blazing with light. Arcane Corps. The Department of Enforcement's special arcane forces. So it wasn't just Operations that had come to collect me.

Seconds passed as each side watched each other warily. I imagined they knew just what they were going up against, the three magic users likely there to protect the soldiers from whatever I could throw at them. Feeling the pulse and roar of the stars waiting for my command, I almost smiled. I didn't think there were nearly enough of them.

Before the stand-off could break, the source of the shriek made its grand entrance. A roiling cloud of black and grey erupted from the elevator shaft, smashing into the ceiling and spilling out into the hall. As it flowed along the surfaces, I noticed movement inside. Eyes widening as I finally saw the truth of the engineer's weapon, I caught Ceile's hand and quickly started backing away, throwing a shield over us that glimmered in golden light.

The cloud was comprised entirely of massive centipedes, all made of the same black metal that the artifacts in the lab had been and lit by dim blue lights along their sides.

Both soldiers and magic users held their ground as the swarm of mechanical arthropods skittered toward them on the ceiling, walls, and floor. As one, the three Arcane Corps wizards made a slashing motion with their left hands, and a shield of sickly purple light expanded out from them to provide cover for the soldiers crouched at their knees. Weapons came up, and I could see blue energy crackle up and down the barrels as they struggled to contain the arcane rounds within.

Before they could fire, I called to the White and the Blue and sent sun flare roiling down the hallway.

The forgotten memories lurking at the back of my mind told me what this would be like, what this power would feel like as I became a conduit for the very energies that had made this world. Crafting the shield had been one thing, but the sheer destructive wave that blasted from my hands and rolled through the passageway toward both swarm and soldiers was something else altogether.

It was glorious.

It made me want more.

Somewhere in the depths, I thought I heard a dark chuckle.

The storm of astral energy hit the shrieking members of the cloud and turned them first to dust, then made the dust go away. One instant, the centipedes were bearing down on us, next, the hallway was clear.

I didn't know when I'd gotten to my feet and started walking toward the Operations soldiers, hands up and pushing the solar wrath through the rest of the swarm. Somewhere behind me, Ceile crouched in the shield I'd left for her, confused and suddenly alone. Now my spell was parallel with the elevator's wreckage, and as it passed by, it caught the parts that were sticking out into the corridor and turned them to dust, too.

I liked that. I found myself sinking ever more power into the wave, and now it was biting into the walls, erasing concrete and metal and plastic with ease. Suddenly, the passageway was quite a bit wider and taller than it had been, bordered by very hot and smooth stone.

One of the wizards and a handful of soldiers were starting to look a little nervous.

The shriek abruptly died off as the last of the centipedes disintegrated, and I brought the wave to a halt only a couple metres or so from the Arcane Corps shield. The raging energy roared, small tendrils of astral power drifting out to snap sizzling back on contact with the purple barrier.

I smiled as I walked forward to stand behind my spell, gaze sweeping over each of the men and women before me. Not a one of them was looking happy to be here in the corridor with me. All three of the wizards must have been thinking that their combined shield wasn't going to be remotely enough. I imagined they hadn't expected me to come out of that elevator with my power intact.

'Would you like to see just what I can do?' I asked, and my voice echoed down the hall, amplified by my magic and briefly drowning out the roar of the flare.

No one answered, so I sneered and started to turn back to go collect Ceile, when I suddenly felt a strange sensation. Something dark and empty, pushing at the edges of my spell. I frowned, looking at the mostly frightened people, feeling shivers run down my spine as the sensation grew, and suddenly the river of astral energy I had been pulling from the sky began to slow. The wizards' shield was suddenly gone, and I cursed as I realized the cause.

Lunaron, something whispered at the back of my head.

Torn between turning and running and sending the flare forward to annihilate everyone, I didn't react in time. The Suns were eclipsed, and all of the energy in my hands faded away. My spell hissed and spat, trying to keep on living even after its life blood was gone, but then it too dissipated, leaving only the smell of ozone behind.

The shock to my system dropped me to my knees. The high pitched whine from earlier was back, and my head felt heavy. So much power, and now that it was gone everything was rushing forward to fill the hole. I thought I heard Ceile yelling my name, but it was all I could do to raise my head.

The Operations soldiers and Arcane Corps wizards had parted down the middle, and another robed figure was walking slowly through the gap. Beneath the hood, I could see the pale face of a young girl, with brilliant hazel eyes. She came forward and stood above me, reaching out to put a hand on my bowed head.

'I'm sorry, Mr. Tundra. You're needed,' she said, sadly, and then everything went black.

112

Dreams. They came and went, nightmares interspersed with memories that up until recently I hadn't known I had. I saw more images of a family that had been everything to me but had destroyed in the end. I saw more of my lonely childhood. I saw more of the early years of me and James' relationship, when a weekend spent chilling on the couch with each other was one of my favourite ways to spend time.

I saw dark days where I hid in a locked room and talked to myself.

Those dreams were intimately familiar. Edgar Lorn staring in a mirror and talking to himself was an awful lot like me talking to the Other.

Floating through the years of my hidden past, I again watched Bill rescue me from the ruins of my home, my burnt and broken body torturing me with each bump and jolt. I watched him carry me to the strange ambulance with its strange paramedics. And then the world vanished.

My next memory was waking up in a hospital as Martin Tundra.

I wondered about the gap. How much time passed during it? What had happened to me? Why did I go into that ambulance as Edgar Lorn and come out someone else?

'Wake up, Mr. Tundra.'

The voice carved through the dreams and I groggily broke free of my sleep and opened my eyes to blue sky and clouds. I found myself lying on my back on a military cot. Beside my bed, the young lunaron sat on a chair, smiling down at me.

Her hood was down, and I got a better look at her face. She couldn't have been more than thirteen. Every lock of her long light brown hair was intricately braided, coming to an end in a thick tail hanging between her shoulder blades. Her brilliant hazel eyes sparkled mischievously. A well-used book lay in her lap, the spine mercilessly broken.

'Hello,' she said.

'Hello,' I said, raggedly.

I sat up slowly, taking time to allow my aching head to adjust, and looked around. I shook my head, incredulously, as I took in my surroundings. The lunaron and I were on the plain bordering Krekt Twelve. We were in the middle of an empty circle of ground, twenty metres of flattened grass ringed by a barricade of Operations soldiers and Arcane Corps wizards. A glowing dome shield glittered over us, maintained by at least ten robed figures spaced evenly around the circle.

Beyond them was an army.

My line of sight wasn't great, but I could still see hundreds of Enforcement personnel busily moving around dozens of airships. Smoke billowed from several spots in the distance, entrances into the Krekt, I imagined. Mostly Military Operations Section, though I could also make out Special Ops men and women scattered around here and there.

'You guys weren't messing around when you came to put me in a box,' I said, watching as groups of soldiers marched up the landing ramps of several airships.

'You are not exactly defenseless, Mr. Tundra, and this is not exactly safe territory,' the lunaron said, gently.

I looked back at her, and frowned. Putting that aside for the moment, I asked, 'Where's Ceile? What've you done to her?'

Smiling, the girl reached over and softly patted my knee. 'Ms. Angael is being cared for by our best necromancer. She will rejoin us once we are ready to go,' she said, her voice friendly.

I sighed with relief, even though I knew I could hardly trust anything the Government had sent my way. 'Alright then. What now?' I said, shaking my head. 'What do I call you?'

The girl's smile went sad again, and now she was shaking her head. 'I'm sorry, Mr. Tundra, but I don't have a name. I'm not allowed to share that kind of information with you, anyway. But I can give you some other answers,' she said. 'First! You may be interested in this.' She reached down next to her and then passed me a mirror.

'They aren't afraid I'll take you hostage or kill you with this thing?' I asked, cocking an eyebrow at her before turning my gaze to the glass. I gasped. It was me in there, but I looked thirty years old. Or rather, what James Lorn might have looked like at thirty years old. All the scars and blemishes and wrinkles were gone, replaced with lightly lined but smooth skin. My hair, beard, and moustache were a pale blond again, no traces of the white or grey that had slowly devoured it over the last two hundred years. My eyes, almost grey just yesterday were now blazing blue.

I let the mirror slowly drop into my lap, and then I gave my arms and legs a once over. Shaking my head, I found them in just as good a shape as my face, and I could feel the strength in them, another thing I'd lost as I'd lived long past my body's expiry date.

When I looked back up at the girl, her smile was dazzling. 'Quite the change! I'll bet it feels good. As for you doing me harm, well, I think you need only consider one thing, Mr. Tundra,' she said. 'Is my life, is my status as a lunaron, worth more than having you, a solaron, under their control?'

I frowned, and for several long seconds we looked at each other silently. She was right, of course. Lunarons were rare, and they served a useful purpose, but if the Government had a solaron, especially one that might live thousands of years, then they had a giant edge up on any enemy that came knocking. They'd give up a hundred lunarons before they let me escape.

Patting my leg again, the girl continued, 'I imagine you're curious about the operation, and all the players. Unfortunately, I don't know much beyond my role here. The man you know as Bill is missing, as are three other members of his team, though we were able to recover the kobold. The little fellow was a bit angry, as apparently Bill tried to kill him, but he'll likely be placated now that he's the only one left to collect the reward.'

I shook my head. All of this was on Bill. He'd been weaving in and out of my life for centuries, causing havoc, and now he had gone to ground again.

'The dwarf force sent by the rebel army was mostly decimated by whatever artifact went off down there. Oh, speaking of that, a number of Operations people owe you their lives, since you were kind enough to annihilate the artifact's swarm. Whether that squad was capable of destroying it or not, you certainly did. I doubt you will see much gratitude, but you should know it exists,' the lunaron said, matter-of-factly.

'The civil war currently affecting the dwarves continues on. I'll bet another group will be sent to find out what happened to the first, but it'll be much too late. The lab level has been purged of essentially everything other than its walls, ceiling, and floor. A very interesting device! It followed you up the elevator shaft, expanding out into every floor on the way, though damage to those was limited,' she continued.

I looked at her curiously. The girl's language fluctuated back and forth between casual and formal on the fly. At least her accent didn't also, listening to Bill speak had been mind-twisting sometimes. 'How old are you? And if you're going to be my chaperone, I'll need something to call you,' I said.

For a moment, the lunaron didn't say anything, just cocked her head and looked at me silently. Then she leaned in close. 'You may call me Chelle. And I am fourteen,' she whispered.

'Alright, Chelle it is. So, what now?' I repeated my question from earlier.

'Well, Mr. Tundra, we are going to wait here while our forces load up. Once most of Enforcement is away, we will collect Ms. Angael and board our own airship for transport to a City facility. Of course, we will have our escorts. A special team will be keeping an eye on us,' the girl said, smiling. 'The Verdant Moon is her name! She's a beautiful ship, not like that ugly Black Ops one I got stuck on during the trip here.'

Her enthusiasm was catching, despite the circumstances. I couldn't help but smile at her. The book in her lap caught my eye again, and I asked, 'What is it you're reading, Chelle?'

The girl's smile split into a big grin, and she lifted the battered book up so I could see it. 'It's called The Great Unlife,' she said, then frowned. 'I don't know the ending! Don't tell me!'

I laughed. 'I haven't heard of that one, Chelle. It sounds depressing,' I said. Then I sobered and asked, 'What's going to happen to me and Ceile at the facility?'

The grin on her face slowly faded, and she shook her head. 'I'm sorry, Mr. Tundra, but that information isn't part of my mission. Technically, the Department's lunarons are part of Black Ops, but we aren't part of Black Ops intelligence,' she said. 'We aren't usually given much background before they send one of us in.'

It felt very odd to be having this conversation with a teenager. 'Do you know the facility's name?' I asked, hoping I'd recognize it so I'd have a clue what I was getting into.

Chelle again looked carefully around before leaning in conspiratorially. 'It's called Whisper Station, Mr. Tundra. I do not know what they do there,' she whispered. She looked frightened.

My eyes widened, and my chest suddenly felt very tight. Maybe the girl didn't know anything about the facility, but I did. Whisper Station. Operated by the Department of Research. They built weapons there. Terrible weapons.

They turned people into monsters there.

113

Followed by a parade of people prepared to turn me into paste if I got rowdy, Chelle and I steadily made our way across the plain toward the airship she'd called the Verdant Moon. Other than the girl, no one else had said anything to me, and there were plenty of unhappy looks being sent my way.

The ship was big and sleek, but while she had several banks of cannons she definitely wasn't military. Almost as large as the dwarf vessel we'd stolen from Krekt Twelve, the Verdant Moon looked like she was built to haul cargo or people. I smirked, thinking it was small consolation that I'd likely be comfortable on my final flight.

My stomach rumbled, and I tried to remember when I'd eaten last. Not since early into our trek through the caverns by the Rook's lands, I thought. As for water, I'd had more than my share in my plummet down door number three. Still, I felt dried out.

As if she'd read my mind, Chelle said, 'You and Ceile will be able to eat once we're aboard. You're to be treated well, unless you disobey. Please don't do that, Mr. Tundra. It will be very unpleasant for you if you do.' The lunaron seemed genuinely concerned, and there was just enough fear in her voice to make me wonder if she had seen some of that unpleasantness herself.

The area under the airship was bustling with activity, with members of every Section in the Department boarding or loading equipment into the vast hold. In the chaos, I spotted some familiar figures, and actually shouted with joy when one of them was not only Ceile, but a completely whole Ceile.

Grinning, my friend rose from her seat and jogged toward me, much to the chagrin of the two serious-looking Black Ops men trying to watch her. All smiles, we wrapped each other in a tight hug, and then Ceile lifted me in the air, laughing.

'You are heavier today!' she joked as she set me down. Looking me over, she nodded slowly. 'You look great, Martin. The chamber really worked.'

I smiled and squeezed her hands. 'You look great, too. No, amazing! Their necromancer did fantastic work,' I said, looking at her pristine hand and eye.

'Hello, Ms. Angael, I'm happy to see you back on your feet,' Chelle said, peeking around from behind me. Ceile smiled at the girl.

'You've met?' I asked, cocking an eyebrow at the two.

Ceile nodded. 'They let me come along with you during the exit from Krekt Twelve. I had much time to speak with our young host,' she said. She winked at Chelle, who giggled.

'Move your group along, lunaron,' a gruff voice growled from behind us. I turned to find a large weretiger moving through the half circle of Operations forces, men and women parting around him like water. He was every bit the nightmare that Nox had been, and towered over everyone even if he wasn't as massive as the big 'wolf. His orange fur was brilliant where it wasn't covered by some kind of black grease, which I assumed was to give the 'tiger some level of camouflage.

I frowned. I knew him, though I couldn't remember from where. 'Hanaak,' I hesitantly said, nodding slowly at the weretiger.

His dour expression vanished as a toothy grin split his face. 'I wondered if you'd remember me. C'mon, you two, the Sorcerer wants to meet you,' he said, draping a big arm over my shoulders and pushing me lightly toward the group Ceile had been waiting with. My friend gave me a curious look but I waved her off. Her eyes narrowed, but Chelle took her arm and pulled her into step behind Hanaak and me with a gentle smile.

As we approached, the swarm of personnel thinned out. Most of our escort split off and headed for several other airships, leaving us guarded by the lunaron, the weretiger, a handful of Operations soldiers, and a lone Arcane Corps member, who looked like he'd rather be anywhere else. Waiting ahead were Ceile's two Black Ops guards, a man and woman in basic Enforcement uniforms, and Weezab.

I felt anger rear its head in the depths when I saw the kobold, a cold rage slinking through my veins. His rags were gone, replaced with traveling gear that fit him well. He watched me impassively as we neared.

The man and woman stepped forward to meet us, and they looked over our shoulders. 'We'll take it from here,' the woman said to the soldiers and wizard. Without fanfare, everyone but the newcomers, Hanaak, and Chelle immediately moved away, headed for the Verdant Moon's loading ramp. I frowned when I noticed that Weezab hadn't left with the others.

'We're running late, Command wants to have a dog and pony show before we head back to the City,' the man said to Hanaak, then turned to me. 'Agents Enak and Paige,' he said, gesturing to himself and the woman. 'Our team has been assigned to bring you to Whisper Station. You've met Hanaak already. You'll meet the Sorcerer once we're aboard.' Turning away and waving over his shoulder, he headed for the personnel ramp.

The rest of our motley crew followed. I noticed Enak and his group all gave the kobold nasty glances as they passed the little fellow. Ceile's look was full of disappointment, but Chelle gave him a friendly smile. I wondered if she knew him or was just that cheerful. Whatever the case, Weezab slid into line a short way behind us.

The Verdant Moon was just as massive inside as it looked from the outside. Whoever had built the airship hadn't seemed to follow any particular design spec, and I was lost not long after we'd scaled the ramp and stepped through the fortified entrance. The passage, wide enough for Hanaak but barely, seemed to turn and go up or down at random. Enak seemed to know where he was going, but Paige looked as confused as me.

Finally, just when I thought we were going to wander the ship until we died, we rounded a corner and found the hall bordered by a number of doors. Crew members came and went from several of them, but our guide led us to an unused one and took us in. The chamber beyond was a large lounge of sorts, full of chairs of all shapes and sizes to sit or sleep in, a simple kitchen, and a large window that covered the entire far wall, giving a spectacular view of the land below.

Curled up in one of the chairs was a dark-skinned man in simple robes and a wide-brimmed hat that was pulled down over his eyes. He was snoring loudly.

Agent Enak stepped to the side, and waved us into the room. 'Have a seat at the table. We have a few things to discuss, and then you may have the run of the room,' he said, his deep voice rumbling. Gesturing across at the two doors opposite the kitchen, he continued, 'There are showers available. Once we're done, you may use those as well.'

Nodding, I looked at Ceile and then took a spot at the table. She sat down next to me, taking my hand as we waited for the others to join us. Chelle chose not to join us, instead taking up a position at my shoulder. Enak sat down across from us, unbuckling his holster, wrapping it up, and dumping it unceremoniously on the table. Agent Paige leaned up against the kitchen counter, and watched us carefully. Hanaak hadn't followed us further into the room, and was now standing in front of the door.

Weezab dragged a chair out from the table at the far corner and then climbed up onto it. The little kobold's head barely reached the top, and I almost laughed as he glared over at me from his undignified position.

When we were settled, Paige spoke. 'The four of us are here to make sure you don't try to harm the lunaron or to otherwise prevent your transport to Whisper. We're authorized to hurt or kill your friend if need be, and to hurt you to a certain extent. I don't want to have to do that, and I'm sure you'd rather I not have to do that,' she said, then leaned forward. 'So, here's the deal. Behave. Use the facilities, get something to eat and drink, have a good sleep. We have a day's flight to the Station, use those hours to rest up.'

She suddenly looked uncomfortable, and shook her head. 'You're really going to want to be rested up.'

When she fell silent, I asked, 'What are they going to do to me? To Ceile?'

She looked askance at me. 'Martin, even if I knew, you know damn well I couldn't tell you. And you know what Research does. What they do at Whisper. Just take my advice and rest,' she said, then looked at Ceile. 'You'll probably remain leverage once we've arrived, Ceile. I don't know what they intend to do with you otherwise.'

Enak nodded, and then said, in an oddly loud tone, 'If the Sorcerer ever shows up, he might have more info for you.'

All the other member of their team had to say in response was another loud snore.

Enak snorted and then got to his feet. 'We'll be underway in a few minutes, there were only a handful of ships left before we boarded,' he said, collecting his weapon and heading for the kitchen.

When he and Agent Paige began talking to each other quietly about the flight, my mind started to wander. If I wanted to stay out of Research's hands, I needed to get me and Ceile off this ship, and that meant getting my magic back.

That meant killing Chelle. I frowned and looked up at the young girl, who smiled sadly back. Was that something I could do? Kill a child to escape?

Something at the back of my head whispered yes.

The Verdant Moon's engines suddenly began to howl, and then the big ship lifted free of the ground. She rolled to one side until we were facing south-east, and then headed out.

I had to give her builders credit. Not a single item in the room rolled or fell, despite the sharp turn. Stabilizing spells sparkled along the edges of everything, keeping anything that wasn't bolted down upright. Our seats at the table had enough give for us to skid them around but wouldn't tip. The lounge chairs bent with the shifting ship, but magic rippled along their supports, allowing them to turn at slightly less extreme angles than the ship's.

Agents Enak and Paige handled the motion well, obviously accustomed to airship travel, but Hanaak had to dig his claws into the floor and reach out for a wall to steady himself. The Arcane Corps wizard hadn't woken, even when his chair had tilted so far over that his hat fell off.

Weezab was still missing, though the way the weretiger kept casting suspiciously glances at one of the washroom doors suggested the little kobold hadn't gone far.

'That's our speech, for the moment. You can get up, stare blissfully out the window, take a nap, whatever. When we arrive at Whisper, we'll be handing you off to Research, though I believe Chelle will be accompanying you all the way to the end,' Enak said, waving vaguely toward the big windscreen and then wandering off to drop unceremoniously into one of the loungers at the far corner of the room. The Agent looked like he was settling into sleep, but his hand rested easily on the grip of his pistol.

Paige didn't move from her position against the wall, but her eyes now spent more time looking out the window than on us. Much like her male counterpart, her hands weren't far from her weapons, though. I wasn't much of a fighter without my magic, even with my strength returned to me, but Ceile was dangerous. I doubted Enforcement or Operations would deposit us into the care of idiots.

Nodding, I gave Ceile's hand a squeeze and then stood. Letting my feet get used to the slight sway of the airship's movement, I turned and went to stand at the windscreen, watching the plains and mountains drift past below. Briefly, I could make out a handful of other ships traveling in our wake, but they soon fanned out and disappeared.

Far to the west, I could see the Rook's mountain, and the grey lands around it. I frowned. Even at this distance, I could tell the stone had expanded quite a way since our encounter with the elemental a couple days ago. As the poisoned plains vanished over the horizon, I wondered if we'd left a threat behind that was even worse than the Scayn.

'It's in the Government's interests that the elemental go about its work,' a quiet voice said from just over my shoulder. Startled, I jerked my head around to find the wizard on his feet and standing beside me. He was dusting his hat off with a sigh. 'They're never the same after they've hit the floor once. I'm Master Wizard Kloe, though you can call me Wade, as that's much easier and doesn't involve as many syllables,' he said, looking up at me and sticking his dark hand out.

He smiled when I took it. 'A pleasure to finally meet you, Martin. These hooligans call me the Sorcerer, which I would appreciate if you didn't,' he said, pointing at the two Agents and the weretiger. The three grinned evilly back. Wade sighed again, then turned to the windscreen and nodded. 'I'm technically in command of this little band of misfits. Technically! As I'm sure one of them had already mentioned, we're here to make sure you get to Research's tender mercies relatively intact, that we're authorized to use force, blah blah blah.' Wade winked at me as he rolled his eyes.

Looking over at Ceile, who had joined us at the window, he nodded and his face went serious. 'You two aren't stupid. I've read everything Operations and Enforcement has on both of you, and I think I know you pretty well. I even tried to get Research's files, which was as much fun as kissing a mrog. You know this ride only ends in two ways,' he whispered. Lifting two fingers, he knocked one of them down. 'One, you play nice, enjoy this time, and then you become Whisper's problem and not mine,' he quietly said, then lowered the second and continued, 'Or two, you do something terrible to Ms. Chelle back there,' he nodded his head at the young lunaron, who had sat down next to Agent Enak and was reading her book again, 'and then my team has to contain you.'

Wade leaned in very close to me. 'I know what you are, Martin. I am ideally suited to stripping magic users of their power, but no one on this ship is under the delusion that I can keep you under wraps for long. The others are under orders to kill Ceile and hurt you if you don't behave, but my instructions are to kill you the instant Chelle is incapacitated,' he whispered. He didn't sound happy about it. 'If I fail, the Verdant Moon has been lined with enough explosive to break the Rook's mountain in half and the captain is to detonate her with all hands aboard.'

The wizard's face twisted with a hint of mischievousness. 'Don't tell the crew, they might take it personally,' he said, then looked back out the window. 'We have a long flight, and I'm bored. So I'm going to tell you both a story. Well, probably a few stories.' He exchanged a quick glance with Hanaak. The weretiger nodded and stepped back until he was leaning against the door, and then the wizard turned away.

He was silent for a long moment, then he slowly began to talk. 'You are a solaron, Martin. The Government had been grooming you to be their greatest weapon for years when something went wrong and you lost yourself. Then they had to start over. They had to find a way to repair the damage, and they had to do it without transferring you into a new body,' he whispered. When I looked at him questioningly, he said, 'You can't transfer a solaron, Martin. Each time someone transfers, their link to the realm between is lessened. For an arcanist or elementalist, this means their power shrinks. For a solaron, this means their power dies.'

Ceile looked dismayed. 'This is not something that is mentioned when transfer is discussed,' she hissed.

Wade shook his head, 'It's a convenient way to keep the population from getting too strong. The Government wouldn't want a whole army of aethons and archons to form over the course of a millennia as no one dies, would they? People might get ideas about making changes to the way things are. This way, the City keeps growing, the Government gets more tax, and they remain nicely and neatly in charge,' he said with a dry chuckle. 'But where was I? Ah, yes. So they had limited time to figure out a way to get you back into fighting form and preferably forever. The regeneration chamber was the answer. I'll bet there was some tears of joy and greedy rubbing of hands in the Government when the artifact was found.'

Then the wizard's expression darkened. 'Of course, things would have been so much simpler to just knock you out and take you directly to the damned thing as soon as we knew what and where it was, but for whatever reason, Command chose to put you into the contractor's hands instead,' he said, then cursed. 'All this test crap, he could have gotten you killed, and for what? We could have put you through the chamber, then done what testing needed to be done.'

He threw his hands up in frustration. 'Why anyone decided to put your care and handling into Peter's hands, I'll never know. Taylor was always a better choice, you two were friends long before Operations decided to slap you and Peter together.'

Wade sighed, then turned and dropped into the nearest lounger. He beckoned for us to join him, waving off my questions. 'Never interrupt the storyteller, my friend. The story might change,' he whispered. When Ceile gently pushed me into the seat next to him, the wizard chuckled and continued. 'Of course, you did us all a favour by helping kill a few things that needed killing. I was happy to hear you killed Peter's black dragon, he really liked it. And the Scayn parasite that ate Woodsholme, that was nice. I hate seeing those things do their work. Nasty bastards.'

'Holy crap. I killed all the gnomes,' I suddenly burst out, as images of the Scayn seed dropping toward the gnome city danced at the back of my head.

The wizard smiled sadly and reached up to grip my shoulder. 'Not all of them, Martin, and we've all done distasteful things in our service, haven't we?' he said, cocking an eyebrow. His tone suggested that there were different degrees of distasteful. Letting me go, he continued on, 'The Rook, that was a mess. The Government wanted it alive, so its growing land would eventually start causing big problems for Krekts Twelve and Thirteen. Command wasn't impressed when Peter took you up against the elemental. It's good that neither of you were killed in the end, but removing the Earth Hammer from the Rook's lap isn't something they're taking lightly. Its lands will grow three times as fast now.'

Shaking his head, he said, 'That's bad news for our long term. Well, it's really bad news for the dwarves' short term, but sometime in the future, we'll have to come back and destroy the elemental or it'll be a problem for us. I hear Operations had an artifact in mind down there in the vault that could do just such a thing, but Peter's cute stunt kind of took that off the table.'

Now I was shaking my head. It seemed like we'd been doing a lot of the City's dirty work, even though we weren't working for the City. There was an awful lot of blood on my hands already, and every time I thought about it, more of Edgar Lorn's - mine, now - memories reared their ugly heads. If it hadn't been for my psychotic break, which had been plenty bloody in and of itself, who knows how many more would have died.

If Wade noticed my discomfort, he didn't show it. 'After everything, you and your group still made it to the artifact vault, though not entirely intact,' the wizard said, and his face was grim. 'Not that I'm surprised. Nox was the only actual Government employee in the lot, and he didn't know they'd put him there. They could have filled your group with Operations men or women, and everything would have been fine, but Peter had to bring his two goons with him, and Operations decided to use two other contractors to keep an eye on them.'

He looked frustrated again. 'So when the kobold is the only one we find, Peter is missing, and all of the others are dead and the artifact vault completely wiped out, we have a bit of a mess to clean up and some questions about just what the bastard was up to down there,' he said in irritation.

Locking eyes with me, the wizard looked at a loss. 'Because there were some scary things in that lab, and I'd like to know where they are.'

115

Wade fell silent, and we sat there staring at each other for a long while. The wizard had offered a lot of information up, and I wasn't sure why. My mind, which had already been running overtime trying to process everything that had been happening, was flat out being crushed. I fought the urge to giggle.

Eventually, the wizard shrugged and looked away. 'Maybe you're curious as to why I'm telling you these things. Well, the truth is that I've been doing this for a long time, and I don't like being told it's classified. I'm tired of it,' he said, quietly. 'Reading your files was sickening. They've been messing with your life for over two hundred years, ever since Peter brought you to their attention, and who knows how long he was messing with it before that.'

He leaned toward me, and stuck a finger out at my chest. 'But the main reason I don't like this job is because of what you are. We usually escort persons of interest. Diplomats. Spies. Whistleblowers. Whatever. You? You're a damn weapon,' he snarled. 'We aren't taking you back to drain you of what you know, we're taking you back so you can annihilate the elves and dwarves and dragons and whatever else the Government considers a threat.'

'Boss,' Paige hissed in warning, nodding over at the washroom doors.

Wade looked over his shoulder at her, fury twisting his face, but nodded. Gradually, he took a deep breath, and when he spoke again his voice was calm. 'So I'm going to tell you all sorts of things, Martin Tundra, and I hope that when you become Whisper's problem, you become a problem for Whisper,' he whispered.

The wizard suddenly stood, and turned to face Ceile and me. 'Now, I need to finish my nap and you two need to, at the very least, take a damn shower. So go do that, and I'll talk a little more later,' he said. With a bow, the man wandered back over to his original spot and collapsed into its clutches.

We watched the wizard until he once again began to snore loudly, and then turned to each other. 'Shall we shower first?' I asked Ceile, who smiled and stood, reaching back to help me up.

The hot water was a luxury after so many days without. Free of my torn clothes, I spent a wonderful ten minutes scrubbing dust, dirt, oil, and miscellaneous from my skin and hair. While I monopolized the shower, Ceile combed over our battered clothing looking for anything useful, dropping the items into the sink and then tossing the clothes into a messy pile on the floor. The Verdant Moon's courtesy included fresh clothing and toiletries, which we took advantage of.

'Where do you think Bill is?' Ceile asked as she dumped my poor cellphone into the sink after fishing it out of the inside of my shredded jacket.

Rubbing at a stubborn patch of grime on my shoulder, I snorted. 'I have no idea. He had to know they wouldn't be pleased with him, especially after he blew up the vault, but he still planned to turn us over. Well, right up until we realized that Weezab had destroyed the engineer's little toy that was keeping me sedate,' I said. Giving up on the dirt, I turned to look at her over the shower door. 'He's still out there, probably with some sort of plan. I'd be surprised if we don't see him and his stupid moustache again.'

Ceile and I both laughed, which felt good. If I ignored for the moment that I was likely headed to my doom, this could have just been me and my dearest friend out on a trip, and even knowing where we were going didn't do much to dull my good mood.

I guess I'd gotten used to being totally screwed.

Conceding defeat and in some sort of definition of clean, I traded spots with Ceile and had a go at my unruly hair and beard while she enjoyed the hot water. I swiped a clear path through the moisture on the mirror and felt an electric shock when I saw the face staring back. I still hadn't adjusted to seeing me looking so young again.

Deep inside, I wondered how long it'd be before what happened to Nox to happen to me.

I stood, inches from the mirror, looking over the strange doppelganger on the other side, fingers tracing over spots that just over a day ago held lines and scars and cuts and cracks. Eyes that were brilliantly blue and unclouded stared back. A chill rippled through my body. I couldn't shake the feeling that something terribly wrong had happened to me. Something that I couldn't undo.

'Martin,' Ceile said, and I turned to find her looking at me curiously over the shower door. 'Are you alright?'

I glanced back at the man in the mirror and then shook my head. 'No, this is going to take some getting used to,' I said, gesturing at myself, who gestured back at me. Ceile looked worried, but turned back to the shower head to continue basking in the heat.

'How do you feel? You look amazing,' she said as she scrubbed her hair. I smiled, then stretched my arms and legs. This body did feel amazing, if I ignored the vague sense of unease.

Having managed to get my hair into a more civilized state, I brushed my teeth. Much to the appreciation of anyone that had to get within ten feet of me, I assumed.

'Martin,' my friend said again. I looked back up at her as I tossed the brush away. 'What you said, how you feel about transfers,' she continued, and her voice was nervous. 'Do you truly believe that?'

Almost two hundred years we'd known each other, and this conversation had to happen here. I leaned against the counter and closed my eyes. 'Yes,' I said, quietly.

Ceile went very still, and for a while, the only sound in the bathroom was the shower water cascading down around her. Then she asked, so quiet that I barely heard her, 'What does that make me, then? What am I?'

I sighed. There was no way for this conversation to go that wasn't going to suck. Opening the shower door, I pulled my friend gently out and sat her down on the toilet seat. Kneeling down in front of her, I took her hands and looked into her eyes. Fear and anger flickered in them.

'I don't know for sure, Ceile. You were born the day the elf Ceile Angael had the rites of transfer cast on her, hoping to transfer herself into this body,' I said, giving her hands a squeeze. 'Everything that she was, everything that made her her, was used to create you. You have her memories, her personality. But you are not her.'

Ceile frowned and tried to let go of my hands, but I held tight. 'Yes, that means that the terrible things you remember didn't happen to you. Does that make them less awful? No. They've shaped you, made you the woman you are today. Made you the woman that has been my best friend for almost two centuries,' I continued. My eyes suddenly started to swim.

'She is gone, then,' Ceile whispered, not entirely a question. Her face had soothed, but now she looked very sad.

'Yes,' I answered anyway, 'Ceile Angael is dead.'

My friend was silent for a long while, her eyes searching mine for something and not finding it. 'And if I were to transfer into a new body?' she asked, very quietly.

I closed my eyes and squeezed her hands again. 'Then you would die, too, and someone new would be born.'

She abruptly leaned forward, pulling me toward her until we were almost nose to nose. 'But that would be horrific! Think of how many people have killed themselves. Think of-' she hoarsely said, before cutting off suddenly. Her eyes focused far away, and when she spoke again, I could barely hear her. 'Martin, what am I?'

I shook my head. 'Something more than Ceile Angael was. Something born of magic. Something amazing born of a terrible sacrifice. And you're my greatest friend and the strongest person I've ever met,' I whispered, with as much certainty as I could muster.

Now there were tears dripping down her cheeks, and she shook her head slowly. 'But how do you know? How do you know about the transfer spells?' she asked.

I shook my head again, and said, 'I don't know. Not for sure. It's what my gut tells me, based on what I know about the magic, what it does, what happens after. I might be wrong, but I don't think so.'

Ceile opened her mouth to speak, but was interrupted by the bathroom door swinging open and then shut very quickly. She looked over my shoulder and surprised both of us with a laugh. I turned to see what she was looking at, and then laughed along with her.

Weezab stood at the door, one scaly hand blocking his sight. 'We need to talk,' he said. 'But could you put some clothes on, first?'

116

Once we'd gotten toweled off and into fresh clothes, we found slightly more comfortable seats on a pile of towels on the floor. Ceile and I leaned back against the wall, tucked in tight with each other, while Weezab paced the floor in front of us, clutching his tail and twitching.

'What do you want, Weezab? You look awfully unhappy for someone that no longer has to split a reward five ways,' I said.

The kobold glared down at me. 'I look unhappy because being cut off from my magic makes me unhappy. Besides, I never had to split my reward, as long as you were returned successfully, I would get what they promised me,' he snarled, quietly. He stopped pacing, and pointed a clawed finger at me. 'No, what we need to discuss is what's going to happen once we get to Whisper Station and everything goes wrong.'

I exchanged a glance with Ceile. 'What do you mean?' she asked the kobold.

Weezab leaned in close. I watched condensation bead and then drip from the scales on his face. 'Listen close, Lorn or Tundra or whoever you ended up, because we don't have much time. The Government wants your power, but not you. They've lost too much time fighting with all of your little cracks and baggage. So Research has developed something that can take your power away from you,' he whispered, eyes narrowing.

I frowned. 'What are you talking about?' I asked.

The kobold smiled nastily. 'It's genius, really. Supposedly, they put you in it, and then it milks you of your magic. You just lie in this machine, drugged out of your mind, and they flip switches and press buttons that tell you what to blow up. Thanks to the regeneration chamber, that'll give Research a weapon that can not only strip the continent of life, but do it for the next twenty thousand years or so,' he said.

Horrified, I said, 'How do you know any of this? Wade said you were just a contractor.'

Weezab barked out a laugh. 'I work for a lot of different people, let's just say. Anyway, Research's little toy is not the problem. Well, not for me. It's a bit of a problem for you, of course. No, what's going to go very wrong once we arrive is that Poe is going to come to get you,' he said.

I shook my head. Navigating around Bill's three names was giving me a headache. 'Why is he coming to get me? Isn't this where we were supposed to end up? Wasn't this the goal?' I demanded, bitterly.

The kobold made calming gestures with his hands, looking over his shoulder. 'Settle down, Martin. The Sorcerer might be a little displeased with his employer at the moment, but I haven't figured out if he and his little team are quite ready for open rebellion,' he said. Looking back at me, the little creature continued, 'Look, it's pretty simple. Peter's been working for the Government for ages, but Poe's been working for himself for eons. Operations and whatnot might think they've got him under their thumb, but we know better, right?'

He suddenly leaned forward again, putting his hands on my knees. 'After all, he's been watching you for the Government since just prior to your little meltdown, but you've known him longer than that, haven't you,' the kobold said. His eyes were feverish.

I was surprised to find myself nodding. At the back of my mind, I saw Bill standing next to me at my mother's grave. 'Yeah. Yes I have. I was a teenager. He looked a bit different, but he was all over the place back then,' I said, hoarsely. More memories danced past, the engineer's influence over my life on display.

Weezab was nodding slowly. 'Well, now we can ask ourselves if the Government recruited Peter to get you to this point, or did Poe use the Government to get you to this point?' he asked. 'And more importantly, what is Poe going to do now that you're here?'

He looked excited, and I frowned again. 'You seem pretty happy about this. Shouldn't you be cheering for the other team?' I said.

The kobold snorted. 'I cheer for whatever team's winning, Martin. I was promised power in return for making sure you made it to Whisper safely, but if Poe tears the whole place down when he pops up again, then I need to look elsewhere for my reward,' he said. Lowering his voice to barely a whisper, the kobold continued, 'Here's the deal. We aren't going to wait to find out what Poe has in mind. We're going to break you out.'

Ceile leaned in, frowning. 'How are we going to do that, Weezab?'

Weezab winked at her, and said, 'Now, now. Can't give you all the details, and I don't have all of them anyway. What you need to know is that I'll get you out, and in return, you'll help me with an errand or two.'

A loud knock at the door made us all jump. 'Kobold, you've had enough time to inspect the cargo. Get out here,' Hanaak's voice rumbled from the other side.

'Do we have a deal?' Weezab hissed.

Ceile looked concerned, but what did I have to lose? 'Deal. We'll expect you,' I whispered. Then I reached out and caught the kobold's hand. 'Don't be late,' I said, pulling the little creature close.

He bared his teeth but nodded. Pulling free roughly, he spun and stomped to the door, throwing it open. The surprised weretiger on the other side rocked back a step before crouching down to look at the kobold in suspicion.

'What were you doing in there?' the 'tiger growled.

'It's above your pay grade, 'thrope,' Weezab snarled, and headed for the kitchen.

Hanaak snorted in amusement, then turned to look at me and Ceile. 'If you're done having your little floor-side chat, you should get something to eat and then sleep,' he said, before returning to his place in front of the room's entrance.

Leaving our towels and old clothes piled up in a corner of the bathroom, I took Ceile's hand and we followed Weezab across the chamber. Agents Paige and Enak watched us go, looking more alert than when we'd gone into the bathroom. Wade was still snoring noisily in his chair. Chelle smiled as we passed her, reaching up to touch my arm gently.

It'd been a long while since I'd had anything to eat, and it felt good to finally have a decent meal. With our hunger sated, Ceile guided me over to one of the larger loungers meant for a therianthrope or larger construct, and with a bit of effort we managed to get wrapped up and comfortable in it. Hanaak shook his head in amusement as he watched us maneuver into the chair. Paige finally moved from her position against the wall, settling into a lounger not far away, and then the weretiger lowered the lights a touch.

Ceile and I lay there, staring out the window, for a long while. The Verdant Moon sailed along, flying above a carpet of cloud, a sea of white that covered every horizon, broken only by the sharp peaks of the Barriers below. Out of our view, the Blue Sun was rocketing toward the land, its dim light growing darker by the minute, until it was just the Moon and the flickering stars lighting our way. Aurora ignited the skies above, ghostly green flame flowing far overhead.

Eventually, my friend's breathing slowed as she drifted off. Tucked in with her, my ear against her chest, I listened to her heartbeat while I watched the stars pulse and blink through the window. A lifetime ago, on the roof of a hotel deep in the City, she and I had watched the stars just like this. We'd only known each other for half an hour at the time, and alcohol had robbed me of the rest of the night, but it was one of my favourite memories.

I twisted my neck to have a look back, and made eye contact with Weezab. The little kobold had almost vanished into the cushions of his lounger, and now just his eyes and snout stuck out from the depths of the chair. He looked thoughtful. We watched each other for a few seconds, and then he nodded at me, looked away and then disappeared into the cushions.

I wanted to stay awake. If Weezab was right and Research intended to bolt me into some machine for the rest of time, then these might be my last few hours. As hard as I tried, though, tiredness crept up on me. My eyes slid shut and when they opened the White Sun was blazing in through the window.

117

The Verdant Moon was still passing over the mountains, heading south east, but we were closer to the ground. I couldn't tell where we were. This deep into the Barriers, there were no landmarks I would recognize. Hell, this far west of the City, the only places I'd ever seen were kilometres underground.

Ceile snored quietly next to me. I smiled as I reached up and touched her cheek gently. Over my friend's shoulder, I could see Hanaak curled up in a chair next to the door. The weretiger was snoring as well, and I shook my head as I wondered how he'd managed to fall asleep. He barely fit in the lounger, his clawed feet jutted way out past the end of the chair, even with him entrenched into its cushions. The claws on his left hand kept clicking together in his sleep.

Enak was still in the lounger he'd picked last night, and when I looked his way, our eyes locked. The Agent looked alert, and nodded at me. I nodded back, and he returned to staring out the window. Across from him, Paige was almost as buried in her chair as Weezab had been. The female Agent was awake as well, but she looked tired and barely acknowledged me when she saw me looking.

I couldn't see the kobold. I assumed he was still hiding in the lounger near the back of the room. Not far from his chair, Chelle was asleep on the floor, curled up against the wall. Wrapped in her robes, she would have looked like a pile of rags if I hadn't known she was there.

Looking back, I found Wade watching me. With a lazy smile, the wizard waved me over. I considered it for a moment, then carefully disentangled myself from Ceile and crossed the room to drop into the seat next to him. We sat in silence for a while, watching the peaks fly past beneath us.

'Tell me something, Martin,' the wizard said after several minutes had passed. I cocked an eyebrow at him and then nodded. 'Your magic. What's it like? The nether I use is supposedly squeezed from the Blue Sun itself, but the energy you use, it's the good stuff. White and Blue, mixed,' he whispered, leaning toward me. His eyes were hungry.

I thought about it for a long moment, then I shrugged. 'I didn't even know I was a solaron until a couple days ago. Too many lost memories. Now, I remember using the magic, remember calling the Suns, but it's an old feeling,' I said, struggling to explain. 'The last while, where I've known I wasn't archon or aethon, feels foreign. The spells are raw, powerful. When I've pulled the energy to me, it's like

I'm the center of the galaxy. Like I could bore a hole to the planet's core. Or cleanse the oceans.'

'Or destroy the planet,' something whispered from the back of my mind.

Wade was nodding, though his expression darkened slightly at that last. 'You wouldn't be the first to try. From what I've heard, every solaron the City has record of had a troubled life. Not that they know of many of you. The last one died decades before you were born, and the one before her, centuries,' he said, quietly. 'So much power, trapped in a non-Elder creature. You could challenge the Horsemen if you chose.'

A shiver rippled down my spine. 'I don't think I'm particularly interested in meeting any of the Four for conversation, much less combat,' I whispered with a nervous laugh.

The wizard looked thoughtful. 'No, I imagine you aren't,' he said after a few seconds, nodding slowly. He turned to look out the windscreen again. 'It's a constant thorn in my side, knowing that despite all my years of study, I will never be any more than a wizard. I'm no archon. I'll never match the raw strength of a geomancer, much less an aethon. And even the weakest solaron could overpower me in a heartbeat.'

'There's a fourteen year old girl over in the corner that is currently overpowering both of us,' I quietly said, smiling.

Wade laughed, very loudly, and then looked very shocked that he had. 'Fair point!' he chuckled. Sobering, he shook his head. 'I've been doing this for a long time, Martin. This group,' he said, nodding at the Agents and Hanaak, 'is only a decade or so old, but I've been around longer than you have.' Seeing my look of surprise, the wizard stuck out an arm and pulled the sleeve of his robe up. Tiny seams ran up the sides of his flesh, visible on his dark skin only because they glowed with a faint blue light. 'Not my idea. I got myself killed in a car accident and my family decided to have me transferred before my body could evict me.'

I knew I had to look horrified, but the wizard just burst into laughter again. 'Martin, Martin, Martin. The look on your face. Yeah, I wasn't very impressed at the time, either, but it's been almost four hundred years. You move on,' he said, letting his sleeve slide back into place and settling back into his chair. 'Look, I've been around long enough to see the City devour the last of the nearby settlements. I was there when Enforcement rolled into Summer's Flame and killed enough of the city's security forces and council to force them into becoming our last District. I was there when we ground the gnoll tribes to dust. I was there when we gave Mei Song that gentle push into the elven city to our south, after we broke her so badly that she couldn't help but explode when she got there.'

Wade looked up at me, and there was a hollowness behind his eyes. 'It gets worse every time I think about it a little more. The City has been destroying everything that might be a threat for centuries. The dwarves are the latest, and the only reason we haven't made them go away is because they've retreated so deep into the ruins that it'll take a real continent-shattering weapon to get them out,' he whispered. His hand darted out, and he poked me in the chest with a finger. 'You, Martin. Once they've got their hands on you, nothing is going to stop them. They'll be able to reach all the way to the Ravenmyre and beyond, right from the comfort of the mega fortress they've been building for a millennia.'

I pushed his hand away, frowning. 'And yet, here you are, helping deliver me to them. Besides, how do you know all of this? You were angry about being told things were classified earlier,' I growled, quietly.

A nasty smile split the man's face. 'Just because they don't tell me everything doesn't mean I have no way of finding out. You're old enough to remember the gnoll invasions and the dragon raids. When was the last time the City's ground-level borders were threatened? My friend, the Government has been slowly stripping this world of anything that isn't itself,' he said. Waving vaguely out the window, the wizard continued, 'The Green Lady is gone. I was busy going out to collect you, so I don't know any details, but she's gone. An attack force quietly left the City last week, and now her lands are empty.'

He shook his head. 'That couldn't have been an easy fight. I wonder how many hundreds of people had to die because the Government needed her dead,' he whispered.

'Why are you telling me all this?' I hissed, leaning in angrily. 'What can I do about it?'

Wade's arms shot out to clutch mine painfully. 'Nothing!' he hissed back. 'Not yet. Not here. We're only an hour or so from Whisper, and there's no way off this ship that doesn't involve some serious incineration.' He leaned forward until we were nose to nose. 'I want you angry. I want you ready. At one point, they have to free your magic so they can turn you into their little puppet. We're going to be there to watch. We're going to be there to give you a little nudge.'

If anything, the man's grin got larger. 'And when we do, you're going to turn their world inside out,' he whispered, then let go of my arms and slid back into the cushions again.

We sat there, staring at each other silently for a long moment. Then I looked around suspiciously and hissed, 'And you think you can trust your team here to not give Research a tip? What about the kobold? What makes you think they aren't ready for trouble? Hell, they have to know Bill is up to something.'

The wizard shook his head, slowly, and his smile faded. 'That's my problem, not yours. Now, sit back and relax. Enjoy some quiet time before everything gets noisy,' he said, closing his eyes.

I sat back in my seat, watching the man. A dark thought occurred to me, and I asked, 'Wade, if you really don't want me falling into Research's hands, why don't you just kill me? The four of you could do that and still escape the ship.'

Wade opened one eye, and for a brief instant his smile returned. 'Because once you've taken Whisper down to the bedrock, you're going to help me with a few things,' he quietly said. Without elaborating, the wizard closed his eye and within a minute was sleeping again.

The White Sun had vanished over the horizon to the south and the Blue Sun well overhead when the Verdant Moon's engines howled and the big airship came to a rest at Whisper Station's massive landing pad. Wade and his group, tailed at a distance by Weezab, led Ceile, Chelle, and I through the ship's labyrinthe halls, coming to a stop at the closed exit hatch.

We hadn't encountered anyone else the whole time. There wasn't anyone waiting outside the recreation room we'd been holed up in. There wasn't anyone in the halls. There wasn't anyone hanging around the landing ramp area. It was just the eight of us. The silent corridors made me wonder if the crew and other passengers had abandoned ship overnight.

There'd been barely a handful of words exchanged between any of us since we'd left the chamber. Even Ceile and I hadn't said much to each other. The air felt oppressively thick, and no one seemed inclined to break the silence.

With a hollow thump, the door slid open, and I was briefly blinded as sunlight blasted in through the gap. Even before the portal had finished moving, Wade was out onto the ramp and walking quickly down to the pavement, followed by Paige, who beckoned for me to follow.

As I set foot onto the landing pad and my eyes adjusted to the light, I saw that the area was almost deserted. A few small attack airships waited silently at the far end, all of them unmarked. A single woman stood not far from us, the blast of the Verdant Moon's engines whipping her hair and jacket into a frenzy. She wore dark, nondescript clothing, and much like the airships, she had no insignia.

The Department of Research operated as ghosts outside its labs.

Wade never hesitated. He walked straight up to the woman, stopping only a metre or so away. The two bowed to each other, and got a few words in before I was close enough to hear what they were saying.

'We'll be taking the subject down to the project level immediately, Master Wizard,' I heard the woman say as I neared. Her voice was mechanical, made all the more so by her having to yell over the airship's roar. 'Is it intact?' she asked, cocking her head and looking at me with electric eyes.

'Better than he's been in two hundred and twelve years, Processor,' Wade growled. Turning to look at us, the wizard waved us forward. 'C'mon, let's go meet the machine.'

The Processor turned on her heel and immediately started walking away. 'Have you briefed it on our safety procedures?' she asked as we fell in line behind her. Before Wade answered, she looked over her shoulder and said, 'Whisper Station's security is enforced by phased units that can move unseen through the facility at high speed. They are equipped with weaponry designed to cause you immense pain but no physical damage. If you disobey, they are authorized to incapacitate you. If you disobey, they are authorized to kill Ceile Angael.'

Looking away, the woman continued, 'As for your magic, you will find it blocked even after Lunaron A34 has left your company. The Station has its own compliment of lunaron support, and you will be passing through their influence as you move through the facility.' She gave Chelle a dirty look. 'Our lunarons are not given the luxury of movement of their own. They provide permanent dead zones to ensure magic does not interfere with our work.'

The young girl suddenly took hold of my hand and tucked in close. There was fear on her face when I looked down. Images of Partridge bolted into the artifact vault's ceiling flickered at the back of my head, the dwarf shifting until he'd been replaced by Chelle's frightened figure. Anger bubbled in my veins.

Whisper Station had a pretty name, but it was anything but. What little I could see of the grounds beyond the airship pad was rough and untamed weeds and scrub. Several plain buildings rose a short way into the sky, uniformly grey-coloured and almost entirely featureless. A handful of windows broke their curved surfaces. Ahead, the concrete dropped, forming into a staircase that descended a few metres to the recessed entrance of a massive bunker, and inside that, a large elevator door.

The Research woman stepped forward and swiped her hand across a flat panel near the door. Instantly there was a low grinding noise, and the door slowly opened. Gesturing for everyone to enter, she followed us in and then swiped her hand across an identical panel inside. A quiet thump later, the door had closed and the elevator was dropping at a quick pace.

The back wall was made of glass, and it was a bit nauseating watching the elevator shaft fly by at this speed. I instead concentrated on the feel of Ceile and Chelle's hands in mine and studying the elevator itself. Thankfully, the car was big, and it wasn't overly claustrophobic with the nine of us in it. Paige and Enak were close, watching Ceile and me carefully, hands on their pistols.

Hanaak leaned casually against the far wall. The 'tiger's arms were folded across his chest, and he was glaring at the floor. I tried to remember where I'd met him before, but couldn't. Next to him, Wade stood at the Processor's shoulder. The wizard looked deep in thought, frowning at the woman beside him.

Weezab just looked mad, standing alone in one corner of the lift.

I wish I knew what he was planning. Between him, Wade, and Bill, I doubted my time here at Whisper would be uneventful. I wondered if the kobold and the wizard were working together. Then I frowned and wondered what the engineer was up to. If all three of them had different plans to get me free, it was going to get really messy.

The elevator shaft abruptly opened up and the view sent my thoughts scattering. I turned and looked out the glass, staring open mouthed at the massive chamber that had been revealed.

'Project Whisper,' the Processor said from behind me.

At the center of the chamber was some kind of gigantic machine. Erupting out of it at every angle and from every direction was a nightmare of pipes and tubes and cables that ran the length of the room, hundreds and hundreds of metres of them that vanished into every nook and cranny. Steam billowed from vents across the machine's surface, hissing out into the air at regular intervals. Arcane energy danced around some of the cables, fuelled by magic users somewhere in the facility.

I didn't know what the machine did, but I knew it was an abomination.

At its base, connected to the machine by a multitude of pipes and other hardware was something I'd seen before. A glass tube, of sorts. Big enough to fit a werewolf.

'That's a regeneration chamber,' I whispered.

'You are incorrect, though the item is based off of similar technology. That is your final resting place. Once you have been installed in it, and fed the proper mixture of drugs, you will be the battery that operates the machine,' the Processor said, her mechanical voice sounding bored. 'Your sentience has caused the Department no end of irritation over the course of your life, and so this has been designed to take advantage of your strength while cutting out that liability.'

I frowned at her over my shoulder. 'You must be a riot at parties,' I said, dryly. The woman chose not to reply.

The project chamber vanished, replaced by the shaft wall once more, and now I idly stared into the blur of concrete and metal. I felt hollow, and a sense of dread was slowly filling up the depths of my mind. I'd known something like this was coming for over a day now, but it was just starting to sink in. We'd come so far, having left the City weeks ago on a quest to regain my youth and avoid my death.

Only to find out we were marching right into it anyway.

The elevator came to a halt not long after the massive test chamber had disappeared above, and the door opened up into a wide room full of medical beds and equipment. All of the beds but one were covered with shrouds. Two people in lab coats stood around the ready one.

They watched us descend the small flight of stairs and move toward them. The Processor brought us to a halt next to the bed. Turning to face us, she said, 'The subject will be prepped here and then taken into the project chamber immediately after. The rest of you will join me in the processing area.' She looked directly at me, and pointed at Ceile. 'If you do not comply, I will begin by removing her limbs. I will strip her of her sight. Then her hearing. And her voice. I will turn her world into a box, a nightmare limbo.'

I snarled and stepped toward the woman. 'And why do I doubt you'll just let her go if I follow the rules?' I said, darkly.

The woman didn't flinch or blink, just continued staring impassively at me. 'Correct. Ceile Angael will be eliminated once you have joined with Whisper,' she said, cocking her head at me. Leaning forward, she continued, 'The difference is that we will be humane about it if you behave.'

Ceile squeezed my hand tightly, but even without looking at her, I knew I wouldn't find fear on her face. She was ready to fight. If the time came, she'd follow me right into the fire, just as we always had.

All the scenarios fired through my mind, all of them ending in our deaths. Without Wade's defection or Weezab's intervention, there was just too much for us to handle. Without my magic, and without knowing more about Whisper's security forces, we couldn't win this fight. I didn't want to just give in, but I didn't want to throw my life away just yet, either.

Finally, I nodded. 'Fine. But I'll want to know she's alright right up until you put me under,' I said. Turning, I enfolded Ceile in a big hug, trying to ignore the dismay on her face. 'This is not the end, my friend. I will see you again,' I whispered in her ear. I felt her nod ever so slightly before we broke away. Looking down at Chelle, I leaned down and kissed her on the forehead. 'Goodbye, Chelle. I hope the book turns out the way you hope it will,' I said, giving her shoulder a squeeze. The young girl looked very sad and gave me a smile.

'Sit,' one of the technicians said, stepping forward and gesturing toward the bed. I nodded, and with a last look at Wade and his group, I threw a leg up onto the chair and skidded myself onto it.

'Come,' I heard the Processor say, and then everyone but the techs and Weezab were following her toward a door at the far end of the chamber. Ceile gave my shoulder a squeeze as she passed. Wade gave me a look that was indecipherable. The others didn't look back.

The strange emptiness that I'd learned to associate with Chelle's presence slowly faded, replaced by a different one. This shadow seemed to flicker, and it was almost like I could just make out the Suns on the other side of it. I wondered if whatever awfulness Research had done to the lunaron responsible had made it vulnerable. I stuck a finger into a crack and felt it slide away. I frowned inside. I might not be stuck in a black hole, but I was still just as imprisoned as I had been when Chelle was nearby.

'Get moving, kobold. Your contract has ended,' the other technician said, scowling at the little creature.

Weezab ignored her, and came up to stand beside me. Reaching up on the tips of his toes, he put both hands and his snout on the arm of my bed and stared balefully at me. 'I'll be around,' he said, suddenly, then dropped to his feet and stalked away.

The techs shook their heads at each other and then got to work. I was given food and water, and the two talked quietly as they checked my vitals. It was odd watching them work, completely free of magic. For the better part of a millennia, humans had walked an arcane path, second only to the gnomes in magical ability, and borrowing or stealing enough science know-how from the dwarves and elves to fill some of the gaps. Sure, I drove a car and watched a TV, but those were novelties, really. My life had, until recently, revolved around the mystic.

But then, Research had always done whatever it needed to adapt.

Other than to ask me to lift an arm or to cough, the man and woman had nothing to say to me, and I was left alone with my thoughts while they poked and prodded. Edgar Lorn's memories waited at the back of my mind, raw and alien, and I picked them over slowly, discovering and remembering at the same time. It was a terrible feeling, not helped by how different I looked now then what I saw when Edgar looked in the mirror.

A dull ache settled in somewhere behind my eyes, and I reached up to rub them. Weeks ago, I'd just been an archon with some, well, quirks. If you can consider fifty missing years and a psychopath sharing my body quirks, anyway. Now I was something far bigger. A solaron. A solaron that had murdered his family and millions more, and then unwittingly changed reality to hide from those crimes. I looked down at my hands, staring into their rejuvenated palms. So much blood had spilled because of me.

No, because of them.

I went very still as the words echoed through my mind. The voice was mine, but I wasn't its source. It skittered along the edges of my brain, then faded into the depths. Hesitantly, watching both techs to see if they were paying attention, I whispered, 'Are - are you there?' under my breath.

There was nothing but the flicker of the memories in response.

My pulse was thumping loudly in my ears. The Other was gone, unravelled during the craziness I'd encountered on the trip. I'd given form to a darker side of myself, given it life. I'd spoken to it and it had replied. I'd thought I shared my body with this monster, when all along the monster had been me. I knew that now.

Every second that passed, the whisper grew fainter and fainter but the words did not. They resounded, bracketing the memories and getting brighter. I turned them over, examining each letter and syllable, and slowly nodded. There was truth in them, and as I sat there, being prepped for a lifetime of drugged imprisonment, they began to fill my mind.

The Government put me on this path.

Bill set me in this direction.

No one would have died if they had left me alone.

My family would still be alive if they had left me alone.

They made me.

This time, the whisper doesn't take my breath away, and though I still searched the murk for that familiar presence, I knew there was nothing there to find. 'They made me,' I repeated, nodding again, ignoring the strange looks the technicians sent my way. It made sense. They'd wanted a weapon, and they'd twisted my mind until it shattered.

Rage set the blood in my veins boiling, and my face split in an evil sneer. Understanding slowly bloomed, backlighting the images of chaos and death that floated listlessly at the back of my mind. The memories that the regeneration chamber had given back to me had also gifted me with a growing self-hatred, but now I understood that that hatred was misplaced.

These people weren't murdered.

They were collateral damage.

Part of me wasn't as convinced by these sudden revelations, but it was quickly buried in the growing fervor I had for them. Hints of fear and distrust were crushed as I grabbed hold of the words and made them mine. I'd been prepared, even if I hadn't admitted it to myself, to die for the blood on my hands. Now, I understood that I was just the instrument, and the people who had used me were the ones that had to be punished.

Something black and ugly slithered along the lunaron's effect, and I felt the emptiness shudder.

Now the thoughts were coming through in a rush, and I breathed deep, trying to settle down. Something didn't feel right, even as I nodded my acceptance of the words. I felt a little shocked by how quickly things were moving, but when I tried to consider what had happened, I found myself drowning in the weight of the belief that I wasn't responsible. I gulped for air, only vaguely aware of the techs clutching my arms, trying to hold me down as I bucked in the bed.

But as darkness slowly crept over my sight and an angry buzzing filled my ears, I found that panic fading and a calm indifference settling in. I just couldn't fight anymore. The anger I had for myself, the anger that was slowly boiling over the people that had pulled my strings, it was rolling outward in a cloud of rage that had replaced my entire world.

Suddenly, it wasn't just about the Government, or about Bill.

The emptiness shuddered again.

When it was just me and the hatred and nothing else, I knew that it was about everyone.

Everyone should have just left me alone.

And so everyone gets to die.

'The anomalies have stopped. Lunaron B56 nearly perished, but we were able to bring an auxiliary example in to assist. The subject has stabilized, vitals are back to base line and it appears to be resting,' I heard an unfamiliar voice say. The words bubble through the darkness of my non-existence.

'What the hell happened? He couldn't have been responsible for that, could he? Lunarons are black holes, you can't just break a black hole,' a different voice said, full of irritation. Each word brings a flicker of light that arcs across my oblivion.

'Unknown. The reaction occurred immediately after the technicians administered the obedience chemical, and the anomalies in the lunaron effect started only seconds later. They claim the subject was speaking to itself during the event, which is not entirely unexpected given its history, but had been deemed unlikely after exposure to the artifact,' the first responded.

I opened my eyes, slowly, and my world resolves into being. The medical chamber was gone, and I found myself tucked carefully into a secured gurney being wheeled along a corridor. My arms, legs, and head were strapped tightly to the bed, which meant the only thing I could see much of was the ceiling passing overhead.

'If it's the drugs, can we risk putting him into Whisper? He needs to be pacified in order for the project to succeed. If a single dose brought his sunny happy side out to play, how do we know a full treatment won't let the Other out?' Second said. A woman, walking somewhere over my right shoulder. She didn't sound like she was pleased to be here.

First clucked her tongue, a metallic sound that matched the dull monotone of her voice. 'The reaction passed, without our intervention. Our calculations show that the chance of a full relapse is almost non-existent. The subject's instabilities remain contained, the balancing persona still intact,' she said from somewhere near my feet.

The two fell silent, and for a short while nothing but the quiet creak of the gurney's wheels filled the hall.

'Even if the Edgar Lorn entity were to surface, the power remains tied to the subject. Once it has joined with the Project, whether Lorn is in charge or Tundra, it will not matter. Inside Whisper, our world does not exist,' First said, breaking the silence.

Their world will not exist.

There was a sharp bang, and then I was rolling through a wide doorway into a massive chamber. From my limited view, I recognized the pipes and cables that hung from the ceiling and climbed the walls. I'd entered Whisper's lair.

Compared to the quiet and calm of the corridor, this place was a riot of noise and light. A low alarm rumbled through a cacophony of voices, hissing gases, the snap and crackle of sparking electricity, and a dozen different thrums and hums that I felt vibrating through my bed. High overhead, scattered among the spider's web of cables and wires were hundreds of flickering lights.

Soon, the top of the machine came into view, spiraling down from the ceiling like some mechanical tornado. There seemed to be no pattern or design to the monstrosity. It was all straight edges but random angles that cycled downward until they came to rest at the foot of the glass tube I'd seen from the elevator.

There had been groups of people gathered around the base as we approached, but they quickly turned and headed for the exits as I was wheeled toward my cell. The alarm got louder and more insistent.

I felt hands running up and down my arms and legs, more poking and prodding. 'I hope you're right,' Second hissed at First. 'He's ready, put him in,' she said, addressing someone else.

My straps fell loose and then I was being lifted free of the bed. My head lolled around painfully, despite my efforts to control it. Whatever they'd shot me up with, it was doing its job. I caught a brief glimpse of the two women, both dressed in basic Research uniforms and watching me quietly. Four others had hold of my body, all in full white lab coats and masks. Only one of them looked at me.

There was terror in his eyes.

Nothing but ash beneath the Suns.

A glass door slid open with a vile hiss, and then I was being tied into a different bed, one that was almost the spitting image of that in the regeneration chamber. The four men and women were rough but quick. Only minutes later, I was alone inside the tube, staring through the transparent top toward the ceiling far above.

'Go!' I heard Second yell from nearby, and then there was the sound of a handful of people running for the exit. For a brief moment, I thought I'd been completely abandoned, but then the woman's face popped into view next to my bed.

'Hello, Mr. Tundra,' she said, her face expressionless. 'I wish I had more time. There is so much we could learn from you.' I felt a sharp pain as she pushed a needle into the soft skin on the inside of my arm. 'They want you lost and vacant, mindlessly spewing destruction across the continent, when we could be looking for ways to fix things.' Her voice was bitter. Reaching up, she pulled a wide mask from the side of the tube and then draped it carefully over my face. Slightly muffled, she continued, 'The energy you use, it created this world. It created every world! Everything that went wrong could be fixed.'

She shook her head, peering at me through my mask. 'We were so close,' she whispered, just loud enough for me to hear. Falling silent, the woman moved in and out of my sight, and I heard switches being flicked and keys being pressed.

Then she reappeared in front of me, and leaned in very close. There was anger in her eyes. 'We did this to you, Mr. Tundra. Remember that,' she hissed, then backed away and vanished. Shortly afterward, I heard the door of the tube slide shut, blocking out everything but the rasp of gas flowing through the mask on my face and my own ragged breathing.

There was a sharp click, and then I felt a painful heat spread outward from the needle in my arm, a jagged fire seeping through my veins. With terrifying swiftness, my mind and body came back to consciousness.

They took them from me.

Fury ripples across my body, and I savagely jerked at my straps. The haze that had held my mind steady while they rolled me out here burnt away in the flames writhing in my blood. I surged up in the bed, slamming against the ends of my restraints and then holding there, straining violently against them. The liquid anger washes over me, pouring from my arm into my chest and then erupting into my head.

In that place between this realm and that between, I felt the ragged emptiness where my magic once waited. With each thunderous heartbeat, I saw waves shimmer along its surface. Alarms began to sound inside my tube, but I was hardly listening, watching that black nothingness pulse as it tried to stand in my way.

A high pitched whine burst into existence inside the tube, and then I felt the whole thing begin to vibrate. A dull thump sounded from the machinery outside that drowned out everything, and after a short pause, came again. It repeated, gaining in frequency until it moaned on in a constant beat. Far above, I saw cables and pipes shake violently and then rock back and forth. Dust fell, quickly blurring my view of the ceiling.

I thrashed as Project Whisper came alive. Brilliant lights flared into existence outside, blinding me, and then everything went tight as I was suddenly slammed back against the bed. Pain ripped through my mind, and now I was nothing but agony and anger. A gap opened in the emptiness between, and energy roared in through it, erupting from my body and lancing into the walls of the tube around me. I screamed as the Suns answered Whisper's call, their blood pouring through me and into the machine's waiting arms.

The world disintegrated, and I found myself floating in that strange limbo once again, orbiting White and Blue as I tumbled through space. A weaving, chaotic line of energy connected me to both stars, and looking over my shoulder, I saw a different line arc from me into the distance, vanishing as the energy passed through some terribly dark point behind. My body shook in the face of all that power, and nothing I did could slow or alter its path. I was just the gateway now.

'Is this really how you're going to let this end, Martin?'

I spun back toward the Suns and found Edgar Lorn floating there in front of me.

121

'I'm glad that here, at the end of everything, I get a chance to talk to myself again,' I said, dryly.

Edgar's face was expressionless, and he shook his head. 'Sadly, my friend, you are not.'

The lines that spiraled between me and the Suns crackled and pulsed with power as I frowned at him. 'What do you mean?' I asked.

'I mean, Martin Tundra, that I am not you. And vice versa,' the man said, then fell silent.

Now I was the one shaking my head. 'Then who are you?' I said.

He chuckled. 'I'm Edgar Lorn, of course,' he answered with a wry smile.

'Aren't I Edgar Lorn?' I asked, confused. It seemed like the universe had decided my life needed to be even more complicated, even at its end.

'No, Martin. You aren't,' Edgar said.

A planet whirled past, briefly obscuring him, before vanishing into the distance. I saw a shroud of shimmering light slowly closing over its surface, devouring the lands below.

Edgar's eyes followed the world until it was gone, then looked back at me. 'There isn't much time. Research might think they've got all the angles covered, but they have no idea what they're dealing with. Whisper is going to come apart at the seams, and we aren't going to have a chance to talk again once it does,' he said.

'I don't understand. Isn't the whole point of everything that's happened that I'm actually you?' I snarled, anger rising. Energy erupted from me, blasting out into space, and I heard an odd wailing noise from the dark place over my shoulder. 'I remember that life! I remember living it!' I howled.

Edgar put his hands up, making soothing gestures. 'Listen to me, Martin. You are not me, despite what you've been led to believe. You have my memories because I needed a place to crash when my body came apart, and you were the unlucky recipient,' he said, coming closer.

'Then who am I?' I demanded.

The man shook his head. 'You're a flesh construct. Of sorts,' he said, gently.

Space did a barrel roll, and Suns and planets and moons spun wildly through the heavens. The lines coiled violently and sparked. The wailing behind me got louder. 'What?' I said, raggedly, as the man and I stood at the center of the chaos.

'I never was very stable, Martin. There were cracks long before the Government got their hands on me, and years of Peter's education just made them worse. When I finally broke, it wasn't pretty. They managed to pull my body out of the carnage, but the damage was done. I was dying, and that meant all of my power would be out of their reach forever,' Edgar said, gesturing out into space. 'Peter had, as he usually does, been planning for that kind of thing. When my body finally died, he had you there, waiting. Him and an army of wizards, that is.'

He stepped yet closer, and leaned in until we were almost nose to nose. 'They tore me out of my corpse and dropped me into your brain,' he whispered. His face was sympathetic.

Anger rippled through my mind, and I clenched my fists. 'Bill said my magic warped my body, changed its looks. Wade said you couldn't transfer a solaron. If I'm not you, then why haven't you talked to me before?' I shouted, the words coming out in a furious rush.

Edgar shook his head. 'Peter is a liar, Martin. He's been telling you what he needed you to hear all along. And poor Wade is just as taken in as you. The whole Government is. They knew so little about solarons, and craved that power. When Peter showed up, and proved that he had information they didn't, they leaned more and more on him. Everything they've done to secure me, they've done on his recommendation,' he said. 'But, technically, Wade's right. You can't transfer a solaron into a construct. What Peter did to you and me was something different.'

The man reached up and tapped his temple. 'You were just supposed to host me for a while, until they could get me into a new model without losing my magic. Nobody's ever done that, Martin! Peter brought that spell to the table, and it killed every wizard involved. At the end of it, you and he were the only ones left standing, but I was more or less safely locked in your head,' he said, excited. 'Of course, nothing's that easy. It messed you up bad, and to make matters worse, we weren't completely separate from each other. You started picking up new tricks, courtesy of my connection to the Suns, and you did it very quickly.'

The galaxy rocked again, and I could hear alarms and smell smoke. Edgar looked over my shoulder, and his eyes got wide. Before I could say anything, he spoke again. 'Look, I'm sorry this is how it had to be. When you started tapping into the Suns, they didn't need me anymore. It's no longer about finding me a new body. They can just use you for the rest of time. I'm just a relic, one more artifact of the past,' he said, shaking his head.

'But I remember it like I was there! James, Nala, Katherine! Mom and Dad! Fifty-two years! If those memories aren't mine, then why can't I remember anything else?' I asked, looking down at my hands.

I didn't recognize them. 'Who am I?' I whispered, looking back up at him.

Edgar shook his head again, and his face was sad. 'I don't know, Martin. Peter didn't explain, and I wasn't in any shape to ask. You were there, and willingly, when they wheeled me into the room. You knew what was about to happen,' he said, quietly. Astral energy raged around him as the lines connecting me to the Suns snapped and vibrated violently. 'Peter knows, Martin! And he's going to come for you. This has been his game all along.'

The alarms and wailing were quickly getting louder, and my chest was feeling tight. 'Why didn't you ever say anything? Why didn't you ever talk to me?' I demanded, yelling over the noise.

'I did, Martin. I just didn't know who I was until the walls started really coming down,' he shouted. The man suddenly reached up and caught hold of my shoulder, and now his face was intense. 'I'm fading, Martin! Peter's spell gave you my strength, and there's nothing left to hold me here. Whatever happens next, I won't be there to help, and so I need to ask you a favour!'

The space around us shuddered, and now I was having trouble breathing. Edgar's grip tightened. 'I've done terrible things, Martin. I've murdered so many people. I didn't mean to! I never wanted to hurt anyone. I just wanted to be left alone,' he shouted. 'All that blood deserves justice, Martin, but I won't be here to feed it. There's no punishment waiting for me in oblivion, regardless of how much I earned it. But Peter! His words stand behind each and every one of the lives I took, Martin!'

He caught hold of my other shoulder and shook me. 'Make him suffer!' he roared.

Then the universe imploded and I found myself back in Whisper's lair. My tube was full of smoke, and I coughed violently. The mask kicked slightly askew, and I could see cracks were forming in the glass walls around me. The chamber rocked, and a bundle of pipe and cable crashed down from somewhere above, smashing into the top of my cell and rolling away into the murk.

Energy was still pouring into the machine from me, but whatever had woken me up hadn't also given me back control. The power raged through my arms, and I felt raw and burnt inside. Tears leaked from my eyes, courtesy of the stinging smoke. Outside, I could see flickering flames in the shadows. Something was obviously not right with Whisper.

There was an explosion from somewhere nearby, and the wall to my side shattered, sending jagged pieces of glass and metal rocketing into the tube. I closed my eyes and tried to jerk my head to the side, narrowly avoiding losing an eye but getting a deep gouge in my cheek as a nasty piece of shrapnel slashed past. Blood very quickly began dripping from my jaw.

I opened my eyes, shook my head and looked around to see the damage. The restraints that had kept my head flat against the bed were gone, hanging cut against the frame. I hadn't been quite so lucky with the others, but at least I could see. Debris littered the inside of the tube, and cracks were slowly skittering along the glass in front of me.

Outside, the smoke whirled and danced, and for a brief moment I caught a glimpse of something moving before the shroud closed in again. The room shook again, and I coughed as the murk thickened and stole away my all-important oxygen. My eyes swam with tears and the world suddenly got distant, with even the roar of the fires and explosions seeming to be very far away.

Then the door to the tube was thrown open, and a battered-looking Agent Paige was at my side. The effect was immediate. A fail safe tripped, and my connection to the Suns and to Whisper was cut off with violent swiftness. The sudden shock threatened to knock me unconscious, and I felt like I was on fire.

With a few slashes of her combat knife, Paige cut me free of the bed, my fall stopped short by the timely assistance of an equally battered-looking Wade. The wizard yelled something into my ear, but I didn't catch it in my daze. There was worry on his face as he pulled me from the damaged tube and dragged me out onto the project floor. At Whisper's base, he gently lowered me to the ground, crouching next to me as Paige slid in on the other side. In the smoke, I thought I saw the form of a big weretiger lurking not far away.

There were dead men around us, all in Research's basic brown uniforms. Most of them had been horribly burnt, and big patches of the concrete in the area were scarred black or even glowing faintly red.

Pale purple lights burst into existence around Wade's left hand and began to drift around his fingers. 'Martin! Can you hear me? Are you alright?' he yelled, his other hand gripping my shoulder tightly. Paige's eyes were darting around the smoke, nervous.

I blinked rapidly, and raised a numb hand to my face to swipe drunkenly at my eyes. 'I- I don't know,' I tried to say. My throat was raw and the words hurt. Hell, everything hurt. Something big collapsed nearby, sending pieces of metal and plastic sliding past.

The wizard must have heard me, as he nodded sadly. 'Well, this is us rescuing you. I probably should have come up with a plan, but we're doing it live instead. Ceile's up ahead. Enak's dead, bastard caught a bullet with his face,' he said, upset. 'I was going to do this quietly, but the instant we killed the first lunaron, the kobold lost his mind.'

Now he shook his head. 'He's on a rampage, and if we don't get the hell out of here, he'll bring the damn place down on our heads.'

122

Sure enough, the lunaron's effect was gone, but even the softest reach for the Suns made my head buzz and my body shake. Whisper hadn't been gentle. As if to mock me, the machine's lights continued to pulse despite the slow destruction of its lair.

With Wade's help, I was up off the ground and limping steadily through the smoke. Paige materialized in and out of the smoke, pistol out and searching for threats. Hanaak was a ghost, and I only knew he was still out there through brief flashes of orange fur in the murk.

'I don't know if Weezab's on our side or not, but so far he's been content to keep his fire aimed at Research. Not that he's being gentle about it. The instant Paige put a blade in that lunaron's back, the project command room exploded. If there's anyone alive on that floor, they're probably not healthy,' the wizard shouted into my ear. He paused long enough to send a lance of killing light shooting into the smoke, answered by a scream from somewhere beyond. 'The whole station is burning now. The kobold's been thorough. This chamber was set to flood with poison in the event anything went wrong, and the little bastard lit the stuff up the instant it started pouring in through the vents.'

Whisper had begun to hum, and a hurried glance over my shoulder saw its lights settle into rhythm with the new song. Wade noticed my look, and he shook his head. 'It's alive, Martin, and it's out of control. The science and engineering people we've run into in the mess are freaking out. Whisper has enough of a charge to do something really bad, and it sounds like that's just what it's going to do,' he said. 'Everyone that isn't here to try and kill us is heading for the surface, screaming like school children.'

I coughed. 'Chelle?' I managed to ask, my voice hoarse.

The wizard gave me a tight smile. 'She's gone. Hanaak took her to the surface before we came knocking. The poor bastards that Research had wired into the damn station couldn't be saved, but there wasn't any reason for the girl to die. The 'tiger sent her east, across the plain. She's smart, she'll get to cover and wait out the storm,' he said.

There was something in his tone of voice, but I couldn't place it. 'So what's the plan?' I asked, searching the smoke for trouble. The haze had closed in around us, and even Whisper's lights had vanished.

'Ceile is holding the elevator, more or less. We found a secondary lift that the kobold hasn't destroyed, in a quieter section of the station. Provided it's intact when we get there, we'll take it up, otherwise, we'll have to take the stairs,' Wade answered. A deep cut on the wizard's forehead was oozing blood down the side of his face. 'Weezab cut

Research's head off when he wiped out the command centre. We're running into scattered units, but with communications down and nobody in charge, it's been a little too easy. They got reckless with Whisper, Martin! They've kept the station even more under wraps than usual, operating with as few personnel as possible.'

He leaned in close, and now there was an evil smile on his face. 'Most of them think you escaped on your own. Hardly anybody wants to come in here looking for you. They know what you are. They might have been ordered to try and recapture you, but leadership has gone dark, and everybody knows the next step after the station is lost is to turn the place to dust,' he said with a smirk.

I shook my head, imagining the explosives lining the walls of the facility. 'So why haven't they killed us all? How long has it been?' I asked.

'Half an hour or so. They pinned us down just outside the project chamber, and it was slow going. As for why they haven't atomized us, my best guess is that either they've lost the ability to do so, or they're a little too invested to let you go,' he shouted. Purple fire erupted from his free hand, catching hold of a soldier that appeared from the smoke and throwing her screaming into the distance.

The haze suddenly gave way, and then we were passing through a pair of shattered doors into a hallway. More dead guards littered the plain white floors, though there were non-combat personnel mixed in with them. These people had died trying to keep Wade and his group from getting in, but judging by the state of them and the corridor, Hanaak had ambushed them from behind.

More than one or two had terror frozen on their faces, but something made me think it wasn't entirely fear of the weretiger. The nightmare scenario for this facility was me getting loose, and it had happened.

Paige and the 'tiger fell in behind us as Wade and I moved through the corpses. The cacophony of the chamber behind us steadily collapsing began to fade, replaced with the low wail of a siren echoing through the lifeless hall. I struggled to keep on my feet, leaning heavily on the wizard as we went.

'Your magic, Martin. Do you have it back?' he asked, looking at me out of the corner of his eye. There was hope in his voice.

I shook my head and shivered. 'It's there, but I can't reach it. Hurts like hell. I don't know what they did to me, but it wasn't nice,' I said, raggedly.

The wizard sighed. 'I figured that was the case. I'm hoping we won't run into full blown resistance, but if we do, I hope you'll have it back. I'm sure Research has one or two archons or aethons kicking around, and I'm not built to take on that kind of firepower,' he said.

Rounding a corner, I saw Ceile drop into a firing position, a pistol aimed at us in each hand. With a huge smile, she leapt to her feet and raced toward us, holstering a pistol with lightning quickness and taking Wade's place under my arm. She gave me a tight hug, and whispered, 'I am happy to see you alive, my friend.'

I gave her a squeeze and a weak smile. 'Barely. I feel like crap. How do I look?' I asked.

'Like you have some new grey hairs,' she said, suddenly frowning. Then she shook her head and pulled me gently in behind Wade as we headed for the elevator. 'Later. The elevator is still intact, and from what I can tell, Weezab has left the structure alone,' she told the wizard.

'Here's hoping it stays that way,' he said, grabbing hold of the dead soldier Ceile had propped up to keep the lift door open and skidding him out of the way. Standing in the doorway, he waved us in. Once Hanaak had ducked past, the wizard slid in and hammered the top level button.

Down the hall, the tone of Whisper's hum suddenly grew in pitch and volume. The corridor started to shake, and I felt the elevator wall begin to vibrate.

'Crap,' Paige whispered as the door slid shut and the lift rose.

Wade spun to look at me and Ceile. 'Whisper's awake, and I don't know what that's going to mean for us. It's not aimed at anything! I don't know if that means it's going to fire into the atmosphere or just blow up. Either of those is very bad. Especially for us!' he hissed. The lights dancing around his fingers flared briefly, then vanished. 'Once we hit the surface, we grab a ship and get the hell out of here, or barring that, we head for the hills. If we can't escape by air, our safest bet is to ride out the storm in the mountains, find a cave system and lie low until Whisper's burnt off everything you gave it.'

Hanaak cursed as the elevator bucked and his head and the ceiling made acquaintance. 'The Moon is long gone, not surprising, but there are a few patrol craft up there that we should be able to fire up and run with. It'll be a packed house, they aren't exactly meant for five, let alone four and a 'thrope, but that's our exit plan,' the big 'tiger growled, rubbing his scalp.

Ceile made the rounds, quietly healing what wounds everyone had, and I felt some of my discombobulation fade as the water magic rained down around me. Wade nodded his thanks as the gash on his head knitted back together and vanished, leaving dried and flaking blood behind. Paige smiled weakly and gave my friend's arm a squeeze. Hanaak just grunted.

The buzz in the metal continued, but as our lift shuddered its way toward the surface, we soon left Whisper's howl and wail behind. I leaned heavily against the side of the car, breathing deep to try and soothe whatever injury the machine had done to me inside. Edgar's words echoed at the back of my head, and somewhere in the depths I felt the rage burning. The fury that had set me alight back in the medical lab was still present, lurking beneath my skin.

My heart was in my stomach as I watched the numbers drop toward zero on the elevator's readout. I was starting to smell smoke again, and I wondered where the kobold was. If the scaly creature was waiting for us up there, I hoped he was going to play nice. He wanted me free, too, but whether or not he wanted to share that prize with someone else was up in the air. Looking around at my saviours, I shook my head. If Weezab decided they were in the way, I didn't know if they were going to survive the encounter, unless Wade got the drop on him.

'Get ready,' the wizard suddenly said, breaking the silence. 'Research has had plenty of time to get people up here, and this is the direction most people were headed to begin with. Plus, that damn kobold is out there somewhere, too.'

Hanaak stepped forward, crouching in front of the door. Paige drew her pistol and stepped to his shoulder, at the ready. Arcane lights ignited at Wade's fingertips. Ceile got under my arm again and guided me gently to the far end of the car, pulling her gun free with her other hand.

I leaned up and gave her a kiss on the cheek, which made her smile. 'Thank you, Ceile,' I whispered, giving her a quick squeeze. 'Thank you for everything.'

A tear leaked down the side of her face, and she returned my hug. 'You are welcome, my friend. I love you,' she said, quietly.

'I love you, too,' I said with a smile, and then we turned to watch the number tick to a halt. The car slowed, and then stopped. The door hissed open, and we all flinched away as blistering heat and smoke billowed in. The hallway outside was engulfed in an inferno.

In the middle of the firestorm was Weezab, and the kobold smiled evilly when he saw me.

'What are you waiting for, idiots? C'mon!' he yelled, waving us forward. The raging flames parted, and fresh air and ash blew in from the corridor.

Hanaak didn't hesitate. The big weretiger charged out of the elevator, tucked in tight to avoid the roaring fires. Paige was right behind him, giving the kobold an indecipherable look as she passed the little creature.

Wade was next, and he paused as he neared Weezab. 'Unless you want to see how well you can firewalk, wizard, you'd best keep your magic to yourself,' the kobold snarled, and the inferno groaned in his grasp. The wizard threw a glance my direction, then nodded and bolted after the 'tiger and Agent.

When Ceile and I staggered up to him, the kobold settled in on my other side and the three of us followed in the others' wakes. 'You look like hell,' he snarled, scanning my face and shaking his head. 'What'd they do to you?'

'Nothing pleasant,' I shouted over the noise. 'I'm free, but reaching for energy isn't working out well for me at the moment. I'm not going to be much use in a fight.'

Weezab growled. 'Well, you'd better keep trying. I've been incinerating anything I see, but you guys took your sweet time getting up here. Who knows what Research has got waiting for us outside, and we can't exactly just hang tight. Whisper is losing its mind down there,' he said, waving over his shoulder.

Ahead, Hanaak and Paige had arrived at the end of the hall. The twisted remains of a big metal door were hanging from the frame, partially melted and pitted with debris. A cold wind was howling in through the gap, and as we approached, I could see a flight of stairs on the opposite side and a hint of a twilight sky beyond.

We huddled down in the cover of the wreckage, and Wade looked over at the kobold. 'Got a plan, kobold?' he hissed. 'Any idea what's out there?'

Weezab shook his head. 'Probably something bad. We're lucky that they apparently want Martin alive, or we'd all be dead already. That gives us pretty good odds that they aren't going to just hit us with something heavy if we poke our heads out,' he said.

'Lunarons?' Paige asked. She was trying to peek out around the door frame.

The kobold barked a laugh. 'I'm going out swinging, so it won't matter if they have an army of them out there. I assume we want to grab an airship, so I'll try and avoid charring those,' he snarled.

Looking over at Wade, his eyes narrowed. 'Watch my back, wizard, and I'll make sure I don't char you and your friends, too.'

Wade smirked, and patted idly at a patch on his robe that had started burning. 'Do what you have to do, Weezab. Just get us out of here,' he said. Hanaak and Paige looked unhappy, but nodded.

The kobold looked at me, and the look on his face was grim. 'Stay close. Feel free to be useful,' he said, and red flames suddenly flickered into existence in his palms. When I nodded, the little creature darted around the corner and scrambled toward the stairs.

I gently pulled Ceile, and we carefully stepped around the debris and followed in Weezab's wake. I was moving easier, no longer needing to lean on my friend as much, but my breath came hard and heavy as we moved out into open air toward the stairs. The wind wailed around us, drowning out the distant shriek of the monster at Whisper Station's heart. Dust and dirt whistled past, blowing in over the edge.

Wade, Hanaak, and Paige closed in behind us, and I saw the wizard's lips and hands moving as he prepared his magic. We hit the bottom of the stairs as the kobold crested the top.

And the sky above ignited in a wave of red flame that rocketed out in every direction, fire lashing out from Weezab's hands into the storm. The shock wave almost took me to my knees, and I had to catch the railing hard to keep from falling. We struggled up the stairs, and came to a halt at the kobold's back as his magic turned the world around us into a living inferno.

A hundred metres away, a massive dome of almost transparent light sparked and pulsed under the onslaught of flame. Inside, a dozen men and women held their hands high, trying to maintain their protection against the kobold's wrath, while another forty gathered around them, weapons raised and aimed at us.

Wade shouted a word of power, and a shield of our own materialized around us. 'There, Weezab! The assault ship!' he yelled in the kobold's ear, pointing out into the storm at a small airship to our left, parked at the edge of the landing pad we'd come in on.

The little creature nodded viciously. 'Let's go!' he snarled, as he sent a string of fireballs rocketing out toward the Research personnel.

In return, the soldiers opened fire, and rounds started cooking off in the furious heat of Weezab's magic or slamming violently against Wade's shield. A cloud of acid rain sprung to life overhead, guided by one of the Research elementalists, but her strength paled against the kobold's, and it hissed away in the wind, a cloud of poisonous gas. The earth rumbled, and a column of stone burst from the ground nearby, lancing into the shimmering wall of the shield next to me. The shock sent Paige tumbling, but Hanaak caught her and set the

Agent right. She nodded thanks and sent a hail of gunfire flying our enemies' way.

The plain had been almost barren to begin with, but Weezab's influence was turning anything that lived to ash and charring the dirt. The wind, whipped to a frenzy by the heat, whirled between our legs and carried the ruin away until we were walking on hard clay and stone. The railing of the stair way began to glow red as we left it behind.

A flash of light from the rear of the Research dome drew my eye, and I looked over in time to see an arcane heavy slug, glimmering wildly as it fought Weezab's magic, blast toward us from behind their ranks. I caught hold of Ceile and pulled her to the ground as the round powered into our shield and exploded.

Wade was strong, and the kobold's magic had robbed the shell of some of its strength, but it still hit like a house. Weezab was lifted free of the ground and tossed away, twirling violently. Wade rolled past, blood pouring from a big gash in his chest. Paige vanished in an eruption of dust and dirt.

Hanaak fell to the ground next to me, the weretiger missing most of his upper half.

I couldn't hear anything but a high pitched whine, and I blinked rapidly as my eyes tried to regain focus. Ceile was close, looking dazed but alive. She shouted something I couldn't hear, clutching my shoulder painfully. I looked over at her, and watched as a storm of gunfire and magic suddenly rained down toward us out of the chaos.

My friend threw herself over me, but at the last second, the oncoming danger burst in an explosion of light and sound as it slammed into a new shield. From underneath Ceile's body, I saw Wade on his side, propped up by an elbow, his free hand held into the air as he desperately maintained the dome. His head kept drooping, and he looked pale and hurt.

Ceile was up, and Agent Paige caught hold of my hand and lifted me up with her. 'Go!' the Enforcement woman yelled, shoving the two of us toward the airship as she turned to help Wade. Above us, Weezab's firestorm had gone mad, tendrils of crimson flame whipping around the plain, carving deep scars in the ground and lancing viciously across the Research shield. The dome flickered briefly, just long enough for the wild magic to turn two soldiers into candles before their protection could return.

A bolt of lightning blasted through our shield, narrowly missing Ceile. Through the murk, I heard Wade scream with the effort of closing the gap, and I knew that it was only because of the kobold's inferno that he hadn't been overwhelmed by the Research people. If they had any aethons or archons, they were probably busy keeping the fire from killing every last one of them.

I put a foot down and almost fell in surprise when it landed on concrete. We'd finally reached the landing pad. I turned to the others to give them some encouragement, just in time to watch a beam of purple light lance through Wade's shield and hit Paige in the back. The Agent never saw it coming. Without so much as a whimper, she disintegrated, collapsing into a cloud of dust that wisped away in the wind.

Deprived of his support, the wizard crashed to the ground, and our shield crackled out of existence as he did. Staggering, I skidded to my knees and caught his arm, the two of us struggling to our feet as death rained down around. Research had apparently decided I wasn't worth keeping alive, and now we were in a lot of trouble.

'We're almost there, hurry!' I yelled. The airship was so close, and I looked wildly back as I tried to keep Wade from falling.

The firestorm was coming apart, but our enemies weren't getting away without a scratch. The wild magic collapsed, tearing through their dome and turning half of them into ash in a heartbeat. The survivors broke ranks, racing toward us through the dissipating fires. Frantically, I called for the Suns, and I howled as astral energy raged into me, the pain threatening to drag me unconscious. I tumbled, falling free of Wade and Ceile, trying to bring the power to bear, but there just wasn't time.

I threw my hands to the sky as bullet and fireball and lightning bolt and death ray plunged from the heavens to meet me.

With a roar of noise that pierced my numbed hearing, the air shimmered and then erupted in an explosion of flame that rippled like water and lit the countryside for kilometres around. Not a single thing made it through, and when I looked over my shoulder, I found a very battered-looking Weezab standing over me, his arms wide and mouth snarling words of power.

The wave of soldiers and magic users broke as the former tried to flee for cover and the latter tried to summon it to them, but the kobold wasn't having any of it. With an evil laugh, he sent the wall of rippling flame rocketing forward, rolling right over every one of the Research men and women. Some of them dropped to the ground, screaming in agony as the kobold's magic charred their flesh. Some of them burst into flame, flailing wildly and rolling in the ash.

Some of them just disappeared, turned to dust in the fire's fury.

In an instant, it was over. The wave flickered and fell apart, and the storm broke. Night fell, the shadows no longer chased away by the flame. The last of our enemies died or dropped unconscious, and then it was just the four of us, huddled on the concrete, kissed by the chill wind.

'You did it, kobold,' Wade said, hoarsely. The wizard coughed as he nodded at Weezab. 'I've never seen that kind of power, it was-'

He never got the chance to finish. The kobold coldly looked over at him, and then lit the wizard on fire.

124

'Weezab, no!' I roared as Wade's body slumped to the ground, smoking. I staggered to my feet, but a flash of flickering fire lifted me off the ground and slammed me down a few metres away. Ceile snarled something, but the kobold caught her and threw her away, too. My friend crashed down painfully, and I heard several vile snaps as she tumbled into the dust.

I managed to prop myself up with an elbow as Weezab stepped slowly toward me, hands spinning lazily as he molded the fire aether into magic. 'I said I'd get you out, I didn't say anything about them. Now, unless you want our friend Ceile over there to experience the same fate, I'd suggest you show a little gratitude and we get the hell out of here before Whisper kills all of us,' he snarled, a wicked grin on his face. Motes of flame spun around his wrists, and I felt the air shiver with heat.

As if to punctuate his words, the ground suddenly shook violently, and the little creature stumbled. He looked a lot less sure of himself as he turned and beckoned me toward the airship. 'C'mon, hurry. I can't imagine why you'd be all that upset that I'd killed one more Government employee, considering he helped bring you in in the first place,' he said, turning away.

Everyone gets to die.

The blood in my veins bubbled, and I felt the rage begin to spill over from the depths. The whisper echoes in the darkness, and I could almost see Edgar Lorn's face in the roiling smoke around us. I took a deep breath, trying to calm myself, and then staggered to my feet. Ignoring Weezab, and trying to ignore my rising fury, I stumbled toward Ceile. My friend hadn't moved since her ungraceful landing.

'Damn it, Martin, leave her!' the kobold shrieked from behind me, and my path was suddenly barred by flame.

I didn't slow. Energy poured in from the Suns, and I walked through the kobold's barrier like it wasn't there. The fire hissed and spit and then fizzled, whispering over my skin without effect. I heard Weezab gasp, and then the world erupted around me.

My hands never moved, and no words touched my lips, but I took the blood of the Suns and encased Ceile and me in a brilliant dome of light. The kobold's fire lashed across its surface, but I just turned slowly to look at him.

'You all made me into this,' I whispered, but my words were carried across the super-heated landing pad by the magic. 'You all get to suffer.'

The kobold snarled, and his face twisted in anger. He shot his hands into the sky, and the firestorm raging around me exploded. Its fury rippled along my shield, but I didn't let it in. Everything around me and Ceile vanished into its fiery grasp, but we were untouched.

Very slowly, I reached out and took hold of the storm. It roared and snapped against me, but my magic held it firm. Gradually, I pushed the fire away, bending it back toward its master.

On the other side of its fury, the kobold suddenly looked very nervous. His face scrunched up in concentration.

The blood in my veins was boiling, and the heat in my face wasn't from the flames. I took a step toward Weezab, and my will pushed the flames ahead of me. I let the shield drop. I was in control now.

The kobold struggled, and I felt his strength through the storm. An archon would have drowned in that strength, turned to ash in an instant. Other aethons wouldn't have fared much better in the face of the little creature's anger.

But I was no aethon. I didn't beg the Suns for their power. I called, and they answered. Astral rage wrapped the firestorm up and slowly folded it over the kobold, despite his efforts. With agonizing sureness, the flames encircled him, until he stood at the center of a sun of his own. Trapped, and with death looming over him, he glared at me.

'We could have been gods together,' he roared, and then with a howl of rage and a violent gesture, he collapsed the storm in on himself. In seconds, his magic turned him to dust and then he and the inferno were gone.

Once again, darkness enveloped the world, and I found myself lying on my back on the landing pad. The concrete was still hot, and I felt the heat burrow through my clothes. I lay there, staring up through the wind at the stars. For a long moment, the gusts and the crackle of burning corpses was all I could hear.

Then a familiar hum worked its way out of the ground.

I sighed, and with a great deal of pain, I managed to get back to my feet. The Suns still raged in my grasp, their energy waiting in the galaxy's worth of roiling spheres that whirled and spun around me. I picked my way carefully through the glowing red sections of concrete, stumbling my way over to Ceile's side. Kneeling down next to her, I reached over and gently rolled my friend onto her back.

Her twisted and broken body made me gasp, and my grip on the Suns failed, sending the energy rocketing back into the spaces between.

Whether Weezab had meant to do the damage or not, it didn't matter. Both legs and an arm were broken, the limbs twisted in tortured ways, the jagged edges of broken construct bone jutting out in bloody ruin. Her skin was torn, shredded by the pavement as she was thrown across it, and her face was a mask of blood and damaged tissue.

There was a rapidly growing pool of red fluid beneath her.

I cried out, and pulled her to me. For several terrifying seconds, I thought she was gone. Then her eyes slowly opened, and she stared up at me, shivering in pain.

'Mar- Martin,' she stuttered, and her intact arm reached up to catch my hand tightly.

'Ceile, you have to heal yourself,' I said, my voice ragged and hoarse. 'I can't. Edgar didn't know how. I can't heal you.'

Her eyes closed, and she coughed violently. Her hand let go of mine, and she traced several lines in the air, whispering as she did. A rain of dim green light flickered weakly across her body, and some of the wounds closed over. I hurriedly tried to arrange her limbs properly, but she shrieked with agony and the magic faded away.

'I can- cannot,' she whispered. 'I do not have the strength.'

I stared down at her, at my greatest friend, and despair overwhelmed the rage. With a cry, I set her gently down and got to my feet. Reaching my arms up into the night sky, I called to White and Blue and their energy poured into me until I lit the area like I was one of them. I froze there, enough power in my hands to destroy a District, turning my gaze back to Ceile's face. My mind raced as I tried to find the right shapes and forms.

'Why can't I fix you?' I begged her. Tears dripped from my cheeks.

I felt empty, and when she smiled and shook her head gently, I sobbed and let the magic go. I dropped to my knees and clutched desperately at her arm. The emptiness spread, and I felt the Suns slowly fade to black, and with them, the light around me. At the last second, I recognized that emptiness, and I looked over my shoulder just as my connection to the realm between disappeared into shadow.

'I'm sorry, Martin. I really am,' Chelle said, standing a handful of metres away. Her arms were hugged tightly around herself, and the young girl looked miserable.

Standing next to her was Bill.

125

'Good work, Chelle. Hello, Martin,' the engineer said, giving the girl a gentle pat on the head and coming forward to stand over me. 'Did you miss me?'

'Bill,' I growled, looking back down at Ceile. 'I'm going to kill you.'

The man chuckled. 'I doubt that, my friend. We should talk,' he said, and promptly kicked me in the back. It caught me by surprise, and wasn't soft. I rolled roughly over Ceile and crashed down into the dust painfully. Bill stepped forward, looming over my friend and smiling sadly.

'My name is Poe. No last name, I've never needed one,' he said. 'We haven't been formally introduced. Peter and Bill are obviously affectations, names used for a single purpose and then cast aside. I've used thousands over the years, of course, it just so happened that my current work required the use of some long term ones.'

Chelle came forward and stood at his shoulder, and he looked up at her with a nod of approval. 'You see, a private collector needed a solaron, and he contracted me to get it for him. They're quite hard to come across, you know,' he said, and frowned. 'It's taken me hundreds of years to get us here, to this point, and you did not make it easy for me.'

He suddenly clapped his hands and smiled. 'I even got the great and terrible Department of Research to do some of my work for me! You see, they really wanted a solaron, too. I needed their resources, and so I gently pointed them in Edgar's direction. Gently! It took a lot of effort to get into their beds with them, the Government isn't exactly prone to bringing outsiders into their blackest lairs,' he said, with a wink.

The ground rumbled, and there was a dull explosion from somewhere below. Bill chuckled again. 'No need to be worried, that thing will spend most of the first ten minutes of its life chewing up the facility and then the atmosphere. We have plenty of time to chat before we have to go,' he said.

I started to get to my feet, my anger rising again, but the engineer pulled a pistol free from his jacket and put it against Ceile's head. 'Now, now, Martin. You just sit there and listen while I tell you everything you need to hear. We'll be off soon enough.'

When I settled back, glaring at him silently, he laughed. Brandishing the pistol, he said, 'Do you like it? It's one of Partridge's designs. Well, everything was one of Partridge's designs, really. Even, this,' he paused, pointing at the metal body he'd stolen from Petrel, 'was his. As was the Red Flag.'

He leaned forward conspiratorially, and grinned. 'Surprised? Figured I'd built all of that myself, maybe? Maybe you think I built the portal generator, too. And the party tricks in my rings,' he laughed. 'You might be surprised to know that not only am I no wizard, but I'm no engineer, either.'

'The far more interesting truth to my tale, Martin and Ceile, is that I am the greatest thief that ever lived. I have lied and stolen and cheated my way to every great success and find I've ever had. I had Partridge build me all of my toys while I had him boxed up, using his own smarts and stolen tech. That portal generator is a beautiful thing, no?' he asked, his tone making it clear that he didn't care if I thought it was or not. 'I found that artifact buried in the plains, and Partridge built me the interface to use it.'

'Of course, Partridge was only a century or so old. Before you came across him, which put me onto his trail, I had to rely on others. Fortunately, a lot of the relics I raided from across the world still worked, like the energy blocker in your watch! That was a fun one, I wondered how long it'd take for you to find it. Thousands of years old, that thing was. Probably the same vintage as the regeneration chamber, come to think of it,' he said, looking thoughtful.

'Bill, who am I?' I asked, before he could continue monologuing.

The thief looked surprised, then smiled. 'Ah, that's the big question, isn't it? You know all about me tinkering with Mr. Edgar Lorn, solaron supreme. He was an excellent prize, but a flawed one. He knew nothing about his power, and he was a pacifist. A broken man. Everything you don't need in a world-eating god, really. As I pushed and prodded him into my client's desired shape, I knew he was a bomb. His mind couldn't handle it, and I had to find a way to put him somewhere safe before he blew himself up,' he said, tapping his temple. 'Of course, you can't just punt him into a construct, that kind of thing lobotomizes a solaron. Something about moving the essence of a creature into a different body does terrible things to their connection with the realm between.'

He shrugged. 'My client pointed me in a slightly different direction. Old spells, ancient magic. Rips someone out of their body and slaps them into someone else's. It wasn't perfect. My trials ended up killing a few hundred people, and turning another hundred or so into vegetables, but only a few weeks before Edgar's meltdown, I succeeded,' the thief said, victory in his voice. 'I immediately killed the subjects and my helper wizards, and then went looking for someone to be the perfect vessel for my solaron.'

'Damn it, Bill,' I snarled. 'Who am I?'

He waggled a finger at me, and said, 'You're just a man, Martin. My client brought you to me. You were strong. Healthy. You were a strong wind elementalist, borderline geomancer level. Your mind was clear and you'd never had mental health issues.' Smirking at me, he continued, 'But more importantly, you were a big family man, and you would do anything to keep them safe.'

My heart fell as my anger rose. 'A family?' I whispered, eyes falling to the ground. Ceile looked up at me, her eyes full of pain and sympathy.

Bill nodded. 'No children, of course. That wasn't your thing. A boyfriend, who you loved dearly. Parents. A brother and a pair of beautiful nieces. A sister and a brother in law that you played darts with on the weekends. You'd die before letting anything happen to them. Which is convenient when I needed a willing subject to do something, well, permanent,' he said. 'You were an amazing man, Martin, and when your family lost you, they were devastated.'

'Then Edgar went and had his little hissy fit. The timing wasn't great, and he was dying. We had to do the ritual fast and it didn't quite take. Almost instantly, he started leaking into your mind, and his magic started messing with you. The reaction killed everyone in the room - which thankfully didn't include me, as I was well down the hall before it blew - and reshaped your body. He should have been in stasis, locked in your brain, but the tricky bastard was semi awake and still playing havoc with reality,' Bill laughed, shaking his head. 'When I walked back into the room, you looked like his husband. Even I was a little shocked.'

'Of course, if the initial spell hadn't robbed you of most of your own memories, Edgar's influence quickly did. You were only thirty-eight years old, but I'll bet you remember almost every year of fifty-two of them right now, don't you?' the thief asked, and he leaned forward to look at me curiously. 'Regardless, the magic had settled down, and while you weren't being the perfect holding cell, Edgar was safe and you weren't coming apart at the seams. It was time to start solving the next problem.'

'Bill, what are we doing here? What was the point of all this?' I asked, shaking my head. I felt numb, though anger lurked not far below it. 'Who is your client?'

The thief ignored me. 'The initial hope was to find a way of getting Edgar into his own new body, or simply to take over yours, but I couldn't find a way to do the former without cutting out the only thing that made him useful to me, and the latter wasn't much more promising. Ancient enchanters used to pursue that kind of magic, but it seems they were mostly charlatans, and I found no other leads,' he said, and he looked sad. 'As the years passed, it became obvious that the more pressing matter was keeping you alive while I looked for the solution.'

'When I realized that you and your imaginary friend were using astral energy rather than nether and aether, I also realized that we might not need Edgar after all. Keeping you alive became the only concern, that and keeping you from deciding to ignore your prejudice against constructs. The last thing we needed was for you to show up in a shiny new model, reduced to just a geomancer and with Edgar's power completely gone.'

'Then I found out Krekt Twelve had dug up a regeneration chamber a century or so ago and set out to make it mine. The dwarves had their way with it, and when their research proved promising, I convinced them to abandon the project, and the lab. Then I got good old Partridge settled and went to work,' Bill said, clapping his hands. 'My client was happy, and the Government was on board, of course. They agreed to my terms, which was important, as I had to run you through the ringer to make sure you were still suitable. They just had to send their little errand boy and girl along for the ride, irritatingly enough.'

He cocked his head and looked down at Ceile. 'I was enthusiastic enough when they picked Weezab. I'd been doing experiments on him for over a decade, so I knew him well enough to know how to get rid of him, if need be. Kor was less great. I didn't know much about the dragon, and apparently neither did Operations, seeing as it appears she was working for the Horseman all along,' the thief said, shaking his head. 'That was a surprise. No wonder she was such a pain in the ass.'

Bill looked back up at me. 'The dwarves were always in my pocket. Petrel more so than Robin, as Partridge built him this wonderful body that Ceile so gracefully offered to me. You, Ms. Angael,' the man suddenly said, shaking his finger at her, 'nearly threw a wrench in the works by letting Robin get so attached to you. That could have ended very poorly, if Petrel or Weezab hadn't made it that far.'

Ceile scowled weakly at him, and the thief chuckled. 'Well, poorly for me, anyway. I imagine Robin would have been happier if it had gone differently.'

The ground rocked violently, and Bill's head looked back over his shoulder at the waiting airships. 'Ah, our time is running low. You should know that everything that has happened, since long before you were born, has happened to bring you here, Martin. This chapter of your story is coming to an end. The final act has begun! And once it too reaches its finale, everything will never be the same again,' he said, smiling.

'Bill,' I said.

'Poe, Martin. Bill is an illusion,' the man said with a grin.

'I'm going to kill you,' I growled, and the anger was back, rolling over me in waves.

Bill burst into laughter. 'Oh, Martin, you should see your face. That was worth this entire adventure,' he said, wiping a tear from his eye. 'Now, our time is up, and I no longer have need of leverage. Goodbye, Ceile Angael.' He smiled, gently, looking down on her.

And then he pulled the trigger.

Bill got slowly to his feet, and tossed his pistol away. The weapon landed with a clatter and skidded roughly across the landing pad before vanishing into a dune of ash and dust.

Ceile's eyes stared lifelessly into the sky, the last remains of her life leaking out through the ruin at the side of her skull. The pool of blood beneath her body gradually became one with that beside her head.

Chelle was frozen in time, hands over her mouth in terror, tears streaming down her face. The wind ruffled and snapped her hood, but she may as well have been made of stone.

I knelt there in the dirt, half of me coated in a fine spray of gore, staring down at my oldest and dearest friend. My arms were numb, hanging at my sides. Far overhead, the stars had disappeared behind a curtain of dark cloud, and a flash of lightning brought a roar of noise cutting through the wind. I barely heard it over the thunder of my own heart, thumping angrily in my veins.

The ground shook violently, and behind Bill one of Whisper Station's buildings rocked and then collapsed in a storm of dust and shattered concrete, and then Whisper itself sang through the wreckage. Its wail mixed with the shriek of the wind, and a column of sickly, pulsing light shot into the sky, tearing through the storm above and lancing out into space.

Bill lifted his arms to the sky, and then looked down at me. 'Listen, Martin!' he yelled. 'A countdown that started thousands of years ago is coming to a close! Everything that matters brought us here, brought everything here, to this place!'

An explosion at the base of the column sent a shock wave rocketing across the ground, skidding the Research airships around and knocking Chelle to her knees. The last two of Whisper Station's buildings collapsed, and a blast of brilliant white light erupted skyward, devouring the column. The eruption roared into the clouds, almost half a kilometre across, and then sparks and new explosions burst along its length. Part of the landing pad sank into the earth, carrying the patrol ships with it, and smoke billowed out of the wound.

I reached out and lightly touched Ceile's cheek. The flesh was cold, and the old hum of magic beneath it was gone.

'The end of this sick world is here, Martin! Can you feel it? Whisper speaks, and the skies scream!' Bill shouted, exultant.

High above, the stolen astral energy was shooting out from the clouds, sending spider webs of sunlight skittering along the sky. A massive bolt of lightning rocketed down from the chaos, slamming into the thief's airship and tearing it apart. The wind howled as it grew in strength, and in the shadows to the west, I saw a dark funnel descend toward the ground.

I looked up at Bill, and then slowly got to my feet. The thief smiled darkly as I did. He beckoned to me with a metal finger. 'We have a few minutes, I imagine. Come then! Have your revenge,' he laughed.

Before he finished speaking, I launched myself at him, leaping over my fallen friend and charging, propelled by fury and hate. I passed by Chelle without slowing, and the young girl never looked my way, still lost in her horror. With savage speed, I attacked the thief, striking at his face and hydraulics.

Bill barely moved, just lashed out once, knocking me senseless, and then lifted me into the air with one hand. I sucked in the frenzied air, trying to clear my head, and tried to pull myself from the thief's grasp, but it was pointless.

'You never were a fighter, Martin. Your power always waited in the realm between. Besides,' the man snarled, lifting one arm out and admiring it, 'did you really think you could hurt me? With your fists?' The thief laughed, and then he started carrying me back toward Ceile and Chelle. Lightning flashed close by, and the man's face lit up evilly. 'No, if you really hoped to kill me, you were going to need your magic.'

We came to a stop standing over Chelle, and Bill casually threw me into the dirt a few metres away. The girl looked up at me, then over her shoulder at the thief. He smiled down at her, gently. 'Are you ready, lunaron? Death has come for you,' he said, just loudly enough to be heard over the wind.

'He'll come for you too, one day,' Chelle said, getting unsteadily to her feet and turning to face him.

The thief barked a laugh, and shook his head. 'Probably sooner than you think, but not in the way you want,' he said. Bending down, he reached over and put his hands on the girl's shoulders.

'Bill! No!' I yelled, raggedly, as I drunkenly stumbled to my feet.

He looked up at me, and now his smile was sad. 'Go on and give to Death his due, and let the game begin anew,' he said, and then snapped Chelle's neck with a violent twist.

The girl's body flopped to the ground, coming to rest curled up against Ceile's. I watched her fall as I staggered toward them, feeling the anger raging underneath the numbness. I stopped, looming over the two, hands clenched, and then I looked up at Bill.

'Call the Suns, Martin. End me,' the thief snarled, and there was almost a longing in his voice.

Instantly, my mind went clear, and for a brief moment I was emotionless, floating in time, suspended in the middle of a silent storm that had frozen in whirling madness. A motionless tornado hung over the landing pad to the northwest. Whisper's stolen power dangled from the heavens, still as glass.

And then the rage boiled over, and the Suns looked down on me and answered my call.

Another instant passed, and now I really was floating, hovering in the air metres above the pavement, on wings of roaring astral energy. A universe of stars orbited me, a world-ending amount of power, waiting for me to sing the song that would annihilate the thief and the station and the City and then everything else. I reached out, and slowly pointed a finger at Bill, and those stars roared down my arm, hungry for release.

Bill never stopped smiling.

In the next instant, when a flare of solar rage had burst from my hand, furiously whipping toward him, the thief was no longer alone, and a wave of terror and despair rocked me, scattering my magic and dropping me unceremoniously to the ground.

Bill stood, smiling, arms raised to the sky, and at his side was a large cloaked figure, astride a pale, skeletal horse.

Fourth and Eldest of the Horsemen, who was also called Time.

Death, the end of all things.

127

The Horseman sat, still as stone, towering over Bill. His empty cowl stared down at me, and my rage evaporated in the grip of icy fear.

The thief gestured at me wildly, and he looked up at Death out of the corner of his eye. 'Here he is, Horseman! Here is your solaron! The deal is done, now give me what I was promised!' he yelled.

In the presence of the Elder creature, even the rage of the tornado and the fury of Whisper's cry were muted, and it seemed as though the chaos was suddenly very far away. Everything moved slower out there, as though we were encased in our own pocket of time.

Death turned to look down at the thief, and I saw Bill cringe. Despite his fear, he continued talking. 'The bargain, Death! Give me what I asked for!'

With agonizing slowness, the Horseman's arm raised from his side, and a single skeletal finger lifted from his tattered robe to point at the thief. Bill's eyes widened, and he started to step away. Before he could, the thief lifted free of the ground, and his head snapped back in a silent scream.

Black smoke wisped from Death's sleeve, and tendrils of darkness snaked forward to wrap around Bill's outstretched arms. The shadows sunk into every crevice, every pore of the thief's metal body, writhing and growing until the surface was shrouded beneath the Horseman's power. The thief's eyes rolled into the back of his head, and then they too disappeared into the smoke.

With an ugly popping noise, those eyes suddenly burst from his sockets and fell to the concrete below him.

The thief screamed, and kept on screaming, and with each ragged syllable of agony, synthetic parts tore free of his body and dropped to the landing pad. A foot clanged noisily on the pavement. Then a knee. An arm bent at a hideous angle and then crashed down. Piece by piece, the thief was unmade, until nothing of him remained but a ghostly figure made of black smoke.

The scream cut off, and the ghost floated there, motionless and silent.

I watched, spell-struck, as the smoke began to unravel, revealing glimpses of pale skin in the depths. Slowly, the figure dropped to the ground, and then the darkness drifted away, leaving behind a skinny, naked man, lying on his side, facing away from me. For a long moment, nothing happened, then he stirred, and rolled unsteadily to his knees.

It was Bill. A very human Bill.

He was completely hairless, which made him look even weirder than he ever had. Trembling, he brought his hands up to his face, and he stared at them, twisting the limbs around so he could see every inch. When he looked up at me, his eyes were filled with awe. 'I can feel the wind, Martin,' he whispered, and a tear rolled down his cheek.

Gingerly, the thief got to his feet, swaying. His face crinkled, and I saw his nostrils flare. 'I can smell, too. That's not as lovely,' he said, his voice growing stronger. He gave one last look at his palms and then let them drop. A smile slowly split his face in two, and the thief looked hungrily at me. 'Now, Death. Give me his power,' the man said, greedily.

But Death wasn't looking at Bill. The Horseman's empty cowl was pointing at me, and when I met that dark gaze, he cocked his head at the thief, and nodded.

The terror that had iced over my veins faded, and the fire returned. Rage rippled across my mind, and I didn't hesitate. In a heartbeat, I was off the ground and charging at Bill, fists clenched and ready. The thief's eyes went wide again, and the smile dropped off his face as uncertainty splashed across it. By the time he realized he'd been betrayed, it was too late.

I never called the Suns. I didn't need them. I was on the man in seconds and beat him to the ground. I wasn't skilled, but it didn't matter. As Death looked on, I pummeled Bill, punching and kicking as the thief weakly tried to fend me off.

It was messy work, lost as I was to my rage. I was vaguely aware that I'd broken most of my fingers breaking most of the bones in his face, but it didn't slow me down. When he managed to grab my hands with his, I head butted him viciously in the nose. It cracked loudly, and blood gushed from his torn nostrils. When he tried to cover his face, I hit him in the neck and chest. Kneed him in the tender places. When he tried to roll away, I kicked him in the side of the knees until his legs bent at angles they were never meant to bend at.

He never said a word.

Eventually, my mind cleared, and I found myself straddling him, covered in both his and my own blood. Pain lanced through my body, through the ruin of my hands. Beneath me, the unconscious and dying man breathed raggedly through broken teeth and a mostly crushed windpipe. I felt disappointment bubble up through the fury. I didn't want him to get away yet. I didn't want him to stop suffering.

An unseen hand lifted me off of him, and threw me sprawling into the dirt. Angrily, I skidding around to glare up at Death, trying to fight the fear that crystallized at the edge of my mind. The Horseman looked back, but his arm once again pointed at Bill, and the thief lifted into the air, dripping blood from his broken limbs and head.

The black smoke lanced out, and when it was finished whirling around him, the man was whole once more, blinking rapidly as he floated in Death's grasp. The darkness split away from him, and before he fell to the ground, suddenly shot at me, wrapping me up in shadow and carrying me into the air.

If I'd felt agony before, it was nothing in the face of the Horseman's power. The smoke raged around my hands, and bone shards clicked and shifted back into place, sealing shut as tissue knitted itself back together and closed over the wounds. My cuts and bruises vanished in flashes of searing pain, and when I dropped to the ground, the smoke dissipating into the wind, I had nothing but dried blood to show for my revenge.

When I looked up at Death from my ungraceful position, he cocked his head at Bill, and nodded.

I lost count of how long we existed in this cycle of pain and healing, of how many times I beat the man to within an inch of his life, only to have the Horseman revive us both and start again. Outside our strange refuge, the storm raged against Whisper's howl, the dark clouds whirling furiously around the column of stolen astral energy. One of the small airships lifted free of the landing pad and skidded through concrete and then earth in the grip of the wild winds of the tornado.

Winds that never touched us as the thief, the Horseman, and I played our savage game of retribution and punishment.

Finally, after Death had thrown me off of Bill yet again, the thief raised an arm weakly toward the Horseman. 'You promised me, Death,' he rasped, 'You promised to make me your Hand, to use the solaron's strength at your command. You promised me immortality.'

In response, the black smoke poured from the Horseman's sleeve and began to hiss toward the thief. Anger lanced across the man's face, and he spat through a furious smile of broken teeth, 'You're full of lies, Horseman! You've twisted your end of the deal. This is no gift of immortality, this is eternal punishment! Take your reward back, Death! Take it, and I hope the solaron declines your kind offer!'

The darkness slowed its approach, and the Horseman's empty gaze turned slightly to look at me. I got steadily to my feet, feeling the blood ooze from my wounds, the shattered bones in my hands cracking and moving against each other in agony. I glared balefully down on Bill's brutalized form, and let the thought of beating him to death again tickle the depths of my mind.

I was surprised when I found my anger fading away and the image of killing him again made me feel ill. I let my arms fall to my sides, and shook my head slowly. 'He's all yours, Death,' I whispered, turning to look down at Ceile's body.

Bill instantly began to scream, but I didn't look away from my friend. There was a hideous sucking noise, followed by the sound of fluid splashing across concrete, and then the shriek cut off abruptly, leaving the Horseman and I in silence.

128

It was done. I swayed there, trembling over Ceile's body, feeling woozy and sad. Then, with a sigh, I let myself slide to the ground, coming to a rest sitting awkwardly by my friend's side. My battered hands lay tangled in a painful mess in my lap. Blood dripped from a gash on my forehead, falling into a small pool by my feet.

I stared into the red murk for a long time.

Gradually, I lifted my head up and looked into the black abyss of Death's cowl. The Horseman made no motion, both him and steed frozen in time, immune from the wind. The storm raged on behind the creature's back. I felt a sliver of fear worm its way into my mind as we watched each other silently.

Bill's twisted and broken corpse lay spread-eagled at the Horseman's side, empty eye sockets glaring up into the raging clouds above.

Slowly Death raised his arm, and as that skeletal limb went up, so did the thief's body. Steadily, Bill floated over to come to a stop at the Horseman's steed's shoulder. The thief's broken arms hung limply next to him, and his head lolled lifelessly to the side. Seconds passed, and Death and his grim marionette stared eyelessly down at me.

Then Bill's head snapped up, his eyes and mouth opened, and black smoke poured from them.

'Hello, Martin,' he said, his voice dull and monotone. His mouth opened and closed roughly, and I could see his tongue moving in the smoke, but his chest didn't draw breath.

'Death,' I said, nodding slowly.

The Horseman didn't move, and his arm remained out and pointed at me. Next to him, Bill spoke again. 'Do you know why you are here, Martin?' the thief asked.

I sighed, and then slowly put my elbows on my knees and lowered my chest forward to rest on them. The movement sent spikes of pain rocketing through my twisted fingers. 'You need the magic I've inherited from Edgar Lorn, Horseman, but I have no idea why,' I said, quietly.

'Four thousand years ago, Martin, the world had once again fallen out of Balance. My brethren and I answered the world's cry for mercy, and the Ride was called. We set out to end her suffering, but we were arrogant, and misjudged the strength of the life that remained on her tortured surface. As we cut the survivors down, culling each species as was needed, a human came forth from one of the underground cities,' Bill said, his jaws clacking together. 'We had never seen the like of his power before, and we hesitated. Reality was reshaping itself around him. He floated before us, the rage of the Suns roaring in his hands, and he defied us. He claimed that the Ride was no part of the natural order, and that it was not our right to govern the life and death of the world.'

The Horseman's head cocked slightly to the side. 'My brother War rose up to strike the man down for his words, but it was too late. War's blow was swift, but the human wasn't as he seemed. While we had been crossing the world's lands, he had already been sending his magic deep into her bones, and high into the spaces above. Even as his body was crushed by War's strike, his essence swept out through the air and into the earth, and we could do nothing but stand and watch as the Ride came unraveled and the world screamed in agony,' Bill said, the words slowly spilling from his dead lips as though the thief was bored with the narration.

I shook my head. 'But you said the world was out of Balance, couldn't you just start again?' I asked.

'No, Martin, we could not. The solaron sought to set her right, and the raw power he wielded was enough to do so. But not in the same way the Ride would have. She was put back into Balance, but though she was no longer dying, she was sick. Diseased. Purification, the Ride, the Horsemen's very purpose is to prevent this world's death, but we cannot heal her if that death is not imminent,' Bill said. 'Our full power is only granted to us if she faces extinction. Now she lies comatose and poisoned, as sickness turns her oceans to acid and earth to dust.'

The Horseman leaned forward to loom over me. 'She will die, Martin, but she will not die for millennia, and by then it will be too late for your species and all the other life that calls her home,' the thief moaned.

I frowned. 'What do you mean?' I asked.

'With each Ride, we cull the world's inhabitants, granting her time to rejuvenate without their influence. There are always survivors, those we leave be and those hidden in the cracks. When the time is right, they rise from their prisons to find the world fresh and alive, and the cycle begins anew. But this time is different, Martin. The cracks are filling with poison. What life was left beyond this continent's shores is quickly dying off. There are settlements out there, small enclaves of civilization from which life would start again once Purification had silenced the old world.'

Death slowly straightened in his saddle. 'Soon, they will be gone, and all that remains will be these lands. But they, too, are doomed. Look, Martin,' Bill said as the Horseman gestured up at the raging light shooting skyward behind him with his free hand, 'The human's weapon has already set the death of their species in motion. Their machine's power is corrupting the air far overhead, corruption that will allow the poison that lurks over the oceans to spill in, and sending its dark light deep into the stone beneath us. In hours, the City will be lost, consumed by the world its leaders sought to conquer. In days, the beaches and mountains at the continent's edges will be lost, shrouded in acidic shadow,' Bill said, monotonously.

'In months, the only life left on this world will be the creatures that burrow deep beneath this land's surface. They will delve further and further, as death seeps in through the ashes of the earth. And they will survive for years. Decades, perhaps. But a century from now, after a lifetime of fleeing from it, the few that remain will perish in the poison's clutches, tired, afraid, hopeless. Once they are gone, the world will be alone, left to rot until Balance is finally lost, allowing the Ride to be called once more.'

The Horseman's hand fell back to his lap. 'And the Horsemen will ride, and the world will be revived once again. But this time, Martin, there will be no life to keep her company. She will be lost, as barren and silent as her siblings. Her magic will fade, the connection between realms above, between, and below will fail, and she will turn to dust. The Horsemen will stand on her tortured surface, bearing vigil as she passes, until even our power is lost, and then only I will remain.'

'When that time comes, Martin, when Balance falls once more, there will be no Horsemen left to bring her back. All that will be left to do is for me to call the End, and then the world and even I will be no more,' Bill said, then fell silent.

I shook my head. 'But shouldn't that mean that Balance is already lost? If all of us dying means the planet will too, shouldn't that be cause enough for the Ride to be called?' I said, my mind racing.

Death's head bowed slightly. 'It is not. Our power is tied to Balance, and Balance is tied to the present. It does not see its end coming. It cannot see ahead to the coming years and decades and centuries. It is mindless and static,' Bill said. His lifeless jaws cracked shut on his tongue, and a chunk of the muscle fell bloodlessly to the ground.

For a long moment, we stared at each other. I felt tired, and I hurt. Sighing, I said, 'You need me to fix this.'

Again the Horseman nodded. 'There have been eight solarons born since the last Ride failed. Of them, Edgar Lorn was the only one with strength enough to correct the damage.'

I frowned into the abyss of the Horseman's cowl. 'I don't understand. Why all the games? What did you need Bill for? Couldn't you have gone to Edgar yourself?' I asked.

Chelle's body jerked suddenly upright, and I watched in horror as the girl floated, feet dragging, over to hover at Death's steed's other shoulder. Black smoke erupted from her slack jaws. When the Horsemen spoke next, both the lunaron and Bill spoke for him in unison.

'Our power is limited, tied to the health of the world. The Horsemen cannot act directly to topple the Balance, not without potentially losing the power we have. I risked much, even through the use of proxies such as the thief, and I have had to do so alone. My sisters Pestilence and Famine believe that my actions bring us closer to oblivion. Pestilence in particular has used her own puppets in an attempt to hamper or sabotage my efforts. My brother War stands in agreement with me, but has chosen not to assist. He marshals his power toward other pursuits, though I do not know what they are,' the two said, Chelle's soft voice marching side by side with the thief's rumbling speech.

'But why all the sidetracking? Why not just have Bill bring Edgar straight to you?' I asked, suddenly angry. 'What did you need to bring me into this for?'

'Edgar Lorn was not ready. As were all his predecessors, he had to be trained and tested. Poe saw his strength immediately, but it would have been a waste to bring him to me as he was. The solaron would have failed, and I would have lost a great deal of power in the endeavour. He had to be ready to use his magic, and he had to be willing to use his magic,' Chelle and Bill chanted.

'Then who am I?' I screamed, struggling to my feet.

'Your name,' Ceile said as she slowly got to her feet, black smoke billowing from her mouth and the gaping hole in the side of her head, 'is Ulf Klen. I spoke of settlements that lie beyond the oceans.' She slid backward until she half-stood, half-floated in front of Death.

'You were born there,' my friend, the lunaron, and the thief said as one.

129

'It was obvious that Edgar would not survive to complete his training. We had need of a vessel, someone strong enough to contain the solaron until a solution could be found. I searched the world for just such a specimen, and found you far to the south west of this land,' the Horseman's chorus said.

'Your people, though human, have evolved beyond the ones that fill the City to our east. Your mind is stronger, more resilient. The holding magic needed that strength, though we had no way of knowing if it would be enough. Poe's tests were promising but Edgar's mind was crumbling quickly, and getting new test subjects across the ocean was a difficult and time consuming process. You were defiant, and it was only after Poe threatened to eliminate your family that you came to the table willingly,' the chorus continued.

Tears came to my eyes as I heard those words come in my friend's lifeless voice. 'My family?' I asked.

Death nodded. 'Yes. You were promised that they would be unharmed in the coming calamity if you behaved, and that you would be returned to them when Edgar's task was done.'

I shook my head, sadly. 'And what did you promise Bill to get him to do your dirty work? He said you promised him immortality. Promised him my power? Are all your promises empty, Horseman?' I asked.

'Poe was a necessary evil, Martin. For my plan to succeed, I had need of servants with talents such as his. I have no love for such creatures. I told him only what he wanted to hear so that he would do as I wished, and now that his work is done, I have no more need of him,' the chorus sang. As those last words reached their lips, Bill's body jerked upright and then slowly turned to dust. When only his bones remained, wreathed in the black smoke, they tumbled wildly from the air and fell crumbling to the concrete.

Ceile moved to take the thief's place. 'It was on his word that you agreed to obey, a word that is worth nothing. But in this case, I will honour the promises he made,' she and Chelle said.

I frowned. 'You will?' I asked, quietly.

'Yes. If you agree to do as I ask, I will return you to your home and to your family, and no further harm will come to you,' the two girls whispered.

My mind reeled. 'But I don't even remember them. And Bill said that I don't look anything like I did. It's been hundreds of years, Horseman! What good are these promises now?' I snarled, hugging myself against the pain.

Death straightened up in his saddle, cocking his head to the side. 'I will repair the damage done to you, Martin. You will be given your memories back, the ones consumed by Edgar's presence. You will regain your old appearance. You will look young to those who wait for you, but they will know you,' the chorus said.

I stared at the ghastly trio. Blood dripped into my right eye, and I reached painfully up to swipe at it with a battered wrist. Behind the Horseman, Whisper's light was expanding, eating the storm and throwing back the tornado. Far above, through the widening gaps in the clouds, I saw spider webs of sickly-looking lightning bolts crackling through space. The web spread slowly through the heavens, stretching toward the City to the east.

Finally, I lowered my head. Tears and blood dripped onto my chest. 'So be it, Death. What do I have to do to save them?' I whispered.

It wasn't Chelle or Ceile that answered. From behind me, twenty flat voices spoke in unison, 'You cannot, Martin.' I spun, the pain threatening to take me to my knees, and found the bodies of the Research men and women standing there, in varying states of destruction. 'You cannot stop the coming storm. This continent and all on it will die. The humans and their weapon have seen to that.'

I snarled, 'Then what the hell am I supposed to do?'

'Destroy it before the weapon does,' the chorus droned.

The newcomers trembled and swayed as they marched past me, coming to rest behind the Horseman in a rough half circle. 'Whisper is powerful, but its strength pales in comparison to yours. Its light is just a catalyst for the disease. It will kill all the life here, but it will not shatter this continent and wound this world. It will not topple the Balance,' they sang. 'Only you can do so. Call on the Suns, Martin, and cut the world deep. Shatter this land, and grind it to dust in the wind. Boil the oceans around it. As sickness pours into her from the illness that remains, the Balance will fail and the Ride will be called,' the dead said.

I watched them, mouth agape. 'There are billions of lives here, Horseman. You want me to kill them all?' I demanded.

Death leaned forward. 'If you do not, then all life on this world will find extinction and then she will be lost,' spilled from twenty dead mouths.

I fell to my knees, and even the pain from my broken hands didn't pierce the numbness that spread over me. I looked down at the mess, at the bloody wreckage of torn flesh and splintered bone. I didn't recognize them. 'Children, Death. There are millions of them in the City. Hundreds of millions! How many more in the dwarven krekts below? In the elven cities? How many lives would you have me take?' I asked.

'They cannot be saved, Martin. Their deaths will mean nothing if you let them live, and everything if you do not,' the chorus said.

I looked up, and Ceile was hovering over me. 'Destroy this continent, Martin. Destroy the Balance. When that work is done, you will return to your family, free to spend the rest of your nigh-eternal days with them, safely hidden beneath the waves as the world is born anew. Generations will pass, but you will be there when your people push through to the surface, to spread forth through green valleys and crystalline lakes. Life will flourish once again, the world healthy and free of the sickness. Magic will be strong, the realm between refreshed and renewed,' she said, alone.

Tears fell freely now, and I shook my head. 'I don't know if I can, Horseman!' I shouted, hoarsely.

'You must. If you do not act, you and everyone on this world will die. She will be lost, blinded to the light of the Suns forever, to rot and suffocate beneath a choking blanket of poison and acid,' Ceile said. She was kneeling in front of me now. 'Your brother and nieces. Your sister. They still live, Martin. Will you let them die, too?'

An image at the back of my head, of two young girls chasing a bizarre looking dog through the grass, whispered through the depths. They looked familiar, but their names lurked just out of reach. A man walked beside me on the path, his arms clutched comfortably in the small of his back, as we chatted about something called the internet. The dog suddenly appeared at my knee, and dropped a toy covered in drool on my sandaled foot. I laughed as I picked the nasty thing up and threw it into the field. The animal howled and vanished after it, and the girls shot off in pursuit, shrieking with delight.

'They're still alive?' I asked, and I felt the alien sensation of hope.

'They are,' Ceile said. 'Your people are long-lived. You have not survived for more than two hundred years because you are unique, Martin. If you had not set foot in the regeneration chamber, and not been subjected to the corrupting influence of Edgar Lorn, you would live another two hundred before you moved on to the realm below.'

I stared into her dead eyes. Her loss cut deep, and I was sure I'd mourn my friend until the end of time.

Above, the storm was fading, but Whisper's power now hung over the nearest borders of the City. Blasts of wild magic began to fall from the web above, and the air got hot and stale. The wind was dying down here, but far overhead, the clouds roiled and flashed as the astral energy devoured everything around it. Lit by the machine's stolen light, I could see a darkness forming in the sky to the west, and I imagined the poisons that shrouded the oceans spilling over their beaches and billowing through the mountains toward us.

Black smoke was writhing around my hands, and I barely noticed as they slowly returned to normal. The oozing blood on my forehead slowed, then stopped. I got to my feet, watching the magic fall from the sky, crashing down into the vast walls around the nearest District, sending waves of dust and debris into the dying air.

'Well, Martin? Will you be my Hand?' Ceile asked, her soft voice dull and dead.

I closed my eyes, and thought of that tattered memory of the dog and the girls and the man. I thought of everything that had brought me here today. I saw Dr. Jacobs smiling at me as I lay on the exam room bed, his hand resting kindly on my shoulder. I saw Nox grin at me evilly as he picked a steam construct up and threw it across the street, the big 'wolf clapping me across the back with a huge smile after the garbage had been thrown out. I saw Ceile smile as we walked through the forest near my home, hand in hand.

Face after face danced behind my eyelids. Petrel and Robin standing on the platform below the Red Flag. Vrarrs Kor walking naked through the trees. Weezab jumping and chittering, hiding his true self. Scayn's bizarre and twisted elven face, grinning as he skittered creepily along the barren Woodsholme street. The Rook staring balefully down from its throne, the strange theater mask devoid of emotion.

Bill standing in the Electric Cat, posed flamboyantly in the middle of his story.

Peter smirking at me from the side of a hospital bed.

Poe smiling triumphantly down at me, Ceile's dead body at his feet.

I saw Edgar Lorn, smiling sadly as he killed his family, unable to stop himself.

I thought about it all, and when I opened my eyes, blazing with the Suns' might, I was smiling, too.

Thanks

To the Beta Team: Erin, Gar, Rye, Shai, and Mom, who suffered through two drafts' worth of five chapter updates and general author drama. The book wouldn't exist without their feedback and suggestions, and I can't thank them enough.

To Jen, who gave me the opportunity to sit down and finish the book on my own terms. Without her generosity and support, I'd still be midway into the second draft and months behind.

And to my parents, who read The Hobbit to me when I was young and helped get me started on this wild journey, decades ago. You gave my creativity and imagination freedom to run wild, and without that, I wouldn't be half the writer I am today. I love you both.